科麦克·麦卡锡小说的混沌世界

Chaos in Cormac McCarthy's Fiction

张小平　著

 吉林大学出版社

·长春·

图书在版编目（CIP）数据

科麦克·麦卡锡小说的混沌世界 / 张小平著. —— 长春：吉林大学出版社，2021.4

ISBN 978-7-5692-8244-3

Ⅰ.①科… Ⅱ.①张… Ⅲ.①科麦克·麦卡锡—小说研究 Ⅳ.①I712.074

中国版本图书馆CIP数据核字(2021)第079811号

书　　名　科麦克·麦卡锡小说的混沌世界
　　　　　KEMAIKE MAIKAXI XIAOSHUO DE HUNDUN SHIJIE

作　　者　张小平　著
策划编辑　米司琪
责任编辑　米司琪
责任校对　闫竞文
装帧设计　文海传媒
出版发行　吉林大学出版社
社　　址　长春市人民大街 4059 号
邮政编码　130021
发行电话　0431-89580028/29/21
网　　址　http://www.jlup.com.cn
电子邮箱　jdcbs@jlu.edu.cn
印　　刷　天津和萱印刷有限公司
开　　本　787mm×1092mm　1/16
印　　张　19
字　　数　316千字
版　　次　2021 年 4 月　第 1 版
印　　次　2021 年 4 月　第 1 次
书　　号　ISBN 978-7-5692-8244-3
定　　价　68.00 元

作者简介

张小平，字明夷，河南洛阳人，大儒张载先生之二十八世裔孙，英语语言文学博士，扬州大学外国语学院教授、博士生导师，河南大学黄河学者特聘教授，英国剑桥大学、美国特拉华大学和诺维奇大学研究和访问学者，扬州大学"新世纪人才工程"和江苏省"青蓝工程"中青年学术带头人，中国外国文学学会英国文学分会和江苏省外国文学研究会理事，国家社会科学基金评审专家，教育部学位授予单位抽检学位论文通讯评议专家等。主持完成国家社会科学基金项目"科麦克·麦卡锡小说研究"，出版著作（含译著和诗集）《当代美国作家科麦克·麦卡锡小说研究》《子非花：柔剑的诗》《美妆的凝视》《尤金·奥尼尔戏剧中的女性形象和角色研究》《英美文学：阅读与批评》《英美文学：诗歌·小说·戏剧》《灰色空间：都市穷人的地下经济》等，在国内外重要学术期刊上发表论文50余篇。

献给我的父母，他们和文字永在

目录

当西方遇见东方——混沌思维与外国文学研究

（自序）

我们身处一个前所未有的万物互联世界，尤其是身处疫情时期的今天，不仅"混沌"成了绕不开的话题，"混沌"的核心本质——蝴蝶效应，也几乎成为我们日常生活的一部分。因而，讨论和思考"混沌"、研究"混沌"与文学批评和创作的关系，有着重要的意义。

一

什么是"混沌"呢？这要从庄子说起。《庄子·内篇·应帝王》有云："南海之帝为倏，北海之帝为忽，中央之帝为浑沌。倏与忽时相与遇于浑沌之地，浑沌待之甚善。倏与忽谋报浑沌之德，曰：'人皆有七窍以视听食息，此独无有，尝试凿之。'日凿一窍，七日而浑沌死。"位于"倏忽"（南北）之间的中央之帝为"混沌"。但是，有所不同的是，现代意义上的"倏忽"是时间概念，有短暂之意，而庄子意义上的"倏忽"则在时间上多了一重空间意义。换言之，"倏忽"之间的"混沌"指的是"时空一体"，准确地说，接近于巴赫金意义上的"时空体"（chronotope），已经有了今天科学意义上的"混沌"之意。

作为中西文化传统上重要的文化原型，"混沌"的"血统"非常古老，是一个旧的概念。中西方的创世神话都有关于"混沌"的传说或记载。在西方，"混沌"一词可追溯到公元前8世纪赫西俄德（Hesiod）的《神谱》，其中"混沌"被描述成"混沌一片"、"造物产生的背景"。古希腊人将"混沌"看作宇宙的本原状态，经常将其与"原始"、"无序"、"黑暗"以及宇宙赖以演化的一种原始物质关联。西方的经典文学作品，也时常将"混沌"看作秩序的对立面。

《圣经》的《创世纪》中，"混沌"与有序、黑暗与光明、荒芜与生命就呈相对关系，此时的"混沌"指的是天地开创前的状态。奥威德的《变形记》中，"混沌"是一种天然的没有形状的状态。弥尔顿的《失乐园》中，"混沌"被视作"自然的先祖"、"无政府的君王"，甚至是深如涡旋的黑暗的统治者。莎士比亚的悲剧《麦克白》中人们对"混沌"的认识，类似我们今天日常生活中谈及的"混沌"，即混乱、无序。实际上，从古老的《圣经》直至19世纪现实主义作家托尔斯泰和乔治·爱略特（George Eliot）的小说中，处处都能发现西方人对"混沌"这一古老的概念及其所孕育的美学的冲动，还停留在破坏与毁灭的认识之上。①

"混沌"这一概念在中国传统文化中的丰富性和活跃度并不逊于西方。总的来说，中国神话传说中的"混沌"基本上也与无序和混乱相关。《山海经》对"混沌"如此记载："有神鸟，其状如黄囊，赤如丹火，六足四翼，浑敦无面目，是识歌舞，实惟帝江也。"此处的"浑敦"便是"混沌"，其无面目的特点与《庄子》所载的处于"倏忽"（南北）之间的"混沌"类似。《神异经•西荒经》也有类似的记载："昆仑西有兽焉，其状如犬，长毛四足，两目不见，两耳而不闻，有腹而无脏，有肠直而不旋。食物轻过。人有德行而往触之，人有凶德而往依凭之，天使其然，名为浑沌。"值得注意的是，与饕餮、穷奇、梼杌四个异兽合称上古四大凶兽之一的"浑沌"，其不见、不闻、直肠子、不消化的特点，与庄子的"混沌"也有共通之处，都有"空"的特性。《三五历纪》提到："天地混沌如鸡子，盘古生在其中。万八千岁，天地开辟，阳清为天，阴浊为地。盘古在其中，一日九变，神于天，圣于地。"此处"混沌"则被用来描述天地未开、状如混沌这一宇宙的表现。《乾凿度》提出了一套宇宙生成论，即浑沦→天地→万物。"浑沦"便是"混沌"，一种宇宙未分离的状态。

众多中国神话传说中的"混沌"，到底哪种是我们要讨论的富有现代科学意义上的"混沌"呢？我们不妨还是回到庄子那里。庄子意义上的"混沌"被

---

① 实际上，并非所有的文学经典作品对"混沌"的认识都是无序、混乱。18世纪英国诗人布莱克 (William Blake) 在他的长诗《天国与地狱的婚姻》中对"混沌"的理解，已经有了科学意义上的"混沌"之内涵，也即"混沌"是有序与无序的中间地带，而有序能从自组织的边缘的无序中涌现。小说家劳伦斯·斯特恩 (Laurence Sterne) 在其经典名著《项狄传》中也有对"混沌"的独特书写，且该小说因对叙事时间的非线性以及叙事内容的非因果逻辑的处理，常被当作后现代主义小说的肇始。

"倏忽"二帝凿七窍而死，言外之意分明指的是，"道"原本浑然一体，无所分界。将"混沌"看作"道"，不禁又要联系老子。《老子》有云："有物混成，先天地生，寂兮廖兮，独立不改，周行而不殆，可以为天下母。"（《老子·第二十五章》）这个可以为天下母的"混成之物"，就是"道"。"道"不仅先于天地，更是宇宙、天地、万物生成、运动、变化和转化的最初根据，是某种"种子"，是"物"、"信"（息）合一，可谓一种二重化存在的原始混沌状态。如此，庄子意义上处于"倏忽"之间的"混沌"，便是"大道"，是"宇宙的原本"、"人类之初"、"人生之始"，实属"无形"、"无名"、"法自然"而自然而然。这一位于"南北"中央、介于"倏忽"之间的"混沌"，其"常无为而无不为……万物将自化"（《老子·第三十七章》）的"自然不为、无不为"的特性，不仅有了上述所说的当代科学意义上朴素的"时空体"之特征，更是因其本质上关于非决定论的复杂自组织思想，揭示了"事物自生演化发展的无目的性、不确定性、随机性的特征"[①]，恰与当代混沌理论对宇宙中动态事物的认识直接相通。

就宇宙的起源来说，中国古代哲学中有很多概念，除了"道"或"混沌"之外，还有"太极"、"气"、"太玄"等，其共同特点就是将宇宙看作具有变化特性的"空"或"无"。《老子》曰："天下万物生于有，有生于无。"（《老子·第四十章》）；"道生一，一生二，二生三，三生万物。万物负阴而抱阳，冲气以为和。"（《老子·第四十二章》）老子对其说的"无"太过模糊，并未多作解释，这也为后世的哲学家对"无"与宇宙之起源关系的解释留了余地。魏晋玄学的代表人物王弼，在他的《老子注》和《周易注》中，就将"有生于无"的思维推向了极端。他不仅以"无"为万物之根本，还以"无"来释"道"，并将"道"归于"无"。当然，至于"无"与"道"的关系，禅宗也有类似思想。禅宗思想中的"空"（"无"）尽管与"有"对立，但在禅宗的认识中却是一种"存在"。正如《金刚经》的偈语所说，"一切有为法，如梦幻泡影，如露亦如电，应作如是观"。有与无，存在与非在，两个看似独立的两极却是一对辩证的矛盾，相互交融，共生发展，无始无终地变幻和循环。

总之，中国传统思想中"混沌"的含义一直在变化，但总的来说，无论是"空"或"道"、"太极"或"无极"、"太玄"或"气"，中国古人对"混

---

① 邬焜：《古代哲学中的信息、系统、复杂性思想》，载商务印书馆 2010 年版，第 134 页。

沌"的理解，尽管相对"简单"，有些朴实，但就"混沌"被看作能与"秩序"彼此做出变化的观念来说，远比西方文化将"混沌"与"秩序"对立的阐释，更接近于现代科学意义上人们对混沌的认识。可以说，早慧的中华文明在"混沌"这一概念的认识上走在了时代的前面。当然，庄周与蝴蝶的"物我两忘"，佛禅思想中的"一花一世界，一叶一菩提"等的万物齐一的整体论思想，以及《周易》与《黄帝内经》对天、地、人的全息统一的看法，都强调了相反相成、阴阳合一、此中有彼、彼中有此、一中有二、二中有一的混沌思维。这样的思维方式与西方传统思维方式重视界定、区分，强调彼此有别，"说一不二"，有显著的差异。

二

如果说传统上人们将"混沌"与"秩序"对立，且在认识上有优劣之分，"秩序"一般相当于"上帝"、"光明的使者"、"规律"、"健康"、"善"、"确定"、"稳定"等，"混沌"则类似于"魔鬼"、"黑暗"、"破坏者"、"疯狂"、"恶"、"疾病"、"不确定"、"不稳定"、"流动"等，那么，我们今天讨论"混沌"，便再也不能将善恶优劣的伦理或道德判断强加在"混沌"身上。随着混沌理论在当代科学领域的兴起，传统中将"秩序"和"混沌"对立且将后者看作负面因素的观点被彻底挑战。

坎贝尔（Ali B. Cambel）指出，"混沌代表的是动态物质中不确定的存在或其随机性的一面，而这样的特性绝没有好坏之分，或是人们不期望出现的那一面——有时，恰恰相反"[1]。如此，"混沌"不仅是秩序的对立面，更是可以创造秩序，两者不分彼此，甚至能够相互转换。借用黑尔斯（N. Katherine Hayles)的术语，"混沌"就是有序的无序或者无序的有序，指的是有序来自无序，无序也可产生有序。[2]因此，"混沌"乃是一种悖论式的存在，"处于完全确定和完全随机之间的一种状态"[3]。简言之，当今的"混沌"远非传统上人们对它的

① Ali. B. Cambel, *Applied Chaos Theory: A Paradigm for Complexity* (New York and London: Academic Press, 1993), p. 15.
② See N. Katherine Hayles (ed.), *Chaos and Order: Complex Dynamics in Literature and Science* (Chicago and London: The Univ. of Chicago Press, 1991), p. 15.
③ Joseph Conte, *Design and Debris: A Chaotics of Postmodern American Fiction* (Tuscaloosa: Univ. of Alabama Press, 2002), p. 24.

认识，更不再是科学发现（尤其是经典科学阶段）中的一种"噪音"，而是内涵更加丰富。作为科学术语，"混沌"指的是貌似随机的事件其背后却有内在的联系，貌似无序实则有序。美国麻省理工学院的动力气象学家洛伦兹（Edward N. Lorenz）就将"混沌"定义为"动态系统中对初始条件或内在变化敏感性的依赖"，指的是根据随机变化而出现的一种过程，尽管"这些行为方式的出现实际上受到确然律的限制"①。可以说，现代科学意义上的"混沌"，已然有了随机性、非线性、不可逆性以及不确定性等特征。

现代科学对"混沌"的革新认识，要追溯到洛伦兹发表于1963年的论文《确定性的非周期流》。在这篇具有划时代意义的论文中，洛伦兹指出，在一个动力系统中，初始条件下微小的变化能带动系统巨大的长期的连锁反应，这也是为何长期的天气预报不能准确预测的原因。洛伦兹的发现，挑战了长期浸淫在牛顿经典科学中人们对世界的认识——一切都能预测，甚至能够确定。然而，洛伦兹这篇论文并没有引起太大反响，1972年，距离他当年论文发表约10年之后，在美国华盛顿特区召开的世界气象研究大会的一个分会场上，洛伦兹再次提出他对"混沌"的洞见。这一次他的发言题目为《可预测性：巴西的一只蝴蝶翅膀的震动能引起德州的飓风吗？》。富有诗意的"蝴蝶"被洛伦兹用来指代"混沌"，实际上洛伦兹起初一直想用海鸥来做意象，当然，动态系统中物质运动的轨迹在相空间的映射确实看起来就是一只翩翩起舞的"蝴蝶"，冥冥之中，这是否是与庄子的"蝴蝶是我我是蝴蝶"发生了"量子纠缠"，我们并不得知。但有趣的是，由于洛伦兹的坚持，"蝴蝶效应"后来竟真地成了科学家们眼中"混沌"的本质，并且有时还被当作混沌理论的隐喻。

作为科学术语，"混沌"真正进入科学界的视线还要等到1975年。这一年，李天岩（Tien-Yien Li）和约克（James A. Yorke）在《美国数学月刊》上联合发表了题为《周期"三"意味着混沌》的论文。论文指出，动态系统会因数"3"的出现从而引发系统的"混沌"性。②可以说，这篇极有开创性的论文从此引发了混沌理论研究的热潮，还由此诞生和发展了一门新兴学科，也即混沌学。不过，混沌理论最终被科学界完全接受并享誉整个科学研究圈，还要归因于众多

---

① Edward N. Lorenz, *The Essence of Chaos* (Washington: Univ. of Washington Press, 1993), p. 24.
② 相比"数字"而言，笔者认为，"数"更为原始，毕竟在数字没有形成之前就有了数的出现。数应该是人类呈现世界的方式之一。数不仅只是简单地用来表示数目，而是兼有语言、文化、符号等多种属性。

科学家的参与和奉献。庞加莱（Henri Poincare）、库恩（Thomas S. Kuhn）、大卫·儒勒（David Ruelle）、罗伯特·肖的研究团队（Robert Shaw Group）、曼德博（Benoit B. Mandelbrot）、费根鲍姆（Mitchell Feigenbaum）等人的研究成果为混沌理论的丰富和完善，做出了卓越的贡献。

雷舍尔（Nicholas Rescher）指出，"从古希腊时期'科学'的古典思想一直到现在，大多数哲学家都把他们对于科学典范的学科观念的渴望——如古希腊的科学——建立在数学之上。他们的目标一直是，要以数学科学的精确性和普遍性回答他们领域中的问题。……这种根据世界偶然表面现象之下的、不能违反的、深刻的必然性，来掌握世界有规律的结构的认知寻求，长久以来就是科学的渴望"[1]。事实如是。人类对复杂世界的把握从来都渴望能有一种规律或一种解释体系，确定性和精确性是终极追求。但实际上，这种渴望是有问题的，西方古典哲学的缺陷不仅在于对确定性承诺的夸大，更是在于夸大了对精确性的承诺。

作为当代新兴学科的代表，混沌学率先确立了复杂性、非线性与随机性在后现代科学中的地位，更是对以牛顿经典力学为核心的机械论科学图景做出变革。混沌理论将科学研究从关注宏观和微观世界转向了日常生活中的动力学，使得科学家们不再将涡旋当做噪音而忽视不谈；同时，混沌理论也将人们的关注点从物理行为的简单的降低模式，转向了复杂的互动系统中。可以说，混沌理论将不确定性、不可预测性第一次纳入宇宙图景，从根本上改变了以牛顿、拉普拉斯（Laplace）和达尔文等观点为基础的决定论以及相应的世界观，世界（包括自然世界和人类世界）不再是一个具有自然规律的、可辨的、可解释的有序框架，实在也不是一个整饬的、排列有序的"花园"或一种有条理的、有着整洁边界的系统，康德主义的因果关系原理也不再被看作人类思维的重要部分，这对我们重新认识宇宙的复杂性以及人类在宇宙的地位有着非凡的意义。

实际上，20世纪确切地说就是后现代主义的世纪。随着爱因斯坦、普朗克、薛定谔等科学家对旧的物理学秩序的打破，康托尔（Cantor）、海丁（Arend Heyting）和曼德博等数学家对旧的数学秩序的挑战，量子力学理论造成因果关系的崩溃，混沌理论的"横空出世"，算得上现代科学的第三次革命，彻底颠覆了传统上人们认为世界是一台精密的机器的观念，不仅出现了新的相对主义，确定性也正被或然性或似真性（plausibility）取代。20世纪以来的我们，可谓"栖

---

① 尼古拉斯·雷舍尔：《复杂性：一种哲学概观》，载上海科技教育出版社2007年版，第237页。

居在一个遍及机会和混沌的世界"①，或者说"是一种自组织的自然趋向，一种从无序到有序，从机遇到规律，从混沌到结构涌现的更高级复杂系统的自然动力学"②占主旋律的世界。总之，我们必须承认，以研究非线性动力系统中事物运行行为的"混沌"为宗旨的混沌理论，早已越过了科学领域的疆界，成了一种我们认知世界以及我们身处的宇宙的一种方法、一种模式。确切地说，是一种新的思维和文化的范式。

<h2 style="text-align:center">三</h2>

混沌理论指出，世界是一个"决定性的混沌"或者说"涡旋"。既然是一个"混沌"，我们生活的世界便不再有绝对规律，也不单纯存在机械进程，而是充满了不确定性并且不可预测。世界不再是一个孤立和封闭的系统，而是万物互联且呈开放性。当然，世界也不再是宏观或者微观之说，而呈整体性和全息性。简言之，现今的混沌理论，已经占领了"宇宙观为僵化的确定性秩序的现代主义过分简单化与宇宙观为无政府主义的、无理性的、完全不受理性约束的后现代主义之空虚之间的中间地带"③。接受世界的"混沌"和"复杂"，并以一种新的理性感受力去认知和把握世界，当务之急，是处于时代浪尖上的我们必须面对和做出调整。

当代科学与后现代主义思潮在对世界认识上的重叠，使得艺术和科学在当代社会踏进了同一片领域，造成了20世纪乃至21世纪美国文学的巨大变化。放眼当今世界，人类正经历一场以国际互联网络为代表的信息革命，加之生命科学、人工智能、材料科学等领域的科技进步，使得人类社会遭遇了前所未有的变革。这无疑对文学艺术的发展有着不可估量的影响。许多当代美国小说都出现了形形色色的"科技文化"主题。电脑科技的发展和计算机网络的出现，都为小说文本的形式提供了广阔的空间。许多有着新的空间形式的小说，如"赛博空间"、"超空间"等，已完全抛弃了传统的叙事观念，甚至用电子文本取代印刷文本。与此共生的是，随着科学和技术的发展，当代美国小说的叙事模式也变得复杂起来。

就美国后现代主义小说的空间形式而言，空间批评理论学者弗兰克（Joseph Frank）对小说叙事"空间并置"的建议，已经有些无力，毕竟后现代主义小说

---

① 尼古拉斯·雷舍尔：《复杂性：一种哲学概观》，载上海科技教育出版社2007年版，第241页。
② 尼古拉斯·雷舍尔：《复杂性：一种哲学概观》，载上海科技教育出版社2007年版，第241页。
③ 尼古拉斯·雷舍尔：《复杂性：一种哲学概观》，载上海科技教育出版社2007年版，第242页。

拥有的大多都是漂浮的能指，根本没有真正的句法和组织可以"参照"，其叙事也不再遵循传统的因果–线性–时间顺序，小说的空间也被呈现得漂浮和异质。换言之，后现代主义小说中的叙事总是"混沌"式的碎片化。不仅如此，混沌理论的空间形式如奇异吸引子（strange attractor）、分形（fractal）、迭代（iteration）、倍周期分岔点（period-doubling bifurcation）、涡旋、自组织（self-organization）等，也被以约翰·巴思（John Barth）、约翰·豪克斯（John Hawkes）、凯西·艾克（Kathy Acker）、托马斯·品钦（Thomas Pynchon）、唐·德里罗（Don DeLillo）、科麦克·麦卡锡（Cormac McCarthy）、保罗·奥斯特（Paul Auster）、理查德·鲍尔斯（Richard Powers）等为代表的一批当代美国作家所运用，用来丰富他们的小说叙事或建构小说的空间形式，使得他们的小说呈现出一种新的动态空间性的"混沌"审美。

对于文学研究者来说，是时候摆脱斯诺（C. P. Snow）所说的"两种文化"的现象了——文学文化与它的科学配对物（即科学文化）渐行渐远。不管怎么说，作为一种新的科学理论，混沌理论已经展示出其对于回顾、重释甚或重记语言、文本、自我、社会以及时空性等方面的作用。实际上，混沌理论"推翻现有的科学观和系统观的这一过程，恰恰与当今文学对于不确定性与不稳定性、能指的自由游戏以及各种各样的重写等新的关注点有了共振"①。不仅如此，混沌理论与人文领域以及当代的文学创作所关注的空间以及空间形式的联系，以及混沌理论与新兴的叙事空间理论家们在对读者介入、整体把握叙事细节，并重新拼贴叙事空间形式等方面强调的共识，无疑对于我们深入认识和研究当代美国小说，尤其是考察当代美国小说的叙事空间形式这一新的艺术表现形式，印证后现代主义文学或者新兴的"后后现代主义"文学的多元与复杂性，不仅富有启发，更是大有益处。

四

在一个充满"混沌"和"随机"的宇宙，我们不能再习惯于"习惯"中，要学会直面我们自身处于其中的、复杂的自然世界中的生活事实，毕竟，混沌理论给予我们的是一种"真实的冲击"。

---

① Gordon E. Slethaug, *Beautiful Chaos: Chaos Theory and Metachaotics in Recent American Fiction* (Albany: State Univ. of New York Press, 2000), p. xii.

黑尔斯（N. Katherine Hayles）认为，混沌学不仅给予我们一种新的认识后现代主义和思考秩序的方法，并且，当代美国小说中明显具有的四大后现代主义特质——非线性、自指性、不可逆性以及自组织，在混沌理论中也相当突出。除了与后结构主义在某种程度上有相似处之外，混沌理论"对总体性的怀疑"，也与后现代主义重要学者如德里达（Jacques Derrida）、詹姆逊（Fredric Jameson）、利奥塔与露丝•伊丽格瑞（Luce Irigary）等的观点不谋而合。此外，混沌理论对迭代、递归循环、非线性与不可预测性等宇宙观的强调，与其他后现代主义理论也有很多相似之处。可以说，混沌理论带给我们的是一种新的思维方式，这种新的复杂的整体的多元的混沌思维，不仅可以让我们重新把握世界的复杂性，更是可以将这种思维方式用来建构一种新的混沌学文学批评。

黑尔斯教授的做法就是一个极佳的范例。作为一个混沌学文学批评的践行者，黑尔斯指出，混沌理论就是"混迹于后现代主义主要特征赖以形成和产生的文化来源中一个著名场地。后现代语境通过提供一种文化和技术的媒介，催化了新科学的形成，这些文化和技术媒介中的主要构成部分，它们相互结合相互促进，使得它们最终不再是单一分离的各个事件，而是涌现出了一种新的认识，那就是，复杂系统中真正起着建构作用的是无序、非线性以及噪音"[1]。在她的著作《被缚的混沌》（*Chaos Bound*, 1990）中，黑尔斯就将混沌理论的概念和相关范畴灵活运用，不仅用来解释当代美国文学，还用来说明科学、文学与文化现象三者之间的重要关联。可以说，黑尔斯在她的这本著作中已经提供了混沌学文学批评的范式，"它们不仅与普通的文学批评范式平行，且使用更加宽泛，（她）还凝练出了一些重要的批评词汇，这些词汇与那些描述物理现象的词汇类似"[2]。

除了黑尔斯，著名学者加塔利（Félix Guattari）的著作《混沌互渗》（*Chaosmos*, 1992），就其书名本身已经不言自喻，并且加塔利在此书中的确化用了混沌理论的多个概念，并对这些概念进行重新创造和改装，使得他着力建构的新的"审美范式"，不仅超越了弗洛伊德和拉康的精神分析理论，还突破了分析者和被分析者的二元独立模式。就拙著《科麦克•麦卡锡小说的混沌世界》而

[1] N. Katherine Hayles, ed., *Chaos and Order: Complex Dynamics in Literature and Science* (Chicago and London: The Univ. of Chicago Press, 1991), p. 5.

[2] Michael Patrick Gillespie, *The Aesthetics of Chaos: Nonlinear Thinking and Contemporary Literary Criticism* (Cainesville: Univ. Press of Florida, 1996), p. 17.

言，本书分析的世界级文学大师麦卡锡不仅在他的小说的叙事内容，更是在小说的叙事形式、叙事策略乃至叙事的空间构型上，都活跃着"混沌"的概念和混沌理论的原则和范畴，从而使得麦卡锡的小说有了独特的"混沌"美学特征。

当然，还要明确的是，麦卡锡在他的经典小说《血色子午线》（*Blood Meridian*, 1992）中早就提出了"眼球民主"（optical democracy）的概念,这显然已不仅仅是混沌思维，更是一种当下被热议的后人类中心主义（post-anthropocentrism）思想。在麦卡锡的小说中，我们发现生命远非被人编码、定义为一个物种，而是被当作一个相互作用的、开放性的过程。这种"有活力的、自组织的生命自身结构的普遍生命力"[1]强调的是一种平等主义，恰是后人类中心主义转向的核心，此种认识不仅是"对作为发达资本主义逻辑，即生命的机会主义跨物种商品化的一个唯物主义的、世俗的、负责的和非感性的回应"[2]，更是"社会与文化理论对另一个文化，也即科学文化取得的巨大进步做出的肯定反应"[3]。换言之，混沌思维与后人类中心主义思想就其对世界呈整体性、互联性等的认识来说，也有千丝万缕的联系，这无疑给予我们了一个新的维度，得以拓展混沌理论在外国文学批评和文化研究新的领域。

实际上，一直笼罩在人类中心主义下的人文学科，正被"一个复杂的、以科学研究和技术信息为主导的知识体系所取代"[4]。这一挑战虽算不上终极危机，但却开辟了人文学科跨学科和跨媒介研究的新纪元，也为"软"科学和"硬"科学之间的新对话指明了新的方向。不仅如此，混沌理论所提出的"自组织"概念以及系统通过其自然的运作能够展现出更高阶规律的"涌现"，恰使处于后现代虚无主义焦虑下的人类，有了走出人类中心主义藩篱的可能。随着人们对后人类状况研究的增强，新的认知主体也会发生变化，不仅出现了人类和非人类、行星和宇宙、自然与人工的复杂综合体，更是出现了环境人文学科、地缘政治和社会经济历史的跨学科融合以及数字人文学科的飞速发展，这一切都需要我们调整思维方式。混沌学可谓恰逢其时，毕竟混沌思维这一新的整体的、复杂的、动态的和全息的思维方式，正是我们赖以运用从而应对日新月异、愈来愈复杂的世界和新的情况。

---

① 参见（意）罗西·布拉伊多蒂：《后人类》，宋根成译，载河南大学出版社2016年版，第87页。
② （意）罗西·布拉伊多蒂：《后人类》，宋根成译，载河南大学出版社2016年版，第87页。
③ （意）罗西·布拉伊多蒂：《后人类》，宋根成译，载河南大学出版社2016年版，第87页。
④ （意）罗西·布拉伊多蒂：《后人类》，宋根成译，载河南大学出版社2016年版，第214页。

古罗马哲学家奥勒留（Marcus A. A. Augustus）在他的《沉思录》中说过：
"不要为将来担忧。如果你必须去到将来，你会带着同样的理由去的，恰似你带
着理由来到现在"。世界永远朝向未来开放。如果说有了"混沌"的存在，我们
身处的世界才有了一切的可能和契机，那么，有着混沌思维装备的我们，建设
"人类命运共同体"或者"全球健康共同体"，追求生态、社会和个人的可持续
发展，也都有了无限的可能和美妙的期待。

"蝴蝶"一直栖居在我们的世界，并早已扇动她的翅膀，不远的将来，会出现
怎样一种美好的复杂的未来呢？

道可道，非常道。

是为自序。

张小平

2020年12月29日于扬州逸庐

Abstract

In our cosmos, chaos is everywhere. Order and disorder, terror and beauty, *yin* and *yang*, symmetry and asymmetry, certainty and uncertainty, all are paradoxical and changeable, hence the world as a beautiful chaos. Cormac McCarthy (1933-), one of the important contemporary American writers, is the explorer and pursuer of the chaos. Until now, McCarthy has won various awards for his achievement in fiction, such as the American National Book Award, the National Book Critics Circle Award, the Pulitzer Prize, the PEN/ Saul Bellow Award for Achievement in American Fiction and so on. Along with Philip Roth, Thomas Pynchon and Don DeLillo, McCarthy is considered as one of the four major American novelists of his time by Harold Bloom. It seems impossible to discuss contemporary American literature without consideration of McCarthy. However, in comparison with another three celebrated writers, who have got comprehensive and systematic studies from Chinese academic circles, McCarthy is still in the obscurity and has been ignored on the Chinese literary critical scene for so many years, though his writing career started in the 1960s.

For McCarthy, his works are set not far beyond his living habitats, from Appalachian rural mountains to Southwestern deserts and prairies, and then to Santa Fe in New Mexico, yet his vision goes beyond the regional constraints and into the wider world. Posited within the context of both postmodernism and chaos theory, two important streams of thoughts in contemporary period, McCarthy's novels address the darkness of humanity, violence of society, denaturing of wilderness, chance and randomness of human life, uncertainty and unpredictability of human destiny, and the disproportion between cause and consequence for the development of events, reflecting the cosmos as a deterministic chaos in the postmodern age. His working as a fellow at Santa Fe Institute, a think tank for international studies of chaos theory and complexity science, makes McCarthy's writings focus on chaos, one of the important issues and concepts in contemporary scientific studies and cultural fields. More than an important concept to discuss, chaos has become both the narrative content and form of McCarthy's novels, making his works remarkable in contemporary American literature. Self-consciously making his narrative form in accordance with his thematic content, McCarthy resorts to principles and patterns of chaos theory to be his narrative strategies and narrative forms, which makes his novels as complex and dynamic as the beautiful chaos, presenting unique aesthetic features.

By means of the dialectic combination of cultural studies, historical examination, close reading of the texts, and analysis of discourse and narrative structures, the dissertation, *Chaos in Cormac McCarthy's Fiction*, makes a full-length study of the issue of chaos in McCarthy's fiction and his world vision of chaos as well as innovation in fictional writings. This dissertation makes application of chaos theory suggested mainly by N. Katherine Hayes, Jo Alyson Parker, David Ruelle and Ilya Prigogine, and some relevant postmodern theories proposed by Frederic Jameson, Jean Baudrillard, Jean-Francois Lyotard, Ihab Hassan and Linda Hutcheon, together with the theory about the spatial form in the fiction suggested by Joseph Frank, to examine how chaos becomes the thematic content of McCarthy's novels, how McCarthy adopts the principles of chaos theory to develop his narration, and how McCarthy constructs his fiction's spatial configuration with the patterns of chaos theory. After a research on McCarthy's major novels, *Child of God* (1974), *Blood Meridian or The Evening Redness in the West* (1985), *All the Pretty Horses* (1992), *The Crossing* (1994), *No Country for Old Men* (2005), and *The Road* (2006), this dissertation points out that McCarthy's novels are as complex and dynamic as the beautiful chaos, and his writerly texts demonstrate the merging of science with arts as the tendency of contemporary American literature in the postmodern consumer society. The exploration of the chaos reflected through narrative content and form in McCarthy's fiction aims to draw an outline for McCarthy's aesthetic world on the one hand, and on the other hand to understand better the complexity of human and natural world and the epistemic development in the contemporary world.

The dissertation consists of "Introduction," four chapters, and "Conclusion."

The Introduction gives a general outline of McCarthy's literary career and achievement and pays emphasis on his importance in the literary world, and then a survey on McCarthy criticism at home and abroad is made to suggest the importance of the present study. In McCarthy criticism, although a few scholars have paid attention to McCarthy's association with contemporary scientific turn, few scholars start a systematic study of chaos in McCarthy's fiction and none of them takes McCarthy's works as an organic whole to explore his "chaotic" narrative and aesthetics of chaos presented in his works. The structure and contents of this dissertation have been briefed in the Introduction.

Chapter One, "Chaos, Spatiality, Postmodernism and McCarthy" gives a general theoretical framework of this dissertation. First, this study distinguishes the concept of chaos in modern science from that of traditional understandings and points out that the concept of chaos has been shifted from its previous indication of disorder and confusion to that of orderly disorder. Then, this study explores chaos theory's origin, content, relations with Chinese traditional thinkings, particularly with thoughts reflected in The Book of Changes, and its postmodernist approaches to literary criticism involved. Furthermore, space and spatial form are introduced in terms of the spatial turn in the humanities and the spatial form in the fictional writings by tracing its development in modernist and postmodernist writings.

Chapter Two, "Order, Disorder and Nonlinearity: Chaos and Wilderness" addresses the dark and violent world in McCarthy's fiction, in which man, nature and society are presented to be chaos and wilderness. As one of the great metaphorsof chaos, wilderness is synonymous with chaos, which is characteristic of orderly disorder or disorderly order and nonlinearity. McCarthy's fictional world is full of paradoxes, in which order accompanies disorder, symmetry coexists with asymmetry, and beauty and terror are symbiotic naturally. First, with the aim to explore the relations of science with literature, especially with fictional writings, this chapter traces the epistemic shift from classical science to modern science in terms of the relationship between order and disorder. Then, from the perspective of chaos, this study takes *Child of God* and *Blood Meridian* as case studies to examine the turbulence of characters as regards the origin, development and results of violence. Some other novels, such as *The Orchard Keeper, Outer Dark, Suttree,* and *The Crossing,* are discussed when associated with some relevant ideas. McCarthy just takes violence to demonstrate the truth of world, which is different from that of his contemporary writers, who construct the truth and actuality by means of language.

Through the detailed exploration of violence for Lester Ballard, a killer-necrophile in *Child of God,* the second section attempts to show how the individual subject is involved in a chaotic system of violence negotiated between social subjects and social reality, in which, man, nature and society are interconnected with one another. Ballard's atavistic regression from a human to a "human animal," from civilization to wilderness suggests that his perversion and violence are not only made from his innate physical and psychological defects, but also from the capitalized Order of his living age and society. Institutional systems, familial background, gender relationship and community are combined to make him violent and morbid. The spatial transferring of his habitation and the metaphor of his identity as animals are taken in the fiction to strengthen his marginalization and nonlinear regression from the society. The presentation of Ballard's atavistic regression from civilization to wilderness aims to refract the evil of society and humanity, and his sacrifice for the modern civilization and the capitalized Order makes *Child of God* an allegory to imagine the human world in the contemporary period.

In *Blood Meridian,* those barbarous American mercenaries take violence as acts of consumption in the consumer society, from which they are self-reflecxive. As a sign of consumption, violence dismantles the relations between man and object, making people surface ones without self-perception. Encoded by the grand narrative of Enlightenment with the masks of knowledge, science, order and rationality, violence is made to be the only "legitimized knowledge" in the wilderness or a new fetishism, changing people into "the captives of the cave," and slaves of violence consumption. McCarthy's wilderness is a chaos space, in which man, fauna and flora, and even natural phenomena, are equally harsh, bloody and dangerous, presenting to be in "optical democracy." In America, violence has its historical, cultural and social contexts, McCarthy's aesthetic presentation of violence in *Blood Meridian* is socially and politically motivated at its core to make a diagnosis of the malaise of his living age and society, and to warn his readers to be aware of and reflect upon violence. After the exploration of violence in the wilderness for McCarthy's works, this chapter points out that violence is a nodal point of McCarthy's complicated textual web, from which wilderness and chaos are presented in the world of man, nature and society. Via violence, one of important cultural and social issues in postmodern world, McCarthy not only casts doubts on the humanity but also challenges against the Western metaphysics of dualism and its epistemology since the Enlightenment. In his construction of the world as orderly disorder and nonlinearity, McCarthy subverts the binaries of subject and object, man and nature, nature and culture, order and disorder, center and margin, making him important in contemporary American literature.

Chapter Three, "Iteration, Indeterminacy and Butterfly Effect: Narrative Strategies as Chaos" focuses on the narrative strategies of McCarthy's fiction, in which three key principles of chaos theory have been applied in his narrative texts: iteration, indeterminacy and butterfly effect. The first section explores how iteration is applied in *Blood Meridian* to shape the genre, characters, land description and language style, and how the fiction is made to be a "chaos sandwich" with the "baker's transformation." To begin with, the definition of iteration and its creation of the complicated patterns in a nonlinear dynamic system are introduced and examined. Mathematicians describe iteration as the "baker's transformation." The infinite iteration of the simple process of stretching and folding produces complicated patterns or designs, so does the narrative. With the device of iteration, *Blood Meridian* is made to be exceptionally complicated. In his iterative use of the literary conventions of the Western literature, McCarthy not only makes his "complicit critique" of the convention of traditional Western through the exposure of the violent and raw reality hidden in its convention and the utopia and ideology imagined and constructed in the Western, but also constructs his own specific generic feature of postmodern Western, hence achieving his transcendence. The fiction's iterative richness is added through intertextuality, which is presented through the characterization of the complicated figure of Judge Holden as the icon of chaos and the flat figure of the Kid. Furthermore, the fiction's chapter headings, language style and landscape description present the feature of iteration, making the fiction both strange and familiar in its aesthetic effect and hence a "chaos sandwich."

The second section examines the indeterminacy presented in both the thematic and textual planes in *The Road*. As an important principle of chaos theory, indeterminacy makes the system transform from order to disorder, and vice verse. Due to its sensitive dependence on initial conditions in a chaotic system, the self-organization system may be emerged in the disorder. Just on the edge of chaos, all the variables will be interacted with each other, making the system complex. Living on the edge of chaos, the "self-organization system" created by the Father is indeterminate and futile due to his problematic strategies in a post-apocalyptic wasteland: identification with "good guys,"making frontiers in the South, memories and stories, cultural rituals, emotional forces, together with chance. Besides, the ambiguous genre and title, open ending, nameless figures, fractured structure and minimalist style of language create indeterminacy in the textual level, which echoes that of its narrative content and "field of literary production."

The third section goes further to discuss the "butterfly effect" in *No Country for Old Men*. As the essence of chaos theory, the butterfly effect not only makes the system nonlinear but also causes the uncertainties in the system's development due to its disproportion between cause and effect. In *No Country for Old Men*, the butterfly effect is taken to present the life and world of protagonists as a deterministic chaos, in which chance plays a great role, indicating the randomness of the human world and the meaningless of life and the problematic factuality of the Newtonian paradigm as well. In correspondence with the chaos in the life of characters, the novel's narrative patterns echo James Yorke's vision of "periodic three implies chaos" through the triplet of plotting events and tripartite structure of the fiction as well as three major characters involved in the tracking-up motion. Besides, the frequent appearance of the imagery of coin tossing strengthens the chaos aspect of the novel, indicating the stochastic probability in human life and world.

Chapter Four, "Strange Attractor, Fractals and Self-Similarities: Spatial Configuration as Chaos" explores the spatial configuration of McCarthy's fiction in light of chaos theory and the device of "reflexive reference" proposed by Joseph Frank, meaning the trials to combine facts with inference in the interpretation of a literary text. The previous two books of the border trilogy are taken as case studies. To begin with, the patterns of chaos theory are generally introduced. As the simulation of the motion of the deterministic chaos, both strange attractor and fractals feature self-similarities in their spatial configuration, though the latter is more remarkable than the former in the characteristic of self-similarity. In contemporary fiction, both can be taken as spatial forms to produce the dynamic spatiality in the narrative.

Strange attractor is taken in *All the Pretty Horses* concerning the frontier journey of John Grady Cole to and from Mexican-American borders, in which attracting points, bifurcation points and self-similarities in the strange attractor are presented. Centering around the utopia ideal of the protagonist, there is a deterministic chaos, in which horses in the wilderness are attracting points. Along with the futile journey of John Grady, Blevins, Alejandra and Dueña Alfonsa are bifurcation points, which facilitate and strengthen the chaos for John Grady's journey, making his life more turbulent than before. Through the presentation of emptiness of John Grady's dream driven by the frontier myth, McCarthy makes his fiction self-reflective, criticizing the very genre of which it is inside. Besides, a large quantities of self-similarities are made from the choice of images, characterization and the narrative structure, creating the multiple-dimensional reflexivity and symmetrical asymmetry in the text globally and locally.

In *The Crossing*, fractals are made on both of the planes of the narrative content and structure. The most remarkable for the fiction is its interpolated tales, which are made to construct self-similarities with the major part of the narrative, as regards its thematic motifs like life, myth and narrative. By means of the organic combination of the major part of the narrative with the interpolated tales and some other minor tales underlying the major tale, McCarthy makes his text into fractals with the multitude of self-similarities, indicating the recursive symmetry across the scale and reflexivity in multiple dimensions. Reflexivity is a narrative about narrative, which is made apparent through the interpolated tales and some minor tales in the fiction, making it convenient for the writer to make comments on what he tells in the major narrative part, and even helpful to explore how to make use of chaos theory to write down a story about chaos. It is such organic complexity in the narrative that makes *The Crossing* outstanding in McCarthy's corpus and even contemporary American fiction.

The Conclusion offers the general understanding of chaos in McCarthy's fiction. Chaos is the core of McCarthy's works, and hence the tension to understand his aesthetic force. McCarthy's scientifically complex vision of world makes him consider life as the deterministic chaos and cosmos as the holistic web, which makes his characters live on the edge of chaos with chance and randomness, and his works into a whole and meanwhile interconnected with American literature tradition. His writerly texts encourage the reader's nonlinear thinking in their participation in the writing, presenting the possibility of "chaotic" narrative in the postmodern age. All in all, McCarthy's concepts of chaos in both life and cosmos and his presentation of chaos in both his thematic content and form have made him a unique and influential figure in contemporary American literature. He will be much more influential in the future, for he is on the "road," still writing.

List of Abbreviations

Throughout this dissertation, parenthetical references to McCarthy's novels use the following abbreviations:

TOK   *The Orchard Keeper* (1965)

OD   *Outer Dark* (1968)

COG   *Child of God* (1974)

S   *Suttree* (1979)

BM   *Blood Meridian,* or *The Evening Redness in the West* (1985)

Horses   *All the Pretty Horses* (1992)

C   *The Crossing* (1994)

TS   *The Stonemason* (1994)

Plain   *Cities of the Plain* (1998)

COM   *No Country for Old Men* (2005)

Road   *The Road* (2006)

Introduction

In a way, art is a theory about the way the world look to human beings. It's abundantly obvious that one doesn't know the world around us in detail. What artists have accomplished is realizing that there's only a small amount of stuff that's important, and then seeing what it was.

Mitchell Feigenbaum, Chaos: Making a New Science

As a prominent phenomenon in literature and culture in the postindustrial society since the 1960s, postmodernism battles against the beliefs of the Enlightenment, with its "incredulity toward metanarrative" (Lyotard xxiv), or its penchant of "dedoxification" (Hutcheon, *The Politics* 3), "decreation/ deconstruction" (Hassan 91), "denaturing" (Hayles, *Chaos Bound* 265) and "delegitimation" (Lyotard 37) of the supposedly universal truths of Western humanism. Likewise, chaos theory challenges against classical science, and takes the cosmos as a deterministic "chaos" with orderly disorder or disorderly order rather than a machine with order, completely overturning the universal truths of classical science in the past over three hundred years. Both are symbiotic and mutually developed in contemporary period. It is in the context of these two trends of thoughts that Cormac McCarthy's writings have been produced and cultivated.

This study is primarily on the fiction of McCarthy, one of the most important American contemporary writers, with an attempt to examine the issue of chaos in his major novels, *Child of God* (1974), *Blood Meridian* (1985), *All the Pretty Horses* (1992), *The Crossing* (1994), *No Country for Old Men* (2005), and *The Road* (2006), and some of his other works may be mentioned if necessary. By taking up the issue of chaos in McCarthy's works, this study intends to investigate the ideas of chaos in his human and natural and aesthetic world presented through his narrative content and form. More than a metaphor, "chaos" will be taken as one of important concepts for the study's theoretical approaches in the exploration of McCarthy's fictional and textual world as regards to his narrative content, strategies and forms.

The inspiration of a study on McCarthy mainly grows out of the imbalance of overseas and Chinese scholarship on this writer. Globally speaking, McCarthy is more and more regarded as one of the most important American writers of the late twentieth century and the early twenty-first century. His fame has become worldwide. It seems impossible to discuss American contemporary novels without mentioning McCarthy. Harold Bloom has named him "one of the four major American novelists of his time, along with Philip Roth, Thomas Pynchon, and Don DeLillo" (Brosi 14). Comparing with the other three important writers in American literature, McCarthy is still in the obscurity in Chinese academic circle and has been ignored on the Chinese literary critical scene for so many years. Meeting the glory of his contribution to literature in the world, we cannot close our eyes, which is why I am stimulated into making a full-length study of McCarthy's works and trying to map out his artistic trajectories and utter a Chinese voice in McCarthy's scholarship.

Before exploring McCarthy's literary works, it is better to briefly know him and his literary career and achievements as well. Meanwhile, a survey on McCarthy criticism at home and abroad is also necessary.

I. McCarthy's Literary Career and Achievements

Charles Joseph McCarthy, Jr. was born into the family of Joseph McCarthy and Gladys McGrail McCarthy, in Providence, Rhode Island, in 1933 and raised in Knoxville, Tennessee, where Joseph McCarthy, Sr., worked as a lawyer in Tennessee Range Authority. McCarthy later took the first name of Cormac, the Gaelic equivalent of Charles, which is said to be "a family nickname given to his father by his Irish aunts" (Frye 2), or get inspiration from his visit to Blarney Castle in County Cork, built in the fifteenth century by an Irish King Cormac Laidir McCarthy, whom he regards as an ancestor (Cant, *Cormac McCarthy* 18). In spite of a small incident in life, we may discover his ambition from childhood.

McCarthy was raised a Roman Catholic and educated in Catholic schools until he entered the University of Tennessee in 1951. In his university years, he has shown his literary gift, and earned the university's Ingram-Merrill Award for creative writing. In 1953, he left it for the U. S. Air Force and stationed in Alaska, where he read extensively, primarily to kill the time and mollify his tedium in the barracks. He returned in 1957 to the University of Tennessee and stayed there briefly without getting a degree. Anyhow, he had other earnings, for two of his short stories, "Wake for Susan" (1959) and "A Drowning Incident" (1960), were published in the University's literary magazine, *The Phoenix*. Some major thematic motifs of his later literary works, such as death, dream and violence, have presented in these two stories. In 1961 McCarthy married his fellow student Lee Holleman, and had a son, Cullen, and in 1964, they divorced.

It is generally thought that McCarthy's fiction has a strong geographical feature. As Sam Shepard remarks, "Imagination is great, as far as it will get you. But it usually doesn't get you any farther than your own experience" (qtd. in Owens 21), writers usually talk about something he is familiar with. His first-period fiction, including *The Orchard Keeper* (1965), *Outer Dark* (1968), *Child of God* (1974) and *Suttree* (1979), is often set in the rural regions of the Appalachian mountain near his hometown, Knoxville, or at least drawn from experiences in his home state of East Tennessee. Though a few works in his earlier period, McCarthy still gets acclaims. The first of McCarthy's fiction was edited by Faulkner's editor Albert Erskine, and published by Random House. He was awarded a $5,000 fellowship by the American Academy of Arts and Letters, the William Faulkner Foundation Award for 1965 and a grant in 1966 from the Rockefeller Foundation, and later Guggenheim fellowship in 1969. Those grants help him survive for almost two decades. In 1967, McCarthy took a trip to Europe and on the boat he met Annie DeLisle and they were married in England that year. In McCarthy's works, the themes of violence, wilderness, human nature and survival are consistent. His early Appalachian fiction follows the tradition of Southern literature created by William Faulkner, Flannery O'Connor and Carson McCullers, which are featured with grotesqueness, surrealism, violence and religious significance.

In 1976, McCarthy moved to El Paso, Texas, and about a year later, he left Annie DeLisle. It is said that his migration is mainly out of his necessity for collection of materials for his new work, *Blood Meridian, or The Evening Redness* in the West (1985). However, such a transitional fiction from Appalachian period to Southwestern one, though taking him so long time, does not receive well from his readers because of its presentation of violence and darkness in humanity, rather, encounters criticism from critics. Some stand on the side of Vereen Bell's "nihilist" thesis as regards to the violence in the novel, and some follow Edwin T. Arnold's defense to take McCarthy as a moralist. Though controversial, it is still regarded as one of the best of McCarthy's oeuvres. Harold Bloom, Professor Emeritus of Yale University, a leading international critic, speaks of it highly, and even takes it together with Melville's *Moby Dick* and Faulkner's *As I Lay Dying* to be known in the history of American literature. Bloom holds that "no other living American novelists, not even Pynchon, has given us a book as strong and memorable as *Blood Meridian*, much as I appreciate Don Dellilo's *Underworld*, Philip Roth's *Zuckerman Bound*, *Sabbath's Theatre*, and *American Pastoral*, and Pynchon's *Gravity's Rainbow* and *Mason & Dixon*" (532).

McCarthy has a wide range of interests, and wilderness in the west attracts him most. In a rare newspaper interview (only three times in his life), he talked with the interviewer about rattlesnakes, and his plan with Edward Abbey[1] to "reintroduce wolf to Southern Arizona" (Woodward, "Venomous Fiction" 30). In most of his early novels, his protagonists would be arranged to go westering in the ending, which seems to suggest that wilderness in the west is a place to deal with their difficulties in life. Oddly in consistence with the westering of his characters, McCarthy also moved to the Southwest of USA at the end of 1970s. In 1981, McCarthy was awarded the prestigious Genius Grant ($236,000) from the McArthur Foundation, recommended by Saul Bellow, Robert Penn Warren, and Shelby Foote, and he was said to be one of the first in the arts to receive this grant. His winning prize gives him a chance to make friends with the Nobel-Prize winner, particle physicist, Murry Gell-Mann, who works at the Santa

---

[1]Edward Abbey (1927-1989) is a contemporary nature writer and the advocator of the preservation of the west, esp. the desert, and one of his well-known environmental writings is *Desert Solitaire* (1968).

Fe Institute.

Human life is also a chaotic system. For McCarthy, this is a "chaos" in his life in that such an incident is so critical in his literary career that his later works are associated with chaos, featuring "scientifically" in the narrative, though we may sense "chaotic" color in his early works because of his own broad interests since childhood and the powerful influence of chaos theory in society. Founded in 1984, Santa Fe Institute is a think tank, where international scholars in a variety of disciplines conduct researches in a wide range of areas from biology to chaos theory. In terms of the studies of chaos theory, there are three schools in the world: the American school, represented by the Santa Fe Institute; European school, represented by Belgian scientist Ilya Prigogine and his followers; Chinese school, represented by the scientist Qian Xuesen. The open and eclectic approaches to a variety of questions at the Santa Fe Institute were attractive to McCarthy, and he became a fellow at the Santa Fe Institute, working among scientists. Almost in the same year, he married Jennifer Winkley and moved to Santa Fe, New Mexico. In McCarthy's own words, "I like being around smart, interesting people," and more important, "it's sobering how investigations into physical phenomenon are done, it makes you more responsible about the way you think" (Woodward, "Cormac Country" 98).

In the wake of his Southwestern motion, his writing makes change, too. Farewell to his early Appalachian fiction, McCarthy shifts to the Western literature,[1] and his Southwestern works are usually considered as new Western or postmodern Western or revisionist Western or apocalyptic Western for critics. His Southwestern "turn" represents "a sudden break with his past, including his family, wife, and career in Southern fiction" (Jarrett, *Cormac McCarthy* 4). For better or worse, we cannot predict his shift at present, yet after all, in his Southwestern period, McCarthy's "fortunes have skyrocketed" (Owens xiii) with the publication of *All the Pretty Horses* in 1992. Such a fiction was awarded both the National Book Award and the National Book

---

[1] As a specific branch of American literature, the Western literature may be written in capital or lowercase letter. The present study takes the spelling in lowercase letter to refer to this subgenre, and the capital letter will be used when written singly. The same is true for the Southern literature when mentioned in the study.

Critics Circle Award, and on the bestseller list of *New York Times*, "becoming that most esteemed of literary creations, a popular novel with serious artistic merit" (Owens xiv). After *All the Pretty Horses*, another two volumes of his border trilogy, *The Crossing* (1994), and *Cities of the Plain* (1998) achieve greatly. McCarthy's Southwestern works are welcomed in the critical community, and the first McCarthy conference was held in 1993 to make studies of him and his writings. Simultaneously, Hollywood discovered his books and edited them into films. Until now, most of his novels have been edited or adapted into cinemas. *All the Pretty Horses* were directed by Billy Bob Thornton and released in 2000. It is commented to be a big success.

In his latest New Mexico period, McCarthy wrote two novels: *No Country for Old Man* (2005) and *The Road* (2006). *No Country for Old Man*, written and directed by Joel and Ethan Coen, received international acclaim for its winning of four Academy Awards from the National Board of Review, the Directors Guild of America, the New York Film Critics Circle, and the Golden Palm at the Cannes Film Festival, besides Oscar Award of Best Picture. In his mid-sixties, McCarthy became the father of John Francis McCarthy, to whom *The Road* is dedicated. This novel gives a portrait of the horrible post-apocalyptic world, in which the love between father and son impresses the reader deeply. *The Road* surpasses *All the Pretty Horses* with its popularity both in the public and academic circles, even rivals with *Blood Meridian* and *The Crossing* for its enthusiastic critical reception, eventually not only winning the Pulitzer Prize, but also Great Britain's James Tait Black Memorial Prize for fiction. It is also made into a winning-prize film in the direction by John Hillcoat.

Besides ten novels, McCarthy has some other works: three screenplays, including *The Gardener's Son* (1976), *Whales and Men* (written in the mid to late 1980s) and *The Counselor* (2013); and two dramas, *The Stonemason* (1994), and *The Sunset Limited* (2006). In June 2007, this camera-shy writer astonished his followers and appeared on daytime television for Oprah's Book Club featuring him on *The Road*. As one of the most popular television talk shows in America, *Oprah's Book Club* enables its recommended writer to become nationally purple one night. With this interview, Knopf printed 950,000 additional paperback of *The Road*, making McCarthy known to every household.

By now, McCarthy has said goodbye to his previous life "far from madding crowd" and becomes a writer with applauses and flowers. *The Road* was ranked in 2010 by the *New York Times* as number one on the list of the 100 best American books of the past ten years, and *Blood Meridian* also sat on the second place on its 2006 list of the best American fiction of the previous quarter century. *Blood Meridian* also was among Time's 100 best English language books (fiction and nonfiction) published from 1923 to 2005. Ralph Ellison comments that "McCarthy is a writer to be read, to be admired, and quite honestly-envied" (book leaf in COG). In 2008, McCarthy won the PEN/Saul Bellow Award for Achievement in American fiction. At present, McCarthy is not only popular in America, but also welcome in Europe, particularly Britain and Germany.

A self-made writer with rich knowledge of science, philosophy, religion, culture and literature, McCarthy attracts the reader with his works and his persona himself as well. A man does what he loves, McCarthy answers Oprah with his special humor, "that's the blessing," because "the 'laws of probability' will put all of us in the lucky and unlucky charts equally like a poker player in Las Vegas or the stock market analyst" (Lincoln 14). McCarthy is still on "the road." From Woodward's second interview with McCarthy in 2005 for Vanity Fair, we learn that there are as many as four or five novels underway for him ("Cormac Country" 100). Perhaps, some day the reader will be "lucky" with McCarthy's another book with unknown depth, we are expecting.

II. McCarthy Studies at Home and Abroad

Although McCarthy's literary career spans almost forty years, yet his reputation is largely confined to his admirers and specialized academic circles until *All the Pretty Horse* (1992) brings him into the general reader's vision and gains popular success and critical acceptance as well. In the light of the acceptance of his works in the public and academic circles, we may divide McCarthy criticism into two periods. The first phase is to assess and canonize him and his works basically, and the second one tends to be mature and diverse in his criticism. The focus of critics in the first period seems like the question, "why McCarthy is so good," and in the second stage, they have paid more attention on "why McCarthy is so important," in other words, to attempt to enlist him as a canon writer in contemporary literature.

Before the 1990s, McCarthy criticism is featured with intense local-color analysis, and in this period, only one full-length book, *The Achievement of Cormac McCarthy* (1988) by Vereen Bell, makes exploration of his works before the publication of *The Border Trilogy*. Bell is a respected Southern literary scholar and his devotion to analysis and evaluation of all the novels published to that date promotes McCarthy to be an excellent Southern writer. In this stage, McCarthy criticism almost holds that he is equivalent or near equivalent with those postbellum modern romance writers in the South, particularly often with William Faulkner, Flannery O'Connor and James Dickey as well.

Since the 1990s, McCarthy criticism has entered a new and mature phase.[1] There appear at least 10 full-length critical books and 6 collections of book-length editions of essays by different authors, and more than 100 essays published in different academic journals, and in USA, almost 28 PhD dissertations and MA theses dealing with McCarthy and his works directly or associating him and his works together with some other writers.[2] McCarthy fans have had their on-line site in 1999, The Cormac McCarthy Society, and founded the academic journal *The Cormac McCarthy Journal*, devoted to the study of McCarthy and his works. In the fall of 1999, the journal Southwestern American Literature published an issue primarily on McCarthy's Western writings, later, in the spring of 2000, The Southern Quarterly published another special McCarthy issue. In this period, critics make use of different points of view and a wide range of critical approaches to explore McCarthy's works, and his screenplays and dramas are involved, too.

Since McCarthy's works have been written since the 1960s, which is generally

---

[1] Rick Wallach asserts that Holloway's *The Late Modernism of Cormac McCarthy* has marked McCarthy criticismto enter into a new and mature phase ("Foreword" 2002), yet before the publication of Holloway's book, Robert Jarrett's *Cormac McCarthy* (1997) and Barcley Owen's *Cormac McCarthy's Western Novels* (2000) have promoted McCarthy criticism to be diverse and objective.

[2] This conclusion is reached after reviewing the online databases of Galegroup, JSTOR, PQDT and ProQuest from the website of XMU Library.

acknowledged as the starting period of postmodernism,[①] thus, the most distinguished and heated debate in McCarthy criticism is on the definition of McCarthy as a postmodern writer. Following Bell's monograph to canonize McCarthy in 1988, Robert Jarrett's Cormac McCarthy (1997) is one groundbreaking critical book to deal with his novels before the publication of Cities of the Plain. In this critical book, Jarrett regards McCarthy as a writer experienced a shift from modernism to postmodernism, and suggests that his works are predominately realistic and modernistic before *Blood Meridian*, and postmodern after it (*Cormac McCarthy* vii-viii). Jarrett's idea is challenged by John Cant, who thinks that labeling McCarthy's works in this manner seems to be too obscure. In light of Lyotard's classical definition of postmodernism as "incredulity toward metanarratives," Cant argues that "one of the unifying themes of McCarthy's works is his depiction of the failure of the 'grand narrative' of American Exceptionalism" (*Cormac McCarty* 5). In *Cormac McCarthy* and the *Myth of American Exceptionalism* (2008), Cant presents a unified vision of McCarthy's output to discuss his rewriting of the grand narrative of American exceptionalism with different forms in his works, and suggests that McCarthy's deliberate organization of his works into the mythic form is to "point out the destructive consequences of structuring the consciousness of individuals by means of powerful mythologies which they are not in a position to live out" (9).

In effect, Cant's contention is to demonstrate McCarthy as a revisionist, which is a major tendency for postmodernist writers in their writings. Cant's argument of McCarthy as a revisionist of American myth echoes in James J. Donahue's dissertation, *Rewriting the American Myth: Post 1960s American Historical Frontier Romances* (2007), which argues that McCarthy's works criticize the inherent racism of Daniel Boone Mythology and rewrite the myth of frontier. Actually, McCarthy's postmodern rewriting of American myth has been discussed before, particularly in Barcley Owens' *Cormac McCarthy's Western Novels* (2000), which is not mentioned in the

---

① Critics have different ideas to chronologize postmodernism, yet just as Prof. Yang Renjing asserts, "Postmodernist novel is the output of World War Two, and the publication of *Catch-22* by Joseph Heller in 1961 has brought black humor onto the literary stage, indicating the beginning of postmodernist novel of American literature" (2).

argumentation from both Cant and Donahue. Owens mainly focuses on violence, one of the major thematic motifs for McCarthy's works. After his exploration of four of McCarthy's Southwestern novels, Owens argues that the violence presented in McCarthy's Western works is to reflect or refract violence in the human mind, and reassess the violence in American culture. For Owens, four of McCarthy's Western novels are McCarthy's criticism of American myths, especially its poisonous effects on young men with its idealism. The ideas of the myth's poisonous effect on young Americans from Owens receive correspondence from Megan Riley McGilchrist. In *The Western Landscape in Cormac McCarthy and Wallace Stegner* (2010), McGilchrist makes exploration of Western landscape and nature in McCarthy's Southwestern novels with the context of post-Vietnam world. McGilchrist argues that "McCarthy's Western landscapes begin from the center of the myths of the west itself" (3), and his works aim to remind the reader of the West as "hollow simulacrum of reality" rather than "the home of heroism and hope" (8).

Different from the critics mentioned above, David Holloway takes McCarthy as a "late modernist," which has been proved in his monograph, *The Late Modernism of Cormac McCarthy* (2002). Holloway suggests that McCarthy's works should not be taken as either modernist, or postmodernist. He draws on Fredric Jameson's category of "transcoding" to associate McCarthy's works with a broader cultural and historical milieu and then assumes that his works are of "late modernism," which is "a kind of writing that embodies aspects of postmodern so as to map a route through and beyond the condition it describes," and "a writing that seizes upon the postmodern so as to use it against itself and negate it dialectically from within" (4). Close to that of Holloway, Georg Guillemin argues that McCarthy's works have had allegorical dimension, yet they are different from the postmodern writing, which "has rehabilitated allegoresis through its use of parable, and typological structure through its use of intertextuality" (10). Meanwhile, Guillemin points out that McCarthy's allegorical "iconography partakes of the realism Mikhail Bakhtin has defined as carnivalesque" (10).

Besides the distinguishment of McCarthy to be a modernist from a postmodernist, some critics argue eclectically. They hold that McCarthy's work is postmodern, or even has transcended postmodernism to found his own specific features. Taking *Blood Meridian* as a case study, Owens notes that in McCarthy's postmodern presentation of violence, some other genres have been combined, too, particularly turn-of-the-naturalism (10). Kenneth Lincoln's vision about McCarthy's works sounds credible and original. In his *Cormac McCarthy: American Canticle* (2009), Lincoln assumes that McCarthy's works are "hyperrealism," because they invite the reader to see into the depths and heights and ironic abruptions. For Lincoln, the term "hyper" implies dimensions of radical data beyond the given consensus, and "hyperspace" posits a physics of time/space beyond three dimensions. Lincoln writes that distortion may reveal hidden depths, and illusion may conjure holographic truths. Though McCarthy's hyper-real fiction presents the reader with the fabrication of reality, yet on further reflection it "stands truer-to-life than flat dimensional 'reality,' that is, art real to the point of abruptive disbelief and breakthrough discovery" (20). In effect, Lincoln's contention is still postmodern, yet eclectic after all. As we know, the fiction always tends to image the reality with "illusion," and postmodernist fiction is still "mimetic" of reality, even though it has to refract rather than reflect, and the reality it presents has been masked with the distortion of the "actuality."

One of the most classic criteria to differentiate modernist fiction from postmodernist one is McHale's definition about the problem of "dominate." McHale argues that literary modernists focus on epistemological concerns—how to interpret the world, while by the postmodern era, the predominant concerns have become ontological and the question changes to ask what the world is (9-11). Based on McHale's definition, Matthew Guinn acknowledges the "transition in McCarthy's work" (110). After his close examination of *Suttree*, Guinn points out McCarthy's differences from many quintessentially postmodern writers, because he "remains aloof from a totally postmodern sensibility" through the combination of "the styles and approaches of both modernist and postmodernist fiction," forging "a form of his own that promise to transcend his own period" (115). Similar to Guinn's idea of integration, Christopher Metress asserts that McCarthy is both a postmodernist and a moralist, In his exploration of *Outer Dark* with the theological vision, Metress holds that as a postmodernist,

"McCarthy dismantles our metanarratives, deconstructs our preconceptions, and throws us into epistemological uncertainty at every turn. As a moralist, however, he is drawn to the mysteries of faith and ... cannot stop wondering in the most passionate and honest way what gives life meaning" (154). Metress's understanding of McCarthy's works seems to be more accurate and more nuanced.

With regards to this conflict in which McCarthy's work is fully embroiled, Holloway's argument is persuasive for us to look at such a problem. He has noted that such terms of classification, "tend to obscure the heterogeneous, conflicted, or contradictory character of the broad tendencies they name" (*The Late Modernism* 14). McGilchrist also speaks reasonably, McCarthy's novels "defy classification ... this is not to say that one may not look at McCarthy in theses critical terms, but simply that he often goes beyond, and between, the parameters of critical definition" (46-7). Both of the critics' ideas may be taken as a conclusion for the argument of McCarthy to be a postmodernist or not.

Associated with the debates over the definition of McCarthy as a postmodern writer, the other question deserves due critical attention in McCarthy criticism: hisclassification as a regionalist. Such a question is a cliche, for it has been argued in the first period of McCarthy criticism since the debut of his first work, but in the second phase, it is still prevalent. Since McCarthy's works are geographically featured, they tend to be categorized into Southern or Western writings. Some critics in the South camp unanimously garner McCarthy as a Southern writer, and they would like to find in each of his novels "something redemptive or regenerative, something affirmative mysteries," supposed to get affirmation in Southern literature (Phillips 435). For instance, Walter Sullivan, one of the esteemed critics of Southern literature, initially welcomes McCarthy as a formidable new talent, and posits his earlier works within the tradition of Southern novels. He even pronounces that "no Southern novelist since William Styron has got off to a better start" (*A Requiem* 70). However, the approval from Southern critics is short-lived, because McCarthy's writings have shifted "westward" after the 1980s, which have had obvious postmodern feature, and in the minds of Southern critics, he quickly transformed to be a "bad guy," which refers to those writers, who "criticize the Southern tradition or uproot the whole tradition" in the definition of Brinkmeyer (qtd. in Li 179). Nell Sullivan even assumes, "McCarthy is the artist not merely bereft of community and myth; he has declared war against these ancient repositories of order and truth" (72). Though Southern critics feel desperate for McCarthy's subversion of Southern literary tradition, they still acknowledge that he has directed a new way for Southern literature and entered into something "postSouthern."[①]

"Political unconscious" haunts McCarthy criticism frequently. In terms of McCarthy as a regionalist, critics in the West camp hold that McCarthy's works are postmodern Western or antiWestern or apocalyptical Western, especially his Southwestern ones. The Western literature is generally mistaken for popular literature in America, so putting McCarthy's works into the tradition of the Western literature might be helpful to promote it to a higher plane with its aesthetic values. Different from the narrow vision of critics in the South camp, scholars in the West camp read McCarthy in a broader tradition. According to them, McCarthy has gone beyond the Western or the Southern and belongs to the Western culture as a whole, especially its philosophical heritage. King James Bible, Shakespeare, Conrad, Dostoyevsky, Hegel, Nietzsche, Heidegger, Kierkegaard, are McCarthy's antecedents. So, we may find that McCarthy studies are usually ideological-leaden. Apart from the ongoing disputes about Southern or Western over McCarthy's novels, some critics represented by Mark A. Eaton suggest a new genre, South-Western, to define McCarthy's novels (Eaton 155-80). John Cant even categorizes McCarthy's earlier works into Appalachian literature, for they are thought to be much "local" than other Southern literature due to their basic displays of lives for poor mountaineers in West Tennessee and their prevalence with violence portrayed in one form or another (Cormac McCarthy 31-6).

Besides the debates on the definition of McCarthy as a postmodernist or regional writer, critics have explored McCarthy and his works with various critical approaches. The Pastoral Visions of Cormac McCarthy (2004) by Georg Guillemin employs the

---

① "PostSouthern" is coined by Lewis P. Simpson to refer to the eclipse of Southern literature's "defining vision of social order at once strongly sacramental and sternly moralistic" (Simpson 255), yet it is later adopted by many critics to describe "an overt form of Southern postmodernism" in contemporary literature (Petrides 4).

approach of ecocriticism to study the evolution of pastoral vision in McCarthy's works from *The Orchard Keeper* to *The Border Trilogy*. Wallis Sanborn's *Animal Presentation in the Fiction of Cormac McCarthy* (2003)[①] echoes Guilemin's research with its focuses on non-human animals, feral and domestic, in McCarthy's fictional natural world. Jay Ellis's *No Place for Home* (2006) brings a Jungian lens to McCarthy's fiction. He links the settings, particularly houses, graves and fences in McCarthy's novels, with the interiority of characters to explore "the underlying rule governing McCarthy's description of space" (4). In addition, some critics, such as Dianne Luce, Nell Sullivan and Megan Riley McGilchrist, employ Feminism approach to examine his works, in which women are discovered to be absent or dead, and the Western landscape to be feminine rather than masculine. Thematic studies of McCarthy's works mainly focus on blood and violence, which are foregrounded. Americanist approach draws on McCarthy's formal debts to Herman Melville, Ernest Hemingway, John Hawks, Flannery O'Connor, Mark Twain and William Faulkner with the aim to enlist McCarthy in American literary tradition. Popular in Euro-American countries, comparison studies have taken McCarthy's contemporary writers, such as E. L. Doctorow, Don DeLillo, John Barth, Tim O'Brain, Toni Morrison, Leslie Marmon Silko, and Wallace Stegner, to make comparisons in terms of the theme, style, gender relations, or aesthetic features in their works.

Besides full-length books by single authors published in McCarthy criticism,several collections of essays by different authors have appeared since the 1990s. All of them present a wide range of different critical points of view on McCarthy and expose his works with a range of theoretical approaches. Published respectively in 1995 and 2002, *Sacred Violence* with two volumes are still influential and significant for McCarthy criticism today. *Perspectives on Cormac McCarthy* (1999), edited by McCarthy scholars, Edwin T. Arnold and Dianne Luce, and some other collections, such as *Myth, Legend, Dust* (2001), *A Cormac McCarthy Companion* (2001), *Cormac McCarthy* (2002), *Modern Critical Views* (2002), appear consecutively, not only

---

① Sanborn's dissertation of *Animal Presentation* has been published in the form of monograph in 2006, yet unavailable for me, and my reference is still his dissertation from the database of PQDT.

enriching McCarthy criticism but also providing suggestions and references for later McCarthy studies.

In comparison with the overseas scholarship on McCarthy, Chinese McCarthy criticism is still in its nascent stage. To my knowledge, there have not been much critical explorations about McCarthy in China, and only simple introduction or comments on McCarthy's works are scattered in three academic books: Li Yang's *Changes of American Southern Literature in the Postmodern Period* (2006), Jiang Ningkang's *Literature and National Identity in Contemporary America* (2008), and Luo Xiaoyun's *American Western Literature* (2009). Li Yang places McCarthy together with some other contemporary Southern writers in the post-1960s context, and mainly explores their challenges against and developments of classic thematic motifs in the Southern literature since "Southern Renascence." Li Yang mainly focuses on McCarthy's Appalachian works, i. e. *The Orchard Keeper*, *Outer Dark*, *Child of God* and *Suttree*, yet due to his general concern of all the post-Southern writers in the postmodern period, Li's study seems hardly elaborate in the study of McCarthy's works, and his conclusion is also made too rough without close textual analysis. Although he aims to examine four of McCarthy's novels, actually, in his monograph, only the novel, *Suttree*, catches his attention, and he simply gives a glance at another three works.

Jiang Ningkang gives an introduction to McCarthy's *The Border Trilogy* in his monograph, and points out that they are aesthetically beautiful and attractive due to their presentation of sublime Western landscape and cowboy's adventures, which caters for the cultural atmosphere in the contemporary period. Besides, the frontier spirit, martial codes and individualism shown in the novels reconstruct American national identity, that's why these novels are welcome in America (191-5). Prof. Jiang's contention is original, yet his topics about the construction of American national identity limit his study of McCarthy's works and makes it stay in the introductory plane. Luo Xiaoyun makes exploration of *The Border Trilogy* through the lens of ecocriticism in his book, and argues that McCarthy's later works have turned towards introspection, because there is no longer frontier for people to explore, with the disappearance of the Western frontier as "safety-valve" proposed in Turner's "Frontier Hypothesis," which is significant for McCarthy's works (162-3). Though persuasive for Prof. Luo's argument, Luo's study does not leave enough space for him to explore McCarthy's works in one book with the focus on the development of American Western literature as a whole.

Nevertheless, from the database of CNKI,[①] we can browse 47 essays on McCarthy and his works in domestic academic journals since 1965, when McCarthy's first novel, *The Orchard Keeper* was published. Most of essays by Chinese critics mainly concern McCarthy's Southwestern novels, esp. his border trilogy, with Jiang Ningkang's "Narrative Aesthetics and Cinematic Representations in Cormac McCarthy's Novels", Pei Yali's "Cormac McCarthy's Fiction and Cinema" and the present dissertation writer's " 'All Tales are One': Fractals in *The Crossing*" as their representatives. Apart from the studies of Prof. Jiang and Prof. Pei and the present writer as well, which explore the cinematographic devices and chaotic narrative configuration taken in the border trilogy, obviously, the approaches to McCarthy's works in Chinese McCarthy scholarship seem to be monotonous. Ecocriticism approach is popular, which might be explained as the pursuit of vogue or simply modeling after the overseas scholarship. Until now, to my knowledge, there is not yet any monograph or Ph.D. dissertation on McCarthy and his works in China.[②] While, thankfully, MA thesis on McCarthy's works has been around, and only in 2011, seven theses are newly added.[③]

All in all, after the exploration of McCarthy studies at home and abroad, we may find that McCarthy scholars miss one important issue, namely, McCarthy's "chaotic" visions about human, natural and aesthetic world, although they have made efforts to define him as a postmodernist or regional writer since the 1990s. Few scholars start a systematic study of chaos in his novels and none of them takes McCarthy's works as an organic whole to explore his "chaotic" narrative, although a few scholars have

① CNKI refers to Chinese National Knowledge Infrastructure, and the database of CNKI almost includes all the essays published in major Chinese academic journals since 1980s.

② The statistics is given until the finishing time of this dissertation, i.e. 2012. At present, more than 8 dissertationshas been done in China on McCarthy and his works.

③ From 2009 to 2010, there was only one MA thesis on *The Road*; while until 2011, it has ascended to 8 ones, in which 3 theses are on the Western fiction, including *The Border Trilogy*, 4 theses about *The Road*, 1 thesis on *No Country for Old Men*. The emerging MA theses in recent years demonstrates that McCarthy has drawn the attention of Chinese academic circle.

paid attention to his association with the contemporary scientific turn. Besides Gordon E. Slethaug's *Beautiful Chaos* (2000), which takes two of McCarthy's novels, *Blood Meridian* and *All the Pretty Horses*, to make exploration of their narrative strategies related with chaos theory, to my knowledge, Jay Ellis' *No Place for Home* (2006), and Steven Frye's *Understanding Cormac McCarthy* (2009) are only books to mention McCarthy's association with chaos theory. In Ellis' book, the complexity (chaos) theory is taken to explain the destines of McCarthy's heroes as wanderers or nomads in the wilderness. Frye's book also touches on the core of McCarthy's philosophical vision of chaos. In his introduction to *No Country for Old Men*, Frye points out the influence of chaos theory, particularly, the "butterfly effect" on the characterization of the villain Anton Chigurh in the fiction (150-64). Besides, McCarthy's paradoxical ideas about the mystery of universe, such as the coexistence of violence, evil and depravity with peace, good and love, are mentioned in Frye's introducing analysis of *Blood Meridian*, *The Crossing*, and *Cities of the Plain*, though he does not associate them with McCarthy's specific vision of world as chaos.

However, in spite of insightful observations, Slethaug does not go deep into a detailed study of McCarthy in a book to discuss chaos in many postmodernist writings; while for Jay Ellis, he merely mentions in his conclusion the significance of complexity theory to explicate the destinies of characters in McCarthy's works, and does not make further exploration in his examination of the spatial constraints of McCarthy's characters. As for Frye, his book is simply written for beginners to have a general understanding of McCarthy and his literary works, so he does not make close examination and showcase the chaos in McCarthy's fiction obviously, neither does he associate the paradoxes of the universe displayed in McCarthy's works with chaos theory. Though their touches on the chaos in McCarthy's writings are impressive and inspiring, they can only give a brush on the surface of McCarthy's profound world. The treasure house of McCarthy's fiction is yet to be further exploited. Reviewing the scholarship on McCarthy at home and abroad, it is hoped that this study can contribute a little to filling up this blank.

III. The Framework of Chaos in Cormac McCarthy's Fiction

The present study is intended to carry on within the general framework of postmodern and chaos theories. It also draws upon some of ideas and approaches from theories about space and spatial form as well as traditional Chinese thinkings. In exploring and mapping the chaos in McCarthy's fiction, it is necessary and helpful to make use of significant convergencies between literary and philosophical, deconstructive and organic, Eastern and Western, scientific and humanist points of views. Thus in order to facilitate the discussion and to maintain a workable intellectual context, the study's treatment of literary works is intertextual sometimes, the study's use of perspectives from Chinese traditional thinkings is illustrative, and the study's account of events in history, or ideas in philosophy and science sometimes is not analytic or critical of these events or ideas themselves, but helpful with my analysis and examination of the complexity of McCarthy's fictional texts. Hopefully, the exploration of McCarthy's idea of chaos reflected in his fiction can be helpful with the understanding of the complexity of human world and natural world as well as his complexity in narrative strategies and spatial configuration, and expectedly, to draw an outline for McCarthy's aesthetic world to understand better the epistemic development in the contemporary world.

This study, apart from Introduction and Conclusion, is divided into four chapters. In Introduction to this dissertation, McCarthy's literary career and achievement are introduced, and a survey on McCarthy criticism at home and abroad has been made so as to suggest the importance of the present study. Chapter One gives a general theoretical framework of this study, and in it, chaos theory's origin, development, content, relations with postmodernism and Chinese traditional thinkings, particularly *The Book of Changes* and approaches to literary criticism are explored and discussed. Meanwhile, another lens of this study, the theories of space and spatial form are introduced, in terms of the "spatial turn" in human sciences and the development of fiction with spatial form from modernism to postmodernism.

Chapter Two addresses the dark and bleak world of McCarthy's fiction, in which man, nature and society are presented to be wilderness and chaos. Both *Child of God* and *Blood Meridian* are explored, and some other novels, such as *The Orchard Keeper, Outer Dark, Suttree, The Crossing*, are mentioned, too, when some relevant ideas are discussed necessarily. This chapter takes violence, one of the important cultural and social issues in postmodern society and age, as focus, and its origin, development and consequences are examined with references to the turbulence of McCarthy's characters from the perspective of chaos. For McCarthy, violence could be taken to demonstrate the truth of reality. Via violence, McCarthy not only casts doubts on the humanity, which is both evil and violent, but also questions the Western metaphysics of dualism and challenges the Western epistemology since the Enlightenment. To some extent, his radical epistemology in his texts subverts the binaries of subject and object, man and nature, nature and culture, order and disorder, center and margin.

Chapter Three explores the narrative strategies of McCarthy's fiction, in which three key principles of chaos theory have been applied in his narrative texts: iteration, indeterminacy, and butterfly effect. The first section makes exploration of the application of iteration in *Blood Meridian*. As a basic mathematical calculation, iteration has been vividly described as the "baker's transformation" by mathematicians. For a nonlinear dynamic system, iteration is one of the important means to map the phase space, and in the process of stretching and folding, complicated patterns or figures might be created through the infinite process of iteration. Concerning the literary text, the device of iteration might be taken to make a narrative text into chaos, complicated and beautiful. *Blood Meridian* presents its iterative shaping in the ambiguity of its genre, characterization, chapter headings, landscape description, andlanguage style, which not only makes the fiction a postmodern Western with its unique generic feature, but also makes the fiction both strange and familiar in its aesthetic effect and hence a "chaos sandwich."

The second section goes on exploring the narrative strategy as indeterminacy in *The Road*. As an important principle of chaos theory, indeterminacy can make the system transform from order to disorder, and vice versa. In this alternative transformation, the self-organization system may be emerged in a chaotic system. Just on the edge of chaos, all the variables will be interacted with each other, making the system complex. As a narrative strategy, indeterminacy is presented on the thematic and textual planes in *The Road*, making the text remarkable in McCarthy's literary works. Living on the edge of chaos, the "self-organization system" created by the Father is indeterminate and futile due to his problematic strategies in a post-apocalyptic wasteland. Besides, the ambiguous genre and title, the open ending, the nameless figures, the fractured structure and minimalist style of language in the novel, create the indeterminacy of the fiction's textual level, which echoes that of its narrative content and its "field of literary production."

Efforts are made further to discuss the narrative strategy as chaos in *No Country for Old Men*, which is examined in the third section. As the essence of chaos theory, butterfly effect not only makes the system nonlinear but also causes the uncertainties in its development due to its disproportion between cause and effect. In *No Country for Old Men*, butterfly effect is taken as an important strategy to present the life and world of protagonists as a deterministic chaos, in which chance and caprice play a great role, indicating the uncertainty of human world and life as an open dissipative system and the problematic reality of Newtonian paradigm as well. By means of the butterfly effect, McCarthy makes his narrative pattern and destinies of characters "chaotic," and thus making his fiction dynamic with complexity.

Chapter Four takes the previous two volumes of the border trilogy as case studies to explore the spatial configuration of McCarthy's fiction as chaos in light of chaos theory and the device of "reflexive reference" proposed by Joseph Frank. With the research of the spatial forms of the previous two books of the border trilogy, the study aims to present that in McCarthy's fiction, patterns of chaos theory have been taken to make McCarthy's fiction characteristic of spatial configuration as chaos.

As the simulation of the motion of the deterministic chaos, strange attractor is taken in *All the Pretty Horses* as narrative form with its concerns of some key points like attracting points, bifurcation points, and self-similarities going through the frontier journey of John Grady Cole. Centering around the dream of the protagonist, there is a deterministic chaos, in which horses in the wilderness are the attracting points or attracting basin. Through the presentation of its emptiness of John Grady's dream and his futile journey, in which Blevins, Alejandra and Dueña Alfonsa are presented as bifurcation points to decide on the chaotic behavior of the deterministic chaos, McCarthy makes his fiction self-reflective, critiquing the very genre of which it is a part. A lot of self-similarities made from the choice of imageries, characterization and narrative structure not only create the multiple reflexivity in the fiction but also make the narrative text symmetrical asymmetry or orderly disorder locally and globally.

The Crossing is remarkable with its spatial configuration as fractals presented in both the narrative content and structure. Fractals feature self-similarities, indicating the recursive symmetry across the scale and reflexivity in multiple dimensions. By means of the complicated combination of the major part of the narrative with the interpolated tales and some other minor tales, McCarthy makes his text into self-similarities across the scale in terms of major thematic motifs like life, myth, and narrative, and hence the spatial configuration as fractals for his narrative text. Via the spatial form of fractals, the self-reflexivity of the narrative gets foregrounded, which not only makes the fiction a postmodern metafiction but also explores how to make use of chaos theory to write down a story about chaos. It is this organic complexity in the narrative that makes *The Crossing* outstanding in McCarthy's corpus and even contemporary American fiction.

In Conclusion, this study's understanding of the chaos in McCarthy's fiction and his remarkable position in American literature would be offered. Chaos is the core of McCarthy's works and hence the tension to understand his aesthetic force. McCarthy's mobility in his life and writings as well as his experience of wilderness and working at Santa Fe Institute make it possible and proper to employ chaos theory to make studies of his profoundly informed novels on the one hand. On the other hand, his scientifically complex vision of world as the deterministic chaos makes him present humans, society and nature as wilderness and chaos, and his adoption of the core principles and patterns of chaos theory as narrative strategies and forms in his works makes his novels as complex and dynamic as the beautiful chaos. Furthermore, his vison of life as narrative and cosmos as the holistic and interconnected web makes his characters live on the edge of chaos, and meanwhile causes his works into a whole and interconnection with American literature tradition. His texts as writerly ones encourage the reader's nonlinear thinking in the process of participation in the writings. All in all, McCarthy's concepts of chaos in the cosmos and life and his presentation of thematic content and narrative form as chaos in his fiction make him a unique and influential figure in the history of contemporary American literature.

Chapter One
Chaos, Spatiality, Postmodernism and McCarthy

Science looked a lot like literary criticism, from across the room.

Richard Powers, Galatea 2.2

As "a highly charged signifier" (Hayles, *Chaos Bound* 9), chaos gets new meanings in contemporary period with its challenge against traditional understandings of life and cosmos, and attracts interests from various areas. Just "like crabgrass on a suburban America lawn" (Barth 284), chaos theory with its key focus on the chaos in a dynamic system, has gone beyond the scientific community and entered the literary and cultural world. Chaos is an important concept in McCarthy's oeuvre, and with this key, we may explore McCarthy's unique "chaotic" narrative within intellectual contexts of postmodernism and chaos theory as well as spatial "turn" in the last half of the 20th century. In view of the chaos's crucial position in the examination of McCarthy's works, what this study attempts to do is to bridge between science and the humanities, science and literature, science and philosophy, literature and spatiality and even the Eastern and the Western, hopefully laying a theoretical framework and workable context for the study's discussion and examination of thematic content and narrative form as chaos in McCarthy's fiction. Therefore, with the aim to facilitate the exploration of McCarthy's fictional texts, this chapter would offer a general introduction of chaos theory's origin, development, content, approaches to literary criticism, relations with postmodernism and the spatial "turn" in contemporary literature, and its "across-scaling self-similarities" with Chinese philosophy, particularly *The Book of Changes*, in terms of their visions about life and the world.

I. Chaos and Chaos Theory

The world in which we live is so extraordinarily diverse in composition, form, and function that any standard classification is impossible. Mountains, rivers, leaves, clouds, coastline and lots of other things in nature coming into our vision every day are seemingly easy to know its formation; however, once observed, they appear to be in irregularities, and yet present self-similarities between scale levels. Nature is so complex that we have to face something uncertain. Even in our personal universe, we cannot predict what will happen in the following moment, though we make good preparations, because we are inextricably linked to our natural environment, and the social and professional institutions with which we are associated. Even though those technological devices we use in our daily life are powerful, perhaps a small effect can have significant consequences. Conversely, a major effort might yield very little. In other words, cause and effect are not proportional. Such a world with complexity is the studying object for chaos theory.

"Chaos" and "chaos theory" are easily confused and used interchangeably. So to begin with, it is necessary to differentiate them. Chaos is a condition, while "chaos theory is a collection of mathematical, numerical, and geometrical techniques that allow us to deal with nonlinear problems to which there are no explicit general solutions" (Cambel 16). Technically speaking, chaos theory is called as nonlinear or non-equilibrium dynamic system theory;[1] while the latter is not as popular as the former, although the former is not very precise, even ambiguous. Oddly, it is its ambiguity that fascinates scientists and common people. Since the 1960s, chaos theory has caught attention of scientists and turned out to be a hit for scholars from different disciplines and was quickly widespread in the 1980s and late 1990s. Now it has become an interdisciplinary subject and involves mathematics, physics, chemistry, mechanics,

---

[1] In effect, chaos science has two branches, one focuses on "deterministic unpredictability" of chaos, in other words, "the order hidden within chaotic system" (Hayles, *Chaos and Order* 12); the other on "self-organization system," meaning that actual order can arise in complex system. With regard to its focus on the interaction of order and disorder at the edge of chaos, the second branch, namely, Prigogine branch, has assumed the name, complexity science in recent years. The present study takes the popular term, "chaos theory" to name both.

dynamics, meteorology, geology, seismology, biology, ecology, and genetics and so on within its rubric, though mathematics and physics are its core subjects. Chaos theory has been garnered by its proponents as the third revolution in the scientific history since Einstein's theory of relativity and quantum mechanics, which brings the shift of paradigm[1] in physics and people's thinking of the cosmos and life.

To a certain extent, chaos theory shoots the holes of "the notion that all can be predicted in the macroscopic natural world, and by extension, in human behavior" (Tabbi & Michael 102), and brings changes of ideas from traditional vision of the world as a mechanical clock with stability, reversibility, certainty and linearity, to the acceptance of "the long-term unpredictability of any future behavior generated by feedback in a nonlinear chaotic system" (Rice 104-5). In the past three hundred years, we looked at the cosmos mechanically, analytically and symmetrically all the time, and yet, thankfully, chaos theory has changed our vision and helped us see the world full of artistic glamour with strange images and intricate interconnection, and learned to appreciate the world in the way closer to that of artists. Now, chaos theory has gone beyond the scientific community and entered into the domains of arts and literature, and the concept of chaos also changes greatly, becoming a new cultural metaphor in the contemporary world.

i. Redefining Chaos

As regards to the concept of chaos, it is not new, rather, ancient still, for it has been mentioned in the creation myths from both oriental and occidental cultures. By Greek accounts, "chaos" labels the pre-creational state of the universe "when order had not yet been imposed on the elements of the Earth" (Grimal 98). Often described as the "nether abyss" or "primitive," "primordial matter … out of which the order of universe is evolved," chaos is, by most mythological accounts, "the first state of universe" (OED), "the oldest of the gods … before the formation of the universe" (Robert Bell 44). The

---

[1] According to Thomas S. Kuhn, the paradigm refers to a set of assumptions, conventions, questions, procedures, theoretical frameworks and modes, which is universally accepted by a group of scientists in a given time. The shift of paradigm is the change in Gestalt or psychological belief rather than the deepening of recognition of the world. (See Kuhn, 1970)

word "chaos" is believed to trace back to Hesiod's *Theogeny* in the 8th century B. C., and chaos is depicted "both as not-form and the background against which the creation takes place" (Hayles, *Chaos Bound* 19).

Similar to that of ancient Greek myth, in which chaos is taken as a kind of primitive matter with confusion and formlessness to create the orderly universe, the concept of chaos is also associated with something disorderly and messy in ancient Chinese myths. *San Wu Li Ji* holds that before the division of the heaven and earth, there lied a Chaos (Hun Dun) in the shape of an egg, from which Pan Gu (Creator in Chinese myth) was born. Later, in *Qian Zao Du*, chaos is mentioned again to refer to a kind of primal atmosphere (Qi in Chinese) or a kind of matter in a mass or a kind of state before the creation of the cosmos. Associated with "disorder" and "confusion," chaos is generally taken as a metaphor to refer to those humans want of wisdom and knowledge in traditional Chinese thinking.

In the oriental and occidental myths, chaos is discovered to be opposite to order. In classical literary works, chaos and order are binary, too, and traditionally, chaos is understood as something bad or undesirable. In Ovid's *Metamorphoses* (1st century, B.C.), chaos is described as the state of nature with shapelessness. Later, in Milton's *Paradise Lost* (1674), we read:

Before their eyes in sudden view appear

The secrets of the hoary deep, a dark

Illimitable ocean without bound,

Without dimension, where length, breadth and height,

And time and place are lost; where eldest Night

And Chaos, Ancestors of Nature, hold

Eternal Anarchy amidst the noise

Of endless wars, and by confusion stand (II, 890-97)

Portrayed as one of "Ancestors of nature," and a crowned "Anarch" as well as the primal ruler over the turbulent abyss, Milton's "imperial Chaos" develops that of the image presented in Ovid's *Metamorphoses* and even the Biblical account of the void from which God creates the cosmos. In Shakespeare's *Othello* (1622), "chaos" is mentioned, too: "Excellent wretch! Perdition catch my soul / But I do love thee! And when I love thee not, / Chaos is come again" (Oth. 3.3. 98-100). *Othello*'s understanding of chaos is similar to that of conversations in our daily life, in which chaos is condemned as some sort of confusion or disorganization. In brief, in the traditional understanding of the order/chaos binary, on the side of order we find "the Christian God, the bringer of light, the Chinese Yang; sanity, goodness, truth, health, certainty, stability and determinacy," and on the side of chaos we find "the Christian devil, the prince of darkness and Siva the destroyer; madness, evil, falsity, illness, uncertainty, flux and indeterminacy" (Boon 39-40).

A bit more complicated than myths, chaos has got more than one layer of signifieds in Chinese philosophy, which is much closer to that of modern science. Seemingly, chaos is associated with something void (Wu in Chinese), or nothing (Kong in Chinese), but in effect, this maelstrom "is at heart a 'source'-the source, in fact, of the universe" (Kundert-Gibbs 19). Shen Yi Jing portrays chaos to be like a kind of dog with long hair on its four legs, and this grotesque and mysterious beast is blind, deaf, even hardly with any internal organs. *The Book of Mountains and Seas* makes account of chaos as a deity named by Di Jiang (or Di Hong) living in Mount Tian, looking "like a leather bag in flame-red, without distinct facial organs in the head" (81). Chaos is now characteristic with something void. "Ying Di Wang" of Chuang Tzu makes correspondence and goes on taking chaos as the symbol of voidness:

In ancient China, there lived three emperors, one was named Shu (Brief), the emperor of the South Sea, the other one was Hu (Sudden), the emperor of the North Sea, and another one, Hun Dun (Chaos) as the emperor of the Centre. One day, Shu and Hu met together in the kingdom of Chaos, Chaos treated them well. For the acknowledgment of goodness of Chaos, Shu and Hu discussed to reply him with seven openings in the human head (i.e. eyes, ears, nostrils and mouth) to make him similar to others, so they began to dig one each day. Seven days later, with the accomplishment of their work, Chaos was dead with seven openings. (Guo 309)

Opposite to order, symbolized by another two emperors, Shu and Hu, Chaos is special for his voidness (lack of openings to see, hear, eat and breathe). To be void is to be simple, thus order can thrive from it; to be void is to be complex, thus everything can be included in it. Once in accordance with others, he becomes nothing and then dead. Such an idea of chaos presents the dialectics of Taoism, and to a certain extent, echoes the understanding of chaos in modern science.

Besides chaos (Hun Dun), some terms, such as "Tao," "Taichi," "Qi," or "Tai Xuan" in Chinese philosophy, are associated with the source of universe, the "void" with "changes" as its nature. As the opening lines of *Tao Te Ching* indicate, "The Tao that can be told, is not the eternal Tao. The name that can be named, is not the eternal Name. The Unnamble is the eternally real. Naming is the origin, of all particular things" (Chap. 1).[1] The "Tao" is nothing, yet it is previous to Being, for the ineffable void of the Tao is source of all things. Similar to Taoism, *The Book of Changes* also takes "void" (Wu Ji) as the progenitor of the world, for it generates the Taichi, and then Yin and Yang, four elements and the sixty-four Hexagrams are produced consecutively. Zen Buddhism, which takes Taoism and Mahayana Buddhism as sources, also pays more attention on the "void" (nothing). If attaining anything void, then people could be perfect with quietness and transcendence, for he has escaped from "having," i.e. thirst in the world. So the void signifies being. In Zen, both being and nonbeing, two interdependent points, intermix and accompany with one another and can be cycled eternally. The four-line stanza in the end of *The Diamond Sutra* says, "All conditioned dharmas (phenomena) are like a dream, an illusion, a bubble and a shadow, like dew and lightening. Thus should you meditate upon them" (Chap 32). Impermanence turns out to be constant, which provides the truth of "changes" of things in the world alternatively: all are in the process of "to be." Of course, the implications of chaos change all the time in Chinese philosophy, yet its understandings of chaos seem to be close to that of modern science, though the former is a bit "simple." The following

---

[1] *Tao Te Ching* has lots of versions in translation, and the present study mainly takes Mitchell's version (1988), yet makes some changes with the present study's own understanding. So, the study just notes its original chapters.

section would offer detailed discussion of the "self-similarities" between *The Book of Changes* and chaos theory.

In the contemporary period, chaos is nothing "noisy" any longer, but has come to be seen as something rich in information, just as Hayles observes, "The more chaotic a system is, the more information it produces. This perception is at the heart of the transvaluation of chaos, for it enables chaos to be conceived as an inexhaustible ocean of information rather than as a void signifying absence" (*Chaos Bound* 8). It is partial for us to say good or bad for order and chaos with moral terms, and traditional ideas of order/chaos have been challenged in the wake of the development of chaos theory. As Cambel comments, "chaos implies the existence of unpredictable or random aspects in dynamic matters, but it is not necessarily bad or undesirable-sometimes quite contrary" (15). Chaos has been changed not to be opposite to order, rather, chaos can produce order, or order may arise in chaos, for both are involved together and even change alternatively. In the term of Hayles, chaos means orderly disorder or disorderly order (Chaos and Order 15), which refers to "a condition that lies between a state of complete determinism and a state of utter randomness" (Conte 24).

ii. Chaos: a New Paradigm

"Chaos," now defined as sensitive dependence on interior changes in initial conditions in a dynamic system, refers to the process that "appears to proceed according to chance even though their behavior is in fact determined by precise laws" (Lorenz 24). It is featured with chance, nonlinearity, irreversibility and indeterminacy.

In the period of classical science, chaos was ignored by scientists as "noise," because order and law were their focuses at that time. By the 19th century, chaos got exploration in thermodynamics. In effect, the equilibrium of thermodynamics is a kind of chaos, which suits for the condition that the temperature, pressure, density and chemical power, almost every point in a closed (conservative) system is hardly different from each other. In other words, chaos is made when the system's entropy gets to the maximum, and the extent of the messy state for particles tends towards a large value, too. The concept of entropy was proposed by Rudolf Clausius in 1850. According to

Clausius, when the entropy of the system strives toward a maximum, it may amount to achieve the equilibrium of heat, causing the "heat death" finally. Actually, the second law of thermodynamics places constraints on the direction of heat's transfer from being available to unavailable, from order to disorder, and finally to irreversibility (heat death), which regresses to the viewpoint of ancient Greeks, taking chaos as the final state of universe. The chaos caused from the equilibrium of thermodynamics is lower-staged, messy, quiet and indifferent in its macroscopic representation, which differs from the chaos in the sense of modern science greatly.

Until 1963, Edward Lorenz, a meteorologist, renewed the concept of chaos in his groundbreaking essay, "Deterministic Non-periodic Flow," which demonstrates that small changes in the initial conditions can produce great consequences subsequently, so that's why the weather-forecasting cannot be precise in the long term. What Lorenz realized is contrary to common sense, i.e. predictability and determinism cultivated by Newtonian science, which "gives a deterministic picture of the world: if we know the state of the universe at some initial time, we should be able to determine its state at any other time" (Ruelle 29). Lorenz has considered randomness and chance ignored by classical science into his studies and posited his studying weather system in an open (dissipative) system. Lorenz's progress can be attributable to the advancement of digital computers in contemporary period, which allows more and more massive calculations of sets of numbers accessible. At present, complicated calculations can be accomplished in seconds with computers, yet before the computer's invention, it may take hundreds of hours for mathematicians to finish the calculations with paper and pencil. More important, computers can be helpful to create graphic images in the screen, which are "keys" to scientists in their studies. Just as one chaos specialist remarks, "It's masochism for a mathematician to do without pictures, how can they see the relationship between that motion and this? How can they develop intuition?" (Gleick 39).

In 1972, Lorenz presented a speech entitled "Predictability: Does the Flapping of a Butterfly's Wings in Brazil Set off a Tornado in Texas?" in a session devoted to the Global Atmosphere Research Program, at the 139th of science, in Washington, D. C.

and then "the butterfly effect" was first touched upon and later taken as the "essence" of chaos and even a metaphor of chaos theory. Seagull was firstly proposed and finally the butterfly was set due to the image of Lorenz attractor similar to a butterfly (see Fig. 1.1). "The butterfly effect," one of the key terms in chaos theory, refers to "sensitive dependence on initial conditions," indicating that "tiny differences in input could quickly become overwhelming differences in output" over time, relatively simple dynamic systems could demonstrate radically different behavior (Gleick 8). In Chinese speaking, we may say, "a small error could lead to disastrous result." English folklore also reflects such a rule: "For want of a nail, the shoe was lost; / For want of a shoe, the horse was lost; / For want of a horse, the rider was lost; / For want of a rider, the battle was lost; / For want of a battle, the kingdom was lost." However, we should note that "butterfly effect" in chaos theory cares much more about the effect's growing exponentially: "A quantity that doubles after a certain time, and then doubles again after the same interval of time, and then again and again, is said to grow exponentially" (Ruelle 39). Exponential growth is also called growth at constant rate, for instance, if we deposit money in the bank at a constant rate of 5%, then the amount will double in about 14 years provided ignoring taxes and inflation.

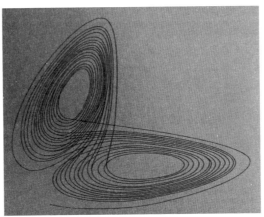

Figure 1.1 The Lorenz Attractor (from Slethaug xxviii)

Take a falling leaf as an example. Classical science tells us that such a leaf is doomed to fall down, yet when, how and where it is, we don't know. The humidity of atmosphere, the velocity of wind, even the tough surface of the ground will be considered to decide on the time, method, and position of this falling leaf. Chaos theory usually presupposes in a dissipative system, in which a source of energy may replace that dissipated with friction; whereas, for classical science, the system is ideational without consideration of friction or some other elements. The famous example taken by chaos theorist is the dripping faucet. At a certain flow rate, the drips may be regular and predictable. While, the system is nonlinear: when a drop detaches from the strings of water, a sudden change in mass occurs, and each drop affects a subsequent drop. If we turn up the flow rate, the system will go chaotic, for the shortened time between drops makes their interaction unpredictable. Both the examples of the falling leaf and the dripping faucet demonstrate that the world as a system cannot be predicted but described, as opposed to the classical paradigm and in conjunction with quantum mechanics, hence the paradox for chaos theory, the science of being "both deterministic and unpredictable" (Hayles, *Chaos Bound* 14).

As a technical term, "chaos" entered the scientific literature in 1975 when Li and York published a paper entitled "Period Three Implies Chaos," in which they characterized certain flows as being "chaotic." While, to make it well-known and accepted in the science community may be attributable to several scientists, such as Henri Poincare, Thomas S. Kuhn, David Ruelle, Robert Shaw Group, Benoit

Mandelbrot and Mitchell Feigenbaum.[1]

Chaos theory necessitates the shift of paradigm for the knowledge of cosmos today, and puts a definitive stop to the idea that the course of the universe is both determinate and predictable, which indicates a decisive break with the classical mode of thinking on the problems of motion and dynamics. Likewise, it returns science from its care of the very large and the very tiny to the dynamics of everyday life, and offers scholars "a method for discussing turbulent events previously dismissed as experimental noise; it shifts our focus away from simple reductive models of physical behaviors and toward complex systems of interaction" (Boon 38). Therefore, chaos theory has now become "not just theory but also method, not just a canon of beliefs but also a way of doing science" (Gleick 38).

iii. Mapping the Phase Space: Strange Attractors and Fractals

Physics is to study the rules of matter's temporal and spatial motion. Besides sensitive dependence on initial conditions (the butterfly effect), which indicates the deterministic chaos in the temporal evolution, another key terms, strange attractors and fractals, in chaos theory, are particularly significant for chaos theory. Both strange attractors and fractals are simulations of the deterministic chaos in the spatial evolution.

---

[1] Henri Poincare, a French mathematician, discussed the question of unpredictability and determinism in a very nontechnical way in his book *Science et Methode* in 1908. Due to the digression of quantum mechanics and lack of the help of digital computers at that time, his work did not draw attention of the science community. Lorenz just furthered his research in the exploration of chaotic deterministic system. But his Poincare Conjecture and Poincare Map as well as the way of iteration to look at the macroscopic problem are still available in chaos theory; Thomas S. Kuhn, a historian of science, is helpful for the development of chaos theory with his book, *The Structure of Scientific Revolution* (1970); David Rulle's essay, "Microscopic Fluctuations and Turbulence," in *Physics Letters* 72 A (1979), caught people's attention on the chaotic behavior in dynamical system and his research in "turbulence" makes contribution to chaos theory; Robert Shaw Group is also called as the Dynamical Systems Collective, which included four young scientists in California Univ. at Santa Cruz: R. Shaw, Doyne Farmer, Norman Parkard, and James Crutchfield. Their collaborative work are presented in the essay, "Strange Attractors, Chaotic Behavior, and Information Flow" in 1981, which was influential in the history of chaos theory; Benoit Mandelbrot's contribution is on the empirical side with his finding in fractal geometry, while Feigenbaum is on the theoretical side with his observation of universal behavior in chaos.

Both are thought to represent the behavior of a chaotic system, and as a geometrical property of the system, the latter presents the geometrical characteristic of the former. Both live in phase space and may be created via iterations or period-doubling bifurcation.

Phase space is one of the most important tools for spatial modeling in physics. According to Kundert-Gibbs, "Phase space is a malleable abstracted space-something like a thin sheet or rubber that can be pulled, bent, and stretched-that contains not only the everyday dimensions of height, length and width, but the associated vectors of motion in each of these three directions" (37). Therefore, "in essence, phase space maps the two most important elements of physics: position and motion together in one space" (ibid). In Gleick's words, phase space "gives a way of turning numbers into pictures, abstracting every bit of essential information from a system of moving parts, mechanical or fluid, and making a flexible road map to all its possibilities" (134). Such a mapping can be helpful to visualize the characteristics of an object's motion graphically by means of the patterns created on the computer screen.

Let's take examples of pendulum and dripping faucet to map the phase space of the object's motion. First, we map the behavior of pendulum (see Fig. 1.2). Suppose in this system there are only two variables: position and velocity. We can take Cartesian geometry to make these variables on an XY axis, one on the horizontal axis, the other on the vertical. Both change continuously, thus making a line of points that traces a loop, repeating itself forever, around and around. The same system with a higher energy level-swinging faster and faster-form a loop in phase space similar to the first, but larger. For such a dynamic motion, every orbit must eventually end up at the same place, the center: velocity 0 and position 0. Such a mapping excludes the friction, yet, if we consider the friction in the motion of the pendulum, the mapping will be different. We may observe that there is a central point attracting the orbits towards it. Instead of looping around forever, they spiral inward to a fixed point (see Fig. 1.3). Therefore, in the case of the pendulum with friction, there will be an attractor as a single fixed point, while in the case of the pendulum without friction, we may observe a periodic orbit, a figure "representing the pendulum's attraction to a particular set of repeating coordinates" (Jo Alyson Parker 12). Fixed point and limit cycle (periodic orbit) are two simpler kinds of "attractors," which have been worked with physicists to represent the "behavior that reached a steady state or repeated itself continuously" (Gleick 134).

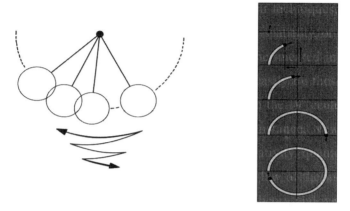

Figure 1.2 Mapping the Behavior of the Pendulum without Friction (from Gleick 136)

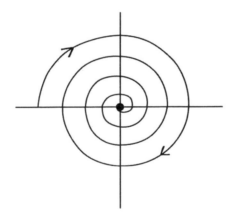

Figure 1.3 Mapping the Behavior of the Pendulum with Friction

Different from fixed points or limit cycles, strange attractor, an important indicator of chaos, is constituted with a collection of infinite points in a multiple-dimensional phase space, which can be simulated with the help of computers. Termed by David Ruelle and F. Takens, strange attractors "exhibit unpredictable and bizarre motions" (Cambel 60). In the mapping of the evolution of a chaotic dynamic system, such as the dripping faucet or weather, we may observe a strange attractor. When we map the dripping faucet, a computer simulation of its motion gives us access to the three variables of the drop's position, velocity, and mass over an indefinite period of time and thus enables to see "the geometry of the attractor describing the motion of a fluid system" (Jo Alyson Parker 13). In the case of dripping faucet, the orbit hovers around certain coordinates within a basin of attraction. Trajectories diverge at times and crowd at other times, but they never repeat themselves exactly, making an evolving shape constituting a Rössler attractor[①] (see Fig. 1.4). All in all, the pendulum's motion is typical of the mode of classically predictable and deterministic motion in the system, no matter how we vary the initial conditions within the basin of attraction, the trajectory will always fall onto the same attractor; whereas, the motion of the dripping faucet typically exemplifies the chaotic system, which "can change from a periodic and predictable to an aperiodic quasi-random pattern of behavior, as a single parameter is varied" (Shaw 1-2).

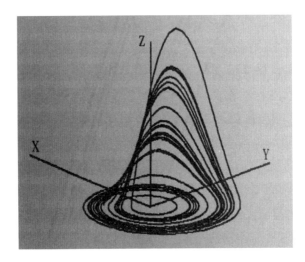

Figure 1.4 The Rössler Attractor (from Cambel 72)

The most interesting strange attractor should be Lorenz attractor, which resembles the beautiful shape of a butterfly with its wings spread, or a peacock with its tail

---

① The Rössler attractor is named after its discoverer, Otto Rössler, a German medical doctor, who comes to chaos by way of chemistry and theoretical biology. The same is true for some other attractors, such as Lorenz attractor, Hénon attractor and so on.

fanned, or a dramatic mask, when mapping onto a computer screen. Such a strange attractor is "a two-dimensional representation of a three-dimensional phenomenon" (Boon 60). Due to the limitation of a paper, we have to present it in a two dimension. Actually, to present such a complicated strange attractor may take thousands, even millions, of iterations imaged on the computer screen, and the image in our vision is via infinite iterations in the high-dimensional phase space. In it, the orbit jumps between two attracting points and the trajectories cross from one "wing" to the other at irregular intervals. The points along the trajectory trace a path around the strange attractor without ever retracing the path, so we cannot predict when the jump will occur, thus the motion remains unstable and aperiodic. For the Lorenz attractor, one of its major characteristics is the combination of stretching and folding, which is similar to the stretching and folding that occur in our kneading of bread dough. After the iterations of stretching and folding, we cannot locate the original point, nor can we know the patterns that those points will take as we perform further iterations.

Scientists and mathematicians have found out that chaotic dynamical systems take other shapes as well, such as Hénon attractor and Japanese attractor. These attractors have complicated geometrical properties, and always with the similar characteristics: "they are folded, stretched, layered, and undergo all sorts of contortions. The trajectories of chaotic attractors diverge, and they are sensitive to initial conditions" (Cambel 70). Usually, they contain a self-similarity across scale through stretching and folding, which is called fractal dimension by the French-American mathematician Benoit B. Mandelbrot.

Dimension is a concept for geometry and space theory. In the phase space, variables are taken to determine the motion state of a system, so the numerals of variables equate dimensions of a phase space. In Euclidean geometry, a point has zero dimension, a line has one dimension, an area has two dimensions and a volume has three dimensions, all integers. In contrast, fractal dimensions may assume non-integers, such as 1.6 for sea anemone, 2.35 for clouds, and so on. Nature is diverse. As a rule, natural objects are not regular and smooth in their shapes, such as triangles, squares, cones, circles, cubes, and straight lines, just as Euclidean geometry teaches us. Irregular shapes, such as coastlines, cloud forms, strange attractors, and border lines between countries, exist in it. They cannot be easily measured, because they are fractals. In other words, they don't have integer dimensions that we use casually each day, rather fractal ones.

The term "fractal" was coined by Mandelbrot with its derivation from the Latin fractus, meaning "to break," and introduced in 1975. He points out:

We ought not … to believe that the banks of ocean are really deformed, because they have not the form of a regular bulwark; not that the mountains are out of shape, because they are not exact pyramids or cones; nor that the stars are unskillfully placed, because they are not all situated at uniform distance. These are not natural irregularities, but with respect to our fancies only; nor are they incommodious to the true sense of life and the designs of man's being on earth. (6)

Basically, a fractal is a pattern which can be presented mathematically, and our natural world presents us with fractals often. The basic shapes of fractal figures cannot change even though we compress or expand them, and "closer inspection reveals more structural detail" (Cambel 176), for they exhibit scaled self-similarity everywhere.

We may notice self-similarities in nature. The typical example of fractals in nature is coastline, and Mandelbrot has found out that the length of British coastline depends on the measure scales he used. Exactly, the length of coastline is scale-dependent. Such a measuring result sounds like chaos: a coastline with ever-increasing length, which is contrary to the assumption from Euclidean geometrythat the size of our measuring stick makes differences to the number we will get. But the fact refuses intuition. When we measure the coastline, "without regard to what size ruler we use to measure the coastline, it will always repeat its angular ins and outs to the same degree, with each scale looking much like every other" (Kundert-Gibbs 46).

The other example of the fractal self-similarity is Mandelbrot set (see Fig. 1.5), which has been taken as the "icon" of chaos theory due to its representation of "nonlinear, nonclosed, self-similar nature" (Kundert-Gibbs 44). In Mandelbrot set, we find lots of nodes connected to the main body of the set. If we zoom in on a small node to the right of the large node at the top of the figure as shown in Fig. 1.6, we may find that is is similar in appearance to those clearly observable in full view. If we zoom in again, this time focusing on a small node to the right of the node at the top of the large node in Fig. 1.6, we again find a similar pattern as shown in Fig. 1.7. If we zoom in again and again, a similar shape presents to our vision, too. In effect, the configuration of Mandelbrot set is made by means of the infinite recursion of similar shape.

Besides Mandelbrot set, some other figures, such as Cantor set (see Fig.1.8), the von Koch snowflake (see Fig.1.9), the Sierpinsky triangle (see Fig. 1.10), and Julia set (see Fig. 1.11), are similar to that of configuration in Mandelbrot set. They are fractals, exhibiting scale-invariance. In other words, when we magnify repeatedly, the various images look the same regardless of size. As Cambel puts it, "fractals are made up of parts that are scale copies of the whole. In other words, there is replication" (186).

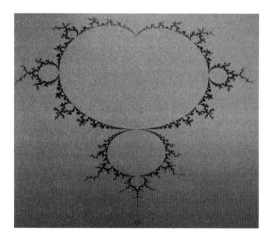

Figure 1.5 The Mandelbrot Set in Full View (from Gleick, "Illustration" 1987)

Figure 1.6 The Detail of Mandelbrot Set-Zoom 1 (from Slethaug 64)

Figure 1.7 The Detail of the Mandelbrot Set-Zoom 2 (from Slethaug 64)

Fractals reveal that in finite space, there are infinite possibilities. And things in the cosmos are similar, yet not of duplication; they are iterated, but not of repetition. In other words, they present holographically: a necessary connection between parts and whole in the system. This recalls Chinese allegory of Chuang Tzu's dreaming of butterfly, in which Chuang Tzu cannot be differentiated from the butterfly, and both are unitary in the process of changing. Zen Buddhism also corresponds: a grain of sand reflects the world, and a leaf images a Buddha, for both are mutually reflexive. Therefore, the fractal's self-similarity is to connect the macro /micro world together through the complex iteration of feedback loop in a dynamic system, and "uniqueness and dissimilarity of differences" are produced (Briggs & Peat 104-5).

Figure 1.8 The Cantor Set

Figure 1.9 The Von Koch Snowflake

Figure 1.10 The Sierpinsky Triangle

Figure 1.11 The Julia Set (from Cambel 183)

Another concept is necessary to discuss when exploring both strange attractor and fractals. Period-doubling bifurcation is the way for a system to enter into the chaotic state from linearity to nonlinearity, or from order to disorder. A bifurcation means "a splitting, a decision point where the system must take one path or another" (Weissert 234). We may note that the original orderly organization does not disappear completely after the bifurcation; rather it may generate infinite self-similar structures. Gleick describes this systematic movement towards chaos clearly: "this bifurcation would come faster and faster—4, 8, 16, 32—and suddenly break off. Beyond a certain point, the 'point of accumulation,' periodically gives way to chaos" (73).

Take a leaf floating down a stream as an example. When the leaf meets a boulder in the middle of the stream, it must go around one way or the other, and at this time, "boulder" constructs a "bifurcation" point. As for which path the system (the leaf's motion) will go, chance determines. Thus we may find that bifurcation is situated at the edge of chaos, from which the chaotic system can experience great transformation, and a "self-organization system" in the term of Ilya Prigogine may occur, meaning that order may "emerge" in chaos, and at this time both order and chaos are complementary. Such a system is called as "dissipative structure," which portrays the universe as a nonlinear or far-from-equilibrium chaos with "complexity and diversity and apparent tendency to evolve in the direction of increased differentiation and complexity" (Porush 56).

As the simulations of deterministic chaos in the spatial evolution and markers of chaos theory, both strange attractors and fractals generate fantastic patterns with symmetrical asymmetry or recursive symmetry across scales, illustrating "the stability and the hidden structure of a system that otherwise seemed patternless" (Gleick 153). Their unique beauty appeals to scientists and writers as well, and in the fourth chapter of the present study, they will be further discussed when concerning the spatial configuration of McCarthy's novels.

II. Chinese Chaos: *The Book of Changes*

As the core of Chinese wisdom, and the source of Chinese tradition and culture, *The Book of Changes* (Zhouyi), can be illustrative of chaos and chaos theory. Written about 3,000 years ago in China,[1] *The Book of Changes* holds the first position among the classics in ancient China,[2] and it has been enshrined by Chinese since its creation. *The Book of Changes* takes human beings as the center, around which the relations of human beings with their living cosmos are studied. Three relations are explored in

---

[1] If we trace the origin of *The Book of Changes* to Fuxi, the inventor of two signs, Yin (- -) and Yang (–), before Chinese characters appeared, then it may have the history of more than 6,500 years. (see <www.huaiyang.gov.cn /Item/Show.asp?m=1&d=3768>)

[2] The classics in China are *The Book of Changes, Book of Poems, Book of Records, Book of Rites,* and *Annals of Spring and Autumn.*

The Book of Changes, i.e., the relation of man and nature, man and society, and man himself. As the treasure of Chinese wisdom, *The Book of Changes* provides crowning inspirations for scholars to explore the cosmos unknown to us, which has been proved to present lots of truths disclosed by modern science, e.g. astronomy, geology, seismology, biology, physics, chemistry, ecology, holography, and genetics and so on.

However, since its birth in ancient China, comments from scholars differ greatly all the time. Some think it mysterious and superstitious with its omens and predictions. Actually, since the appearance of *I Zhuan* by Confucius, its nature has been changed. And its original function as vehicle for divination has been shifted to be secondary, even though it was taken to make predictions in Zhou Dynasty. Historically, with the publication of a series of books to interpret *The Book of Changes*, such as Wang Bi's *The Annotation of Zhouyi*, Zhu Xi's *The Original Meaning of Zhouyi*, Wang Yangming's *Zhouyi Wai Zhuan*, and Wang Fuzi's *Zhouyi Nei and Wai Zhuan*, *The Book of Changes* has been counted as the classic of Chinese philosophy.

The present study concerns philosophical ideas in *The Book of Changes* with regard to its correspondences and associations with chaos theory in their visions about the universe and human world and human himself, hoping to be helpful with the understandings of chaos theory and thus the chaos in McCarthy's fiction. To make *The Book of Changes* and chaos theory into dialogue seems adventurous due to vast gulf between them in terms of their temporal and cultural milieus, yet it is significant anyhow, for it is generally acknowledged that Chinese traditional thinking is one of the sources to inspire Western philosophers and scientists,[①] and more important, *The Book of Changes* may be counted as Chinese chaos theory.

The Book of Changes is made up of two parts, *Ching* and *Zhuan*. The first part is also titled as *Yi* (Change) or *I Ching,* which was said to be written in Shang Dynasty and completed in West Zhou Dynasty, and the second one as *Zhuan* (*I Zhuan* or *I Da Zhuan*), including ten essays, which was reported to be written by Confucius in Spring and Autumn and Warring States Era to make interpretations of *I Ching*. It is generally

① For instance, the philosopher Carl G. Jung got the inspiration from *The Book of Changes* and then had his idea of "synchronicity"; the scientist Ilya Prigogine acknowledged that Chinese traditional thinking is helpful with his science of complexity in one of his lectures in Beijing.

acknowledged that *The Book of Changes* was attributable to scholars in different periods, specifically, Fuxi conceived the hexagrams, King Wen doubled the hexagrams, Duke Zhou wrote Yaoci (Line Text) and Confucius wrote *Ten Wings* (i.e. *Zhuan* made up of a collection of ten essays). In the narrow sense, *I Ching* is considered as the synonym to *The Book of Changes*, which is popular for foreign scholars. The present study takes *The Book of Changes* to name *Zhouyi*.

Consider the key terms of *The Book of Changes*, in which we could find out their associations and correspondences with chaos theory. The first term is the Taichi (Primordial Polarity). The first part of *Xi Tzu* has said that "in *The Book of Changes*, there comes the Taichi and the Taichi produces Yin and Yang (Yin, here refers to Yin element, i.e. Yin Yao in Chinese, so does Yang), and then Yin and Yang generate four images (four elements, i.e. Young Yin, Old Yin, Young Yang, Old Yang) and after these four images, the eight trigrams are made."[1] Each trigram is made up of three binary elements, and these eight trigrams go on developing into the sixty-four hexagrams. The scheme is developed in stages. Following the Taichi, some other key terms are important to make a comprehension of *The Book of Changes*, such as "Yin and Yang," "the five phase locations" (Wu Xing)[2] made up of metal, wood, water, fire and earth, "the Heavenly and Earthly Stems," and "the eight trigrams" constituted from Heaven (Qian), Earth (Kun), Thunder (Zhen), Water (Kan), Mountain (Gen), Wind (Xun), Fire (Li), and Lake (Dui). These key terms are associated with each other and combined in *The Book of Changes*, which are of value and help for us to understand its views about the relations of humans and their surroundings.

As the "gestalt" of *The Book of Changes*, the Taichi is an important spatial model to show its vision about the cosmos and human world. The popular figure for the Taich is "the fish of Yin and Yang." In the circle is the Taichi, and the circle is divided into two areas, black and white. In the black areas there is one white dot and vice verse.

---

① *I Zhuan* is a collection of ten essays, in which two parts of *Xi Tzu* are included. Each of these essays are in less than 10,000 words, so the study does not note when mentioning.

② The five phase locations, named by Wu Xing in Chinese, were wrongly taken to refer to five elements in nature, and the present study takes the term of physics, "phase locations," to make it true to its original meaning in Chinese hopefully.

The white represents Yang, which is located in the South and the black represents Yin, which is in the North. Yin and Yang constantly change and transform into each other, provided one part's power and energy are stronger than those of the other. Both move and alternate dynamically in the state space of the Taichi, just like that of the alternation between order and disorder in the deterministic chaos. Besides, if we enlarge the dot (white or black) in the Taichi, another figure of the Taichi will appear, and such a process can be reiterated infinitely, then we may get lots of fractals of the Taichi. Actually, the Taichi typically represents the across-scaling self-similarities of things in the cosmos from galaxies to DNA.

As its title implies, *The Book of Changes* is a book about changes. *Tao Te Ching* has suggested that all things contain Yin and Yang and it is the blending of two that generates harmony and balance of the world (Chap. 42), which indicates that there are two polarities in one thing, whose alternate transformations depend on the change of one of variables in one polarity. In the preface to *The Original Meaning of Zhouyi*, Zhu Xi also points out that "all things are born from Yin and Yang. *The Book of Changes* is mainly about the ways of Yin and Yang, from which the trigrams are produced" (1). Zhu's words make the paradoxical essence of Yin and Yang clear: both Yin and Yang are not only contradictory to, but also complementary with each other, which presents the rule of the universe.

The ideas of Yin and Yang in *The Book of Changes* are close to that of chaos theory in terms of their visions about the laws of man and cosmos, particularly orderly disorder or disorderly order for the deterministic chaos. Just as Hayles puts it, "In chaos theory chaos may either lead to order, as it does with self-organizing systems, or in yin/yang fashion it may have deep structures of order encoded within it" (*Chaos and Order* 3). Yin and Yang construct a whole, and both are hardly separated from each other. Yin can change into Yang, and vice verse. If some new variables are added in the system of the Taichi, then Yin can grow up progressively from the lower stage to the higher one, i.e. from the Young Yin to the Old Yin; similarly, Yang can be turned into the Old Yang from the Young Yang. The changes of Yin and Yang seem to be similar to that of the Lorenz attractor in a dynamical system, which oscillates between two attracting basins, sometimes crossing, sometimes separating, which sensitively depends on the changes of variables in the system.

The Book of Changes pays its emphasis on chance. By chance, it means that *The Book of Changes* makes combination of both time and opportunity (Shi and Ji in Chinese), in that they are thought to be mutually affected, especially in certain temporal-spatial spot. We may take the trigger in a gun as a metaphor to demonstrate its importance in telling one's destiny, and the act of click in a brief moment decides on one's life. Similar to the understanding of chaos theory about life as a deterministic chaos, it is hard for one to control his destiny, because of its nonlinearity and indeterminacy due to its sensitive dependence on initial conditions in a nonlinear dynamic system.

As the source of the world, the Taichi is superior to Yin and Yang, for the Taichi is "Tao," i.e. the law of the world. In *The Book of Changes*, the rules of Heaven, Earth and Humans constitute that of the world, which works as *Tao Te Ching* assumes, "The ways of man are conditioned by those of earth. The ways of earth, by those of heaven, the ways of heaven, by those of Tao, and the ways of Tao by the unconditioned" (Chap 25). In other words, the cosmos's balance decides on the harmonious relations of heaven, earth and humans, for they are holistic, and mutually conditioned and restricted. Only in accordance with the law of nature, the world can be made harmonious and balanced. Such a holistic viewpoint about the cosmos, including Heaven, Earth and Humans, is almost the same as that of chaos theory: the world is interconnected, organic, and dynamic, and small changes may cause great effects for the development of things, sometimes even catastrophic effects.

Consider the "five phase locations" in *The Book of Changes*. In the minds of ancient Chinese, these five phase locations make up the natural and human world as well as the organs in the human body, which are combined into organic systems. These five phase locations are not isolated from each other; on the contrary, they promote and constrain each other. Their mutual relations signify the complexity of the world. In details, wood generates fire, fire generates earth, earth generates metal, metal generates water, water generates wood; meanwhile, water restricts fire, fire restricts metal, metal restricts wood, wood restricts earth, and earth restricts water, building up a cycle and whole (see Fig. 1.12). From the ideas of five phase locations, things in the world can be divided into five parts or five types. The number five is the criteria to categorize everything in the world, which could be presented in the following, such as five locations (east, west, South, north and center), five materials (metal, wood, water, fire, and earth), five tastes (bitter, hot, sour, sweet and salty), five notes (Gong, Shang, Jue, Zhi, and Yu, musical notes in traditional Chinese music), five colors (black, red, blue, green, and yellow), five periods (spring, summer, autumn, winter, and long-summer).[1] Similarly, the five phase locations also correspond with organs in the human body, such as five facial features, made up of eyes, ears, nose, mouth and tongue. Some other things are associated with the figure "five": five livestock (cattle, sheep, dog, pig and chicken), five fruits (peach, pear, apricot, plum, date), five crops (hemp, millet, wheat, beans, rice), five figures (head, two arms and two legs) and so on, which constitute an organic system in the world. The five phase locations care more about dynamic changes than the static state, and the system than the isolation in the universe. Basing on ideas of these five phase locations, nature may be seen as a system rather than a machine, and the world in which we live is not to be static, simple, reversible, deterministic, and changeless in the ideas of classical physics, but is a picture with complexity, irreversibility, chance and changes, as chaos theory describes.

---

[1] The season in the modern sense refers to spring, summer, autumn and winter, four in total; while, for ancient Chinese, everything could be divided into five, so the Long-Summer is added to make the season five ones.

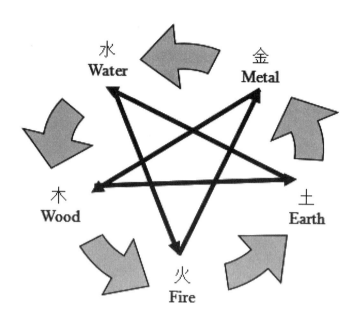

Figure 1.12 The Relationship of Five Phase Locations

As mentioned above, *The Book of Changes* looks at the world with imagination rather than scientific examination, for it was developed in the ancient time after all, when people knew little about the cosmos. For the ancient Chinese, the images of elements and texts were rudimentary to make exploration of the world outside them. Though simple in the mode, it can be made complicatedly in its transformation. These trigrams generated from the basic elements (Yin Yao and Yang Yao) are dynamic, for they vary all the time in different time periods and spatial spots, which reflects the world with complex images in the process of the transformation. Each trigram has three lines, and they can yield the sixty-four hexagrams through different lists and organizations of lines of Yin and Yang. More than that, with six lines to a hexagram, and four possible values to each line, "the number of combinations available to describe different situations comes out to be 4096, or 4k in computerese. The dynamics of change has expanded the sixty-four static hexagrams into more than four thousand patterns of development" (Huang 6).

Interestingly, the changing of trigrams and hexagrams is similar to that of Mandelbrot's fractals, so does the transformation of the Taichi, which is a kind of fractal with certain self-similarity. In the chaotic system, one of the major ways to achieve the state of chaos is via period doubling bifurcation. Similarly, the process of the development of the Taichi, from the Wu Ji (void) to the Taichi (one), then to two elements (*yin* and *yang*), then to four ones, then to eight trigrams, then to sixty-four hexagrams, then to the infinite, is close to that of the system in bifurcations, after which all grow up exponentially in the process of iteration.

The Book of Changes is none other than the sixty-four hexagrams, which are constituted with two parts, the graph (i.e. the imagery of the elements) and text. The text sometimes tells a story, sometimes gives an omen; but it always says things in human terms. For each element in the pattern of a hexagram, there is a text; and for each hexagram, there is a text accompanied with it, too. They may be interpreted differently by the reader with different intellectual and living backgrounds, and more than that, the variance in the understanding of the graph and text depends on its own dynamic changes in the spot of temporal-spatiality, that's why the interpretation of the world and events from *The Book of Changes* is both determinate and indeterminate. Actually, imagination plays great role in our understanding of *The Book of Changes*, because it describes the universe with imageries, so insights, even epiphany, are helpful in the practice.

For the interconnection of the eight trigrams, two patterns are helpful: one is the Primordial, or "Earlier Heaven" (Fuxi Bagua) (see Fig.1.13), and the other is the Manifested, or "Later Heaven" (Wenswang Bagua) (see Fig.1.14). We may note that it is partial to simply understand the eight trigrams as eight natural phenomena in the universe, for they are complicated enough to find correspondence in astronomy, astrology, geography, geometry and anatomy. More important, the temporal and spatial are included in the trigrams, implying that time passes in the space and space changes with time. To be specific, it refers to four time periods, four seasons, five phase locations, eight positions and so on. For example, the trigram of Thunder (Zhen) refers to the east and spring, where and when everything is vigorous and prosperous; the trigram of Lake (Dui) refers to the west and autumn, where and when everything is dreary and desolate.

Figure 1.13 The Primordial or "Fuxi Bagua"

Figure 1.14 The Manifested or "Wenwang Bagua"

The First Part of *Xi Tzu* says, "With the movement of the sun and the moon, there appears winter and summer." As we know, the movement of the sun and the moon signifies the spatial changes, while the alternation of winter and summer is a kind of temporal progress. Xu Daoyi assumes, "in ancient China, the temporal is confused with the spatial, and the time's passing just signifies the changes of the motion of the sun and the moon in a dynamic system" (117). It's apparent that Xu misses the point that it is the combination of temporality with spatiality to examine things in the world that makes *The Book of Changes* remarkable, because its interpretation of objects in the motion is close to Bakhtin's "chronotope," which pays emphasis on the temporal-spatial combination with the basis of Einstein's temporal-spatial vision. More exactly, the interpretation of things in the world from *The Book of Changes* is much closer to the mapping of phase space with strange attractor. As the simulation of matter's motion in the phase space, the strange attractor is "simultaneously a spatial configuration and a temporal continuum-a spatialization of temporal process and a temporalization of spatial form" (Jo Alyson Parker 26). Besides, the arrangement of the eight trigrams from Heaven to Earth foregrounds the nonlinearity of the development of things in the universe, for they develop without absolute causality, which demonstrates its vision similar to chaos theory for *The Book of Changes* again.

At present, more and more scholars have been aware of the importance of *The Book of Changes* concerning its interpretations of the world close to modern science. With regard to its key terms discussed above, *The Book of Changes* provides us with lots of truths about the world. Ontologically speaking, *The Book of Changes* suggests that the world is both certain and uncertain; epistemologically speaking, *The Book of Changes* holds that the world can be recognized, yet it is hard to describe exactly. As for things in progress, *The Book of Changes* thinks it certain to develop, yet chance decides on its certainty or uncertainty in the development. Close to chaos theory, the world is described as the paradox of determinacy and indeterminacy in *The Book of Changes*.

III. Literary Criticism and Chaos Theory

Karl Marx once points out that natural science is the basis of knowledge, and he even anticipates that both natural and social science would be combined into oneness in *Economic and Philosophical Manuscripts of 1844* (qtd. in Shen 309). Michel Foucault also asserts that the humanities can "take Mathematics as their tools" to make their research procedures and results into certain kinds of figures (*The Order* 349). Though Lyotard argues in *The Postmodern Condition* that science and literature are two kinds of discourse, yet there is still a tendency of disciplines-crossing and disciplines-transplanting in contemporary period. Chaos theory brings the world with a "future shock."[①] Since it burst onto the scene in the late 1980s and early 1990s, chaos theory has "demonstrated that it is not simply a passing fad but a viable and important means for generating new insights within all disciplines" (Jo Alyson Parker 17-8).

To be honest, it is not strange to connect "hard science" with literature, though adventurous. Some fictional writers have taken chaos theory as the themes of their works, such as Tom Stoppard's *Arcadia* (1993), Richard Powers' *Galatea* 2.2 (1995), and Michael Crichton's *The Jurassic Park* (1990), Darren Aronosky has made it a mind-bogging film in 1998, which were popular in the general public and academic circle. Chaos theory also provides inspirations for critics in their literary criticism. As far as I know, some scholars such as N. Katherine Hayles, Alexander Argyros, Jo Alyson Parker, Thomas P. Weissert, Gordon E. Slethaug, Thomas Jackson Rice, John L. Kundert-Gibbs and Joseph Conte have sought to transfer the concepts or other aspects of chaos theory into their discipline, and some of them also made applications of chaos theory in literary criticism.

Among them, one of the most well-known scholars is Hayles, who observes that chaos theory is

one site within the culture where the premise characteristic of postmodernism are inscribed. The postmodern context catalyzed the formation of the new science by providing a cultural and technological milieu in which the component parts came together and mutually reinforced each other until they were no longer isolated events

---

① This phrase is suggested by the futurist, Alvin Toffle in his well-known book, *Future Shock* (1970).

but an emergent awareness of the constructive roles that disorder, nonlinearity, and noise play in complex systems. (*Chaos and Order* 5)

Hayles assumes that chaos science provides us with a new way to consider postmodernism and both are in the same cultural milieu. In her vision, four attributes in the contemporary fiction distinctively postmodern are also prominent in chaotic systems: nonlinearity, self-reflexivity, irreversibility and self-organization. In her groundbreaking discussions of the affinities of chaos theory and postmodern literature as well as postmodern theories, Hayles argues that chaos theory "provides a new way to think about order, conceptualizing it not as a totalized condition but as the replication of symmetries that also allows for asymmetries and un-predictabilities" (*Chaos and Order* 10-1). Besides its similarities with poststructuralism, chaos theory's "suspicion of globalization" is similar to those suggested by Jacques Derrida, Frederic Jameson, Jean-Francois Lyotard, and Lucc Irigaray. More than that, its emphasis on iteration, recursive looping, nonlinearity, and un-predicability, makes it similar to other postmodern theories. In her *Chaos Bound* (1990), Hayles derives methods from chaos theory to interpret contemporary literature and applies the fundamental concepts of chaos theory in her explanations of interconnections in science, literature and other cultural phenomenon. She also "offers broad paradigmatic parallels as a way of suggesting a vocabulary for literature akin to that which delineates physical phenomenon" (Gillespie 17) and makes practice in her literary criticism. All in all, Hayles completely takes chaos theory as postmodernism for their similar cultural milieu and chaos theory's convergence with postmodernist literature and postmodern theories.

Hayles' contentions get correspondence with that of Rice and Kundert-Gibbs. Rice observes that as a rule, the history of Anglo-American literary theory in the 20th century roughly parallels the developments in the science, yet in their paradigm shifts, there still exists a chronological "red shift," i.e. a lag of several decades for the literary academy's assimilation with scientific theories. However, chaos theory is a shock in that it is simultaneous with some theories, particularly "new historicism," which studies literature in all its contexts and views the literary works not only in terms of the reader and the text itself, but also in terms of its relations with the complex multiply realities, sharing the fundamental assumptions of chaos theory and the broader emerging field of sciences of complexities (Rice 109-10). In light of chaos theory's "destabilization of the old, commonplace paradigm and the revisioning of the fringes," and its idea of the relative progress of things from order to disorder or from disorder to order, Kundert-Gibbs holds that chaos theory overlaps with some postmodern theories, such as feminism, deconstruction, post-colonialism, ecocriticism, and gender studies, due to their similarities in the dismantling of the stereotyped Cartesian binary opposition in Western thinking (51).

Just as Jo Alyson Parker points out, "literary theorists are not claiming to be scientists; they are instead laying claim to a conceptual trove that enhances literary studies-and enhances science as well" (20). Parker assumes that "by drawing on scientific concepts literary theorists find new ways of articulating and apprehending the complex workings of a literary text," for "new concepts lead to new ways of seeing" (ibid). Based on Parker's idea, the application of chaos theory in literary criticism is advantageous to combine the form with the content in the critical examination, which can avoid the weak points of both structuralism and post-structuralism, because the former takes the text as a close one, paying more attention to the form, while the latter makes the text go from "the prison of language" into the "political unconscious," paying more attention to its social and historical contexts. Feminism, post-colonialism and gay studies are good cases, for they care more about the work's political and social contexts than the form of the text, hence diverging from the aesthetic aim of literary works. Besides, a literary text is usually involved with the writer, the text, the world and the reader. Once the text is produced, it may expect the participation of the reader, and then the text may be transformed into three ones: the written text, the pretext, referring to that of collections of materials of the writer before writing, and the post-text, referring to that made after the interpretation of the reader. Chaos theory cares much more about the observer's perspective, so in the process of criticism, it is reasonable to combine three texts into oneness.

With regard to the advantages from the criticism of "chaotics,"[1] Gillespie takes his side with Jo Alyson Parker. He directly criticizes other criticisms to be like "the blind men describing the elephant, each topical or ideological effort at criticism tend to distort perceptions of the work under consideration, and each produces a fragmented impression that never blends into a complete picture" (13). For him, chaotics criticism is "a strategy that enables a genuine acceptance of pluralism, one that reflects the way reading encounters literature," and it is also "a system of criticism grounded upon the way a typical reading simultaneously sustains a range of different response to a work without giving primacy to them" (ibid).

Both Parker and Gillespie consider chaotics criticism as "a new hypothesis," leading away from either/or thinking, and its interest in plurality reasserts itself. Just as Gillespie puts it, "simple input often led to complex results, and consequently, the possibility making accurate predictions of results based upon a perceived sense of their causes became increasingly unlikely" (17). For Gillespie, nonlinear thinking is expected when doing criticism. By nonlinear thinking, Gillespie means that there is no absolute or mechanical viewpoint to consider, rather reader's response and participation are involved in the process of criticism. Gillespie and Parker trace their criticism to the holistic nature of chaos theory, which takes the world as an organic system, in which any microscopic random fluctuations can bring about macroscopic transformation.

Besides Hayles, Parker and Gillespie, some other scholars make application of chaos theory in their practice of literary criticism. Until now, specific texts or sets of texts, from Shakespearean drama to *The Bluest Eye* (1970) by Toni Morrison, have been reexamined with chaos theory. In *Strange Attractors* (1995), Harriett Hawkins makes comparisons of Shakespearean drama and Milton's *Paradise Lost* with popular novels, and suggests that these popular novels' "refashioning" or parodies of these classics are one of ways to make applications of chaos theory, for these novels may be counted as "fractals" of the classics. Hawkins even makes assumptions that those classics are strange attractors, in which cultural "attractors" are involved. For Hawkins,

---

[1] Chaotics is the term by Hayles, which is said to be suggested by Ihab Hassan (Hayles, *Chaos and Order* 7).

"passion" is also a kind of strange attractor, and then these passionate women, such as Desdemona, Cleopatra, become strange attractors, too.

Scholars have various understandings of chaos theory in their literary criticism. For example, Kundert-Gibbs pays emphasis on the relative nature of chaos theory, and thus he links Zen Buddhism with chaos theory to make studies of Beckett's drama because of their common concerns of "void." According to Kundert-Gibbs, the "void" is "far from being a negative or nihilistic shift," rather, "a more positive one," where "the knowledge of a socially created reality allow us, à la Zen, to step back from the bipolar categories of order /disorder, creation /destruction, etc., and see our world as essentially unitary instead" (20). Gordon E. Slethaug takes chaos theory to be affinitive with postmodernism in his examination of contemporary American fiction through the lens of chaos theory. His *Beautiful Chaos* (2000) is a milestone monograph, which details basic assumptions about orderly and dynamic systems and the various manifestations of chaos theory in postmodernist literature. Kevin A. Boon's *Chaos Theory and the Interpretation of Literary Texts* (1997) works like that of Slethaug. In his exploration of Vonnegut's postmodern narrative, Boon contends that there exist "orderly disorder" and "disorderly order" in Vonnegut's fiction. His opinions about postmodern novel's "orderly disorder" in the narrative form and thematic presentation get developed by Joseph Conte.

In his erudite monograph, *Design and Debris* (2002), Conte employs chaos theory to explore postmodern fiction, and some of works from writers, such as John Hawkes, Kathy Acker, John Barth, Robert Coover, Don DeLillo and Thomas Pynchon, are examined. He argues that between postmodern fiction and chaos science, despite in two disciplines, there have been a homologous development, in which both move independently but share convictions regarding orderly disorder. Conte demonstrates how the paradigm shift from modernism to postmodernism has led postmodernist writers to embrace science in their treatment of complexity in the world and society. In literary modernism the artists still attempt to impose order and coherence on a disorderly, random, and inchoate world, while for literary postmodernism, the artists try to delineate the process of "orderly disorder" (Conte 7). The understandings of "orderly disorder" from both Conte and Boon are attributable to Hayles, who contends that in chaos theory there are two layers of connotation: first, there are orders hidden within the superficial chaos; second, in the chaotic process of transformation, there exists some "self-organizations," i.e. patterns, therefore, order may arise out of dynamic changes of a complex system (*Chaos Bound* 8-17).

To sum up, just like the discrepancy in people's understandings of postmodernism, there are a great variety of ideas about the application of chaos theory in literary criticism, which proves the nature and glamour of chaos and chaos theory. Nothing is stable and absolute. The ideas of Hayles about the affinities between chaos theory and postmodernism, between chaos theory and postmodernist writings, suggestions of Parker and Gillespie about the comprehension of chaotics criticism with its advantages of the combination of narrative form and content in literary criticism, and Gillespie's proposal about nonlinear thinking in literary criticism, and some other critics' significant practices in literary criticism, are beneficial to interpret different genres of literary works, and of course, inspirational for the exploration of McCarthy's fiction with dynamic complexity.

IV. Space, Spatial Form and Chaos

Chaos theory is interdisciplinary, and its involvement in the narrative with spatial form makes contemporary writings much more complex than ever before. For understanding better the dynamic complexity of McCarthy's fiction, especially its spatial configuration as chaos, a brief review of "spatial turn" in the humanities and literary writings in the last half of the twentieth century is necessary. "Spatial turn" was a tendency for academic circles at the end of the 20th century. Foucault anticipated in 1967 that "The present age may be the age of space instead. ... We are in the era simultaneous, of juxtaposition, of the near and far, of the side by side, of the scattered" ("Of Other Spaces" 22-7). Similarly, Frederic Jameson claims that "the dominant cultural mode is one defined by categories of space; we inhabit the synchronic, rather than the diachronic" (qtd. in Hebdige 16). Consistent with "spatial turn" in the humanities, fictional writings also shift toward the spatial in the 20th century. With their destabilization of causal-linear-chronological conventions, postmodernist writers even make their works "consistently spatial in their organization and purpose" (Klinkowitz 47), advancing the experimentation trend of their modernist precursors to the extreme. The turn toward the spatial in literary writings not only echoes what W. T. Michell has identified as "pictorial turn" in philosophy and arts, but also recalls the sensibility for space and spatiality in the more overtly political manifestations since the 1960s, characterized by Guy Debort's "society's spectacle," Foucault's notion of surveillance, and Baudrillard's culture of simulation. Additionally, such a spatial turn in literary writings also reinforces the field concept[①] of modern science that emerges about the same time (Tabbi & Wutz 11).

Etymologically, space derives from Latin spatium, which means "gap" or "distance." Space has long been regarded in two ways: "on the one hand, at a microscopic level, as the gaps between things, which keep them apart; on the other hand, at a macroscopic level, as the larger container into which all things are inserted" (West-Palov 15). Such an understanding of space originates from Euclidean geometry, which determines Western thinking in the era of classical science. Both Plato and Aristotle think that space is an objective container, without any nature. For Kant, there are "not spaces but Space-one infinite continuous Unit" (Curtis 163). Opposite to time's "richness, fecundity, life, dialectic" (Foucault, *Power* 70), space is traditionally considered to be "neutral, insignificant, meaningless and homogeneous" (West-Palov 16), nothing significant for philosophy or sciences.

Einstein's theory of relativity changes the concepts of space and time in Newtonian physics, and his idea of spatialized time and temporalized space makes the space less neutral or homogeneous than ever before. Chaos theory advances Einstein's theory and pays more emphasis on the matter's motion in temporalized space, as we mention in the first section of this chapter. In consistence with the changes of scientific knowledge about time and space, philosophers also lash out at Kantian philosophy. In modernism period, William James and Henri Bergson are relevant. James thinks of it impossible for

---

① The field concept was central to several disciplines during the first half of the 20th century, which implies that "reality consists not of discrete objects located in space but rather of an underlying field whose interactions produce both objects and space" (Hayles, *Chaos Bound* xi).

Kantian uniform space, while Bergson insists on the distinction between time and space and makes emphasis of time in people's consciousness. His concept of temporal "durée" influences the whole generation of modernist writings, such as the narrative technique of stream of consciousness, making the literature have a turn from the representation of the outside to that of the inside. Since the 1960s, space has gone into the vision of French thinkers, such as Heidegger, Derrida, Kristeva, Foucault, Deleuze, and Henry Lefbvre. In the English-speaking world, such a "spatial turn" was heralded by cultural geographers, such as Harvey David, Derek Gregory, John Urry, Mike Crang, Edward Soja and Doreen Massey, with their series of monographs about space published in the past decades.

Heidegger asserts that the world does not exist in the space; rather, space exists in the world. So, space becomes a kind of "being," which can produce "places" from desolation and hence the possibility of "dwelling" (Lai 168). Derrida suggests a neologism, "spacing," which denotes "the active, productive character of space" (West-Palov 17), so space/spacing can be changed from its original container, "dead, fixed, the undialectical, the immobile" to a new "medium with its own consistency and above all, its own productive agency" (Foucault, *Power* 70). In *Of Other Spaces* (1986), Foucault suggests the notion of "heterotopias." In his point of view, some places like prison, factory, barracks, whorehouse, theatre, library, museum and asylum contain "heterotopias," where the space of the other is presented and the other's rebellions could be found, so it seems that they are fluid, just like "a place without a place" (27). For Foucault, our present life is still constrained by a series of spatial either/or: private space/public space, family space/social space, cultural space/practical space, leisure space/ work space and so on. And power works in the space, for the space is the basis of the practice of power. The new "trinity" of space, knowledge and power[1] makes the space hierarchical, because the space is generally constructed rather than natural or the made.

Foucault's idea of space as "productivity" and "production" gets developed by Henri Lefbvre, who assumes that space is the very fabric of social existence, a medium

---

[1] Foucault is generally known with his "trinity" of knowledge, power and subject.

woven of relations of subjects and their actions and surroundings. Space is not a pre-existing receptacle for human action any more, but the production of human action; space, in turn, may exert its own variety of agency, modeling the human actors who have configured it. In *The Production of Space* (1974), Lefbvre proposes a "trialectics," in which physical space, spiritual space and social space are included. Among them, social space is the most important, for it covers the historicity, sociality and spatiality. Via the concept of space, Lefbvre makes his critique of capitalism society, which is different from Karl Marx's adoption of the relations of productive force and productive relations to observe the essence of capitalism society. For Lefbvre, the society can be produced by space, though social space is produced by the society (Lu 490). Therefor, space becomes both the producer and the product.

Lefbvre's seminal contribution to spatial theory has been extensively acknowledged by Edward Soja. Soja proposes a postmodern reconstruction of human geography, which centers on ideas of "how we interpret the land we inhabit, how we are changed or altered because of our dealings with it, and how we interact with it" (Barrera 24). In *Postmodern Geographies* (1989), Soja also asserts that the production of space is a social process. He thinks it necessary to make distinction "between space per se, space as a contextual given, and socially-based spatiality, the created space of social organization and production" (79). For Soja, space is a social product, rather than a physical construct. Human patterns of being-in-the-world exist simultaneously and dialectically in time and space and are necessary to understand power struggles that extend through time and along geographical space.

In short, in the humanities, ideas of the space have been moved away from notions of space as "the material/ phenomenal rather than the abstract. ...[as] being rather than becoming" towards a conceptualization of being fluid and dynamic (West-Palov 22). Such a "turn" of intellectual inquiry is significant because all the significance are considered as something produced, or something specific to time and space, in one word, all emerge out of the context. So each of concepts associated with space, such as location, context, contours and dimension, cannot be ignored, especially in the spatial analysis, for they are hardly taken as something physical or abstract, but an interpretable text, from which power, hierarchy, hegemony and identity could be discovered (Crang 51). Geopolitics is such a subject, which studies "the political behavior in the space" through the link of space with politics (Geoffrey Parker 44).

In accordance with the traditional absence and silence of space in the humanities, conventional narrative also simply takes space as landscape descriptions to break down the temporal flow, or setting, upon which the narrative is carried out, in that literary writings are generally counted as temporal art. Lessing's *Laocoön* distinguishes music and literature from painting and sculpture. For Lessing, time is fluid, so literary works, particularly the fiction, develop temporally, and the sequence of events develops along the chronological axis for the purpose of telling a "story"; whereas, painting, sculpture, and architecture are spatial arts in essence, which are synchronic, reversible and visual (Lessing 51-82). Though the narrative with spatial structure or with space as themes does exist in the history of literature, it has been ignored by the scholars all the time. In the 1920s, in light of Einstein's theory of relativity, Bakhtin suggested his important concept of "chronotope" to combine "topos" and "chronos," two major narrative components, together; however, his idea did not catch the attention of scholars at that time. Until Joseph Frank's essay, *Spatial Form in Modern Fiction*, was published in 1945, the spatial form in the narrative has become visible and attentive. In this essay, Frank suggests a new theory to make exploration of modernist writings.

To some extent, Joseph Frank's theory may be considered as the product of modernism. In the 20th century, scientific and technical development and bloody world wars shattered people's sense of time, space and home, and strengthened alienation, absurdity and fragmentation in the human world. The structural device of the twentieth-century literature that seems "most newly obtrusive is fragmentation, which is analogue for the felt fragmentation of twentieth-century culture" (Rabkin 95). In modernist fiction, the predominance of causal-chronological sequence has become seriously weakened. Some modernist masters, such as Proust, Kafka, Faulkner, Joyce, Hemingway, and Woolf, discard the conventional notion of their precursors, and in their fiction they no longer mirror the physical details of the external world within a progressive, continuous, causal and linear structure, rather they pay much attention to the sub-consciousness or unconsciousness of their characters in light of Bergson's concept of "durée" or private time to expose psychological space and time and "simulate" the dreams or the flux of thoughts or "stream of consciousness" in one's inner mind. So different techniques, such as the temporal-spatial juxtaposition, the intersection of temporal-spatiality, or cinematic montage to make time and space come back and forth, are experimented in their writings. However, their experimentation cannot be understood easily by those critics familiar with those narrative strategies of the realistic fiction in the 19th century. Just as the shift of paradigm in the scientific community does, for instance, Newtonian physics encounters the challenge from Einstein's theory of relativity, quantum mechanics meets with the revision of chaos theory, and the second law of thermodynamics has been proved to be contradictory to Darwin's evolution theory and wrong in its portraiture of the future of the whole universe, literary criticism also suffers the crisis in its encounter with new modes of writings. In response to the requirements of his age, Frank's theory of spatial form provides a new methodology for the interpretation of modernist writings.

Modernist masters are good at the creation of spatial form in their works. Imagists like Ezra Pound, T. S. Eliot, e. e. cummings and T. E. Hulme, at the beginning of the 20th century, made good use of the juxtaposition and superimposition of images in their poetry to create the spatial beauty by arousing the reader's visual perception. They borrowed spatial strategies and techniques from Chinese traditional poetry and Japanese haiku to bring about spatial form in their poetry. Pound's famous poem, "In a Station of the Metro" (The apparition of these faces in the crowd / petals on a wet, black bough) impresses the reader with a beautiful impressionist painting, which is achieved via the juxtaposition and superimposition of images.

Imagism poetry inspires Joseph Frank. Pound's famous definition of image, that which presents an intellectual or emotional complex in an instant of time, implies that literature can be made into the visual art. Joseph Frank observes that modernist poetry "undermines the inherent consecutiveness of language, forcing the reader to perceive the elements of the poem not as unrolling in time but as juxtaposed in space" (Smitten 17). By way of the "suppression of causal/temporal connectives, those words and word groups by which a literary work is tied to external reality and to the tradition of mimesis" (ibid), the whole character of the literary work can be altered, which forces the reader to perceive it in a new and unconventional way. Based on Joseph Frank, "juxtaposition" is an important way to make the syntax of the fictional work synchronic among the seemingly disconnected words or word groups.

Joseph Frank takes the scene of country fair in *Madame Bovary* (1857) by Gustave Flaubert as an ideal case, in which the traditional narrative syntax is disrupted through the shift of simultaneous actions back and forth, making different associations of characters involved in this scene "juxtaposed" and independent of the progress of the narrative, hence spatial form in the fiction. As "an eternal monument to go beyond time," *Remembrance of Things Past* (1913-1927) by Marcel Proust achieves its spatial effect through presenting events or characters discontinuously, forcing his reader to juxtapose different images of characters in an instant moment (Frank 11-5). James Joyce's *Ulysses* (1936) impresses the reader with a "picture of Dublin seen as a whole" with his techniques of "distributed exposition," "reference" and "cross-reference" to construct his narrative, which makes his reader connect different fragments with each other and associate them with their complementary parts through the device of "reflexive reference" (Frank 7).

No novel can be perfectly temporal or spatial, for "they all involve simultaneity, flashbacks, or jumps in time, and they almost never ignore time completely" (Smitten 20), thus in a fiction of spatial form, its departures from pure temporality, or from causal/temporal sequence ask the reader to "map out in his mind the system of internal references and relationships to understand the meaning of any single event" (ibid), or combine the separate parts together into a whole. According to Frank, the reader's perception is a necessity, that is to say, the reader is asked to participate in the writing, and his responses towards the text are helpful to map out a pattern or a picture in his mind, and his "spatial feeling" or "spatial intuition" is requested to appreciate or examine the literary text with spatial form. For those complicated modernist writings, the reader have to read repetitively to achieve his "reflexive reference."

Joseph Frank's term "reflexive reference" is similar to "Guan Xiang" in Zen

Buddhism, which asks a person to map the state of a concept in the mind in his meditation, and it is also close to the mapping of trajectories of matter's motion in a dynamic system on a computer screen for chaos scientists, in which iteration is requested. Gadamer's hermeneutics may be helpful to understand such a term. First, take the text as an open system, in which the horizons of both the reader and the text mix together, even infiltrating mutually. Then, reiterate the process of understanding of the text, through which the textual meaning can be produced. To put it simply, the reader is asked "to suspend the process of individual reference temporarily until the entire pattern of internal reference can be apprehended as a unity" (Frank 6). Only making the reference of one part of the work to another one, then "units of meaning are referred to each other reflexively in a moment of time" (qtd. in Smitten 21), which may work out the syntax of a narrative with spatial form.

In addition, both "cross-reference" and "reflexive reference" could be combined to organize these disparate single parts into a whole, creating a form of synchronicity. Such a way of "reference" or "cross-reference" or "reflexive reference" may be extended to any other works of the same author in light of the intertextual or intratexual allusions of works. Only when a literary work is viewed multiple-dimensionally, can the gestalt of writings be created. According to Curtis, a gestalt relates to the text what Saussure's langue relates to parole. When we read a text with spatial form, we will have a relationship, text: gestalt :: parole: langue (Curtis 176). In brief, in Joseph Frank's theory of spatial form, we may note the combination of the approaches of structuralism, phenomenology and hermeneutics.

Joseph Frank's innovative theory gets developed by scholars, who provide a variety of techniques and patterns to make analysis of literary works, mostly modernist ones, such as "framing," "story-within-the story," "leitmotif," "paratactic device," "parallel chapters," "authorial illusion" and so on. The gestalt of literary works in the reader's mind is different, for example, *The Sound and the Fury* (1929) is discovered to be like "an impressionist painting" in the mind of Joseph Frank, while it is felt like "a series of concentric circles" by Eric S. Rabkin (98). Mickesen even takes orange to image some fiction featuring with the spatial narrative, and he writes, "Spatial form novels are not carrots, growing cumulatively and without interruption toward a climatic green effusion; rather, they are oranges with a number of similar segments, going nowhere or in circles focused on a single subject (core)" (65).

As Ihab Hassan points out that, "modernism and postmodernism are not separated by an Iron Curtain or Chinese Wall" (88). Hassan means that there are tangled relations between modernism and postmodernism. Brian McHale also suggests that "postmodernism follows from modernism, in some sense, more than it follows after modernism" (5). So postmodernist narratives are "not the direct result of linear and progressive development of modernist writings, rather, they practice exactly the same aesthetic characteristics" (Zhan vi). Postmodernist writers continue with experimental techniques of their modernist predecessors, even go further. In their writings, the spatial-temporal congruity are shattered to be much more "fragmented," in order to "simulate" the "fragmented" reality with the loss of historical sense, temporal perception and unity of identity for individuals produced by a new state of "cultural development of the logic of late capitalism" since the 1960s (Jameson 46). For modernist writers, in spite of the fragmentation of their world, they still believe in something objective, so inner mind becomes their final "Eden." Dream, memory or something subconscious or unconscious, turn out to be another reality in their writings. While, for postmodernist writers, since the author has been "dead," his hierarchy over the text has been lost, either. Facing the text with indeterminacy and word game, the reader may interpret the text with his free association, because all texts are reproductions or reflections of previous texts in Kristeva's understanding. Free interpretation equals to no interpretation, for "their works cancel themselves, make fun of their continuing creation, refuse interpretation, and engage both the author and reader in self-reflexive game-playing" (Klinkowitz 40).

According to Linda Hutcheon, postmodernist fiction should be characterized by what she calls "historigraphic metafiction" (*A Poetics* ix). Such a genre of fiction has a very outstanding feature, that is to "discard conventional notions of character, action, thematic development, narrative sequence, and ultimately illusion itself ('suspension of disbelief') in favor of a fully self-conscious form of writing" (Klinkowitz 39). Authors like Vladimir Nabokov, William Gass, William Gaddis, Ronald Sukenick and Cormac McCarthy, are masters of metafiction. In their writings, they are involved into the texts, and sometimes they may become one of characters in the fiction, sometimes they may talk about their actual writings in their books with the aim to expose the fictitiousness of their works, and hence a sense of comedy and play produced for the work to succeed. Nabokov has asserted that "one of the functions of all my novels is to prove that the novel in general does not exist" (115). McCarthy also speaks of the narrative's fictionality in *The Crossing*, "all is telling" (C 155). For them, writing is to play the game with the world and they could invent "realities" throughout their works. Anyway, it is such a pure self-reflexiveness that "has made this new writing dominantly spatial in form" (Klinkowitz 40).

With regard to the spatial form in the postmodernist fiction, Frank's proposal of "juxtaposition" is not sufficient, because in their works, there are only floating signifiers, and nothing about the syntax and organization can be "referenced," the narrative in postmodernist writings becomes chaotic (disorderly) fragmentation. However, his advocation of reference, cross reference and reflexive reference is still helpful to explore spatial form in the narrative. In postmodernist writings, the narrative is no longer causal-linear-chronological, and the space is presented to be floating and heterogeneous. Despite spatial form taken in the narrative, in modernist writings, the narrative sequence is still exhibited to show the world in progress and space is taken as a relief from the ongoing action of time; while in postmodernist writings, spatial form is left to be the only way to demonstrate their recognition of the world. So in "the schizoid text" (McHale 190), the reader's "reflexive reference" just brings him with a simple "collage," perhaps.

With the development of computer technology recently, contemporary fiction have got some new features. There appear some fiction with new spatial forms, such as "cybertext," and "hypertext," which completely discard conventional notions of narrative, and even replace printing text with electronic one. By means of all kinds of new media, such as web or hypertext software, or special-devised story-space, these new types of fiction present much more complicated spatial form than ever before. In these hypertext fiction, spatial form has been changed completely to a "labyrinth" with "forking paths," where "the reader's self-guided tour through a series of linked and interrelated 'lexias' (or blocks of text) departs sharply from the model of a single, linear narrative compelled by the printed page" (Geyh et al 511).

In sum, contemporary fiction becomes more and more complex in the narrative form with the development of technology and science. Chaos theory's spatial patterns, such as strange attractors, fractals, bifurcations and turbulence, have been employed by some of contemporary American writers, such as John Barth, John Hawkes, Kathy Acker, Thomas Pynchon and Cormac McCarthy, to name a few, to enrich their narrative or construct their fiction's spatial form, making their fiction present the aesthetic characteristics of dynamic spatiality. Anyhow, as a new science, chaos theory has demonstrated its ways to help to review, reinterpret and reinscribe language, text, self, society and even temporal-spatiality. Its process of "overturning established views of science and systems chimes with the emphasis of literature of the day on uncertainty and indeterminacy, free play of signifier, and rewritings of various sorts" (Slethaug xii), and additionally, its association with space and spatial form concerned in the humanities and literary writings in contemporary period will be enlightening for our examinations of contemporary fiction doubtlessly.

Chapter Two
Order, Disorder and Nonlinearity: Chaos and Wilderness

True words are not beautiful / Beautiful words are not truthful.

Lao Tsu, Tao Te Ching

A smooth river flows in the mountain or in the woods, and a boulder in it will make the river go back and forth in eddies and swirls, sometimes against the macro flow of the piece, following now one stream, now another. It is true that nature is nonlinear, and turbulence is one of her best symbols.[①] In our cosmos, regularity coexists with irregularity, order accompanies disorder, of course, symmetry and asymmetry, beauty and terror are symbiotic naturally, which is what chaos theory tells us. If we take cosmos as the Taichi, yin and yang, order and disorder constitute it, both are not opposite to each other, rather, they are complementary. According to chaos theory, orderly disorder, an oxymoron by itself, constitutes our living universe. McCarthy's fictional world is full of such paradoxes, as the "chaotic" nature implies. In this chapter, I would like to address the world of human beings and nature presented in McCarthy's fiction as wilderness and chaos with specific reference to *Child of God* (1973) and *Blood Meridian* (1985) and if necessary, some other novels may be mentioned in the discussion.

McCarthy's world is dark and bleak, even bloody and violent, which is considered as some critics, particularly Vereen Bell, to be "nihilism." However, just

---

① As important as the butterfly for chaos theory, "turbulence" is also a metaphor cited frequently to refer to the behavior of chaos in nonlinear dynamic system. The scientists David Ruelle and Ilya Prigogine contribute to chaos theory with their researches in the "turbulence."

as Aristotle defines the great tragedy as something beautiful torn into pieces in front of the audience, the greatest literature usually enables us to "look into the very heart of darkness by making of the intolerable a thing of beauty" (Winchell, 1990).[1] For McCarthy, wilderness is synonymous with chaos, characteristic with orderly disorder and nonlinearity. McCarthy's fiction seems to suggest that nature, people and society are in the situation of "wilderness inside and outside."[2] As we know, the octopus does look hideous, yet we cannot ignore it, for it indeed exists in nature, constructing the chaotic cosmos together with something beautiful. Its ugliness images us human beings, which is of motivation for McCarthy to be "mimetic" of orderly disorder and nonlinearity in nature, human being and society in the postmodern time. McCarthy's fiction may give his reader what W. B. Yeats might have called terrible beauty.

Before our exploration of McCarthy's fictional world as wilderness and chaos, it is of necessity to observe the epistemic shift from classical science to modern science, in terms of the relations of order and disorder with the change of human knowledge of our living cosmos, hopefully understanding better the effect of the crosstalk between science and literature on literary writings.

I. Epistemic Shift

In terms of the issue of order and disorder, people have been obsessed with it since ancient time. Since Copernicus's heliocentric model overturned Ptolemy's geocentric theory, human beings have been liberated from the fetters and constraints of the medieval Christian theology, which believes that nature, as the creation of God, is unified and orderly. Renaissance thinkers and artists focus on the dignity of human beings and people's reason is emphasized because it is thought to be capable of controlling the passion. For these thinkers, order could be known by human beings,

---

① Winchell's essay is republished in the web, so the present study just notes its original publishing year. The case is true to that of Pitts and Schopen quoted in this study.

② Georg Guillemin notes that *Child of God* is a novel "about wilderness inside and out" (37). This study further develops Guillemin's contention and argues that McCarthy's characters are wild in nature, and the world, natural and human, is wild, too. They seem to be of wilderness and chaos from inside to outside, which reflects the factuality of world in the age of the post 1960s.

though God is generally believed to create order. The Renaissance value of reason is carried on into the age of Enlightenment. With the development of the theory of falling bodies of Galileo and Cartesian mathematics as well as Newtonian mechanics, people's reason, rationalization and heroic mechanism become central to Enlightenment thought, from which man can be able to understand the universe and improve his own condition. Classical or modern science considers the cosmos to be "clockwork," and seeks to "portray nature a unified, deterministic, rational, and simple system, ruled by unalterable laws" (Grubic 124). Modernity (Renaissance and Enlightenment are also named by modernity) is still fundamentally on order, and man believe that the power of knowledge could overcome ignorance and disorder. Design and symmetry are thought to be of beauty and simplicity. Accompanied with modern science, determinism and reductionism are prevalent in Western thought. Art follows science usually. Literary realism and naturalism assume that the reality may be "represented" in literature, for it may be recognized by human beings, so in realistic fiction, the causal-linear-chronological narrative structure is popular.

In the late 19th and early 20th century, the Newtonian paradigm was challenged by electro-magnetics, thermodynamics, relativity theory, quantum mechanics, and chaos theory. Albert Einstein's Theory of Relativity (1905) that discards the concept of absolute motion, Werner Heisenberg's Uncertainty Principle (1927) that implicates the observer as a presence in any system of measurement, and Niels Bohr's Principle of Complementarity (1927) that treats the logical contradiction of light as wave and photon as complementary, reinforce the dysfunction of the Newtonian cosmic model and the enlightenment project along with it, and undermine the deterministic logic of natural world and "the linear reasoning of proportional causality, continuity, and objectivity that supported realism" (Conte 7). Furthermore, in the 20th century, with the development of industrialization, urbanization and modernization, not only the environment was deteriorated by people's desire of economic interests, but also human beings were made inhuman and nonhuman by the capitalistic system. Alienation and fragmentation became the common sentimentality in modern period. Apart from this, two great wars, genocide and the atomic bomb strongly suggest that the project of modernity, science, reason and order, might be flawed, though they have been respected before. For literary modernism, since the world is altered to be in disorder and fragmentation, "representationalism" is hardly possible in literary works, so it starts to promote "a self-conscious and more intuitive aesthetic" (Conte 7). The fiction of stream of consciousness, the imagist poetry, absurdist theatre, cubism, Dadaism, and surrealism are experiments for writers. Despite this, modernist writers still hold that they may impose order and coherence on a disorderly, random and inchoate world, and order and coherence can be discovered in their writings.

The "order-obsession" inherited from Newtonian science in Western culture and thought was completely overturned by the postmodern science in the second half of the 20th century. In *The Postmodern Condition*, Lyotard asserts that science has reached a "crisis of determinism" (53). The quantum mechanics, nonlinear dynamics, Mandelbrot's fractal geometry, and René Thom's catastrophe theory are thought by Lyotard to represent an epistemic shift, i.e. a change in the condition of knowledge. Lyotard concludes,

Postmodern science-by concerning itself with such things as undecidables, the limits of precise control, conflicts characterized by incomplete information, 'fracta,' catastrophes, and pragmatic paradoxes-is theorizing its own evolution as discontinuous, catastrophic, non-rectifiable, and paradoxical. It is changing the meaning of the word knowledge, while expressing how such a change can take place. It is producing not the known, but the unknown. (60)

In the postmodern age, science no longer limits its attention on objects and condition, rather, nature re-enchants and redraws the attention of scientists with its instability, irregularity and beauty shown in its variety of natural phenomena. Chaos theory believes that the world is unpredictable with probabilities and uncertainties rather than of absolute laws and mechanic process, of interconnected webs rather than of isolated, closed systems and frictionless planes, holistic rather than global or local. There are clear parallels between the realities of individual life and human history. In short, postmodern science has a paradigm shift "from nonlinearity as a grotesque exception in a deterministic universe, to a world in which orderly disorder is plentiful and predictability a rarity" (Conte 10).

Frederic Jameson suggests three periods of capitalistic development in relevance to three literary stages, market capitalism to realism, the monopoly stage or imperialism to modernism, and multinational or late capitalism to postmodernism (35-6), which is the application of Marxist principle of economic base and superstructure. In terms of the relationship between science and literature, it seems to me that another tripartite scheme that Newtonian mechanics, Einstein's relativity theory and chaos theory are in relevance to realism, modernism and postmodernism respectively is much proper. For postmodernism literature, Cartesian rationalism and mind/body dualism and Newtonian "clockwork hegemony" termed by Kellert no longer control their minds (Grubic 166), and literary eclecticism featured with inclusiveness and openness finds the "carnivalization" as its strong alley in their works. In postmodernist works, linear-causal-chronological narrative structure has been broken up, and chaotic fragmentation becomes its composition. No center, or history, or origin could be found, but the floating of perpetual "presents" and collages of pure "signifiers." Reality could be found no longer, but "hyper-reality," or "simulation," or "illusion," or "actuality" in place of the "representation." The postmodern writer "both anticipates and fervently illustrates theories of chaotic behavior and unpredictability before their adoption by the academy as a legitimized narrative" (Conte 10).

Taken as a whole, within the intellectual context of the epistemic shift, McCarthy's fiction displays his observation of man, nature and society as chaos and wilderness, chimes with the major rhythm of his living age and society. His fictional world with darkness and violence presents the truth of the world as the turbulence of orderly disorder and nonlinearity, which will be explored in the following section.

II. From Civilization to Wilderness: Nonlinearity in *Child of God*

The majority of McCarthy scholarship focus on his Southwestern novels, and his earlier Appalachian novels have not had as much critical attention. However, just as Edwin T. Arnold observes that McCarthy's books "speak to one another whatever their setting and, with each response, deepen and expand and give shape to McCarthy's overall artistic vision" ("The Mosaic" 18), McCarthy's earlier books anticipate his overall works in that they show how the individual subject is involved in a chaotic system of violence negotiated between social subjects and social reality, in which, man, nature and society are interconnected with one another. Therefore, it is significant and necessary to take *Child of God* as a case study to explore questions mentioned above, which will be helpful with the understanding of the chaos going throughout McCarthy's fiction.

Child of God is about 27-year-old Lester Ballard, a mountaineer living in Sevier County, Tennessee. Due to his incapability of paying the property taxes, he is ostracized from his property and house by the county government, which starts his degradation and transformation into a serial killer and a grotesque necrophile. To our shock, in the fiction, such a murderer and necrophile turns out to be a "hero," going to the center from the margin, and the fiction directly addresses him as "a child of God much like yourself perhaps" (COG 4). Although postmodern literature is obsessed with marginality, to tell the story of such a "rebel," who challenges against the taboos of a civilized society, warrants our attention.

Truth is closely associated with turbulence, while turbulence, though independent, cannot separate from the river which makes it. More important, in the turbulence, both the inside and outside cannot be separate from each other, but merge together. Seemingly, as a transgressor, Ballard is on his own; however, his actions signify "the totality of violence as a governing system that structures social reality" (Weiss 74). *Child of God* is produced in the turbulent years of America, when Watergate Incident made people question the justice and credibility of government; social unrest, change and revolution, such as student movement, civil rights and feminism movements, sex revolution, rock 'n roll, almost tore up the streets of the country; the 12-year-long Vietnam war brought in loss and trauma to Americans; armaments competition and atomic annihilation produced the ruins and "silent spring" of the whole country.

With the perspective of chaos to examine the turbulence of Ballard's life, it seems to me that its origin, development and result are of chaos and the disproportion between cause and consequence decides on its nonlinearity. Ballard's atavistic regression from a human to a "human animal," from civilization to wilderness suggests that his perversion and violence not only result from his inborn tendency of violence and quick temper, but also from the capitalized order of his living age and society. Institutional systems, familial background, gender relationship and community are combined to make him violent and morbid. In the presentation of a monster "hero" or a killer-necrophile, McCarthy aims to make Ballard refract the evil of society and humanity, and thus *Child of God is* made to be an allegory to imagine the human world in the age of post- "9.11."

i. Violence, Turbulence and Over–determination

In the cultural milieu of postmodern relativism, truth has been problematic. For McCarthy, violence is not only the consequence of truth, but also it is truth. Located in Western literary tradition, McCarthy's oeuvre flooded with terror and violence is not unusual. Like his precursors, such as the Homeric epics, which are full of armed violence and personal suffering, or Shakespearean tragedies, particularly, *King Lear*, in which Edmund stomps out Gloucester's eyes with his boot heel, or Joseph Heller's *Catch* 22, which portrays the battle absurdities, or Toni Morrison's *Beloved*, which records a bloody story of the infanticide, violence is one of major thematic motifs for McCarthy's works. Most of his characters are involved in the turbulence of violence, in which they struggle, fight, destroy and deteriorate, and yet chance and uncertainty make their destinies much more complicated and ambiguous. Lester Ballard is not an exception.

Ballard's violence is not presented directly, and the fiction just invites the reader's imagination. In his shelter cavern, "a chamber in which the bodies of a number of people [are] arranged on stone ledges in attitudes of repose" evidences his brutality (COG 195). The fiction gives detailed presentation of his killing by three times totally: First, after the failure of making sexual assault of Ruebel's daughter, he shoots her out of the window and then sets fire on his friend's house, leaving the idiot child sitting on the floor to burn up; second, on his way of hunting in the mountain, he shoots a boy through the neck, then fires at the base of the skull of the boy's girl, and then rapes her still warm body in the weeds; third, after his murder of Greer, who buys his father's land in the auction, he leaves out with "a wig" fashioned "from a dried human scalp" (COG 173). In a word, Ballard is a murderer, rapist, sadist, arsonist, necrophile and savage.

Human life is a complex dynamic system, in which "there are simply too many variables involved in the complex networks of parameters that influence each moment of [human] lives" (Boon 18). Ballard's propensity of violence since childhood has decided on his difference from the others, yet after all, he is a social person, whose behavior has to be limited by laws, morality, ethics, taboos, and some other social codes. Only when some of variables in the social system alter, may his violence become possible. The ironsmith in the fiction speaks right, "it's like a lot of things … do the least part of it wrong and ye'd just as well to do it all wrong" (COG 74). A small perturbation may cause great changes in the system. In respect to Ballard's life process and his involvement into the turbulence of violence, it might be argued that the factors from both the given and the made should be combined together in the analysis of his nonlinear development. In other words, multiple elements in his living world and his own physical and psychological propensity decide on the turbulence of his life.

The orphanhood is one of causes for Ballard to be a transgressor. Most of McCarthy's protagonists are orphans. John Wesley Rattner, Culla Holme, the Kid, John Grady Cole, and Billy Parham do not have mother or father or both. One of the unnamed narrators tells, "They say he never was right after his daddy killed hisself [sic]. They was just the one boy. The mother had run off, I don't know where to nor who with" (COG 21). Evil seeds have been sowed in Ballard when he is young. Want of caring parents in a normal family, and witness of his father's sinful hanging in the barn are crucial for a young boy to go astray in his later development. Nobody pays him love and care; neither does he understand how to love others reciprocally. His orphanhood starts at the age of 8 or 9, and how he has spent his boyhood in the later ten years is blank in the narration, and in the minds of his neighbors, he is only "a petty annoyance" (COG 4).

The state apparatus represented by the government of Sevier County also causes Ballard's atavistic regression. When he is too poor to pay the property taxes, the local government does not provide him with any assistance to deal with his difficulty, but sells his family's house and property by force, though he still lives there, facilitating his marginality.[①] The American Constitution says that the government is of the people, by the people, for the people, yet it is such a government that dispossesses him and makes him homeless, enhancing his weakness and marginality, and meanwhile planting the seed of his later crime. Just as Rikard puts it, "Ballard loses all the advantages of his traditional white male privilege-land ownership, occupational stability, social interaction, sexual privilege, and cultural as well as monetary currency. … he becomes a mountain-poor-white-trash pariah" (189).

The fact that the local government evicts Ballard from his land makes his destiny recall the historical context of Appalachian industrialization. K. Wesley Berry lists connections between McCarthy's work and its Appalachian environment in details. According to Berry, the subsistence farmers in Appalachian mountainous areas have been exploited and dispossessed since the 1870s, when the agents of timber industry came there to search for lumber, and later at the turn of the 20th century, coal industry entered the country and bought the farmer's lands, facilitating the bankruptcy of the local farmers. Both the timber and coal companies obtained the mineral rights to the land and left the mountaineers with little more to claim than taxes. Lots of farmers had to desert their ancestral farms and found jobs in the coal camps. Moreover, the coal camps, through an unjust control of tax assessment, passed the tax burdens back to those landowners, making them ill afford the area's services. The burden of property taxes forces lots of farmers to sell their lands to absolve their tax debts (Berry 62-3).

---

① The ongoing "Occupy Wall Street Movement" in America started from Sept. 17, 2011, and has lasted for more than half a year. Although the movement has various aims, the capitalized order gets attacked due to its production of social and economic injustice, unemployment, and homelessness. In New York, most of people are driven out of house due to bankruptcy. Bankers and profiteers take chances to buy houses from those failed to pay off the loan from the bank and to make profits by means of auction. On Oct. 13, 2011, lots of protesters were organized to protest against the collateral auctions held there weekly in front of the Court of Kings County in New York. (See <http://grwww. net/portal.php?mod=view&aid=14544>) Though *Child of God* was written in 1973, the essence of the capitalist society does not change, and the instance of Ballard's losing his house is still significant at present.

Furthermore, in Dianne C. Luce's study of *The Orchard Keeper* (1965), she quotes the local historian C. P. White's essay, "Commercial and Industrial Trends since 1865" to evidence the intrusion of industrialization into East Tennessee by the mid-twentieth century. Four phenomena have been identified: the opening of the Alcoa Aluminum plant; the establishment of the Great Smoky Mountains National Park; the advent of the TVA; the development of atomic energy (Luce, *Reading the World* 3). Besides the dispossession of farmers from the industrialization, with the advent of the New Deal, TVA, and the national parks system, the Federal government got involvement with the Appalachian land grab: "Federal intervention in Appalachia before 1930 included the designation of national forests from 1911 and the establishment of the Great Smoky Mountains National Park in 1926. Both involved government purchase of land, often from the timber companies after they had felled the trees but also by compulsion from families that had not previously sold out to those companies" (qtd. in Rikard's note 181). So it may be argued that Ballard's dispossession is not alone and isolated, but historically significant, for it indicates the combination of industrial interests with "legal confusions about overlapping land deeds to the disadvantage of the mountaineer" (ibid).

Driving Ballard out of the town and then acquisition of his profitable property seems to be enjoyable for the townspeople, for the auction turns out to be their "carnival." The exposition of the novel witnesses such a "spectacle":

They came like a caravan of carnival folk up through the swales of broomstraw and across the hill in the morning sun, the truck rocking and pitching in the ruts and the musicians on chairs in the truck bed teetering and tuning their instruments the fat man with guitar grinning and gesturing to others in a car behind and bending to give a note to the fiddler who turned a fiddlepeg and listened with a wrinkled face. (COG 3)

When Ballard attempts to stop the auction with his rifle, Buster, one of the townspeople in Sevier County, gives a blow to Ballard's head with the handle of ax in advance, making Ballard flat on the ground and "bleeding at the ears" (COG 9), dragged out of the town in the truck. The "ax" is one of the important symbols for pioneering in the wilderness, and Ballard's injury from the "ax" foreshadows his later retreat into wilderness.

In terms of Ballard's situation, "over-determination"[1] could explicate it clearly. Besides the government, the legal system in Sevier County is another cause of Ballard's later degradation. These state apparatuses abuse their power, which could be evidenced from an incident in Ballard's life. In his wandering in the woods, Ballard meets a drunken woman lying on the ground, so he wakes her up, and reminds her of coldness at night. It is a pity that the woman misunderstands his goodness. She runs to the police office and charges him with rape. Ballard is not guilty, though he tears the woman's nightgown off brutally and even gives her a slap due to the woman's cursing; however, intuition takes in place of the fact,[2] the sheriff takes his crime for granted, because "a mountain-poor-white-trash pariah" is thought to be a natural suspect, for whom it is not necessary to make any investigation. Ballard gets imprisonment for nine days. Out of the jail, he has got some other indictments from the sheriff: "Let's see: failure to comply with a court order, public disturbance, assault and battery, public drunk, rape. I guess murder is next on the list, ain't it?" (COG 56). Unfortunately, the prediction of the sheriff maps out the trajectories of Ballard's later development.

From a victim of the capitalized order to a victimizer, Ballard kills, steals, rapesand avenges on the authority and ordinary people, whose violence can be counted as "grotesque violence" in the term of Kevin Stadt. By grotesque violence, it means that Ballard's violent actions are "misplaced and aimed at a target which did not provoke it in the first place" (Stadt 3). Ballard's modeling after the style of the police to rob and

---

[1] Louis Althusser's "over-determination" suggests that multiple elements or variables decide on the society's development, and each element or variable is necessary for the development of events in the complex system of conflicts, which are "complex, structural and unbalanced" (Zhao 558). Such an idea about the development of society or individuals is analogous to that of chaos theory.

[2] McCarthy's critique of capitalized order via the case of Ballard echoes that of John Grady in *All the Pretty Horses*, in which the evil captain at La Encantada tells John Grady that "we can make truth here," when he could not find out evidences to charge him with the theft of horses. Both the sheriff and the captain posit themselves superior to the law, presenting the corruption of legal system.

shoot the pair of lovers on the mountain turnaround is one of cases for his "grotesque violence," yet, if observed closely, his superficial grotesque violence just refracts the effect of violence from legal system on him in the deep plane of his mind. Boon suggests that the dynamic system of human life operates "in the gap between order and disorder" (18), neither is preferable if going to the extreme. Unfortunately, Ballard's life system is not made right with his grotesque violence.

As indifferent as the secular world in which Ballard lives, church is not caring and warm for Ballard, either. After the exile from his land and community, Ballard hopes that the church will embrace him with love and care. However, when he walks into the Six Mile Church, what he encounters is still coldness and ignorance from those church-goers. In the process of the congregation, those careless "puppets" does not make any response towards his snuffling from a cold, and "nobody expect [s] he would stop if God himself look [s] back askance so no one look [s]" (COG 32). The estrangement from religion quickens his regression from the society with civilization.

Child of God is structured around Ballard as the focus of the novel, from which violence and corruption of the whole system radiate. Weiss speaks right, "as [Ballard's] violence intensifies, the overall violence of the social system and its constituent social subjects is revealed" (78). Like those small Southern towns in the writings of Faulkner, Sevier County is peopled with morbid, depraved, abject and violent figures. For instance, in the fair, cheaters cheat cheaters. Good marksmanship makes Ballard win always in the game, which irritates the pitchman so that he changes the rules of the game and drives Ballard away. The dumpkeeper, a savage and violent friend of Ballard, lives in the garbage, and has nine daughters, whose names are "out of an old medical dictionary gleaned from the rubbish he picked." He does not remember their age, neither does he know "whether they should go out with boys or not." His daughters "[fall] pregnant one by one," leaving a group of babies in his house. Much more absurdly, one day in the woods, he watches "two figures humping away," and then rushes from behind the tree to "beat the girl with the stick he carried," and shockingly the father rapes his daughter finally (COG 26-8). Here, the presentation of details in the dumpkeeper's family life is to reveal that Ballard's friend is as abject as him. They are what Julia Kristeva describes as the abject, who is "weary of fruitless attempts to identify with something on the outside, finds the impossible within; when it finds that the impossible constitutes its very being, that it is none other than abject" (5). Thus, a life in abjection is a forfeited existence lived in exclusion from one's self. Both Ballard and the dumpkeeper are transgressors of social and ethical codes of behavior and in their morbid behavior "an overwhelming absence of self and social knowledge" is expressed. "Abjection breaks down subjective boundaries between individuals. The transgression of the other is felt as one's own, and thus the violence of one social subject is the violence of the everyman" (Weiss 85, 86).

Just like the literal meaning of the garbage in which the dumpkeeper lives and the rubbish dictionary to name the girls indicates, Ballard's community is corrupted in the morality and ethics, as what he calls by "a chickenshit town" (COG 56) constitutes his living background. Although those persons live in the periphery of the society, they construct the identity and consciousness of the community. Ballard is not completely different from them, though he is made to be an "other," ignored and alienated. In effect, Ballard is "a nodal point" as Frederic Jameson would say, through which the social order, community and social subjects are connected and constructed. As a witness, Ballard evidences his community's morbid and violent behavior. Most of the inhabitants in Sevier County appear to be abnormal. For instance, Grasham "[sings] the chickenshit blues" at his wife's funeral (COG 22); Kirby, the moonshiner, is too drunk to find out his own whiskey for the customer; the idiot child in the dumpkeeper's house (his own child and grandchild) tears off the legs of the robin gifted by Ballard and chews them in the mouth. The list could go on. When Sevier County is in flood, the townspeople rob rather than help mutually. In brief, the morbid community cultivates Ballard's violence and perversion.

The gender relationship cannot be excluded from the consideration of Ballard's nonlinear development. In terms of his grotesque "necrophilia," Dianne C. Luce asserts that loss of mother in the childhood affects his normal relationship with the female, for "many of whom had lost parents to death when they were young, and for whom the corpse represented the lost mother" ("The Cave" 173). Loss of mother in the childhood might frustrate him, which shadows his normal relationship with the female in adulthood, yet the morbidity of the gender relationship in his living community, such as incest and adultery, enhances his sexual disorder. In the story he encounters or witnesses such incidents by three times. Moreover, the false charge from the drunken woman in the woods and refusal of his stupid "courtship" from the dumpkeeper's daughter reinforce his sense of frustration in his attempt to communicate with them. Even though these women are wantons, he cannot converse with them normally.

Ballard's situation illustrates that "want and aggressivity are chronologically separable but logically coextensive" (Kristeva 39). For want of opportunity, acknowledgment and integrity of an individual subject, Ballard resorts to voyeurism and control of the female by force (7 women are killed totally). What he does is like that of the idiot child, who "constraints the bird by eating the legs of the bird," Ballard may "kill the child's mother so he can keep her" (Ellis, *No Place* 90). With his retreat into the depth of wilderness, Ballard becomes a divided person, because "the schizoid individual fears a real live dialectical relationship with real live people. He can relate himself only to depersonalized persons, to phantoms of his own phantasies (images), perhaps to things, perhaps to animals" (Laing 77). In the wilderness, he is presented not only to be with supernatural power to make orders to natural phenomena but also to be a morbid serial killer-necrophile.

As Prigogine remarks, "we cannot define man in isolation; his behavior depends on the structure of the society of which he is a member, and vice versa" (*Order Out of Chaos* 42). Apparently, Ballard is structured or constructed in the society. His involvement with the turbulence in life is the result of multiple elements explored above. As a small nodal point in the web of social relations, his violence cannot separate from his wilderness-like living community and society. He is doomed. His marginalization and nonlinear regression from the society get strengthened from several narrative devices employed in the novel, including spatial constraint, metaphors of his identity as animals and the shift of narrative points of view, which may be explored in the following part.

ii. Spatial Constraint, Animal Metaphors and Atavistic Regression

Ballard's transferring of his habitats echoes his nonlinear regression from civilization to wilderness. With his retreat into wilderness progressively, from house to cabin, from cave to the "bowels of the mountain" (COG 135), the extent of his alienation from the society and atavistic regression improves gradually, too. Loss of his ancestral house is the first step for his marginalization, because the house is one of the important spatial icons for human civilization. Driven out of the town, Ballard has to live in a dilapidated shed in the suburb, which is a mile away from the road. In the front, weeds sprout as high as the house eaves, and travelers could see the "gray shake roof and the chimney, nothing more" (COG 14). In this stage, Ballard still tries to make his living place civilized as a man does. For instance, he sweeps out the dung of beasts and mud in the shed, burns a spider hung in the hearth, casts off the nests of wasps, and then drags a small thin mattress into the cabin. Before sleeping, he even rolls himself a cigarette and reads the outdated news of newspapers gathered in the shed. Though far away from crowds, he still tends to keep contact with the civilized society.

It is in this shattered shed that Ballard has his happy yet transient "family life." He brings back a female body from the mountain turnaround in Frog Mountain and takes it as his "bride." We may note that sexuality is not his primal purpose, though he has sex with the dead body several times; rather, it is his desire for communication and family life that leads to his transgression of social codes and rebellion against taboos of civilization, which can be demonstrated from textual evidences. In the store of the town, Ballard buys a red dress for his dead lover and even does shopping to get preparation for a dinner. Then, he makes a good fire to warm the room. He dresses his dead lover up, arranges "her in different positions and [goes] out and peer[s] in the window at her. After a while he just [sits] holding her, his hands feeling her body under the new clothes. He undress [es] her very slowly, talking to her" (COG 103). Apparently, his peering in the window at her is his fantasy of the family life, yet it is pity that his family life is only a "simulacrum," for his living cabin is simply "peopled" with a big teddy bear, a rifle and a dead body. Although "he pour [s] into that waxen ear everything he'd ever thought of saying to a woman" (COG 88), Ballard is still a lonely outcast.

In the second section of the fiction, Ballard degrades quickly. He becomes a cave refuge, for his living cabin gets burned by accident. As for his living situation in the cave, nothing is mentioned in the narration. Nevertheless, his murdering starts from his being a cave dweller. In the third section, his distance from crowds is made larger. In order to escape from the police's chase, he moves into a cavern in the wilderness. The entrance to the cavern is small enough to crawl through, and then a mile off, then farther, all underground, then through a tunnel, we read that he "climbed up a chimney to a corridor above the steam and entered into a tall and bellshaped cavern" in which he stays with his "saint" bodies. "The smell of the water beside him in the trough rich with minerals and past the chalken dung of he knew not what animals" (COG 134, 135). In the small cabin, Ballard still tries to make it habitable, and his living room is at least segregated from his outhouse, around which weeds are taller enough to shelter him from the travelers on the road; whereas, in the cave, the living room and the outhouse are linked together.

The shift of the habitats symbolizes Ballard's alienation from society. According to Freudian psychology, the cave usually symbolizes the female. Nell Sullivan notes that, "the caves resemble the generative female body" (76). Besides, the narrator addresses the bodies in the cavern as "saints." Seemingly, those females are sacrifices of Ballard's violence, with whom they achieve new identities, and of course, just due to their existence, Ballard's situation is presented to be so fiercely and ironically tragic. It might be argued that Ballard's retreat into wilderness symbolizes his atavistic regression to the maternal "womb." The cavern in which he is sheltered corresponds with his situation. In this underground "catacombs," there is "a long room filled with bones. Ballard circle[s] this ancient ossuary kicking at the ruins. The brown and pitted armatures of bison, elk. A jaguar's skull whose one remaining eyetooth he [pries] out and [secures] in the bib pockets of his overalls" (COG 188). As we know, bison, elk and jaguar were extinguished from American continent in the 19th century, so it is strongly ironic that in this underground cavern, Ballard, a "hunter" (a man-gatherer), encounters another "hunter" (Western civilization), which is apparently much more powerful than him.

The atavistic regression implicates death. The womb-like cavern does not symbolize rebirth, but ruin. In McCarthy's fiction, the earth mother is no longer the protector or fecund producer or tranquil retreat for nostalgia, but the "wasteland" in the pen of T. S. Eliot. The landscape of *Child of God* is similar to that of the rest of McCarthy's novels: horrible, cruel, vicious and bloody. The natural wilderness in which Lester lives mirrors the violence, even parallels the "wilderness" in the society: watching two hawks Ballard "did not know how hawks mated but he knew that all things fought" (COG 169). Outside his shabby cabin on the edge of society, for instance, "black saplings stood like knives" (COG 93); inside his cave, "a fautline in the vault's ceiling appeared with a row of dripping limestone teeth," and he could see through a "smokehole" where remote stars "burned cold and absolute" (COG 133). The snow outside the cave witnesses "struggles, scenes of death," and animals' faces look horrible with "berrystains where birds shat crimson mutes upon the snow like blood" (COG 138), even timid rats are bold enough to disturb him. In the "womb," in which he falls down, stacks of bones and water with smell of decay indicate that this is his burying tomb rather than producing womb. As Ellis assumes, "His need for a home leads to his enclosure in a womb-grave that would be a threatening enclosure for anyone. Ballard's retreat into a hiding place in a primeval shelter runs him back toward death" (*No Place* 109).

Unlike his ancestral pioneers, who are said to be the immigrants of Celtic Irish, Ballard is unfortunate, though he possesses traits traditionally associated with American frontiersmen, including "his armed individualism, his perverted consumerism, his clumsy improvisation, and his resilience as the underdog" (Luce, "The Cave" 185). So, Ballard is merely an anachronistic "hero" in the wilderness in that Appalachian mountain has been ruined with the industrialization and urbanization. Berry writes that "Appalachia is revealed as a place both beautiful and ruined, a land of scant patches of virgin woodlands juxtaposed with the scars of more than two centuries of pioneering" (4). The landscape has been alien in the narration, "going up a track of a road through the quarry woods where all lay enormous blocks and tablets of stone weathered gray and grown with deep green moss, toppled monoliths among the trees and vines like traces of an older race" (COG 25). Man has made natural environment enemies, and floods in Sevier Country perhaps are good evidences. To make Ballard an anachronistic "hero" in the wilderness is in effect the parody of the ideals or heroes of American frontiers, such as the image of Daniel Boone or Cooper's Natty Bumppo, and the fiction's subtext subverts a traditional image of the frontiersman in the wilderness.

McCarthy's knowledge of wilderness is rich, and his boyhood activities include "hunting and trapping, sleeping on the screened porch in the summer, and escaping the house at night to roam the countryside" (Luce, *Reading the World* 3), which makes him familiar with animals in the wilderness. In his fiction, animals are usually taken to map the situation of characters, which occurs in his earlier work. In *Outer Dark* (1968), Rinthy is compared to be a wounded bird during her labor and later a careless hog to indicate her irresponsibility for her child's being killed by the evil Triune. In *Child of God*, animals are taken to parallel the identity of Ballard in the process of the nonlinearity of his atavistic regression, recalling his spatial constraint.

Ballard's appearance is delineated to be as wretched as animals when he enters into the reader's vision. With his retreat into the wilderness, he finishes his transformation from a man to an "animal." Moving to the shed on the edge of the town starts his regression, for the barren cabin is the dens of predators like foxhounds, black snakes, foxes, possums, spiders, wasps and mosquitoes before his arrival. So to drive them away and occupy their dens not only symbolizes Ballard's change of identity from man to "animal," but also implicates his pathetic exile from human society. It is also ironic that those predators change from house-owners to "homeless" ones, which recalls his eviction from a violent society. At night, foxhounds "flood into the cabin yard," and circle the room with "rising volume dog on dog," and even "two more dogs [come] through the door" to attack him (COG 24). Insects even take advantage of his weakness, making him "lying with his fingers plugged in the bores of his ears against the strident cheeping of the myriad black crickets" (COG 23). In order to stay alive, the penniless Ballard has to steal turnips, potatoes or corns in the valley gardens like "a rutting hog" (COG 79). Later, he is presented to be "like an owl" (COG 105), sitting on the hearth to get warmth in the early morning because of his cabin's burning up, and in order to escape coldness, "he'd long been given to talking to himself but he [does not] say a word" (ibid). Disaster frequents Ballard. Flood in Sevier County soaks his only mattress with water. His cry in agony that echoes "from the walls of the grotto like the mutterings of a band of sympathetic apes" (COG 159) sounds pitiful. In the underground cavern, his body becomes the lair of mice and insects in his illusion: "He heard the mice scurry in the dark. Perhaps they'd nest in his skull, … His bones polished clean as eggshells, centipedes sleeping" there (COG 189). All in all, Ballard experiences his regressing "metamorphosis" from a landowner to a marginal person, then to a predator (killer), to a hog (a thief), to an owl (a loner), to an ape (the ancestor of humans), to a skeleton as the dwelling of mice.

The shift of narrative perspectives also strengthens Ballard's marginalization and regression. As Andrew Bartlett notes, "the aesthetic power of *Child of God* results from McCarthy's superb regulations of narrative distance and perspective" (4). The change of the narrator's position, from which we see Ballard, corresponds with his process of "othering" in the society and community. The first section in the fiction is constituted with seven textual fragments to "see" Ballard, in which narrators are dwellers in Sevier County. The subtext of the fiction gives a hint that a curious interlocutor makes his inquiries about Ballard, and then the "heteroglossia" made up of Ballard's behavior and clan lineage is "seen" (heard). In their attempts to construct Ballard's identity to be "the other," these dwellers construct their own identities, too. As we have talked in the previous part, the community in which Ballard lives is not distinguishable from him in violence, evil and morbidity. Being "crazy," Ballard is silent in this section, we cannot hear any voice from him. In effect, his discursive power has been dispossessed with the dispossession of his house from the authority of Sevier County. In the second section, the narrative point of view is shifted to the omniscient point of view from the gossiping of unnamed narrators, which provides the convenience for the reader to follow Ballard's actions in the wilderness, to "watch" his morbidity as what Ballard usually does with voyeurism, and simultaneously to witness his loneliness and hardship struggling with fire, snow, flood and other disasters when far away from crowds. With his retreat into wilderness, Ballard changes to be "inhuman." He has the mysterious superpower to address animals or plants or dead bodies or natural phenomena in the wilderness. As Foucault notes, modern instruments of penalty are hardly distinguishable in terms of their particular forms, and all the factories, schools, barracks and hospitals resemble prisons ("Panopticism" 228). The third section no longer focuses on Ballard, and the narrative perspective alternates between Ballard and the sheriff, for Ballard is completely reified to be both the "game" of the sheriff and the studying "subject" of the medical school. The shift of narrative points of view is in accordance with Ballard's identity as "objects," reinforcing the extent of his being controlled from society.

After "newly born" from the underground catacomb, he has no way out. Unexpectedly, he chooses the hospital in which he stayed before the escape as his final retreat; likewise, illogically, he is not charged with any crime after the arrest. All are in chaos, uncertain and nonlinear. Finally, he is sent to the state hospital, and "put in a cage next door but one to a demented gentleman who used to open folks' skulls and eat the brains inside with a spoon" (COG 193). In the minds of his living society, Ballad is no more a "human," but a crazy animal. After death, he is moved from the constraining hospital to a teaching one, where "he was preserved with formalin," then "was laid out on a slab and flayed, eviscerated, dissected. His head was sawed open and the brains removed. His muscles were stripped from his bones. His heart was taken out. His entrails were hauled forth and delineated" (COG 194). Three months later, "when the class was closed Ballard was scraped from the table into a plastic bag and taken with others of his kind to a cemetery outside the city and there interred" (COG 194). Such is what "the child of God" ends, and he is "sacrificed" by the society at last. The narrative tone of his ending is technical, and "the passage reads more like the medieval torture and execution of some grievous heretic than the practices of modern science" (Cant, *Cormac McCarthy* 97). Ballard does not walk out his life's "turbulence," but is finally devoured by the "river" to produce it. From house to cabin, from cabin to cave, from cage to bag, Ballard, with his retreat to the margin of society, finishes his life constrained by the violence of social system and state apparatus, regressing from civilization to wilderness, from man to "monster," from a social subject to an abject, then a studying "subject." The shift of narrative perspective corresponds with the objectification of his identity, foregrounding his being controlled from the society.

iii. *Child of God* as an Allegory

Although Ballard is a necrophilic mass-killer, transgressor and social pariah, the narrator still feels for his situation in the narration, drawing attention of the reader to the humanity in him. All are like what John Lang remarks, "Ballard's actions are often shocking but they are not, unfortunately, unique. ... McCarthy reminds us of his protagonist's underlying humanity" (94). Ballard's humanity can be shown from textual evidences. For instance, on his way to the dumpkeeper's house, Ballard meets a group of robins, after which he "[falls] and [rises] and [runs] laughing. He [catches] and [holds] one warm and feather [s] in his palm with the heart of it beating there just so" (COG 76). At this moment, he seems to be a young boy, naughty and lovely. Even as a cave refuge, he still holds nostalgia to live in the countryside. Walking on the mountain road, he is even moved by a man, a mule wagon and the gray fields, and "squatting there he let [s] his head drop between his knees and he [begins] to cry" (COG 170). Out of the underground cavern, Ballard meets a bus, in which a small boy sitting in the last rear looks out of the window with his nose puttied against the glass. Such a scene makes Ballard feel disturbed: "he was trying to fix in his mind where he'd seen the boy when it came to him that the boy looked like himself. This gave him the fidgets and though he tried to shake the image of the face in the glass it would not go" (COG 191). Here the narration makes use of the dialogic method to mix the voices of the narrator, writer and the character's inner mind together, foregrounding his humanity because Ballard can be able to make confession and even epiphany in his life. The little boy might be the foil of Ballard before degradation; more exactly, his once pure "doppelganger." Kevin Stadt speaks right, "McCarthy makes Lester a monster, but a human one" (128).

McCarthy takes a sociopath as the center of the novel, which is to warn that we human beings are evil. Sevier County has its history of violence, and that of White Caps and Blue Bills are introduced from the narration of Ballard's neighborhood. Both groups attempt to punish those transgressors with the purpose to define the morality of community, yet both fight with each other to achieve moral and legal control of

Sevier County, which produces more violence through their violent curbing. Out of the reader's expectation, Ballard's crimes are immune to punish. He always escapes from the police and wanders around the periphery of Sevier County, though several times he could have been caught. Until he kills Greer, one of the landowners in Sevier County, does the police make decision to arrest him. In effect, the social system and community of Sevier County are complicit with Ballard in his regression from civilization to wilderness. Edward Soja distinguishes the space from spatiality, according to him, space is "a contextual given," whereas spatiality is "socially-based," meaning "the created space of social organization and production" (79). So it may be argued that Ballard's degradation is partly socially-decided.

Capitalized order not only constraints human beings, but also produces the alienation and aberration. McCarthy speaks philosophically in one of his rare interviews,

There's no such thing as life without bloodshed, I think the notion that the species can be improved in some way, that everyone could live in harmony, is really dangerous idea. Those who are afflicted with this notion are the first ones to give up their souls, their freedom. You desire that it be that way will enslave you and make your life vacuous. (Woodward, "Venomous Fiction" 31)

His words indicate that violence warrants attention and meditation. Violence is taken as discursive power for the privileged, while for the underprivileged, it is also the means to achieve power.

As the "evil fruit" produced from all kinds of morbid and violent social relations in which he is involved, Ballard is doomed to sacrifice for the evil of human beings. Just as one of the unnamed narrators comments, "you can trace em [sic] back to Adam if you want and goddam if he didn't outstrip em all" (COG 81). As the top of the sin of Adam, Ballard images the degradation and violence of human beings. René Girard asserts that the "sacrifice" serves to "protect the entire community from its own violence," and "the purpose of the sacrifice is to restore harmony to the community and reinforce the social fabric" (8). Jonathan Culler also presents the similar vision about the function of the "sacrifice," which is taken as one of social reinforcement against aberration. For Culler, to maintain necessary civic distinction, "the pharmakos is cast out as the representative of the evil that afflicts the city: cast out so as to make evil return to the outside from which it comes and to assert the importance of the distinction between inside and outside" (143). The pharmakos is "scapegoat" in Greek, a synonym of the "sacrifice."

Indeed, Biblical allusions are scattered in the fiction. The sheriff tells the deputy, "you ain's [sic] seen a old man with a long beard buildin [sic] a great big boat anywheres have ye?" (COG 161). And an old woman also says, "it's a judgment. Wages of sin and all that" (164). Flood is usually one of the symbolic means for God to punish man with evil. Looking at Sevier County in the flood, the dialogue of the Deputy with an old man is significant. In comparison with the flood in 1885, they converse, "you think people were meaner then than they are now? the deputy said. ... No, he said. I don't. I think people are the same from the day God first made one" (COG 168). Weiss speaks right, "The heavy rains that flood Sevier County act as a theological and moral punishment not only to Ballard's actions but also to the community as a whole" (90). The flood has been over for almost a century (the fiction doesn't tell its concrete temporal setting, but mentions that Ballard was dead in 1965), yet the morality of Sevier County does not improve any much, rather, they "would have to be rotten to the core" (COG 164). Such might be the message from the fiction as an allegory.

III. Orderly Disorder and Disorderly Order: Violence in *Blood Meridian*

William Gaddis notes that, "there may be something in the notion that every writer writes only one book and writes it over and over again" (Grove B10). Violence is just that "book" for McCarthy to visit and revisit once again, from the death of John Wesley's father in *The Orchard Keeper* to vast images of destruction in *Blood Meridian*, from John Grady's disembowelment in *Cities of the Plain* to the cannibalism in The Road. Though different in tone or content superficially, McCarthy's novels are still similar in some thematic motifs, particularly violence presented in the postmodern American society. Like that of *Child of God*, violence still haunts in *Blood Meridian*, from which chaos is presented in man, nature and society. Similar to the critical attention on *Child of God*, whose presentation of morbidity and violence has caused many reviewers and critics to dismiss the novel as pulp fiction unworthy of serious exploration,[①] *Blood Meridian's* ambivalence and its rendering of violence as well as its blend of horrific description and philosophical pronouncements also bring about lots of critiques from McCarthy scholarship.[②] Though the bloodiest novel in McCarthy's works, *Blood Meridian* is still more appreciated by literary critics than his other novels due to its ambiguity and complexity as well as its integration of aesthetic beauty and horror, and has been taken as a "touchstone by which McCarthy readers define themselves" (Arnold and Luce 9).

Violence is a nodal point of the textual web, from which McCarthy makes his questioning of humanity and critique of Enlightenment and modernity as well. This study takes violence as the focus and structure of the text and meanwhile posits it in the context of postmodernism, and tries to point out that in McCarthy's fictional world of man and nature, wilderness and chaos are inside and out. Violence is taken as a means to create order in the disorderly world, yet results in the world to be much more disorderly. Violence blurs everything, and makes the world a chaos. If *Child of God* makes us feel that we are evil; while after the reading of *Blood Meridian*, we may sense that man is not only evil but also violent. In effect, for McCarthy, man as empirical-

---

① For instance, Richard Brickner claims that *Child of God* is "an essentially sentimental novel that no matter how sternly it strives to be tragic is never more than morose" (6-7).

② For instance, Walter Sullivan poses the question: "what do we make of this phenomenon, a mind that dwells unremittingly on evil and a prose that conveys these thoughts with the tongue of an angel?" ("About" 652) transcendent subject has been dead.[①] Via violence, McCarthy not only questions the Western metaphysics of dualism but also challenges the Western epistemology since Enlightenment, and to some extent, the radical epistemology of *Blood Meridian* subverts all dualism of subject and object, man and nature, nature and culture, order and disorder, center and margin.

i. Violence, Humanity and "Optical Democracy"

Violence occupies most of textual space in *Blood Meridian* and even becomes the landscape of the novel, just as Peter Joseph puts it, "one gluts upon a baroque of thieving, raping, shooting, slashing, hanging, scalping, burning, bashing, hacking, stabbing ..." (16). Unlike that of *Child of God*, in which the writer just invites the reader to imagine, the violence in *Blood Meridian* turns out to be "the condition of every day" (Weiss 18). The novel follows the Kid, a 14-year-old boy, as he navigates his way through a horrific landscape filled with Indian "savages," bloodthirsty scalp hunters, ruined churches, deformed creatures, inhospitable terrains, and decayed and dead animals and humans along Texas-Mexico border, to demonstrate the chaos of human and natural world.

One hermit the Kid comes cross speaks of the nature of human beings, "You can find meanness in the least of creatures, but when God made man the devil was at his elbow. A creature that can do anything. Make a machine. And a machine to make a machine. And evil that can run itself a thousand years, no need to turn it" (BM 19). The hermit means that man is evil. In the text, no matter they are whites or non-whites, Americans or non-Americans (Mexicans and Indians), all are evil and violent, which implies that nothing savage or cultured in the traditional dualism of Western

---

① Human nature is understood with complication and diversification. Karl Marx asserts that man is alienated in the capitalized society, and for Marx, human nature is the summation of all social relations in reality. Immanuel Kant argues that man is the rational subject in moral practice. Ernst Cassirer thinks of man as animals of sign, and his idea gets developed by Baudrillard in his discussion of consumption and hyper-reality of postmodern society. With the proposition that "God is dead" made by Nietzsche, Foucault assumes that in postmodern society, man is dead. This study thinks that McCarthy's idea of man is similar to that of Foucault, challenging man in capital letter since Enlightenment, which takes man as something rational, empirical and transcendent.

metaphysics is associated with skin color or race. The boundary between center and margin blurs, for all are wild and disorderly. In an interview about the film *The Road* (2006), the director Tony Hillcoat claims that McCarthy "explains to him that [*Blood Meridian* is] very much about the worst in human nature" (qtd. in Collett-White, 2009), which illuminates the hidden implication of the fiction behind its superficially bloody spectacles.

Violence may be divided into something logical and illogical in view of the balance between its objectives and consequences. Captain White, Judge Holden, Glanton and their mercenaries are commissioned to kill and scalp as many Apaches as possible in the Western territories with the aim to protect Mexicans from the harassment and attacks from the Apache bandits. Though immoral and unjust, their killing and scalping are logical at least, for they kill for money and bounty. However, with the elevation of their violence, all are killed, no matter who are Apache Indians, or Comanche Indians, or Mexicans, their employers and protectors in the term of contracts, or Americans, their comrades-in-war and peers. Though immoral and intolerable, their actions are still logical, for they are in accordance with the basic principle of economics, i.e. to pursue the maximization of profit at the minimum cost. The question is that in the text lots of illogical violence are neither out of economic profits nor for psychological satisfaction,[①] and in effect, they kill irrationally. For instance, some are done without any reason, just to wipe out everything, to destroy the whole community and its culture, even to slaughter the elderly, women, children, or small animals. More complicatedly, to the reader's shock, the man to kill or the man to be killed makes no response in the process of killing. Denis Donoghue claims such types of illogical violence as "motiveless malignity" (406), while Kevin Stadt considers them as "grotesque violence" (116-9). Despite that, it is still hard to elucidate these irrational phenomena. Concerning a postmodern novel, it is outmoded and improper to make its analysis in terms of cause and effect. For *Blood Meridian*, everything seems to

---

① Humanism economics pays emphasis on the achievement of psychological satisfaction in the economical actions, and its basic principle is to satisfy one's purpose of being joyful through the acquisition of materials. Therefore, to kill is analogous to obtain the objects, which satisfies oneself psychologically.

be absurd and it is hard to make distinguishment of evil from good in terms of morality and ethics. Violence is acts of consumption and for those barbarous gangs, it is more a sign of consumption. The victims they kill and scalp are their consuming "objects," and just in their reification of these victims, they are objectified, too. Violence turns out to be a blank signifier without any signifieds.

According to Baudrillard, the postmodern society is a consumer society, which features "affluence" and "consumption," and the function of material goods has been shifted from use value to consumption value. In traditional society, the articles we buy from the store are out of consideration of their use value, in which the relations of man and object are consumed; while, in consumer society, what we consume are "imageries" of objects, namely, signs. Baudrillard suggests,

Consumption is neither a material practice, nor a phenomenology of "affluence." It is not defined by the food we eat, the clothes we wear, the car we drive, nor by the visual and oral substance of images and messages, but in the organization of all this as signifying substance. Consumption is the virtual totality of all objects and messages presently constituted in a more or less coherent discourse. (25)

Actually, consumption is a new "language equivalence," an organized discursive system, and "a systematic act of the manipulation of signs" (ibid).

Although set in the aftermath of Mexican-American war, and *Blood Meridian* indeed sources from Samuel E. Chamberlain's *My Confession* published in 1856, the text is not about nineteenth-century America or Mexico, but addresses the present contemporary society actually. The mission of the Glanton gang is to kill the Apache bandits in the border areas and thus winning bounties from the governor of Chihuahua, yet they kill everything. For them, Indians are not the only attacked objects, rather the whole village, community, and even culture are wiped out from the earth in their bloody destruction. To kill is to consume, and for the gang, violence has become purposeless, but the sign of consumption, from which they are reflective:

Glanton rode his horse completely through the first wickiup trampling the occupants underfoot. Figures were scrambling out of the low doorways. The raiders went through the village at full gallop and turned and came back. ... Already a number of the huts were afire and a whole enfilade of refugees had begun streaming north along the shore wailing crazily with the riders among them like herdsman clubbing down the laggards first. ... one of the Delawares emerged from the smoke with a naked infant dangling in each hand and squatted at a ring of midden stones and swung them by the heels each in turn and bashed their heads against the stones ... they moved among the dead harvesting the long black locks with their knives ... one of the Delawares passed with a collection of heads like some strange vendor bound for market, the hair twisted about his wrist and the heads dangling and turning together. (BM 155-7)

This sequence is one of the examples in the novel, from which we may argue that "the aim of violence is not an object, but a means for a self-reflexive pursuit" (Weiss 20).

Following Baudrillard's vision about consumption, we could understand the violence in the text plausibly. For an object, in order to become object of consumption, the object must become sign; that is in some way it must become external to a relation that it now only signifies, a-signed arbitrarily and non-coherently to this concrete relation, yet obtaining its coherence, and consequently its meaning, from an abstract and systematic relation to all other object signs. It is in this way that it becomes "personalized," and enters in this series, etc.: it is never consumed in its materiality, but in its difference. (Baudrillard 25)

That's to say, individuality can be achieved through consumption of material goods,and in the process of communication with objects, human communication can be accomplished, too. Therefore, the relations of man and object are changed to that of man and man in this situation.

In the Glanton's gang, there are two Jacksons. One is white, the other is black. During the supper at one night, the white Jackson warns the black Jackson to go away with a gesture, which irritates the black. No more words between each other, just minimal dialogue, "you aim to shoot me? ... it that your final say?" is left. Then the black steps out of the darkness from the fire bearing the bowieknife in both hands and with a single stroke cuts off the white's head. For black Jackson, violence is the sign to achieve his "personality" and also the "language" to accomplish his communication with the white. More than that, violence foregrounds his individuality and meanwhile helps him acquire his identity. Such a "sign value" of violence has been internalized with the gang, for they make no response, just move away when facing the murder between peers. In the dawn when they set out, "the headless man [is] sitting there like a murdered anchorite discalced in ashes and dark. Someone [takes] his gun but the boots [stand] where he'd put them" (BM 107).

Once objects are transformed into signs, emotional response might be erased in the violent encounter. In one episode, in which Glanton gang meet an old Mexican woman when they ride into a small town, there is obviously lack of emotion from both the killer and the killed:

The woman looked up. Neither courage nor heartsink in those old eyes. He pointed with his left hand and she turned to follow his hand with her gaze and he put the pistol to her head and fired. The explosion filled all that sad little park. Some of the horses shied and stepped. A fistsized hole erupted out of the far side of the woman's head in a great vomit of gore and she pitched over and lay slain in her blood without remedy. ... He took a shinning knife from his belt and stepped to where the old woman lay and took up her hair and twisted it about his wrist and passed the blade of the knife about her skull and ripped away the scalp. (BM 98)

The scalped woman is lack of emotional response, and the surrounding persons, including Glanton men, town dwellers, Mexican warriors, are involved without any emotion, either. They are like puppets without any response towards such a bloody scene. The detailed textual evidence is to prove that figures in the text are surface ones, nothing about coldness or indifference from humanity. The relationship of agent and victim has been erased, only the floating signs are left in the consumption of violence.

Indifference is everywhere in the text when encountering violence. Captain

White and his mercenaries come across a bush hung with dead babies, while these "castaways" just stop side by side and then pass away without any response. Such an encounter happens after they are attacked by the Comanches. Though the text doesn't present the origins of these killed babies, it is still supposed that they are either Mexicans or Whites rather than Indians. There are numerous cases where Glanton's gang encounter violence from nature or antagonists or peers, and their responses are the unanimous silence, and often, for example, they just camp and lie down "to sleep among the dead," and there is "nothing moved in that high wilderness save the wind" (BM 153, 138). Stadt speaks right, "The very narrative itself, on every page, frames the savagery as if it were natural, inevitable, and unremarkable. The matter-of-fact attitude makes the violence even worse than if the characters were traumatized by such scenes" (109-110).

According to Frederic Jameson, man is "dead" and loses his subjectivity in the postmodern time. If there are anxiety and alienation in the modern society, while in the postmodern society, there is no emotion any longer. Scream and anomie cannot be discovered, because bourgeois ego, or monad, has been ended, which is called by Jameson as "the waning of affect" (14-5). Jameson's argument might explicate the violent condition in *Blood Meridian*. Emotions, such as fear, horror and anxiety, are effaced in the world of violence. After the effacement of emotions, human subject may become fragmented and "dead," and thus his relations with the world may be changed, too. The vision of Jameson echoes that of Baudrillard in the latter's understanding of the consumption in the consumer society, which makes people slave of objects after the loss of subjectivity. Once violence becomes unconscious, then it may be natural for one to be of inertness. Man is made to be empty in that they are nothing with three dimensions, but surface without self-perception.

For McCarthy, the violence of humanity is just one aspect of his "optical democracy," in which the fauna, flora, landscape and even natural phenomena are equally harsh. Between man and nature, there is "unguessed kinship," for both are dark and violent (BM 247). Such kinships are explained well from one case, where the kid comes upon a single tree burning through the night in the middle of the desert:

A heraldic tree that the passing storm had left afire. The solitary pilgrim drew up before it had traveled far to be here and he knelt in the hot sand and held his numbed hands out while all about in that circle attended companies of lesser auxiliaries rousted forth into the inordinate day, small owls that crouched silently and stood from foot and tarantulas and solpugas and vinegarroons and the vicious mygale spiders and beaded lizards with mouths black as chowdog's, deadly to man, and the little desert basilisks that jet blood from their eyes and the small sandvipers like seemly gods, silent and the same, in Jeda, in Babylon. (BM 215)

Around this flame, man shares a primal bond with the horrifying creatures in the wilderness. The narration presents the wildness of nature outside human beings. In *Blood Meridian*, the wilderness in the West is no longer Thoreau's *Walden* as retreat or Hawthorn's forests as regeneration, rather the inferno in Dante's *Divine Comedy*. Nature seems to be dark and wild in the text, and it fuses violently together with human beings.

Similar to the darkness of humanity, the wilderness is bloody and dangerous, too. In the desert, schools of coyotes and wolves follow the wretched "pilgrims" and "the little prairie vipers rattle among the scrub," and in the evening, the eyes of great pale lobos "shifted and winked out there on the edge of the firelight," "the cries of owls and the howls of old dog wolf" are the only sound in the silence, and at night blood brat attacks them and even crafts in the wounded Sproul's neck and drinks his blood. This "evil terrain" is "ancient and naked," barren and hostile, where the sun is "urine colored" in the morning, and then at noon it changes to be bloody and rises "out of nothing like the head of a great red phallus until it cleared the unseen rim and sat squat and pulsing and malevolent behind them" as they ride on, and the moon is "like a blind cat's eye up over the rim of the world," even the shadows of stones in the evening are "like tentacles to bind them to the darkness yet to come" (BM 61, 45, 89, 138, 47, 44-5, 152, 45). Moreover, on this "terra damnata," nature seems to be deceptive with its mirage, when the Kid watches "an immense lake," with "the distant blue mountains," a hawk, and trees, and "a distant city very white against the blue and shaded hills," yet in the morning, when he wakes up on the same spot and rises to see that in truth there is "no city and no trees and no lake only a barren dusty plain." Besides, the wilderness is also an arena of even stranger natural spectacles, where one could hear "the dull bloom of rock falling somewhere far ... in the awful darkness inside the world," where the raiders are unexpectedly "visited with a plague of hail out of a faultless sky" with the size of "small lucent eggs," where "the rocks would cook the flesh from your hand" (BM 62, 111, 152, 138). In brief, McCarthy's wilderness is analogous to violence of human beings, which features with the turbulence of orderly disorder. In the wilderness, nothing can be distinguishable between evil and good, just as the narration writes, "In the neuter austerity of that terrain all phenomena were bequeathed a strange equality and no one thing nor spider nor stone nor blade of grass could put forth claim to precedence" (BM 247). However, in the kinship between man and nature, the most horrifying animal of all creatures in McCarthy's fictional universe is still the one with two legs.

In effect, since McCarthy's first novel, nature has been presented to be strange and mysterious, and also the relationship of man and nature is forged. The most prominent example in *The Orchard Keeper* (1965) is the tree in the prologue that has grown around a fence in such a way that the latter cannot be dislodged from the former, even with the saw. This scene has received much critical attention and has been read as either as an instance of nature adapting to human infringement (Ragan 15) or of nature's inevitable triumph over "human vanity" (Winchell 296) or of that "man and nature [are] interfused" (Vereen M. Bell 22). The worker in the novel even asserts that the fence has "growed [sic] all through the tree" rather than vice versa (TOK, "Prologue"). Owens-Murphy speaks right, such a scene gives one example of "humanity's inextricability from nature," and between man and nature "a symbiotic relationship" exists, "one is not necessarily privileged or valued over the other" (158), though man and nature struggle with each other always.

Moreover, in *The Outer Dark*, the merging of humans with the natural world is presented in a shockingly beautiful passage, in which the body of the tinker, who has been hung from a tree by the Triune and begins to decompose:

The tinker in his burial tree was a wonder to the birds. The vultures that came by day to nose with their hooked beaks among his buttons and pockets like outrageous pets soon left him naked of his rags and fresh alike. Black mandrake sprang beneath the tree as it will where the seed of the hanged falls and in spring a new branch pierced his breast and flowered in a green boutonniere perennial beneath his yellow grin. (OD 238)

The morbidity and violence of this passage are tempered by its surprisingly gentle depiction of nature, though the tree "pierces" the tinker's body with its branches, because flowers form a "green boutonniere" over him and the vultures are even likened to "pets" that "nose" him with their beaks, and far from being sinister, the tinker's corpse becomes "an emblem of tranquility and cosmic harmony" (Guillemin 72). Obviously, such a depiction of the symbiotic relationship between man and nature is a typical embodiment of McCarthy's viewpoint about the cosmos, in which everything is equal and there is no hierarchy and even the boundary between subject and object or margin and center is erased and transgressed once the conditions are changed. Just like the tinker, when he lives, we cannot say he is good or evil, at least, concerning his taking away the baby of Culla and Rinthy and refusal to pass the baby to it's mother's arms, he is evil, yet death changes him for he is made to merge into nature and even to be nutritious and poetic for the fauna and flora. The world seems to be back to its original and primitive state, i.e. chaos, pure and simple.

McCarthy's last Appalachian novel *Suttree* (1979) features such a paradoxical relation between men and nature. The Tennessee river in the text is as paradoxical as the Ganges River in India, both sacred and obscene. Bathing and washing in the Ganges river coexists with decomposed corpses or skeletons of man and animals, which creates a strange scene.[①] It seems that life and death are from and in the river. The protagonist Suttree lives in a shabby boathouse along the bank of Tennessee river and makes his living by fishing after he gives up his middle-class family life. The

---

① The strange scene of the Ganges River can be presented from lots of pictures in the web. (See <www.image.baidu.com/i?tn=baiduimage&ct=201326592&lm>)

river sustains Suttree and his friends such as an Indian, who dines from turtles, Wanda and her father Reese, who support themselves by fishing mussels in the river; while it is littered with trash as well as a number of corpses, including a suicide, a baby (S 10, 306). People urinate in the river (S 307). For the poor, the river is also the burial ground, for example, Leonard's father is buried there for the purpose of continuing with his pension from the government (S 250-2); Wanda, Suttree's only pure girlfriend in his love history, is devoured by the floods and the river is her temporary cemetery. As Owens-Murphy notes, the river is the symbol of "an industrial wasteland" (170), more than that, it is a sign of the "city wilderness," which is grossly contaminated, featuring "gouts of sewage faintly working, gray clots of nameless waste and yellow condoms roiling slowly out of the murk like some giant form of fluke or tapeworm" (S 7). To sum up, McCarthy's wilderness is actually a chaos space, defined by Hayles as "a new territory" which is "assimilated into neither order nor disorder" ("Chaos" 306). Chaos space breaks down the binaries, and meanwhile tends to oppose an "either/or" mode of thinking.

ii. Violence, Codes and Modernity

In *Blood Meridian*, violence is a sign of consumption, making people surface ones. Violence is encoded and constructed with blood epistemology and hence the only "legitimized knowledge" in the wilderness to be worshiped. Just like media and advisement in the consumer society, which encode the objects, making people slaves of signs, Enlightenment as grand narrative also encodes violence with the masks of knowledge, science, order and rationality, which creates fetishism of violence, making people consume violence towards man and nature submissively. So, via violence, one of the most important social problems in the postmodern society, McCarthy not only questions humanity, but also makes his critique of modernity.

Violence as consumption follows Baudrillard's thesis of consumer and the consumption of objects. In the process of consumption, material goods are not objects for satisfaction or needs, but signs. The persons to be killed by Glanton's gang are no longer victims, but a group of signs, too. Baudrillard defines consumerism in the postmodern era as follows:

We can conceive of consumption as a characteristic mode of industrial civilization on the condition that we separate it fundamentally from its current meaning as a process of satisfaction or needs. Consumption is not a passive mode of assimilation (absorption) and appropriation which we can oppose to an active mode of production, in order to bring to bear naive concepts of action (an alienation). From the outside, we must clearly state the consumption is an active mode of relations (not only to objects, but to the collectivity and to the world), a systematic mode of activity and a global response on which whole cultural system is founded. (24)

In postmodern society, media and advertisement are complicit to urge people to consume beyond their needs, though what they consume is only "imagery," or "illusion." People's desire for consumption could not be satisfied forever in the affect of media, which not only produces desires for consumption, but also changes the individual into the self-regulating "subject" (consumer) through the mechanism of "interpellation." To a certain extent, the working mechanism of media and advertisement is similar to that of ideology, which works on human mind and behavior imperceptibly. Consumption has become the "unconscious" inherent in consumers. The same is true for those American mercenaries in the text. Once violence becomes a sign, it has lost its reference to concrete objects and shifted to be a non-referential signifier. Violence no longer meets an objective, and in a non-referential modality of violence, their lust for blood could not be satisfied easily, and on the contrary, the violence will get improved. In the system of consumption, no one can stand outside and all subjects are equivalent in their involvement with such a closed system, and actually, every one is sign. Violence subverts the dualism of victim and agent, subject and object, man and nature. Man becomes objects, or the desired objects. In the unconscious, man has been alienated completely.

If the sign value of objects gets consumed, objects have to be encoded initially. According to Baudrillard, there are two means to encode the objects. In terms of subjects, man has the propensity to be different from the other, and it is desirable for a normal man to acquire individuality, identity and personality. The coded sign is helpful to distinguish people from others. For instance, fashionable dress, deluxe automobile and luxury house implicate one's social status and identity, because dress, cars and mansion have been encoded with taste, nobility and wealth. The possession of the coded objects implies the ownership of these coded signs. With the object's modification into a sign of system, "certain social structure will be produced, which will urge, even force people to consume, hence the slaves of consumption" (Zhang 141). In terms of objects, the mass media facilitates the codification of objects, and helps the objects transform to signs. In such a social structure of signs, people have to consume. Once most of consumers accept the codes of objects from the mass media, the objects as signs will be thought to be compulsory, and thus getting consumption naturally. Therefore, consumers are changed to be "captives of the cave" in the allegory of "cave" from Plato's The *Republic*. What they see and need is not something real, but their own shadows refracted on the wall. In the consumer society, the reality has become hyper-real with "simulacrum" and "simulation," and nothing is different for the real or imagined, virtual or artificial.

In *Blood Meridian*, violence is a sign, and it is encoded and constructed. Judge Holden underscores the blood epistemology. When talking about the way of raising children, he says, "at a young age, ... they should be put in a pit with wild dogs. They should be set to puzzle out from their proper clues the one of three doors that does not harbor wild lions. They should be made to run naked in the desert until ..." (BM 146). For him, "men are born for games. Nothing else" (BM 249). Judge is the instigator and practitioner of violence in the text, for instance, he buys two puppies from a young boy in the town, then throws them down into the river over the bridge. Moreover, in the text, he is a cold-blooded killer and rapist of young boys. In Judge's mind, by killing puppies, just as with children, he is actually doing what is only right.

In order to legitimize the blood epistemology, God and Christianity need to be challenged. In Judge's vision, "Books lie," for God "speaks in stone and trees, the bone of things" (BM 116), so "war is only trade we honor here" (BM 248); otherwise, man is only another kind of clay. For Judge, blood is the only logic or truth of the world. Refusing Christian ethics and morality, he builds up his religion of war and expounds it, "War endures. As well as men what they think of stone. War was always here. Before man was, war waited for him. The ultimate trade awaiting its ultimate practitioner" (BM 248). Not only is war eternal and sacred, but in a world of total anarchy, war is the only thing that is sacred, for he argues, "war is the truest form of divination. ...War is the ultimate game because war is at last a forcing of the unity of existence. War is god" (BM 249). Guillemin speaks right, "[Judge's] tirade ... turns terrorism into dogma" (97). In effect, more than dogma, war has been taken as a kind of the complex of idea, faith, concept, more exactly, religion.

As one of ideological state apparatuses, the purpose of religion (war) is "to persuade [people] to take it as 'truth'; while, actually, it serves for certain kind of secret and specific benefits of power" (Žižek 13). In its working mechanism, those gangs are "interpellated" into its system, and made to be submissive and indifferent "subjects" (killers). Although in the end of text, perhaps influenced by the ex-priest, the only person in the gang to know Judge's sinister purpose, the Kid has a bit of awakening of human nature in his confession made to an old woman in the rocks with promise to send her back home, it is late, because "she was just a dried shell and she had been dead in that place for years" (BM 315). In the text, McCarthy does scorn at Christianity, and those victims are taken as "monks" or "anchronites" with metaphor or simile, for instance. In Judge's words, morality is constructed, for "moral law is an invention of mankind for the disenfranchisement of the powerful in favor of the weak" (BM 250), so the power of will precedes the morality of Christianity. In contrast with the destruction and desolation of churches and slaughter of churchmen, war becomes the only legitimized religion or faith in the textual world. The hermit's judgment of humanity echoes, "a machine to make a machine" (BM 19), which results in blood and violence. The presentation of Judge as a crazy Hitler-like war-worshiper or God of war-as-religion is not to show that McCarthy is an advocator of violence, but to warn us and criticize violence fetishism. God does not create violence, but man himself makes violence prevalent in the earth.

The fetishism of signs is not new in human world. In the ancient society, due to the limitation of knowledge of universe outside human beings, different signs are created to pay homage for ancient people. For instance, "dragon" is Chinese totem, and the figure of "Taichi" is taken to drive out evil spirits. In the postmodern society, the fetish has attained in all aspects of culture and objects are signs to be worshiped. In a chaotic cosmos, violence is a sign to be worshiped, too. Once blood epistemology is acknowledged by most people, fetishism of violence will be set up and becomes the only "legitimized knowledge" in the chaotic cosmos. Nobody questions its legitimacy, for it is produced by power, which may create reality and truth. The necklace of human ears worn by Brown is a good sign of violence. After his being hanged, such a strange "heathen" necklace is shifted to the Kid, who treasures it until his death. For Glanton's gang, violence can reward them with money, drinks, whores and respect from Mexicans. Blood, lust and violence condition their life. Cowardice, compassion and clemency are absent from the lexicon of these bandits, for they are internalized with martial codes. For instance, Sproule's hysteric response with the blood bat's attack in the desert brings upon the Kid's disdain; the Kid's "mindless violence" gets appreciation from Judge, who gives the Kid smiles when meeting at the very beginning (BM 3); Judge feels disturbed with the Kid's clemency in his withdrawal of the arrow from Brown's thigh, which directly leads to the Kid's tragic death in the outhouse in the end, though he is taken as a good assassin (or heir) to cultivate.[①] The list may go on. Many critics discuss about the relationship of the Kid and Judge as father and son. Bowers refers to Judge as "the Kid's adopted father" (12) and Parkers describes him as the Kid's "surrogate father" (110). The relationship of father/son between the Kid and Judge is nothing important for the present study, yet in Judge's logic, sympathy and weakness shown in the Kid are not suitable for a warrior. So, the Kid has to be "excluded from the dance" of Judge's war-as-religion, for the Kid is only "a false dancer" (BM 332). He criticizes the Kid's clemency in the rage, and attributes the ruins of Glanton's gang to him, "it was you and none other who shaped events along such a calamitous course" (BM

---

① The Kid's ambiguous end receives critical attention, yet the accepted thesis is that the kid was killed by Judge, although no one seems to agree exactly how the act takes place.

306), which might be argued to be an excuse for the Kid's extermination by Judge. The Kid, in effect, becomes the "scapegoat" of violence fetishism finally, though he survives attacks from the Comanches, the Apaches, the Yumas and the Mexican Army.

Violence fetishism is accepted by different ethnic groups in the text, and even becomes "collective unconscious." Brown, a white American, on his way back from the bar, pours "a pitcher of aguardiente over a young soldier and [sets] him afire with his cigar" to make that man burned up and then "blacken and shriveled in the mud like an enormous spider" (BM 268), though no antagonism exists in them before. The welcomed Mexican riders go through the town, who wear "scapulars or necklace of dried and blackened human ears" (BM 78). They are not only "armed with weapons of every description," but also their horses are with bridles "woven up from human hair and decorated with human teeth" (ibid). Native Americans are brutal, too. They kill and even emasculate their enemies. The Glanton gang come across five wagons with dead Mexican riders killed by Indians, "some by their beards were men but yet wore strange menstrual wounds between their legs and no man's parts for these had been cut away and hung dark and strange from out their grinning mouths" (BM 153). In another scene, two of the missing scouts from Glangton's gang are hanged upside down from a paloverde tree by Indians: "They were skewed through the cords of their heels with sharpened shuttles of green wood and they hung gray and naked above the dead ashes of the coals where they'd been roasted until their heads had charred and the brains bubbled in the skulls and steam sang from their nose holes" (BM 226-7). Violence not only erases differences between nations, colors and races, but also dismantles binaries of margin and center, subject and object. All are "yahoos" in Judge's own remarks (BM 160).

In the text, violence is a sign to be encoded subjectively. Most members of the Glanton gang are evil with malignant violence. Violence is a means for them to achieve prominent position in the gang, which is like that of consumption of object's sign. Judge is a perfect example. Though his origin is an enigma, nobody in the gang makes sure when and where they have seen him, yet he seems to be seated in the list of number two, and always rides ahead with Captain Glanton in the gang. Judge is an encyclopedia-typed character. He can speak five languages, and excels at legality, archaeology, botanics, paleontology, geology, astronomy, history, philosophy and religion, and has been to international cultural centers, Paris and London, in his time. However, his leading position in the gang is achieved through his violent and cold-blooded behavior. In the initial scene in which we see him through the eyes of the Kid, "an enormous man dressed in an oilcloth slicker" enters the tent, and he is "bald as a stone," and has "no trace of beard" and "no brows to his eyes nor lashes to them," and is close to "seven feet in height" (BM 6), then quickly disrupts a religious congregation totally by announcing that the preacher is not only an "imposter," but also "wanted by the law" for "a variety of charges," and among them "the most recent of which involved a girl of eleven years" and a "goat" which he had "congress with" (BM 6-7). Judge's appalling accusations result in the preacher's being shot by the angry mob, and total havoc among the congregation: "... people were pouring out, women screaming, folk stumbling, folk trampled underfoot in the mud" (BM 7). The bloody confusion made by Judge gets a reward with a drink bought by a man in the bar, where he happily tells them, "I never laid eyes on the man before today. Never even heard of him" (BM 8). The preacher becomes a "sacrifice," which helps with Judge's winning authority from the crowds and meanwhile setting up his war-of-religion through "a ritual," which, in Judge's point of view, "includes the letting of blood" (BM 329). Judge's violence is more discursive than physical. In the end, he has become the icon of warlord. Black Jackson, the imbecile and Judge, become another evil Triune in the wilderness. This new, strange and evil Trinity totally subverts the image of God in Christianity. Just as Steve Shaviro remarks of Judge and his companions, "we might be tempted to say that whereas all the other characters kill casually and thoughtlessly, out of greed or blood lust or some other trivial cause, only the judge kills out of will and conviction and a deep commitment to the cause and the canons of Western rationality" (147).

Like consumption, violence is also "a systematic act of the manipulation of signs" (Baudrillard 25). The consumption of violence from Judge and his bandits cannot separate from Western rationality, which encodes violence, and changes man to be the consumers of violence. Western rationality originates from Enlightenment. As one of the origins of modern civilization, Enlightenment thought "embraces the idea of progress, and actively seeks that break with history and tradition which modernity espouses" (Harvey 12). Prof. Zhan Shukui holds that "modernity is the inevitable result of Enlightenment," and modernity can be defined as "the new comprehensive civilization which developed generally in but not limited to Europe and North America over the last several centuries and fully evident by the early twentieth century" (8). In effect, Enlightenment is synonymous with modernity, which aims to liberate humankind from ignorance, disorder and irrationality with the power of knowledge, order and science. According to Mary Klages, modernity is fundamentally about order, about creating order out of chaos (qtd. in Sun 46). In brief, its assumption is that creating more rationality is conductive to creating more order, and that the more ordered a society is, the better it will function. Though modernity brings about great achievements for human life and society, it also produces lots of problems. It seems to me that *Blood Meridian* is McCarthy's "The Dialectics of Enlightenment."[1] Within the subtext of his fiction, he makes critique of modernity. Nick Monk notes that Judge is "the supreme avatar" (83) of European Enlightenment. Besides him, Glanton and Captain White also engage with the project of Western modernity. So in the person of Judge and his companies, McCarthy gives a literary reply to "what is Enlightenment?" and "what is man like?".

What is man like? Such a riddle of Sphinx tortures philosophers and literary writers for generation after generation. Ancient Greek philosophers, particularly Socrates, Aristotle and Pythagoras, hold that man is a rational being. For Enlightenment philosophers, man is not only the center of universe, but also the "measure of all things," (Protagoras's adage). Cartesian and Newtonian thoughts even celebrate and promote human beings with rationality to be the prime of the universe. Knowledge and freedom are counted as the goal of a rational man. In *Blood Meridian*, rationalism is presented to be dangerous. For McCarthy, rationality may be taken as a means to control others and nature for the purpose of satisfying one's desire. Rationality does differentiate man from nature and simultaneously helps man know more about nature, yet rationalism aims to make nature yield. McCarthy is against rationalism, modernity

---

[1] *The Dialectics of Enlightenment* is coauthored by M. Horkheimer and T. W. Adorno.

and modern civilization, which is one of major thematic motifs beginning with his first novel, *The Orchard Keeper*, in which Arthur Ownby's shooting at the Tank on the top of Smokie Mountain set by the government is a perfect example to challenge modernity represented by "machines in the garden." In his deconstruction of grand narrative of the Enlightenment, McCarthy fulfills his construction of postmodern epistemology.

For Judge Holden, man is the "suzerian of the earth," which means "a keeper or overload" of nature, because "these anonymous creatures" may seem "little or nothing in the world." However, he is aware that man has to control them through the knowledge of them, for "the smallest crumb can devour us" (BM 198-9). He argues:

Whatever exists, he said. Whatever in creation exists without my knowledge exists without my consent. ... And yet everywhere upon it are pockets of autonomous life. Autonomous. In order for it to be mine nothing must be permitted to occur upon it save by my dispensation. ... The man who believes that the secrets of the world are forever hidden lives in mystery and fear. Superstition will drag him down. The rain will erode the deeds of his life. But that man who sets himself the task of singling out the thread of order from the tapestry will by the decision alone have taken charge of the world and it is only by such taking charge that he will effect a way to dictate the terms of his own life. (BM 198-9)

Judge's hegemonic ideas are typical of that of Eurocentric modernity. His advocation of knowledge, science, order, will of power and violence towards controlling others and nature with the aim to remove the obstacles to modernization, and assumption of modern (European) civilization as the most civilized and superior civilization, are presented clearly in the above when he answers the question of Todavine, who does not understand Judge's acts of taxidermy of one of every species of bird they encounter. In the text, Judge always expresses his desire to "know" and control. He collects specimens of different creatures, plants and also makes sketches of different mineral ores, or artifacts of ancient civilization or different categories of people with equal attentiveness, scrutiny and care for detail. One of the examples is his physiognomy study of a local idiot, which seems to differentiate from races: "The judge reached and took hold of man's head in his hands and began to explore its contours. The man's eyes darted about and he held on to the judge's wrists. The judge has his entire head in his grip like an immense and dangerous faith healer" (BM 238).

Judge's doings are close to that of Captain White. Both hold Eurocentrism. In his recruiting of the mercenaries, White strengthens the racism and "manifest destiny" in his dealing with Mexico and Mexicans:

What we are dealing with is a race of degenerates. A mongrel race, little better than niggers. And maybe no better. There is no government in Mexico. Hell, there is no God in Mexico. ... we are dealing with a people manifestly incapable of governing themselves. And do you know what happens with people who cannot govern themselves? That's right. Others come in to govern for them. (BM 34)

Captain White and Glanton Gang are commissioned by Mexican government to wipe out the Indian bandits for the purpose of creating peace and order in the border areas, yet their violence makes the world into chaos and wilderness, much more disorderly than ever before. Dramatically, Captain White hopes to govern Mexicans, who are thought to be degenerate and foolish in terms of his social Darwinism vision, yet he is beheaded with the head in the big jar by Mexican "degenerates" (BM 34). The ambitious and arrogant Glanton acts like a powerful "feudal baron" (BM 275), yet ends his life with being split into the thrapple by the head of Yumas. Their violent death is doomed due to their adherence to the violence encoded by Enlightenment, modernity and Eurocentric civilization.

The coded violence makes Judge and his band of filibusters hunters of Indians and nature. For them, "the stuff of creation may be shaped to man's will" (BM 5). Judge even announces that "The freedom of birds is an insult to me. I'd have them all in zoos" (BM 199). As Sara Spurgeon puts it, "human will clothed in the sacred rhetoric of science, far from insignificant, is the most powerful force in the novel. If only nature can enslave man, only man can enslave nature, even if by doing so he leaves a sky as empty of birds as the plains now are of buffalo" (91). Though dark and bloody for McCarthy's wilderness, in effect, humankind is still the most horrifying animal in it. In one passage, an old hunter camped with the Kid (now a man) told him of the buffalo on the plains:

... the animals by the thousands and tens of thousands and the hides pegged out over actual square miles of ground and the teams of skinners spelling one another around the clock and the shooting and shooting weeks and months till the bore shot slick and the stock shot loose at the tang and their shoulders were yellow and blue to the elbow and the tandem wagons groaned away over the prairie twenty and twenty-two ox teams and the flint hides by the ton and hundred ton and the meat rotting on the ground and the air whining with flies and the buzzards and ravens and the night a horror of snarling and feeding with the wolves half crazed and wallowing in the carrion. (BM 316-7)

Such a scene of slaughtering of buffaloes for the benefits of humankind in their development of modern civilization could be a brilliant condensation for McCarthy's counter-memory of the winning of the West, his revision of frontier history and his critique of modernity and anthropocentrism and the capitalized Order as well. The consumption and control of natural resources produces large quantities of bones, skeletons and rotten meat scattered on the prairie, which turn out to be trash or waste thrown away by the human beings. Such a delineation of the bleak relationship between man and nature is typical of the phenomenon of late capitalism society, which is a bitter satire towards the frontier wilderness. Due to the overuse of natural world, the frontier wilderness has been degraded into a new waste land full of nightmarish spectacle. When meeting man with guns and powder, nature has to become captives and preys. Birds are driven to the zoo and animals are changed to be playthings in the circus. For example, a gigantic white bear, "an avatar of the natural world" (Spurgeon 89), is forced later by man to be a dancer with the girl's tutu on the Beehive Saloon stage to the music of a little girl's organ, and finally killed by a drunkard and died in the blood. The bear's death seems insignificant for those ignorant audience and its shedding of blood just creates another bloody spectacle, which is similar to the enormous mountains of bones of animals stretching across the prairies miles long. They are doomed to become the "sacrifices" for human development.

The chaos theory's systematic and holistic ideas towards the cosmos correspond with ecocriticism as regards its major concern of relations between man and nature. In terms of relations between man and nature in McCarthy's fiction, the relations of human beings warrant attention, for all the rest of relations in the cosmos depend on the relations of human beings, which are crucial for us to discern the essence of things by looking through the superficial phenomenon. In *The Crossing* (1994), the she-wolf turns out to be a "spectacle" in a Mexican circus to fight with some hunting dogs to please man, which is against Billy Parham's kind promise to send her back to her living mountains. The violence of humanity always prevails over the brutality of nature. Just as David Harvey points out, "postmodernism also ought to be looked at as mimetic of the social, economic, and political practices in society. ... Furthermore, it is just as surely dangerous to presuppose the postmodernism is solely mimetic rather than an aesthetic intervention in politics, economy, and social life in its own right" (113-5). McCarthy's aesthetic presentation of human violence encoded from the perspectives of both subject and object is socially and politically motivated at its core. Without doubt, the strong injection of his fiction into our common sensibility may have its consequences. In Judge's words, McCarthy reminds us of shadows of violence in contemporary society, for "man's memories are uncertain and the past that was differs little from the past that was not" (BM 330).

iii. Violence as Unique Structure of Truth

"Has the rain a father? Or who hath begotten the drops of dew?" (Job 38: 28-30). Violence in *Blood Meridian* has its cultural and historical context. Violence happens everyday, and for McCarthy, American history "is fundamentally defined by violence-it is revisable, but only so far as it takes this central truth into account" (Stadt 106). In

American history, there are too many wars. Only in view of its plunder and attacks of native Americans, more than one hundred wars broke out in American history. From 1945 to 1990, in terms of its participation in or involvement with overseas wars, there were 124 ones. From 1991 till the end of last century, almost 40 wars happened. Simply in the present century, two local wars took place, one was to be against Iraq, the other Republic of Afghanistan. It is calculated that USA has been involved in or directly launched a war every 18.8 year on average before WWII; while, after WWII, the frequency of its starting the war improves with the promotion of its national power, and every 2.1 year on average it would wage a war. During the cold war, the average time of its unleashing the war is 2.6 years, and after the cold war, 1.4 years.[①]

War brings about trauma for Americans. The 12-year-long Vietnam War makes Americans suffer the taste of failure at the first time in American history and cast doubts on their identity as God's elects. The reflection of Vietnam War was a tendency in the 1980s, when the novel was written. No wonder why some of critics have paralleled the fiction with Vietnam War.[②] However, the present study argues that McCarthy posits his text in a much broader cultural and historical context with the cult of violence in American society, and also his purpose is to question the "mindless violence" of humanity. As for Vietnam War, it is only one of factors to be considered. For McCarthy, violence is as ubiquitous as any other form of common sense, for scalping has been a common human practice for at least 300,000 years, as one of the epigraphs to the novel suggests. In the vision of McCarthy, it is absurd to find out "the string in the maze" of human and natural world via violence (BM 245), for it results in the chaos. Likewise, for the purpose of satisfying one's lust and desire for power and order, to intrude, intervene, control or constrain the world with military power with the masks of democracy, science, freedom and order, is doomed to fail, only leaving the society with chaos and wilderness.

McCarthy is a poet, for "all a poet can do today is warn" (qtd. in Lincoln 176);

---

① The statistical figures cited in the study are sourced from <www. zhidao. baidu.com/question/5874436.html>

② Owens, McGilchrist and Brewton parallel the novel with the war of Vietnam. (See Owens, 2000; McGilchrist, 2010; Brewton,"The Changing" 121-43.)

McCarthy is also a philosopher, for "a philosopher has to stand opposite to his age, never obeys; it is the mission for him to be a critic and diagnostician without dread, just like what Socrates does" (qtd. in Hu 10-1). Violence is a sign, which is encoded by modernity and modern civilization. Without awareness of dangers and deception of violence fetishism, man would be controlled and restrained for ever; likewise, without worries of destruction of the earth from Man in the capital letter, the relations of man and nature are doomed in "optical democracy" rather than in balance and harmony. The text's ambiguous ending writes, Judge, the icon of Enlightenment and warlord, still "dances in light and shadow," and "he never sleeps. ... he is dancing, dancing. He says that he will never die" (BM 335). Such a design of the ending may be the possible reply to the Kid's question of the identity of Judge, "what's he a judge of ?"(BM 135). Man, nature and society, encoded by Enlightenment, are what he judges. Judge doesn't die from our society. McCarthy not only warns us to be aware of dangers of war and violence, past and present, whenever, but also reminds us of the specter of Enlightenment, which still haunts our mind and life, producing "captives of cave." To some extent, McCarthy unveils his society and age, and thus criticizing the malady of his society and age seriously.

In sum, McCarthy's fiction is no longer preoccupied with dualistic assumption that the world is either good or bad, either order or disorder, either center or margin, either subject or object, either beauty or ugliness, rather, it is flooded with paradoxes, ambiguities and nonlinearity. McCarthy is important because he focuses his eyes on the contemporary social culture. His propensity to address the most important cultural and social issue renders much weight and importance to his texts. In his fiction, man, nature and society are presented with characteristics of wilderness and chaos, which is his attempt to question and dismantle the capitalized Order. McCarthy is not a writer with pessimistic or misanthropic vision about humanity, but a writer with earnest love for human beings. What he has done in his fiction is what Jonathan Swift has dealt with human beings more than two hundred years before, though human beings are taken as ugly and obscene "yahoos." In his fictional world, the presentation of violence, blood, deformation and morbidity is to make a diagnosis of the malaise of his living postmodern age and society, and attempt to warn us of violence or evil in ourselves. His subversion of the grand narrative of Enlightenment is to disclose its essence of violence and deception, and much more importantly, to construct an objective truth with his unique structure of violence, for it is not merely a consequence of truth, it is the truth.

Chapter Three
Iteration, Indeterminacy and the Butterfly Effect: Narrative Strategies as Chaos

Chaos is exciting because it opens up the possibility of simplifying complicated phenomenon. Chaos is worrying because it introduces new doubts about the traditional model-building procedures of science. Chaos is fascinating because of its interplay of mathematics, science and technology. But above all chaos is beautiful. This is no accident. It is visible evidence of the beauty of mathematics… which here spills over into the everyday world of human senses.

Ian Stewart, Does God Play Dice?

As N. Katherine Hayles remarks, "writers who are relatively ignorant of the new science nevertheless participate in the cultural matrix and so, willy-nilly, encounters in some form the matrix's underlying paradigm" (*The Cosmic Web* 26). John Barth corresponds with Hayles and holds that, as a new science, chaos theory has come to "infect literary theory," and "may even have promise for the practice of literature itself, as part of a working aesthetic for writers, as well as for the illumination of existing works whose authors were quite innocent of chaology" (284). As a new paradigm in contemporary scientific and cultural fields, chaos theory gives insights for McCarthy and his contemporaries, such as John Barth, Don DeLillo and Thomas Pynchon, to name a few. As the study's introduction mentions, McCarthy's life as a fellow at Santa Fe Institute since the 1980s makes him encounter chaos theory and friend of scientists in chaos science. In accordance with the thematic content as chaos and wilderness, some of major principles of chaos theory, such as iteration, indeterminacy and the butterfly effect are taken as narrative strategies to imbue McCarthy's fiction with the aesthetic characteristics of chaos: complex and dynamic.

This chapter takes his typical works, *Blood Meridian* (1985), *The Road* (2006) and *No Country for Old Men* (2005) as case studies to provide a panoramic review of McCarthy's narrative strategies, and to prove the efficacy of chaos theory in the definition of his works as beautiful chaos.

I. Iteration and "Chaos Sandwich": *Blood Meridian*

Simplicity is a kind of beauty, of course, complexity is a kind of beauty, too, just as the diversity of nature shows us. Paradoxically, complexity is produced by simplicity, which could be accomplished by iteration. By means of the iteration of simple formula, complex patterns or figures could be produced. *Blood Meridian* is controversial, yet it is also exceptional, which may be attributed to its textual ambiguity and complexity. *Blood Meridian's* beauty of complexity is produced by iteration, one of the basic modes to produce the complex patterns of the phase space in a chaotic system. It is by means of the iterative shaping of the fiction's genre, characters, landscape and language style that *Blood Meridian* is made to be a unique "chaos sandwich," strange and familiar, complex and dynamic.

Figure 1.8 The Cantor Set

Figure 1.9 The Von Koch Snowflake

i. What is Iteration?

To embark on the exploration of the fiction's exceptionality, it is necessary to know what is iteration. Let us consider the Cantor set. As shown in Fig.1.8, we start with a straight line that may have any length. For convenience we consider a line with unit length. We remove the middle section, but leave the two remaining sections, which are each one-third of the length. Next we divide each of these lines to three, and again remove the middle third. We continue the iterative process to infinity, then the number of remaining sections will tend to infinity, too. Through such an iterative process, "we may get an infinite number of points that we know to have zero dimension" (Cambel 179). The changing process of trigrams and hexagrams in *Books of Changes* is similar to the process of iteration, which produces more complicated patterns than its original two elements. The Koch snowflake, the Julia set and the famous Mandelbrot set are made via similar methods, as shown in Fig.1.9, Fig.1.11 and Fig.1.5 respectively, though the iterative process of computation for Mandelbrot set is a bit more complicated, which may be performed in the computer using a particular software program.

Figure 1.11 The Julia Set (from Cambel 183)

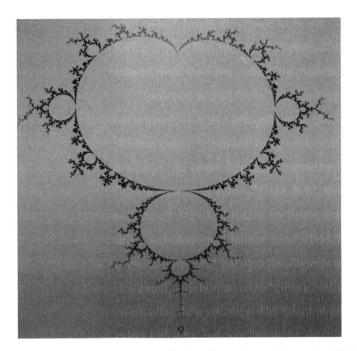

Figure 1.5 The Mandelbrot Set in Full View (from Gleick, "Illustration" 1987)

Iteration is a basic mathematical calculation, which performs repeatedly. When associated with the studies of nonlinear dynamics system, iteration is the basic technique for scientists to take to map out the matter's motion in the phase space, and it is generally performed with the use of superfast computers. For a dynamicist, "such iteration entails calculating the state of a dynamical system as it evolves through time. The process is recursive-that is, the output of a particular calculation becomes the input for the next" (Jo Alyson Parker 69). Kundert-Gibbs' observation of the behavior of a time-dependent system gives us insights. It we start some system at position X_0 and velocity V_0, and proceed to calculate the position and velocity after time T, we have done one iteration. Next, we take the output position and velocity (X_t and V_t) and put them into the same equation, calculate the equation after time 2T and generate our next position and velocity (X_{2t} and V_{2t}). Continue this feedback loop, "where the output of last calculations acts as the input for the next one, then we can 'draw' the behavior of the system for an indefinite period of time" (Kundert-Gibbs 44).

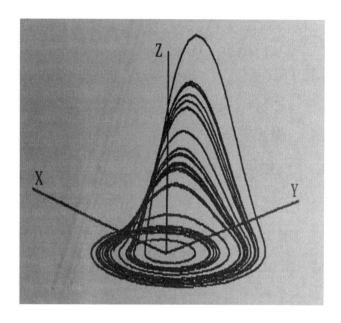

Figure 1.4 The Rössler Attractor (from Cambel 72)

Vividly described, iteration is like "the baker's transformation" described by mathematicians,[①] which is close to the process of producing Rössler attractor as shown in Fig.1.4. In Rössler's own words, this technique is a "sausage in a sausage in a sausage in a sausage" (Gleick 141). Such a process of stretching, folding and squeezing could produce complicated patterns or figures, in which the original shape is impossible to ascertain, exactly speaking, the original "point attractor" could not be identified, for it has been deeply buried and irrecoverable; nevertheless, the original point attractor may be glimpsed in some distorted way during the new iterative reversion, hence making the new pattern strange and familiar. According to Slethaug, the baker's transformation or the process of making sausage could produce intermittence, or the "chaos sandwich," which "gives a glimpse of an ordered state surrounded by chaotic conditions or a glimpse of a chaotic state surrounded by orderly conditions" (133).

---

① "Baker's transformation" is also called Bernoulli shift, the "salt water taffy analog," or "Arnold's Cat" (Cambel 74). In Slethaug's *Beautiful Chaos*, he takes "baker's transformation" as Otto Rössler's hypothesis and mapping, which may be a mistake. A. B. Cambel thinks that "the stretching and folding processes are typical of strange attractors that depict the geometry of the dynamics" (76), and Ian Stewart also asserts that the stretching and folding are the geometric essence of chaos (147).

However, this is a partial story. Some other phenomena will be accompanied in the process of stretching and folding and squeezing in a far-from-equilibrium system. One point should be noted that the calculation of iteration is featured with nonlinearity and unity, and the computation made by means of infinite iteration is not integer in the dimension, but fractal dimension. That is to say, sometimes iteration will produce the fractal, in other words, self-similarity in the patterns or figures, for instance, strange attractors or Mandelbrot set as markers of chaos system. In these figures, recursions of the similar or same image will be infinite. It is akin to "simulacra" in Baudrillard's examination of contemporary consumer society, in which each image merely builds upon its preceding images, i.e. copies of other copies without origin and ultimacy, hence the "hyper-real" coming into existence. For literary writings, such a recursion of similar story or form or structure creates "mise en abyme," or "Chinese boxes," or "Russian dolls," or framing tales (tales-in-the-tale) in the narrative form, which presents the mode of self-referentiality in postmodernist fiction. McCarthy's *The Crossing* belongs to such a mode of recursion, which we may discuss in the fourth chapter of this study.

Chaos system is uncertain, just as Ian Stewart points out, stretching and folding is "the geometric essence of chaos," yet, as for "what's coming" in the process of stretching and folding, "that's unpredictability" (147, 143). Therefore, what appears after iteration depends on the controlling of the process of iteration, which accounts for sensitive dependence on initial conditions in the dynamic system. Kundert-Gibbs speaks right, "no matter how powerful our computers or how finely we look at the set, it will always contain new surprises and figures" in the result of iteration (45). In the chaotic system, there appear different results by means of iteration. In general, two results are prevalent: one is the self-similar fractal in the language of chaos theory, or "mise en abyme" in the language of literary criticism; the other is uncertain and nonlinear, "conveying the sense of a distorting 'mise en abyme', ... which convey difference, not identicality" (Slethaug 133). The latter situation suits for McCarthy's *Blood Meridian*, which pays much more attention on its differences from rather than identicality with its conventions in its stretching and folding of generic conventions in its characterization, language and structure.

ii. *Blood Meridian* and Western Fiction

Blood Meridian's genre is ambiguous. Most of critics take it as postmodern Western or new Western or anti-Western. Rick Rebein holds that the publication of Larry McMurtry's *Lonesome Dove* and McCarthy's *Blood Meridian* witnessed the birth of new Western in 1985. He even points out that the outstanding feature of this new writing is its hybridization, and the new Western "explores the borders between realism and modernism, the Bildunsroman and the picaresque narrative, Old West mythology and New West revision, the oral tradition and the written tradition" (113). Susan Kollin also notes the fiction's hybridization, and she argues that *Blood Meridian* is an anti-Western, because McCarthy "brings elements of the Southern grotesque to bear on Western themes and conventions," and then transforms the genre, "showing the Western as deeply dependent on the contributions and concerns of Southern literature" (558). Slethaug asserts that *Blood Meridian* "inhabits a familiar literary form in order to question and subvert its conventions and ideologies" of the traditional Western, "through its unrestrained and bloody violence" (132). Robert Jarrett considers the novel as a revisionary Western, which "revises the earlier tradition of the Western in a postmodern fashion, reusing and parodying elements of the [Western] genre and of the historical record in order to critique the historical myth of our traditional narratives of the West" (*Cormac McCarthy* 69).

Just as we have discussed in the second chapter, violence is the text's "totality," through which McCarthy presents a world of chaos and wilderness, featuring with orderly disorder and nonlinearity. Apart from this, in his presentation of the most malevolent character of Judge Holden and his bands of American mercenaries, McCarthy criticizes Eurocentric modernity. Through its violence and its "incredulity towards metanarrative," *Blood Meridian* seems to be firmly located within the tradition of the postmodern Western novel. However, we should note that *Blood Meridian*, as a postmodern Western, belongs to the kind of work that Linda Hutcheon calls a "complicit critique" (*The Politics* 11), which self-consciously uses the literary conventions of the Western literature to expose its violent and raw reality concealed by those conventions. By means of iteration, or "the baker's transformation," McCarthy subverts the convention of the traditional Western in his critique of utopia and ideology imagined and constructed in the Western, and then transcends it in the construction of his specific generic feature.

In order to understand better how McCarthy subverts the conventions of Western literature and how he constructs his own generic feature, it is necessary to know the characteristics of Western literature briefly. As a genre of quintessential American literature, it is hard to define Western precisely. Western is usually divided into high-brow (serious or literary) Western and low-brow one (Handley 334). Broadly speaking, it refers to the fiction in the west with a vast and diverse region and a variety of ethnicity and culture (Maguire 437-64). Narrowly speaking, Western merely refers to low-brow (popular) Western, which includes Western adventure, dime Western and formulaic Western. Popular Western is also called as traditional Western, whose structure is formulaic and thematic motifs are desire and dream of the public. Western fiction is usually divided roughly into that written before and after the end of frontier in 1890 regardless of the time the Western literature is thought to have begun.

Western fiction develops from narratives of exploration and settlement in the 19th century and the novel of the frontier, a subgenre initiated by Charles Brockden Brown's *Wieland* (1798) and made internationally famous by James Fenimore Cooper's *Leather-stocking Tales* (1823-41) (Maguire 437). Frontier novels care much more about the descriptions of landscape, in which land assumes the same importance as characters. In this subgenre, cultural clashes between European and Native Americans are prominent with the process of the settlement, so action, adventure and violence are filled in the novels of frontier. Besides an emphasis on the land, action and adventure, cultural clashes, a hero who "champions good, fights evil, and deplores the passing of the wilderness," most of frontier novels and novels of the west also feature "a world either without women or with women in only minor roles" (Maguire 438). Dime novels and formulaic version of Western in the late 19th and 20th centuries also lay the basis for the development of Western fiction.

In these novels, frontier heroes such as Daniel Boone and Kit Carson are glorified and popular heroes such as Buffalo Bill Cody are created, which depicts the West as "a prelapsarian garden and space of retreat for the American hero," thus winning the popular imagination (Kollin 562). Zane Gray's *Riders of the Purple Sage* (1912) and Owen Wister's *The Virginian* (1902) are classic popular Westerns, in which the cowboy is imagined to be "a hero without wings" and "the last romantic figures upon [American] soil," or "one of the nature's aristocracy" (Maguire 439). As American new Adams, these heroic cowboys are transformed into "the nation's most important frontier figure and symbol of innocence" in the nation's fantasy (Kollin 564). The iconic images of cowboys are also spawned through President Theodore Roosevelt, the historian Frederick Jackson Turner,[①] and some other popular Western writers, who promote this belief to be "a kind of national dogma in the early 20th century" (Handley 336).

After the World War II, the Western fiction has changed to be "counter-west" in Handley's words. It not only counters the romanticized west, the legacies of Western settlement, migration and myths that have created expectations yet could not be fulfilled in Western settings, but also reexamines the Western past, which could be presented from several writers of literary Western, such as Wallace Stegner, Larry McMurtry, Cormac McCarthy and Leslie Marmon Silko (Handley 339-41). Though the Western literature is not monolithic, based on Handley's argument, Western fiction still feature something common: first, addressing the "historical past" from the legacy of American conquest, settlement and the encounters among different ethical groups; second, focusing on "how human experience in new environments 'roughed up' and redefined literary genres and conventions"; third, landscape, place and nature as hallmarks of much Western literature; finally, demonstrating "the long-standing clashes among romantic, realist, and naturalist genres and styles, through which the claims of history and the allure of the romantic Western myth collide" (Handley 335). Western's

---

① The historian Frederick Jackson Turner is well-known for his "frontier hypothesis," delivered in his "The Significance of the Frontier in American History" in 1893. For Turner, as a "safety valve," the frontier is also "the meeting point between savagery and civilization" (Smith 251). According to Turner, the west creates American character itself and reveals the process of progress for USA (Campbell, *The Culture* 7).

popularity in the 20th century also attributes to medias. Hollywood, televisions, radios and some other medias get profits from the genre and meanwhile advance the popularity of Western in USA and even overseas countries, from which national identity as something democratic and self-reliant and idealistic has been constructed. Besides, in the Western literature, frontier and westering myths with its ideologies such as "manifest destiny" and "American exceptionalism" have been set up and gradually become the "collective unconscious" of Americans.

For convenience of the study, we may make a rough summary of some key elements hinted in the traditional Western literature, such as violence, nature (landscape or land or wilderness), heroes (cowboys), morality (clashes between good and evil, civilization and wilderness), and frontier or Westering myths, to demonstrate what and how McCarthy plays with in his fiction.

iii. Iterative Shaping: Genre, Characters, Land and Language

Genre, Characters and Iteration

Blood Meridian features hybridization, in which different genres, such as Western fiction, picaresque novel, war novel and historical romance, are mixed. McCarthy's west is a chaos, in which the distinction between good and evil has been erased, only overwhelming amoralism or indeed immoralism stands out. In this moral vacuum, those Anglo-American white mercenaries are cruel and violent, and their goals of coming to the West is to eliminate other races from the earth, yet these violent killers are considered as "pilgrims" in the west, which is greatly ironic of the nation's sacred origins. Indians are no longer "noble savages" in Cooper's *Leather-stocking Tales* or "the other" simply misunderstood and mistreated in some films such as Kevin Costner's *Dances with Wolves*, or formulaic works about ideals in the West, but "a legion of horribles" and "a horde from the hell" (BM 52, 53), equally violent and savage killers, no matter what tribes they are from, the Apaches, Comanches, or Yumas. The binary collisions between civilization and wilderness as the hallmark of frontier space are nullified. Violence is everywhere and blood seems to be a constant in the textual system, which gives the reader a disturbing "thrill" in Barcley Owens' words (xiii) or produces "hymns of violence" in Shaviro's accusation (145). The "virgin land"[①] or "the Garden of God"[②] of the mythologized old west has been obscured by blood, which defies not only order and pattern, but also regeneration and restoration, and transformed into the "evil terrain" (BM 89), implying the failure of the west as utopia and the atmosphere of chaos both in the mid-nineteenth century in terms of the novel's temporal setting and in the mid-1980s as regards the novel's actual writing background.

McCarthy seems to be self-consciously about iterations and recursions in his descriptions of heroes in the West. In the text, Judge comments on the humans, who are not self-contained continuum but iteration of others, "whether in my book or not, every man is tabernacled in every other and he in exchange and so on in an endless complexity of being and witness to the uttermost edge of the world" (BM 141). The heroes in the west are no longer young, innocent and noble cowboys, but some butchers or scalp-hunters or women-rapists or buffalo-extinguishers, though as heroic and adventurous as cowboys still. They go to the West, yet they do not regenerate through violence; they conquer the frontier, yet they do not claim redemption in their violent conquest, either. In effect, they offer nothing in the way of the so-called heroism, but reward with bounties, money and cheers from those ignorant people through their barbarous eliminations of native inhabitants. Likewise, they get nothing except darkness, violence and death from the west, one of geographical spaces in North American continent much mythologized as "a zone of absolute freedom from external restraint of whatever material or psychic kind" (Holloway 147). It is an irony most memorably evoked in the case of the consumptive Sproule, who claims that his coming out to the west is "for [his] health" (BM 58). Just as Robert Jarrett argues, opposed to Cooper's "good" killer Natty Bumppo or the hero represented in John Wayne's cowboy gunfighters or Clint Eastwood's more naturalistic revision of Wayne's gunfighters, in *Blood Meridian* all characters have "hearts of clay" and are led to their eventual doom by the fallen vision of ... Judge Holden and John Joel Glanton. (*Cormac McCarthy* 69)

① "Virgin land" is termed by Henry Nash Smith in his influential book, *Virgin Land*, in which attitudes of people on the west in the 19th century are discussed in his analysis of dime novel.

② Natty Bumpoo in Fenimore Cooper's *Leather-Stocking Tales* takes the west as "the Garden of God."

By means of these "anti-heroes," McCarthy questions the myth of progress, and the national trust of frontier heroes who fight for the public's democracy, freedom and civilization. Likewise, his use of violence in these heroes, not merely "complicates the tradition of the Western hero" (Kollin 564), but makes the Western's conventions problematic, and criticizes its construction of cultural imaginations in the public in its own feedback loop.

Modeled on the picaresque novel, the text is made up with a collection of episodes and incidents that could in themselves follow almost any order. Almost all episodes are violent, except a few occasions, in which a little glory of humanity emerges behind brutality and savagery, for instance, the Kid's refusing to execute dying Shelby with serious wounds, Toadvine's cursing of Judge's lack of humanity, and the Kid's questioning the whereabouts of the expriest after their departure in the Yuma attack. These violent events are not significant for the plot's progression, and for the most part of the text, the tone is similarly cool and aloof. The plot moves, yet it does not thicken. Seemingly, the novel does not seek to resolve any conflicts, and it is merely to describe rather than to narrate (Phillips 443). Progress, sequence and causalities are illusions, which may be reflected from the fragmented episodes in the text. These episodes are in recursions, and almost any episode is "an iteration of the kid's various encounters and the conflicts between the members of Glanton's gang and their opponents" (Slethaug 135). Only McCarthy's signature[1] sentence "they rode on" reminds the reader of the iteration of similar episode in another cycle. In the end of the novel, nearly everyone is dead, killed, or murdered, or hanged, or shot, or executed, with the exception of the expriest, a Catholic, who disappears and the judge, a symbol of warlord, who escapes and dances in the chaotic world.

The central conflicts of the war novel, according to Tobey C. Herzog, are something "between moral freedom and restraint, chaos and control, idealism and reality, truth and lies, technology and primitive culture" (25). *Blood Meridian* evokes the literary form of war novel, and in it, it is full of physical and metaphysical darkness: violence, lust, power, vengeance and chaos. Modeled on war novel, the fiction is

[1] By signature, it means that each text has its idiomaticity, and it is termed by Jacques Derrida.

contextualized in the aftermath of Mexican-American war in the 19th century. The novel does present lots of bloody battle scenes, senseless slaughters and cold-blooded killer Indians and Indian killers. However, there is no distinction between the just and unjust party in the war, and all the involved are villains, simply the iteration of "horribles" in the cycle (BM 52). Usually, war may bring about trauma in the men who join the war, yet, it is curious that none of the characters suffer trauma. Even if they have, they refuse to address. Tobin, a priest, keeps silent, although he is present when churches are destructed, burned and desecrated by those mercenaries. The Kid does not suffer trauma, either, although he lives a life of blood, murder and slaughter. Furthermore, agency cannot be found in the characters except the judge, and they look like "great clay voodoo dolls made animate" (BM 13). Agency is usually related to bravery and stoicism, which recalls the archetype of Hemingway's heroes, yet for McCarthy's heroes, there is no stoicism, no choice in reactions, no response towards killing and being killed, twisting and negating the image of traditional war hero.

By means of the stretching, folding and squeezing of these generic forms, McCarthy blurs the boundaries of genres, and makes his work a "kaleidoscopic chaos" (Phillips 438). More than that, the text's iterative shaping may be embodied in the fiction's flat characterization. Just as we talked about in the previous chapter, the characters in *Blood Meridian* are surface ones. They are wanderers without exact names, even though some of them have, yet they are named either by the first or the last names comically. Some of the important figures, such as the Kid, the expriest, the judge, are named strangely, even without any origin. The reader is made to be as curious as the Kid, who always wonders what the "judge" judges. The text documents the Kid's journey from east to west, from Tennessee to California without any aim and purpose, yet he is always titled by "the Kid" from his appearance in the text at the age of 14 in 1848 until 1878, when he is an adult at the age of 45, his title just makes a simple change from "the Kid" to "the man." The Kid remains nameless, which not only suggests his lack of real identity to echo the book's general atmosphere of chaos, but also indicates the similarities of characters, "as if each could replace another without the reader's being aware of the endless iterations" (Slethaug 134).

The characterization of the Kid gives another instance for the text's iteration. Some critics compare the Kid with Huckleberry Finn or Ike McCaslin of Faulkner's *The Bear*, for they are young boys, and both the Kid and Huck are at 14. It seems that the Kid promises to develop in the adverse conditions for the book's evoking of the tradition of Bildunsroman in some literary forms, such as Western fiction, picaresque novel and road novel, yet his development is out of the reader's expectation. For Huck, his journey west represents escape and freedom; while for the Kid, his passage west falls into blood and violence. In effect, the Kid is simply a corrupted reversal of Huck Finn. In the introduction to the character, the Kid "can neither read not write and in him broods already a taste for mindless violence. All history present in that visage, the child the father of the man" (BM 3). Wordsworth's poem is taken to satirize the corruptions of history and its penchant for violence present in the young boy. The Kid is portrayed as violent and dangerous from birth, and his brutality makes his mother his first victim, for he "did incubate in her own bosom the creature who would carry her off" (BM 3). In the end of the text, he hardly makes any development, rather, in his manhood, he slays a fifteen-year-old young boy named by Elrod when they meet on the north Texas plains. For Ike, his encounter with the bear symbolizes his performance of the rite of adulthood, which makes him pay awe towards nature, and thus becoming mature; while for the Kid, his encounter with the bear twice in the text does not alter his clay-like heart, but responds with silence and indifference. The Kid does not get any peace from nature, or harvests any spiritual transcendence from nature as Ike does, but converges with the wilderness in their violence, brutality and hostility. Throughout the novel, the Kid does not make any transformation. Unlike those heroes in the Western or war novel, he rides an old mule without tail or hair initially, then takes over the horse from a dead man when he joins the Glanton's gang. To describe the "hero" as the Kid, McCarthy seems to counter the conventions of cowboys in the traditional Western fiction. Though the text follows his motion in the wilderness, in effect, he is not the protagonist of the novel, in which only episodes of bloody events iterate again and again in the omniscient narration.

As regards the Kid's development in the text, critics have different ideas. Sean

M. George asserts that the Kid is static, and "by the end of the novel, the Kid doesn't improve his station. ... His capacity for violence and his worldview and his station in life are not changed through his interaction with the judge" (114). Susan Kollin holds that the Kid takes part in all kinds of massacres willingly, and he becomes a man "as defiled and savage as the adult men" in the end (566). To kill willingly implies that he is an individual with agency, and his becoming as violent as those adults indicates his transformation. The present study tends to stand on the side of George. The Kid does not develop throughout the novel, though a series of events occur to him in his wilderness journey, for instance, he helps with pulling the arrow out of Brown's thigh, refuses to shoot dying Shelby, becomes a priest with the Bible, and even wears Brown's necklace of human ears, after the disappearance of the expriest and death of Brown. His acts appear to be compassionate or sympathetic or nostalgic with his peers, yet they could not demonstrate the awakening of human conscience in him. His refusal of taking chances to kill the judge may be understood as his want of choice or no choice at all, because the end is the same: death or violence. It is still doubtful and ambiguous whether he is tired of violence or regains human consciousness or regains his conscience in the end, and after all, McCarthy does not give his reader any sense of future for the west. Rather than a questing hero, the Kid is "never more than a sacrificial victim" (Pitts, 1998) of a chaotic and random universe. His inability of development pushes the Western, war novel and picaresque novel to new limits, and the iterative shaping of characters adds some new traits for these genres.

McCarthy has always been unforthcoming about his intentions in his writings, but has admitted that "all great writers read all other great writers" (Lincoln 9). In one of his rare interviews, he speaks, "The ugly fact is that books are made out of books. The novel depends for its life on the novels that have been written" (Woodward, "Venomous Fiction" 31). Indeed, in Blood Meridian, part of the iterative richness is its intertextuality, which could be presented in the figure of Judge Holden. He is both fictional version of a historical personage and an amalgamation of numerous archetypes from different literary writings.

Critics have taken pains to trace the origins of such a complicated and mysterious figure in literary tradition. Slethaug observes that the figure of Judge is the combination of different figures, such as Melville's Ahab "in his defiance in the face of the universe," or Milton's Satan, who challenges the authority of God with his fallen angels (137, 138). Kollin notes that McCarthy revisits the literary history of the American empire, with the character Judge "becoming a pastiche of imperial figures such as Joseph Conrad's Kurtz and Herman Melville's Ahab" (568). Chris Dacus argues that Judge is not a real person, for he seems little changed or none in almost thirty years, but rather is like Melville's white whale, which is "death, god, the devil, the unknown, light and darkness, i.e. the Whole within itself all contradictions and opposites" (10-1). Rick Wallach even reads Judge as the incarnation of Hindu deity Shiva, "who dances the dance of war and cosmic destruction" ("Judge Holden" 5). Neil Campbell compares Judge to Ulysses, because both seek the unknowable truth through danger, exploration, murder and mayhem ("Beyond" 55-64).

In effect, from the text, it might be argued that Judge is the icon of chaos, the turbulence in nature, for he is the whole of paradoxes, both God and Satan, both Apollo and Dionysus, both life and death, both history constructor and destroyer, both a gentleman and a fraud. He controls discursive power with knowledge, science and history and is capable of the creation of both order and disorder, and he is even an ideal frontiersman and a master of magical tricks. He is well "versed in all philosophy and multilingual, yet still naked, bestial, crouching, and sweating by the campfire" (Owens 62). In the novel, he submits to nothing. Any normative institutions from American or Mexican governments or Indian tribes, even weather, or time cannot limit or affect him. He is the only survivor of the chaotic world. In him, we could find "traces" of the archetypes of the west, yet Derrida's "différence" is produced through the text's intertextual allusions.

Judge's mystery is like the turbulence beyond resolution, which could be reflected from the Kid's dream:

A great shambling mutant, silent and serene. Whatever his antecedents he was something wholly other than their sum, not was there system by which to divide him back into his origins for he would not go. Whoever would seek out his history through what unraveling of loins and ledgerbooks must stand at last darkened and dumb at the shore of a void without terminus or origin and whatever science he might bring to bear upon the dusty primal matter blowing down out of the millennia will discover no trace of any ultimate atavistic egg by which to reckon his commencing. (BM 309-10)

Judge is grotesque. A great-sized albino, he looks "like something newly born" (BM 335). While, he is more an ultimate kid with "mindless violence" than an innocent child (BM 3). He tells the Kid, "what joins the man together ... is not sharing of bread but the sharing of enemies" (BM 307). As demonstrated in the second chapter of the present study, Judge is the epitome of warlord, who believes in Nietzsche's will-to-power, "if war is not holy, man is nothing but ancient clay" (BM 307). As a genius, he always appears to be an European gentleman, carrying an umbrella with him when walking in the desert, which is "made from rotted scrapes of hide stretched over a framework of rib bones bound with strips of tug" (BM 333), impressing the reader with revulsion due to its being morbid and grotesque. In spite of a gentleman, he is always naked in the text. In one episode, he is reported to be "naked atop the walls, immense and pale in the revelations of lightening, striding the perimeter up there and declining in the old epic mode" (BM 118), in the ruins of a mining village at the height of a lightening storm, which recalls Melville's Ahab standing on the deck of the Pequod in a lighting storm.

As desirous as Ahab in the ambition of dominating nature, he not only hopes to be "suzerain" of birds and animals, but also desecrates nature. One of the most horrible episodes for him to debase nature is his help with Glanton's gang to produce gunpowder to destroy the Indians in the desert with his mysterious power. Judge first tells the men "that our earth ... was round like an egg and contained all good things within her" (BM 131), with an aim to "disseminate" the idea that man is the supervisor of nature, then he instructs the men to produce gunpowder with charcoal, the niter from the bat crave, and sulfur from the mouth of volcano. Tobin recalls, "what we'd be required to bleed into it like freemasons but it was not so," and those scalp-hunters follow Judge to pour forth their own bodies in the form of urine instead of blood into the hole of the earth, "like the disciples of a new faith" (BM 130):

We were half mad anyways. All lined up. ... we hauled forth our members and at it we went and the judge on his knees kneadin the mass with his naked arms and the piss was splashin about and he was cryin out to us to piss, man, piss for your very souls for cant you see the redskins yonder, and laughin the while and workin up this great mass in a foul black dough, a devil's batter by the stink of it and him not a bloody dark pastryman himself ... . (BM 131-2)

The judge now educates his men to perform the "gang-raping" of the mother earth in a very horrific way, though they spew the piss instead of seamen. His wisdom and evil make him both God and Satan, both mad Yehweh and Lucifer.

As bloody and lusty as Conrad's Kurtz, Judge has transgressed over the boundaries of civilization with his darkness in mind. The text presents his raping and killing of young kids at least three times. In one small town destroyed by the Glanton gang, a Mexican girl is abducted. Though no mention is made of Judge, yet his handiwork is evident: "Parts of her clothes were found torn and bloodied under the north wall, over which she could be thrown. In the desert were drag marks. A shoe" (BM 239). Shortly, a Mexican girl chained to a post is discovered when Glanton rides into Yuma. Judge is reported to stand "on the rise in silhouettes against the evening sun like some great balden archimandrite. He [is] wrapped in a mantle of free-flowing cloth beneath which he [is] naked" (BM 273). Shortly after this incident, the Glanton gang are attacked by the Yumas, who find "the idiot and a girl of perhaps twelve years cowering naked in the floor. Behind them also naked [stands] the judge" (BM 275), when they break the door into his room. This aberrant pedophile never hides his crimes, roaming around naked much of the time after his action.

According to Briggs and Peat, in most of cultures, clowns, demons, or transfigures are taken as epitomes of chaos, for they are as sly as surviving foxes and usually good at witchcrafts (9). Indeed, as a master of magical tricks, Judge could fling gold coins away from him and have them return on their own. Besides, he loves playing games and the ritual of death. Finally he outlasts all his companies and even survives from time and weather. However, it should be noted that Ahab is finally destroyed by nature symbolized by white whale, and Kurtz ruined by his lust and spiritual darkness; whereas the judge still dances, escaping any punishment physically or metaphysically, which leaves enigma irresolvable through "baker's transformation" of the text, making the west and Western problematic.

Moreover, Judge is "obsessed with the logic that underpins expansion" (Kollin 568). He is not only a good story-teller to theorize the mission and simplify abstract ideas, but also a historian to chronicle the events with his ledger-book. As an embodiment of ration and order, Judge knows best the importance of textual authority. He always carries a ledger to record and sketch everything with details, and then destroys it ultimately. Neil Campbell asserts that the judge "is obsessed by a desire to control his own fate .... The judge keeps a ledger in which he rewrites what was into what could be and thereby wrests control of the past by authoring it" ("Beyond" 58-9). The rewriting of the past makes Judge not merely control his own fate, but also manipulate everyone and everything he meets. "Words are things," so to author the text is to dominate, to "disseminate" at his will, hence manipulating the fates of his own and others with discursive power. He has made successful trials in his charge against the preacher to set up his authority and accusation of the Kid's guilt to kill him with excuses. For him, since "Man's memories are uncertain and the past that was differs little from the past that was not" (BM 330), it is convenient to write (or speak) freely after destroying the original text, which could claim his authority textually. In some sense, his ledger plays the role of history, which is constructed by the winners, and via his ledger, the judge transforms himself to be a myth-maker.

The historical writing or myth-making is selective, and Judge's ledger-book just contains what he hopes to pass down to the posterity. Near the town of El Paso, the American gang discovers lots of paintings and etchings of Indian tribes about men, animals and their chase in the rocks. Judge is busy with copying out "those certain ones into his book," and among these paintings, he traces out the very ones he requires with assurance. After that, "he [rises] and with a piece of broken chert he scapple[s] away one of the designs, leaving no trace of it only a raw place on the stone where it had been" (BM 173). Here the judge only chooses what he needs, and retains what he records, then his ledger becomes the only authoritative. His doings give evidence of history as merely revisable texts having been selected and erased, which is the logic and strategy taken by colonialists usually. With "books" (before it is the Bible, at present it is history) in one hand, he holds the gun in the other. In the text, the judge is indeed ambidextrous. Both writings and gunfire are successful tools to deracinate other peoples for Anglo-American colonialists in historical and cultural records. James J. Donohue compares the judge's "textual enterprise" with that of American frontier mythology, and he suggests that "the narratives that the frontier has left out ... are not ignored by accident, but by design" (280). Donohue's ideas echo in the Judge's statement, "it was his intention to expunge them [his notes and sketches] from the memory of men" (BM 140).

Writing produces counter-memory, which is an act of war by itself. If we take the judge as a myth-maker, and consider his process of writing (myth-making) analogous with that of frontier narratives, then the novel's implied doubts of ideology working in the conventions of the Western is apparent. As a master of story-teller, Judge justifies all his actions:

A man seeks his own destiny and no other, said the judge. Will or nill. Any man who could discover his own fate and elect therefore some opposite course could only come at last to that self-same reckoning at the same appointed time, for each man's destiny is as large as the world he inhabits and contains within it all opposites as well. This desert upon which so many have been broken is vast and calls for largeness of heart but it is also empty. It is hard, it is barren. Its very nature is stone. (BM 330)

Judge's words hardly reflect his personality. Just as Dana Phillips notes, "the speech of McCarthy's protagonists is no longer, then, an index of characterological or personal traits, ... but simply a historical and literary artifact" (449), for this grotesque figure, it is language that speaks him, rather than he speaks language. Although his justification sounds Emersonian, it has been consumed by his evil. His demon-like nature is detected by the expriest, who claims that he has seen his "little cloven hoof-prints in the stone" (BM 131).

In his essay, "The West as Utopia and Myth," Gerald D. Nash points out the multiple roles of the West played in America throughout its history, and the West has been interpreted differently by different generations. Nash quotes the words of Western historian Earl Pomeroy to prove that the discovery of the West depends on the cultural baggage of the beholder, and at present, the West is still a mirror for contemporary Americans to provide a reflection of how they would like to see themselves (69-75). So, to search for the West is to define oneself, McCarthy knows it better. His westering after his final Appalachian fiction, Suttree, corresponds with writings since the 1960s, which tends to revisit and reflect the west as myth, such as E. L. Doctorow's *Welcome to Hard Times* (1996), John Barth's *The Sot-Weed Factor* (1987) and Thomas Pynchon's *Mason & Dixon* (1997). McCarthy speaks to Woodward, ""there isn't a place in the world you can go where they don't know about cowboys and Indians and the myth of the West" (Woodward, "Venomous Fiction" 31). Therefore, by means of stretching and folding of archetypes of the West to present his figures, McCarthy attempts to reveal the worst sides of these characters, and thus defining his time. Likewise, in the iterative shaping of the genre of his fiction, McCarthy constructs the complexity of his novel, making it unique with aesthetic characteristics of being strange and familiar.

Land, Language and "Chaos Sandwich"

In the process of iteration, some incremental information will be added, which is as Hayles remarks, "The iterative procedure produces the undecidables that radically destabilize meaning" (*Chaos Bound* 182). The text's iterative technique not only creates the effect of being strange and familiar, subverting the conventions of traditional Western and meanwhile exposing the weak points of literary forms that the text parodies, but also produces the aesthetic characteristic of "the chaos sandwich," which is shown in the novel's chapter headings, land descriptions and language style.

The novel is set in the 19th century, and thus the structure of the nineteenth-century fiction is taken to convey a sense of antique manner, which reflects through the novel's chapter headings. The chapters are marked with Roman numerals, and at the head of each chapter, a list of topics are included in sequence, which invokes the practice of common nineteenth-century fiction in its "providing a synopsis of events at the head of the chapter" (Slethaug 134). However, just as we mentioned before, McCarthy's text presents the iteration of similar episodes, so in spite of the sequence of events arranged in the heading of each chapter, they "tend to flatten them, making each entry, whatever its degree of significance, equal to the rest" (ibid). Similar to John Barth's parody of the structure of the eighteenth-century fiction Tom Jones in *The Sot-Weed Factor* with the aim to refashion his own, McCarthy recalls signature chapter headings in the nineteenth-century fiction for the purpose to ridicule its inflated views about order. Through the obvious iteration of that used in the 19th century fiction, he reinvents the past without privileging it.

Land is one of the important elements for Western fiction. In *Blood Meridian*, land speaks for itself, even acts for itself. Just as we discussed in the previous chapter,the fiction's vast wilderness in the West is in "optical democracy," and it is as violent and bloody as those heroes wandering in it, evoking the world as chaos, nothing different for nature and culture. However, the text's iteration of the landscape's bleakness and darkness may produce the sense of "chaos sandwich," which appeals to beauty and sublime of the West in most of romanticized Westerns, and meanwhile pays emphasis on the order and beauty in the midst of chaos. One of the typical passages gives evidence:

They rode on into the mountains and their way took them through high pine forests, wind in the trees, lonely birdcalls. The shoeless mules slaloming through the dry grass and pine needles. In the blue coulees on the north slopes narrow tailings of old snow. They rode up switchbacks through a lonely aspen wood where the fallen leaves lay like golden disclets in the damp black trail. The leaves shifted in a million spangles down the pale corridors and Glanton took one and turned it like a tiny fan by its stem and held it and let it fall and its perfection was not lost on him. They rode through a narrow draw where the leaves were shingled up in ice and they crossed a high saddle at sunset where wild doves were rocketing down the wind and passing through the gap a few feet off the ground, veering wildly among the ponies and dropping off down into the blue gulf below. (BM 136-7)

Such a peace of the natural scene is abruptly disturbed by a "lean blond bear" out of the dark forest, who attacks the men and catches one of the Delawares and then disappears into the dark trees with "his hostage" (ibid). Similar instance in the text also foregrounds the "chaos sandwich" of nature:

The jagged mountains were pure blue in the dawn and everywhere birds twittered and the sun when it rose caught the moon in the west so that they lay opposed to each other across the earth, the sun white-hot and the moon a pale replica, as if they were the ends of a common bore beyond whose terminals burned worlds past all reckoning. (BM 86)

The beauty and quietness of landscape are terminated by the antagonism between the sun and the moon, whose opposition changes the kindness of natural scene into hostility. It seems that nature is of chaos, full of paradoxes of order and disorder.

The fiction's language is "highly wrought," or "gorgeous" (Moran 37; Shaviro 143). Apparently, it conveys a sense of iteration. For illustration, we need go no further than the novel's opening paragraph: "See the child. He is pale and <u>thin</u>, he wears a <u>thin</u> and ragged linen shirt he stokes the scullery fire. Outside lie dark turned fields with rags of snow and darker woods beyond that harbor yet a few last wolves" (my emphasis, BM 3).[1] The passage is remarkable with its lyrical rhythms, which is made by the repetition subtly of "thin," and "ragged," and "dark," and less subtly of "he" (the child). In the second sentence, the word, "thin" is repeated to deliver the situation of the child, being pale and thin, then new information is added to make his situation much

---

[1] To mark the words in italics or with different kinds of underlines is to demonstrate the iteration of words or phrases in one sentence or the whole passage, creating the specific style of language via the iteration.

clear, "a thin and ragged linen shirt" wearing on him. In the third one, the word "dark" is taken to describe the fields turned dark by the dusk, then "darker" is taken to improve its original extent, yet it has referred to something concrete, "the woods." Besides, unconventional punctuation disturbs the simplicity of sentences, quickening the reader's eye faster than ever across the words. The iterative technique makes the passage as faintly odd as quietly beautiful.

The other instance witnesses the effect of iteration of language: "they rode for days through the rain and they rode through rain and hail and rain again" (my emphasis, BM 186). The repetition of the word "rain" gets some incremental information: "rain and hail and rain again," and the repetition of similar sentence structure in one simple sentence creates the atmosphere of dullness for the weather and filibusters' marching. Another instance stands out in the text. The recursion of a one-sentence "they went on" with its variation, e.g. "he went on," "they rode on," in the whole text turns out to be McCarthy's signature writing (BM 11, 22, 44). Based on Schopen's statistical analysis, from Chapter seven to Chapter nineteen, such a sentence occurs nearly forty times, and in the final four chapters, more than a dozen (Schopen, 1995). Although none of these is of particular dramatic or thematic significance, this pattern of the iteration of a one-sentence or phrase connects the separated episodes into a whole in the narrative.

In the novel, the mixture of laconic style of Western fiction with profound philosophical meditations is frequent in the dialogue of characters, which makes the fiction strange and familiar. The dialogue of characters in the novel evokes the tradition of the Western. For instance, when the kid meets a hermit who treats him with board and lodging and in the hermit's conversation with the kid, cliche topics of the traditional Western are repeated again, "they is [sic] four things that can destroy the earth, he said. Women, whiskey, money, and niggers" (BM 18), which recalls the dialogue of Rawlins with John Grady in *All the Pretty horses* during their journey to Mexico: "A goodlookin [sic] horse is like a goodlookin [sic] woman. ... They're more trouble than what they're worth. What a man needs is just one that will get the job done" (Horses 89). However, just as Slethaug observes that in *Blood Meridian*, "the frontiersman do not restrict themselves to observations about the weather, the law, bandits, Indians, and other such topics of Western dialogue" (142), but expand their topics to much more profound philosophical observations on humanity, life, religion and cosmos, which is obviously evidenced from the rhetorical Judge. Likewise, for a ragged hermit in the desert, he also has his deep theological meditations ignored in the traditional Western: "The way of the transgressor is hard. God made this world, but he didn't make it to suit everybody, did he? ... it ain't the heart of a creature that is bound in the way that God has set for it. You can find meanness in the least of creatures, but when God made man the devil was at his elbow" (BM 19).

Moreover, the mixture of the minimalist style with the complicated, ambiguous sentence structure in the prose also makes the novel deviate from the traditional Western, creating the effect of the "chaos sandwich." Still take the passage at the very beginning of the novel as an instance:

See the child. ... His folk are known for hewers of wood and drawers of water but in truth his father has been a schoolmaster. He lies in drink, he quotes from poets whose names are now lost. The boy crouches by the fire and watches him.

Night of your birth. Thirty-three. The Leonids they were called. God how the stars did fall. I looked for blackness, holes in the heavens. The Dipper stove.

The mother died these fourteen years did incubate in her own bosom the creature who could carry her off. The father never speaks her name, the child does not know it. He has a sister in this world that he will not see again. He watches, pale and unwashed. He can neither read nor write and in him broods already a taste for mindless violence. All history presents in that visage, the child the father of the man. (BM 3)

Obviously, this is not the familiar rhetoric of the popular Western, but is aesthetically poetic. In it, "see the child" echoes the Biblical phrase, "Ecce Homo," or "Ecce Puer" (Isaiah 41:1), and the Biblical idiom of "hewers of wood and drawers of waters" shifts the register of discourse. In the penultimate sentence in the first quoted paragraph, the reference of "he" is ambiguous. The tone of the passage is also wicked, corresponding with the wicked visage of the character the Kid, who seems to wait for something wicked to happen. Besides, the sentence of telling the age of the Kid "is not linear but circuitous and circumambulatory" (Slethaug 143), which is complicated by its strange comparison of the Kid's birth with meteor showers and even allusions to such astronomical phenomena as black holes. Meteor showers are described in the imagery of classical astronomy, such as the Leonids and the Dipper, which creates "a further gap between the rhetoric of popular fiction and this poetic iteration" (ibid).

Oblique reference to astronomic phenomena happens in another time, when the Kid's dying from the embrace of the judge in the outhouse: "Stars were falling across the sky myriad and random, speeding along brief vectors form their origins in night to their destinies in dust and nothingness" (BM 333). It is known that the Leonids and the Dipper are not fixed and stable heavenly bodies, but flux ones. McCarthy links the birth and death of one ordinary people with changes of heavenly bodies, making people share with the chaos of the natural world on the one hand, and on the other hand, giving the sense of randomness and unpredictability of life, foregrounding the inherent chaos of the novel.

Simplicity and complexity are never stable, and complexity is usually produced by simplicity, as the chaos implies. As an important principle of chaos theory, iteration makes use of the information from the feed-back loop to make its "baker's transformation" by infinite times, and then complicated patterns can be produced in the phase space of a chaotic system. Likewise, in the narrative, iterative shaping with conventions not only magnifies their latent uncertainties but also creates something new, producing the effect of "chaos sandwich," strange from and familiar with its original ones. By means of iteration, McCarthy could go in and out of the conventions of the Western literature freely, and expose the "symptom" of the West as utopia and myth, hence the accomplishment of his complicit critique of the traditional Western. In *Blood Meridian*, through his iterative shaping of genre, characters, language and land, McCarthy not only goes beyond the constraints of the traditional Western, but also constructs his specific generic features in the postmodern Western novel, presenting the actuality of chaos inherent in his living society and age. Likewise, by means of his "baker's transformation," he blurs the boundary lines of genres and creates his complex and dynamic "chaos sandwich" in the fiction. This might be the reason that Harold Bloom takes *Blood Meridian* as one of the classical works in contemporary American literature, for "it is the ultimate Western, not to be surpassed" (532).

II. Indeterminacy in *The Road*

Just as the alternate changes of simplicity and complexity indicate, nothing in our living cosmos is determinate and eternal. "Simple systems give rise to complex behavior. Complex systems give rise to simple behavior. And most important, the laws of complexity hold universally" (Gleick 304). Yin and yang, order and disorder, being and non-being, good and evil, culture and wilderness, all can be changed alternatively, if some of variables are altered in one dynamic system. In effect, in our living world, indeterminacy is the constant, while the determinacy is a rarity. In one word, everything in the cosmos lives on the edge of chaos.

McCarthy's fascination with the world in chaos once again presents in his Pulitzer-winning tenth novel. *The Road* (2006) is about a pair of nameless father and son journeying towards the South with their shopping cart to seek warmth to survive from the forth-coming winter in a post-apocalyptic wasteland. Comparing with the dark and bloody world in *Blood Meridian*, the world depicted in *The Road* is much bleaker, even in the sense of returning to its primitive state, chaos: everything has been destroyed, whatever; no plants, no animals, only a solitary dog wandering in the desolate street; all the traces of human civilization have been erased from the earth, save that ash and dust are everywhere from the sky to the ground, from the city to the farm, from the inner land to the sea coast. In this "cauterized terrain" (Road 14), "the dead outnumber the living in a shocking proportion and of those few living humans, most are barely humans at all" (Kunsa 57), for they have been corrupted and degraded to cannibalism. All in all, in such a "barren, silent, and godless" (Road 4) chaotic world, certainty has been ended, and everything is probable and indeterminate.

According to complexity theory (the later development of chaos theory), when the system enters into the chaos, the edge of chaos is rather complex, in which all the variables interact with each other, and order may emerge from disorder and then a self-organization system will be made automatically. Different from the close system depicted by the second law of thermodynamics, in which the entropy state of the motion of matters is determinate, while in a far-from-equilibrium open system, the motion of matters is much more complex, in which the alternation between order and disorder is uncertain, which depends on chance. The social system is analogous to a far-from-equilibrium open system, which decides on its universality of changes. Actually, McCarthy posits the wasteland journey of his protagonists on the edge of chaos. Living on the edge of chaos is doomed to be indeterminate and chancy.

As one of the important principles of chaos theory, indeterminacy is not merely presented at the thematic level of the fiction, but also displayed on the fiction's textual plane, which evokes the indeterminacy of his fiction's producing contexts. This section aims to examine the indeterminacy in McCarthy's experimental novel, *The Road*, hopefully understanding the complexity of McCarthy's textual world, and meanwhile knowing better how his narrative strategies as chaos demonstrate the complexity of human and natural world.

i. Indeterminacy and Postmodern Science

Before the exploration of the indeterminacy in the fiction, it is of necessity to have a brief review of the development of indeterminacy principle in the postmodern science and the humanities as well as social sciences with the aim to facilitate my discussion of McCarthy's narrative strategy as chaos in *The Road*.

Chaos theory is the destruction of scientific discourses since the 17th century with its key principle of indeterminacy and is a kind of postmodern science by itself. Postmodern science as a term is coined by Jean-Francois Lyotard, who gives a description of the characteristics of postmodern science that "the continuous differentiable function is losing its preeminence as a paradigm of knowledge and prediction" (60). Postmodern science "is producing not the known, but unknown. And it suggests a model of legitimation that has nothing to do with maximized performance, but has as its basis difference understood as paralogy" (ibid). According to Lyotard, thermodynamics, quantum mechanics, and atomic physics belong to postmodern science, and he even canonizes René Thom[①] and Benoit Mandelbrot as practitioners of postmodern science. Perhaps Lyotard did not know chaos theory at that time, after all, his book, *The Postmodern Condition*, was written in 1979, when chaos theory was not popular, but he mentioned Mandelbrot's fractal geometry by "fracta" (60). As the icon of the chaotic process in the nonlinear dynamic system, Mandelbrot's fractals not only present us with the irregularities of the world as frequency, but also "seem so aptly to sum up the endless fragmentations of postmodernity, with mathematics now dumping the strategy of approximating the ideal and unchanging forms of a Euclidean world with a geometry of endless change and differentiation" (Grant 70-1). Besides, Mandelbrot's measuring of British coastline concludes that the length of coastline is scale-dependent, which gives an overwhelming evidence that the world we live in is now uncertain and thus demonstrably postmodern.

The world as indeterminacy has been evidenced in quantum mechanics from the microscopic perspective. Heisenberg's Uncertain Principle in 1927 reminds us that there are greatly differences between physical world and the ideal world constructed from people's daily experience, because the exact position and velocity of a quantum particle could never be measured simultaneously. Niels Bohr's Principle of Complementarity proposed in 1927 gives insights to Heisenberg's Uncertain Principle. For Bohr, the elementary matter in fact behaves both as particles and waves, and then the paralogy in some phenomena could be heuristically viewed under the aspect of complementarity. In fact, the uncanny and unpredictable nature of sub-atomic reactions could be illustrated through the Taoist principle of *yin* and *yang*, the complementary nature of opposites. Just as Rice asserts, Bohr's concept of wave-particle duality makes contribution to "contemporary culture: at the subatomic level the very act of observation, by the means available to us, will affect the nature of what we observe" (151). Rice's idea echoes Ihab Hassan, who mentions the influence of new physics in *The Postmodern Turn*: causality and objectivity have been proved to be dubious and of a fiction transposed from classical concepts (58). Although limited to sub-atomic behavior, quantum

---

① René Thom (1923-2002), a French mathematician, is the founder of catastrophe theory, one of the origins for chaos theory.

mechanics rests its view of universe on the uncertainties of chance probabilities, which is fundamentally contrary to Einsteinian Special and General Relativity basing on the deterministic vision of the cosmos.

Chaos theory's development demonstrates the indeterminacy of universe once again from the macroscopic perspective, which has not been explored by quantum mechanics. Chaos theory emerges "from the experimental observation of unpredictable behavior in deterministic phenomena, deeply embedded order creating chaos," and its synthesis of determinacy and chance gives a much more perfect interpretation of the universe than that of quantum mechanics, which arises from "the hypothesis that deeply embedded uncertainty produces the apparent order of things" (Rice 92). For chaos theory, God indeed plays dice,[①] and in the alternate flux between order and disorder in the dynamic system in nature, stochastic probability plays a crucial role. The motion of dynamic systems depends on its initial conditions sensitively, highlighting "the importance of stochastic events at every level, from the molecular to the global" (Hayles, *Chaos and Order* 12). Chaos theory understands the world as the paradox of deterministic unpredictability, destroying totally the myth of the Laplace's "demon": the universe follows a regular pattern, and its final state could be determined and predicted if the initial state is given.

Moreover, the irreversibility of cosmos demonstrates the indeterminacy of universe from the cosmological perspective, challenging against determinism, mechanism and reductionism of classical science. Such an idea is first introduced by the concept of entropy associated with the second law of thermodynamics, describing the gradual leveling of energy in the universe, the irreversible tendency of a thermodynamic system to move from a state of molecular organization capable of producing work to a state of random, disorganized, uniform molecular movement. Developing studies of irreversibility of cosmos in the close system with equilibrium, the new scientific theories of chaos and complexity demonstrate the irreversibility of time as arrows in a far-from-equilibrium open system. For theories of chaos and complexity, the evolution

---

① The sentence that "God does not play dice" is Einstein's famous rejection of the probabilistic Copenhagen Interpretation of quantum theory.

of cosmos is not as reversible as that understood by classical physics, which likens the universe to a mechanical operation, hence easily plotting "the movements of planets, like billiard games, whether they move forward or backward, here or there, now or a million years from now" (Kuberski 30).

Scientific studies provide us with a new image of nature, which is not a determinate or simple submissive system to subdue at our will and control, instead it will make sensitive responses when confronting with us. Just as Prigogine asserts that the new statement from the new laws of nature is based on probability (*End of Certainty* 23). The "postmodern turn" of natural science is consistent with that of the humanities and social sciences. In the 20th century, the "linguistic turn" of philosophy from the epistemological ration-orientation to language-orientation brings about the recognition of the world as a web of floating signs. According to Saussure, words are signs. Language as a sign system is not a symbol equivalent to objects in the reality; likewise, language is not the reflection of world and experiences. Saussure's separation of the sign from the referent demonstrates that the relations of the signifier as the sound image of word and the signified as the designation of word are arbitrary, meaning that the significance of language depends on differences between language elements. Saussurean linguistics subverts the traditional vision of language as reflection of the world, and hence challenging against the deterministic world portrayed by Newtonian mechanics.

Saussurean linguistics has been developed and appropriated by post-structuralists to "support the deconstructive view that all utterance is ungrounded and indeterminate" (Hayles, *Chaos Bound* 268). For post-structuralists, language is a web without any order, in which lots of clues are interacted and tangled with each other, and nothing orderly could be distinguished. According to Derrida, "writing is not merely written marks but any signifying practice that endures through time and functions to divide the world into the self and other" (Hayles, *Chaos Bound* 178). Inspired from Freudian idea of the psyche as a writing pad, in which the earliest experiences of childhood are like the marks on the sheet, disappearing with the child's growing up, but traces in the wax, Derrida assumes that writings cannot be excluded from the traces within the psyche besides those marks on the page. The Derridean trace remains inaccessible to direct verbalization, for it resides "at a deeper level than words can reach. It is 'always already' present, the elusive and ineffable difference from which all subsequent inscription derives" (Hayles, *Chaos Bound* 179). In this sense, Derrida "opens writing to radical indeterminacy" (ibid). Moreover, for Derrida, the "always already" formula indicates that there is no origin, because the significance not only "differs" but also "defers." Derrida's neologism of "différance" indicates that it is an illusion to find out the origin, because all the signification has been submerged into the chain of signifiers, no matter how far we go back, we never come upon the original difference. Since "there is nothing outside the text," the world will be textual and fictional, hence determinism receding from the flux of language.

Philosophers also cast doubts on the functions of language, from which the determinacy of world gets questioned. Wittgenstein's thesis of language as game emphasizes on the multiple functions of language and also language's versatility. By language-game, Wittgenstein means that language is analogous to game or language is produced by means of game, thus shifting the determinacy of language's significance to something indeterminate. Since the significance of language itself is not stable but relational and changeable, then it is problematic for the function of language to present or represent the reality of the world and its relation with the reality needs questioning, too. Language is no longer a devoting mirror to reflect the world, and the shift of language from the image of world to the game leads to the fact that language no longer represents the world; instead, language decides on and shapes the reality. Heidegger speaks right, "where word breaks off, no thing may be" (Grant 65). As a social currency of thought with great influence on contemporary society, culture and arts, postmodernism arising in the 1960s challenges all the metanarratives in the traditional society with its radical attitudes of denial and doubts and even announces that indeterminacy is its essence, hence dismantling all the constructions and order in the real life and all the power discourses in the West.

To sum up, indeterminacy features contemporary science, culture, arts and society. Just as Hassan puts it, indetermanence (indeterminacy immanence) goes through the whole postmodern society and has powerful capacity of deconstruction, moving "a vast will to unmaking, affecting the body politic, the body cognitive, the erotic body, the individual psyche-the entire realm of discourse" (92). Hassan writes, "As in scientific so in cultural thought, indeterminacy fills the space between the will to unmaking (dispersal, deconstruction, discontinuity, etc.) and its opposite, the integrative will," and indeterminacy is "neither a fashionable nor a factitious term but rather a decisive element in the new order of our knowledge" (65, 71).

The following part is to analyze the indeterminacy throughout the narrative text of McCarthy's latest novel, *The Road*, presented in both the thematic and textual level.

ii. Indeterminacy and Edge of Chaos

Different from that of *Blood Meridian*, in which good and evil fuse together, the chaotic world of *The Road* presents the intense struggle of good with evil, and the criteria to distinguish them have gone to the foundational core of human civilization, cannibalism or not. Struggling on the edge of chaos, the nameless father attempts to constitute a self-organization system with his son. To identify with "good guys" rather than "bad guys" (cannibals) is the first step to constitute a self-organization system in the chaotic world. Next, some other strategies are taken to strengthen their self-organization system: first, frontier Southward to survive from coldness; second, memories, stories and rituals taken to shape the reality, hence internalizing the son's belief to "carry the fire" even meeting with starving, freezing, and threatening at every turn on the road; third, remember to "talk to me," to build up the dialogic relationship; fourth, emotional forces, such as love, courage and sacrifice, to encourage his son to go on with the "fire"; finally, chance. On the edge of chaos, chance decides on the stability of the self-organization system through its affect on the alternate flux of order and disorder. In the novel, each literal encounter with live humans (nine times in total) for the father and son poses a direct challenge to their self-organization system. Furthermore, the father has had a fantasy that his son may be blessed with chance and then "goodness will find the little boy" (Road 281).

In *The Road*, McCarthy once again falls in the traditional geocentric concern of much of American literature in the postmodern phase, in which "space is, and always has been, of paramount importance to American imagination" (Walsh 49). Contrary to McCarthy's previous novels, in which all the protagonists go westering with an attempt to deal with their difficulties in the reality, *The Road* makes both the father and son journey through an ash-laden and savage wilderness toward their "Southern frontier," hoping to accomplish their dream of survival from the holocaust in a post-apocalyptic world. For the characters in the fiction, the South,[①] rather than the West, is what they are eager to access. The South is not only taken as "the physical frontier and goal, but also as an imaginative refuge" (Walsh 53) for both the father and son to shelter from the coldness of the winter in the following days. The climate in the South is their major concern, which is thought to be warmer and better for survival, and there some kind of life may be found to prevail. As we mentioned in the study's introduction, chaos theory is analogous to *The Book of Changes*, particularly their mapping of matter's motion with the "image" (Xiang in Chinese). The South presents itself as the image of the trigram Li (Fire), which indicates fire, sun, warmth, brightness, civilization, beauty. Coincidentally, in the father's narrative, the South has been counted as an utopia in a post-apocalyptic world, which is close to the implication of the trigram Li.

As an important strategy to construct their self-organization system, the father's stories always present the South to be an ideal place. The son also longs to be told about the South from the very beginning of the story and in the later stage, he even develops his own fantasies about "how things would be in the South" (Road 54). Besides stories, the father's memories are also important to strengthen their hope in the South. "Man's memories are uncertain, and the past that was differs little from the past that was not" (BM 330), the judge's words echo the father's practice on the edge of chaos. To a certain extent, the father is similar to the judge, for both are aware of language's importance in its shaping of the reality. In the novel, memories of the father are usually colored with "a flowing wood where birds flew ... over the blue sky" or sitting with his lover in the cinema, which is opposite to the grayness of the world plagued with the ash and dust

---

① The present study takes the South in capital letter to make emphasis of its relevance with the West when associated with the frontier, or frontier spirit, and the rest are in lowercase letter.

or "mummied dead everywhere (Road 18, 24). In his childhood memory, the South is a pristine, pastoral and civilized place, which can be a redemptive place for both him and his son to escape from the disaster and suffering in a post-apocalyptic wasteland. Recalling a day spent picking up the firewood with his uncle in a lake near his uncle's farm, the father remembers that "This was the perfect day of his childhood. This was the day to shape the days upon" (Road 13).

In the post-apocalyptic world, narrative is the only left for the father to construct a self-organization system, even though it is questioned by the son in the later stage of their journey, for in the stories there are always good and helpful people, while in the reality, savages or cannibals are encountered everywhere. Likewise, in the memories, all are beautiful and colorful, while in the reality, there abound "vestiges of written and spoken words whose references no longer exist" (Woodson, "Mapping" 92), and the state of the language is described as "the sacred idiom shorn of its referents and so of its reality" (Road 89). Besides, the landscape for both the father and son to traverse is no longer "some pastoral sanctuary, nor is it one of the 'gardens of the world'; rather, it is a bleak, lifeless and threatening post-apocalyptic horror-scape" (Walsh 52). When they arrive at the seacoast of their dreamy South after plenty of hardship borne by them, what they see and sense is as cold, desolate and chaotic as "the horror-scape" witnessed in their trek across the country: deserted boats and dead bodies of humans and non-humans floating in the gray and silent sea, no fish, no gulls, no shorebirds, no sustenance, no hope anymore. In the sea there drifts a Spanish sailing vessel about a hundred feet offshore, in which nothing associated with hope and sustenance could be found, only death and emptiness stay there. The shore has become "one vast salt sepulcher. Senseless. Senseless" (Road 222). More terribly, the father is dying with sickness when they get to the South. The South is imagined as an ideal place to survive from the winter, yet all are out of their expectation, which demonstrates that the world is deterministically unpredictable. Besides, the iteration of hardship or disasters or despair experienced in their journey adds uncertainties for their self-organization system. Likewise, the imbalance between the ideal and the reality causes their self-organization system to be unstable.

Rather than hope, freedom and happiness indicated in the myth of frontier, the South as new frontier turns out to be as bleak and blank as some other places in the chaotic world, which makes the work significant culturally. Similar to what he does in *Blood Meridian*, McCarty makes the frontier myth problematic in *The Road*, too. In his presentation of the frontier (the West or South) as utopia, he also discloses its essence as dystopia, hence exposing the blankness and fictionality of the frontier myth in American society and culture.

Postmodern novel tend to depict the world in indeterminacy, McCarthy is no exception. However, different from his contemporaries, who believe in the exhaustion of literature and thus take language games to create the indeterminacy, McCarthy still believes in language. As a good story-teller, in *The Road*, the father even takes language to its sacred extent, though he lacks the syntactic elegance of the judge in *Blood Meridian*. Besides making use of narrative to construct the South as utopia, he also takes heroic stories to encourage his son to believe in "goodness" and "fire" in their hearts so that he will not give up, even though tortures and sufferings are constant in their hard life. For the father, he even falls back on the heroic stoicism to cultivate his son, as we may see from his imploring his son to keep trying, for "this is what the good guys do. They keep trying. They don't give up," and his practice of being a stoic hero in his keeping on "getting up" for each morning (Road 137, 272). The sentence, "we are carrying the fire," appears frequently in their dialogue, and in the father's stories, heroes with the fire are told always. In the novel, "fire" and "light" are synonymous, symbolizing civilization or culture. So the father considers his son as a messianic or Promethean figure or Jesus Christ to sacrifice himself or to keep on his duty for the purpose of passing on "the fire" to the future, which can be evidenced from the text. Just before the father's death, the son brings the water to his father, and in the father's obscure vision, "there was light all about [the son]," and "when [the son] moved, the light moved with him" (Road 277). In the first stage of their journey, the father teaches his son to learn how to shoot and even preserves the last bullet for his son in order not to make his son the victim of cannibals. While, with the development of the father's stories, his desire of the protection of his son to continue with living in the post-apocalyptic world has become much stronger, and he even shifts his wish from realistic requirement to spiritual pursuit. With the changes of his wish, the fire even develops to signify "vitality that burns within the ardent heart, the mystery that is the spark of life itself" (Cant, *Cormac McCarthy* 270-1). Before departing from the world, he imparts his last instructions to the boy by telling his young son to keep the fire with him all the time. The boy questions the father, "Is it real? The fire?." The father's answer is decisive: "Yes it is. ... It's inside you. It was always there. I can see it" (Road 279). Fire and light become synonymous with goodness in the novel finally. *The Road* does present the power of language to create the reality, yet on the other hand, McCarthy often obscures it.

The father knows the problematic nature of language, and in his mind, he is aware of what he does every day is "a lie," and those things he makes up are "not true either and the telling [makes] him feel bad" (Road 238, 54). In the end, the father does not believe in the worth of stories or his own efficacy as a story-teller, which could be revealed from the the father's interior. For example, when the son asks what will happen to them, the father answers the boy, "you'll be right," but the following narrative sentence undercuts that verbal assurance: "He was terrified" (Road 208). In the father's memories, all lose its original meanings, for "all that was left was the feeling of it" in the fiction's direct revealment of the father's inner mind (Road 154). For the boy, he has abandoned his studies, and even feels tired to listen to stories. When the father asks him to tell him a story, the boy refuses by saying that all of the man's stories are happy in the endings, while in reality he does not know any stories with happy endings. In their passage towards the South, they encounter a library, where all the volumes are soggy and useless on the floor. Once language becomes obscure and blank, its references are problematic, too. Of course, the self-organization system strengthened by the father's stories may become unstable and indeterminate.

McCarthy's novels are usually acknowledged by most critics to be nihilistic or pessimistic, while his tenth novel tends to be greatly different. In *The Road*, we may sense hope and good vaguely appearing in the human world, even though everything has been broken up and hardship has become the constant in the chaotic world. Just as

Lydia R. Cooper assumes, "'goodness may have all the concrete substance of gossamer but its role in this post-apocalyptic universe is foregrounded in a way that is perhaps unique in McCarthy's corpus" (157), in *The Road*, McCarthy explores the meaning of man's existence in an extreme situation. The vision of Peter L. Berger, a known contemporary American sociologist of religion, gives us insights in his book, *The Sacred Canopy* (1991). Berger asserts that a man has different identities in life, such as father, husband, teacher and citizen, which depends on its dialogic relations with child, wife, student and state respectively. It is in these dialogic relations with others that one may be identified, which may make his world true to him, hence the significance of existence. While one's significance of existence has to be kept in the world's order, which is produced through certain principles and values abode by each individual in it. Once the order is disrupted, his dialogic relations with others may be disrupted, too. Human world is usually weak and unstable, and its order may encounter disruption due to the break-up of man's dialogic relations when some chancy events occur, such as the death of the person in question, or the family disruption, or disease, or disaster, or crime, and so on (Berger 22-5). All of these extreme situations are considered as "margin situation" by existentialists. Once in the "margin situation," man's dialogic relations with others will fall apart, which may make him feel desperate, anxious and meaningless to live in the world, and cast doubts over and negation of previous laws, principles and values, hence the loss of the significance of existence (Berger 53).

Berger's vision about man's state in the "margin situation" is analogous to that of man on the edge of chaos in *The Road*. When the world is destroyed suddenly without the nameless reason and all turn out to be indeterminate in the chaos cosmos, the wife fears to be caught, raped, and eaten by cannibals so that she commits suicide with an attempt to end the perplexity of existence. Different from her, the father chooses to persist in, though he knows better the loneliness, pains, anxiety and horror when encountering the rupture with the pre-apocalyptic world. In order to achieve his self-identification, he not only insists on reminding his son of the responsibility for "carrying the fire" as a good guy, but also passes on such a belief to his young son through his stories and memories. Just as Thomas H. Schaub asserts that the father's repeated version that "we are carrying the fire" is "a strategy rather than a belief, a recourse to religious language and forms in the absence of any foundation for them in the world" (161). When passage South and language turn out to be fantasy and blank signifiers, another strategy is taken to continue with their self-organization system. Before his death, the father does not forget to tell his son to remember to "talk to me" (Road 279). Here, the "me" may be the father, for the father always reminds his son of "each the other's world entire" even after his death (Road 6), and of the goodness (fire) inside himself; or the "me" may be God, for to talk to God means to keep on with one's belief. Not all the postmodernist novels talk about something secular, and transcendence is still their concern. McCarthy's contemporaries, such as Thomas Pynchon, John Barth, and Don DeLillo, have done like what McCarthy does in his latest novel with the tradition of post-apocalyptic literature to re-enchant transcendence after their disenchantment with indeterminacy, nihilism, and even languages games. Therefore, based on Berger's vision, what the father attempts to achieve through the strategy of "talk[ing] to me" is that his son born in the post-apocalyptic world could build up a new dialogic relation in himself and thus have a new relationship with the world to resist the craziness and meaninglessness outside, hence regaining the significance of existence.

When everything is broken up, survival may become the sacred principle for the few living in the post-apocalyptic world. Indeed, *The Road* frequently mentions eating or dining for the father and son by more than 40 times. Survival becomes the basic requirement for their life. Although survival principle becomes obscure with the social, cultural and moral construction, it still works in the reality, and even comes to the reality principle gradually. For a man, how he behaves may be more or less influenced by survival and reality principles. Besides escaping from cannibals, hunger and coldness are another challenge for the father and son to live in the post-apocalyptic world. In his famous book, *The Decline of the West*, Osward Spingler asserts that hunger could destroy all the great things, because "hunger may produce the ugly and obscene horror towards life, which is sufficient to destroy the civilized world terribly, and just in this moment starts the competition of human animals for the survival" (728).

In *The Road*, survival principle produces man's competition for food and thus the division of "good" and "bad" guys. Those bad guys even take some captives to preserve in the cave, whose style is like that of the preserving of food in the human society. More terribly, they may keep some women to produce more babies as food in the future, that is why the wife prefers death to life in this terrible world. In McCarthy's oeuvre, this is not the first time to present cannibalism, especially infant cannibalism. In *Outer Dark*, after the illegitimate baby of Culla and Rinthy is cut to death by the throat, the mute one in the Triune kneels forward to drink the blood in the throat. In *The Road*, both the father and the boy see "a charred human infant headless and gutted and blackened on a spit" (Road 198). In such a "margin situation," "to be good," though hardly possible, still supports the father to go on. With the goodness, their self-organization system could be kept stable and orderly. With the goodness, man will not be submissive to the outside world. With the goodness, man will persist in his being distinguished from the bad (cannibalism). Occasionally when reality principle prevails over his pursuit of "goodness," the father may change his determination. For example, the father does not help Ely,[①] a ninety-year-old half-blind old man wandering lonely on the road; he even grabs all that the thief steals from them and his original owning, which casts his son with doubt over his goodness. Nevertheless, the father is like "the catcher in the rye," and his belief in goodness helps him pave the "road" for his son with tender love and care, who finally meets a family with goodness, and keeps on going "on the road" with the "fire" (goodness).

Besides taking story-telling as a strategy to create the reality, the father also resorts to some signs to define the "goodness," hoping that his definition of "goodness" and persistence with the manners of civilized humanity will be transmitted to his young boy and even to the world of the future. According to Ernst Cassirer, signs are important to distinguish human beings from animals, because the latter lacks the symbolized

---

① Ely is one of small and historic cities in the United Kingdom, where one can find very ancient church with the history almost more than 800 years in the downtown, of course, the tourists could taste very typical and traditional afternoon tea in a tea house named by Peacock. Cormac McCarthy has been to the United Kingdom and once acknowledged his name to be after his English ancestor, one of the Kings in Scotland. The reason that he makes his character such an ancient name is perhaps to pay homage to his ancestry, and obviously, Ely is really very old in the novel.

imagination and wisdom. Without signs, man's life will be limited to physical needs and practical benefits, and thus not being able to find out the "road" towards an idealized world (52-3). The first physical action for the novel is the father's preparation of the meal. Waking up from the gray light in the barren world, the father gathers their few provisions and returns to their overnight camp "with their plates and some cornmeal cakes in a plastic bag and a plastic bottle of syrup. He spread [s] the small tarp they used for a table on the ground and [lays] everything out" (Road 5). This gesture is a highly significant on the father's part, for "he performs the centuries-old ritual of preparing the meal as the sign of civilized humanity" (Wilhelm 132). At one point, the father discovers a hidden bunker full of food stuffs, clothing, toiletries, and other survival gear, where they lead a rather happy and transient civilized life in a seemingly cataclysmic world. The father builds a fire in the dinning room, cooks canned goods, and serves the food in "bone china bowls" on the dinning table (Road 145). They take baths in the bathroom and wear clean clothes and sit at a table with a candle between them and eat with utensils. After the dinner, they drink coffee and sit "on the cot with a checkerboard between them" and play checkers before going to bed (Road 148). The father's recreation of a familiar tableau from the vanished world is to attempt to maintain a meaningful connection to human culture, which is a strategy or means to survive in this raw new world and keep him and his son from the wild and savage world, where the cannibalism continuously looms. More importantly, his replication of the signs of the civilization is to construct a symbolic "road" stretching from the past, where signs are meaningful. And the father ultimately acknowledges that his play-acting of old charades of civilization may be just proof of his "placing hopes where he's no reason to hope" (Road 154).

The self-organization system is indeterminate for it is constructed by the father with different problematic strategies. Similar to doubts over those means mentioned above, McCarthy's emphasis on the importance of signs foregrounds their blankness, obscuring all the probable on the edge of chaos. In the later stage of the journey, the father throws away the billfold with him, in which his wife's photograph, his driver's license, some cash and credit cards in the past world become nothing with any referents.

Also in the wasteland, those abandoned gas stations, houses, farms, boats, trains, cars, supermarkets, and those burned buildings in the city and town are nothing with any signification of human, or industrial, or agricultural, or commercial civilization, whatever. The typical example can be referred to from a can of Coca-Cola lying on the floor of an abandoned supermarket. As an icon of the commercial civilization of USA, the Coca has been altered to be blank and empty in its signification. The sign's ambiguity can be sensed in the changes of the young boy's assessment of the pre-apocalyptic relic from his first sight of it at the supermarket to his drink of it at the bunker in the later stage: "What's it?"; then, it is "really good," and then, "It's the Real Thing," which echoes the advertising slogan of the corporation of Coca-Cola in different periods (Donnelly 70-3). To a certain extent, such a parody of the advertisement is McCarthy's satire of commercial civilization. Without question, it strengthens and even foregrounds the blankness of the signs. By means of the presentation of the blankness of the signs in the post-apocalyptic world, McCarthy makes it uncertain to take the sign as one of the strategies to construct the self-organization system, which is made to be indeterminate, too.

iii. Indeterminacy and Textual Strategy

The Road also presents indeterminacy in its textual level. First, the novel's title deserves attention. The "road" itself is uncertain, for it is full of changes and uncertainties as an open system. Both the father and son have to walk on the "road" to seek survival in the post-apocalyptic world, which depends on chance. Indeed, several chancy encounters occur in their journey. Some are dangerous, for instance, in their encounter of a large group of scavengers, one of whom discovers them accidentally when the father moves into the trees to relieve himself, and grabs the son and later is shot by the father when both struggle with each other; and in another instance, both the father and son enter into a cave full of captives waiting to be slaughtered and eaten by some cannibals, and with the same luck, both escape from the ambushers around the house. Some are fortunate, for instance, first, in the bunker, then, in the abandoned farm, and finally, in the deserted ship in the lead-colored sea, where the father discovers food and other stuffs necessary for their survival. It might be argued that to title the novel "the road" signifies the indeterminacy of people's destiny in a post-apocalyptic world, physically and metaphorically. More than that, the road as the title of the novel is greatly significant. The father takes lots of strategies mentioned above to attempt to construct a "road" for the son and even associates the past with the present by means of cultural rituals to transmit the significance of existence, so his hope can be understood to keep the son to go on walking on the "road" and passing on the civilization to the future.

The ambiguity of the novel's title corresponds naturally with the open ending in the novel. After the father's death, it is chancy for the son to meet a family with a man, wife, and girl. After the knowledge of them as "good guys" rather than cannibals, the son walks together with his new family. It seems that they constitute a full or complete family making up with father, mother and children. Different from the usual presentation of the broken family in McCarthy's oeuvre, in which the father is failed,[1] and the mother is absent from death or desertion, *The Road* is the first time for McCarthy to present a full family to his readers, though it is not perfect. After all, the surrogate mother is nice to give the son freedom to "talk to God but the best thing was to talk to his father" (Road 286), and the surrogate father returns him his father's gun, which indicates that the world is not peaceful, but possible for competition and war.

---

[1] Since his first novel, McCarthy has settled down the image of the father as a failed one. In *The Orchard Keeper*, the failures of Mildred Rattner cannot keep his half-wild son to have a loving home. In *Outer Dark*, Culla Holme witnesses his illicit baby was killed and eaten by the evil Triune, yet did nothing with blindness and indifference. *In Child of God*, the failed father's hanging produces a trauma in Lester Ballard's psyche since his childhood, and later directly causes his morbid violence in his adulthood. In *Blood Meridian*, the Kid's biological father as a drunkard cultivates him to be of "mindless violence" in the childhood, and his surrogate father, the judge, doesn't teach him anything moral and good; and on the contrary, in the end, the judge, a foster father, rapes and kills him in the outhouse. In *The Border Trilogy*, the fathers of cowboys, John Grady and Billy, are failed, too. As a retired veteran, John Grady's father lacks the capacity for the sustainment of the farm from his wife's father and hence producing the tragic destiny of his son when going to Mexico to seek for the finishing of his dream to be a cowboy; Billy's father, though skilled for a frontiersman, dies early, hence leaving both Billy and his brother Boyd wandering lonely in their boyhood on the borders or in a foreign country.

More importantly, as a new man, the son has grown up to be "the best guy," who has power and capacity to walk on the "road."

Concerning the ending of the novel, McCarthy's critics have paid efforts to make exploration. Some think that the novel's ending gives a hope for the future of the son. Jay Ellis argues that the novel's ending enacts a small promise of hope against that dimming away of the world, because it provides the reader with a full family, in which there is love beyond a father and son, hence leaving the hope for the son and his new surrogate family (*No Place* 36-7). Ellis' vision about the hope for the ending of the novel is supported by some other critics, yet they cast doubts on its credibility, especially the arrangement of the son's meeting of the shotgun-toting man and his family, and in Snyder's term, such an ending is "an unexpected surprise ending" (83). Some critics think that this novel is not different from some other McCarthy's novels, though it nevertheless excludes the same kind of vital pessimism presented in McCarthy's entire canon. Euan Gallivan suggests that the novel's ending gives a cautious sense of hope in a most misleading way. That the boy follows the surrogate family to go on is made from his want of choice, and his walking together with the family demonstrates the boy's blind trust in the family, which professes to be the good guys, for "there is nothing in the novel's narrative trajectory to suggest that their continued journey will be any easier than that which occupies the pages of the text" (104-5). Randall S.Wihelm's vision corresponds with that of Gallivan. Wilhelm asserts, "Despite the novel's bleakness, McCarthy ... offers the potential for hope in this final movement, but it is a qualified position, for the austere conclusion ultimately yields little certainty as to what will become of the boy or his newfound protectors" (142).

To sum up, the ending of the novel is neither optimistic nor pessimistic as critics view, rather, optimistically pessimistic. It seems that critics missed one crucial point played by McCarthy throughout his novel: chance. McCarthy once said, "the 'laws of probability' will put all of us in the lucky and unlucky charts equally like a poker player in Las Vegas or the stock market analyst" (Lincoln 14), he means that chance makes life full of probable improbabilities. If chance is considered, whether the boy's future destiny is certain or not, both are reasonable. After all, as a new man, he is "on the road." It is said that humans have been destroyed on the earth by nine times,[①] yet, they survived from destruction each time. The son's future refers to that of human beings, and the uncertainty of the ending of the novel conveys McCarthy's care for and meditation over humanity and their living situation: in spite of the uncertainty of hope, we human beings cannot give up. Anyhow, the road is still long, and we have to hold fast to those human qualities such as love, hope and courage rigidly, which is the law of human being's development. It is in such a cycle that human beings go forward. In the very ending of the novel, the natural depiction in a short passage presents the beauty and peace of the pastoral landscape in a pre-apocalyptic world. The juxtaposition of the past with the present foregrounds the uncertainty of the human's existence. Perhaps this is the significance of the novel with the title, "the road."

The uncertainty of the novel's ending tends to associate with the nameless characters. Different from *Suttree*, in which there are more than 150 characters with names, and *Blood Meridian*, in which there are more or less 100 characters with names, though some of the main characters are titled strangely as we discussed in the first section of this chapter, *The Road* presents its protagonists without any concrete names, only titling them the father and son. Such a strategy makes the figures of the novel uncertain and abstract, hence universality in its significance. Besides the nameless protagonists, the novel does present a minor character, an old man named by Ely; however, his name is simply a lie. His talks with the nameless father illustrate the paradoxical nature of language with its power of construction and deconstruction of the reality:

I don't want anybody talking about me. To say where I was or what I said when I was there. I mean, you could talk about me maybe. But nobody could say that it was me. I could be anybody. I think in times like these the less said the better. (Road 171-2)

---

① It is certain that human beings have been destroyed in the human history, yet there are various views about its overall times. According to Chinese historical recordings, human beings have been destroyed by nine times (See Hancock, 2008); whereas, the Bible says that human beings have been destroyed by three times; and four times from Indians, and seven times from Buddhism.

With the uncertainty of figures, the novel foregrounds the indeterminacy of the destiny of human beings in a far-from-equilibrium open system, and meanwhile corresponds with the uncertainty of the ending of the novel, reinforcing the significance of the novel's title. Human beings are still "on the road," which is as Ely says, "I was always on the road. You cant stay in one place. ... I just keep going" (Road 168).

Furthermore, the catastrophe to produce the end of world is uncertain and ambiguous, recalling the general voice of indeterminacy in the novel. The text just mentions that "the clock stopped at 1:17. A long shear of light and then a series of low concussions. ... A dull rose glow in the window glass" (Road 52). On the association of the atomic bombing presented in *The Crossing*, most of critics suggest that the disaster is from nuclear explosion.[①] In the text, the wasteland is covered with ash and dust, and traces of something burned in the fire are everywhere within sight, which demonstrates that the fire-thesis is partly persuasive. In his interview with David Kushner, McCarthy suggests that "the ash-covered world in the novel is the result of a meteor hit," although, Kushner says, McCarthy admitted in his opinion, "his mind is on humans destroying each other before an environmental catastrophe sets in" (Para. 43). Besides the fire, the unending coldness of winter from rain and snow produces the hardship for the survival of both the father and son in the text. Recalling Robert Frost's ambivalence towards ice and fire in his well-known poem, whatever events or disasters, made from various "civilized" actions of human beings on the earth in the contemporary age, such as the improvement of scientific technology, the excess of the consumption of nature for human beings and wars, are the primary cause of the end of the world. In sum, the reason's uncertainty emphasizes the inevitability of the world's end.

The structure of the novel is consistent with the uncertainties of human being's journey in the post-apocalyptic world. The novel "consists of a continuous sequence of discrete paragraphs, some only a few lines in length, none occupying much more than a single page" (Cant, *Cormac McCarthy* 267). In the novel, "there are no chapters; paragraphs are separated by spaces that would occupy three lines of text: occasionally a

---

① For instance, some early reviewers, like Phil Christman, assume that the shearing light which heralded the end of *The Road* 's human age, was a nuclear holocaust (40).

pause is hinted by the indication of an ellipsis at the beginning or end of the page" (Cant, *Cormac McCarthy* 267). The journey itself is of a series of short stages, comprising a continuous whole. The fractured narrative structure of the novel with broken sentences and paragraphs tends to reflect the nature of the journey which constitutes the action of the novel. As we know, time's arrow is irreversible, and then the division of chapters in the novel is compositional. So no division of chapters better presents the flux of motion of matters (both the nameless father and son) in an open system, and meanwhile adds the sense of indeterminacy for walking on the road. The paragraphs constituting the fiction are separated by white spaces on the page, indicating "a break in topic, scene, or temporality either in the form of dream sequence, memory, meditation, or action" (Weiss 232), which helps McCarthy present textually the randomness of the motion in a chaotic system. Besides, the novel's minimalist style shown in the brief and repetitive dialogues of characters without quotation marks, and large quantities of short sentences, noun phrases and participles, also linguistically characterize the profound nullification central to the journey in a post-apocalyptic wasteland.

McCarthy's fiction refuses to be categorized simply. Similar to the ambiguity of the genre for *Blood Meridian*, McCarthy scholarship has a heated argument over the genre of his latest novel, which has been posited by critics in different narrative tradition, such as the Southern, Western, apocalyptic literature, road or journey narrative, elegy, progress allegory, even trauma literature and slavery narrative and so on. However, it seems to the present study that these critics' attempts to draw a line for McCarthy's oeuvre miss one of the important characteristics of postmodernism literature: indeterminacy. In fact, not being able to categorize into any genre of the novel is one of the significant features for McCarthy's postmodernism writings. According to Charles Newman, in postmodernism, "genre continues to be botanized, subindexed ... marketing device tend to reinforce the fragmentation initiated by aesthetic innovation by further segmenting the audience" (115). Newman means that the boundaries of genres in postmodernism have been blurred and faded, so that genres in postmodernism literature have lost their conventional fixed definition.

If considered as a Southern novel with the emphasis on redemption, *The Road* indeed presents us with the sense of hope for the humanity in the post-apocalyptic wasteland through the father's strategies of language and cultural rituals, yet just as we mentioned before, such a hope's obscurity could be presented from the father's doubts over the deceiving nature of language and the obscure ending of the novel. If taken as a Western one, *The Road* is at most "a prototypical Western," for the novel rejects "the heroic mythology of manifest destiny and endless expansion" (Graulund 65, 66). Additionally, in the novel, we cannot find the heroic adventures from that of both the nameless father and son. It seems that their frontier "telos" is vague, and also their frontier is the South rather than the West, the dystopia rather than the utopia. Both the father and son always move on the road to survive with chance and fortune. In fact, they get nowhere. Just as Graulund asserts, "They are always 'on the road,' but the point of being on the road rapidly dissolve into meaningless" (67). So, it might be argued that the novel is neither Southern nor Western. As for other genres categorized by critics, it is not necessary to check them one by one. However, the multiplicity of the genres to define the novel just evidences the novel's indeterminacy textually. Just as Lyotard points out, the postmodern literature is "the unpresentable in presentation itself ... which searches for new presentations, not in order to enjoy them but in order to impart a stronger sense of the unpresentable" (81). Lyotard's words help with the understanding of McCarthy's latest novel. With the hybridization of different genres, McCarthy presents something unpresentable, and with the strategy of the "cross-over" of different genres, he demonstrates the unmistakable indeterminacy in the text.

As an experimental novel, the indeterminacy of *The Road* is consistent with its "field of literary production."[①] McCarthy got the inspiration of the writing of *The Road* in a very specific moment when he checked into an old hotel in El Paso with his young son, John, probably not long after September 11, 2001, and stood looking at the quiet city at about two or three in the early morning out of their room's window, hearing

---

① The term of the "field of literary production" is made from Pierre Bourdieu (1932-2002), who suggests that to study literature means to construct a series of "buildings in the paper," thus, in our exploration of literary writings, they should be contextualized and historicized, meaning that literature has to be posited in certain spatial and relational structures, hence being explored from both of the internal and external fields.

the lonesome sound of trains and imagining what El Paso might look like in fifty or a hundred years. With a son at his old age, McCarthy seems to add a bit warmth and love in his latest novel, in which the paternal love and care for the young son could be sensed. Worrying about his own son's destiny after his death urges McCarthy to imagine the end of world and the human existence in a post-apocalyptic world, and El Paso seems to be transformed into some port city in the South in the novel.

Besides McCarthy's personal background, the indeterminacy of the novel cannot separate from its social context. In the contemporary period, "the aftermath of 9/11, the sorry mess of Iraq war, ... the specter of global warming and ecological disaster" create the sense of eschatology for people in USA (Walsh 48). Moreover, McCarthy's literary contemporaries, such as John Barth, Thomas Pynchon and Don DeLillo, resort to the post-apocalyptic literature to depict the end of the world and present their anxiety over the future of human beings. McCarthy's contemporary scientists also convey the sense of pessimism towards the world. For instance, the second law of thermodynamics suggests that at the end of the entropic process, heat energy will be non-transferable because everything will contain an equal quantity of energy. In this equilibrium, life will cease, which is the so-called heat death. Zamoria assumes that "Entropy is perhaps the modern scientific equivalent of apocalyptic concerns, but it is far more pessimistic in its view of time, history, and man's relation to temporal reality than apocalypse" (22). Chaos theory challenges the classical science's ideas about the world as certainty, and suggests that the world is a deterministic chaos, full of improbabilities and uncertainties, so that all the hardships and perplexities of life on the edge of chaos are made from indeterminacy and chance.

All in all, the novel's "field of literary production" echoes the indeterminacy present on its thematic and textual levels. With such a personal, social, cultural, and historical milieu, we may understand the significance of the novel, which not only reflects McCarthy's meditation on his living world and age, but also shows his care of the destiny of human beings in the chaotic system. For us human beings, we are still "on the road," which depends on our attitudes towards life and cosmos with indeterminacy. To accept it rather than resist it, such is what McCarthy's experimental novel indicates through the principle of chaos theory.

III. Chance and Chaos: the Butterfly Effect in *No Country for Old Men*

Classical mechanics tells us how the universe evolves over the course of time and "gives a completely deterministic picture of the world: if we know the state of the universe at some (arbitrarily chosen) initial time, we should be able to determine its state at any other time" (Ruelle 29). However, in the contemporary period, all are changed. The deterministic picture of the macroscopic natural world and, by extension, in human behavior, is shattered in front of chaos theory. "Although systems can be deterministic, we may not be able to predict their future state-certainly not the future state of the extremely complex system that constitutes human behavior" (Jo Alyson Parker 115). In brief, sensitive dependence on initial conditions occurs in the cosmos everywhere from the microscopic particles to macroscopic galaxies, even to everyday complexities.

No Country for Old Men is McCarthy's ninth novel. The novel mainly tells the story of Moss's journey along the border of Texas and Mexico struggling to escape from being chased and killed by a psychopathic killer, Anton Chigurh and the sheriff, Ed Tom Bell, in the wake of his stealing of drug money by chance. Moss's encounter with bloody scene of drug dealers in the desert and his subsequent stealing of drug money about 2.4 million dollars make him and his family as well as lots of people associated with or without him, such as motel desk clerks, corporate executives, policemen, drug-runners, hired killers, motorists, passers-by in the street, girls, kids, involved in his life's chaotic system, producing large and bloody effect with "all the pretty corpses"[①] in the novel (Cant, *Cormac McCarthy* 246). In other words, the moment Moss steals drug money capriciously from the failed drug-dealing scene has been "the flapping of wings for the butterfly," and its later transcendence beyond his personal world to involve the society into a violent "tornado" is entirely unpredictable and uncontrollable,

① McCarthy's 1992 novel is titled by *All the Pretty Horses*, which is adapted humorously and precisely by John Cant.

which depends on chance in the process of chaotic system. In *No Country for Old Men*, McCarthy posits his characters in a chaotic system, and by means of the unfortunate destiny of Llewellyn Moss, McCarthy presents the problematic picture of Newtonian paradigm in postmodern time and society. In Moss's life process, chaos is ubiquitous, and seemingly all are attributed to butterfly effect.

This section may go on with talking about McCarthy's narrative strategies as chaos, and the narrative pattern and the uncertainty of the destiny of characters displayed in *No Country for Old Men* are taken to demonstrate that McCarthy's fiction follows the principles of chaos theory, particularly butterfly effect, making his fiction a dynamic one.

i. The Butterfly Effect and Chaotic Cosmos

As the essence or metaphor of chaos theory, butterfly effect refers to sensitive dependence on initial conditions in a chaotic system. For the linear dynamics of Newtonian physics, small causes bring out small effects, and big causes have big effects; whereas, for the nonlinear dynamics of chaos theory, small changes or perturbations may unpredictably and drastically produce large-scale effects and then alter the complex systems completely. Functioning as a nonlinear system, weather system is a typical example, in which small causes could be amplified to lead to large-scale effects. Such a phenomenon in nature has been realized by Edward Lorenz and hence the coined term "butterfly effect."

Life is also a nonlinear dynamic system, a chance encounter or a trivial decision in the process of life sometimes can dramatically alter one's life courses and thus creating complexity in one's life. That is to say, the disproportion of cause and effect in the human behavior leads to the nonlinear development of events in a chaotic system. Just as Chigurh, an evil character in the novel, says to Carla Jean, Moss's wife, before taking her life, "Every moment in your life is a turning and every one is a choosing. Somewhere you made a choice. All followed this. The accounting is scrupulous. The shape is drawn. No line can be erased. ... A person's path through the world seldom changes and even more seldom will it change abruptly" (COM 259). Chigurh means that life is a chaotic system, in which determinism and free will coexist; however, as for where one's life goes, accident and chance operate in it.

Chigurh's words evoke Gleick's observation of the snowflake's formation, a common natural phenomenon in the chaotic cosmos. Gleick writes,

As a growing snowflake falls to earth, typically floating in the wind for an hour or more, the choices made by the branching tips at any instant depend sensitively on such things as the temperature, the humidity, and the presence of impurities in the atmosphere. The six tips of a single snowflake, spreading within a millimeter space, feel the same temperatures, and because the laws of growth are purely deterministic, they maintain a near perfect symmetry. But the nature of turbulent air is such that any pair of snowflake will experience very different paths. (311)

In effect, sensitive dependence on initial conditions (butterfly effect) not only serves to destroy but also serves to create. Concerning the consequence of the development of things in the cosmos, chance is crucial in all dynamic systems, which not merely suits for natural phenomena but also operates in human life.

Comparing with *Blood Meridian* and *The Road*, *No Country for Old Men* is not very outstanding in terms of its artistic achievement, yet concerning the present study with the focus on the chaos in McCarthy's fiction, it is exceptional in that it pays more emphasis on chance and chaos in human life and our living cosmos. Chaos theory's principle, particularly the butterfly effect, has been woven into the fiction's fabric. However, so far, such an important aspect of the fiction seems to be ignored by the mainstream of McCarthy criticism.

Similar to most of McCarthy's canon, *No Country for Old Men* also provokes controversy, though it still garners general critical acclaim. William Deresiewicz, one of the early reviewers, derides the novel, which he thought to be "superficial and perfunctory" as the dubious product of a Catholic sensibility (1). Joyce Carol Oates delivers a review based on a superficial reading of the novel that contains several textual inaccuracies. For Oates, the novel is "suffused with the malevolent Eros of male violence" and reads "like a prose film by Quentin Tarantino" (8).

Despite the denouncement, some critics admire the novel. They have examined it with various approaches. John Cant, Jay Ellis, David Cremean and John Vanderheide make psychological approaches to the novel. Cant and Ellis bring Freudian and Jungian lens to the novel. Cant mainly makes analysis of the Oedipus complex in the novel, and notes "the Oedipal theme ... in abeyance" in the novel ("Oedipus" 49). Cant attributes such a thematic progression to McCarthy's own advancing age and assumes that McCarthy "has begun to feel that he no longer has to strive to usurp the voice of the literary fathers" ("Oedipus" 52). Ellis mainly makes analysis of Moss and Bell and their metaphoric father-son relationship, and he writes, "The book collapses under the weight of the son and father anxiety that is only forestalled by the fetishism and violence preoccupying its opening" (*No Place* 136). Cremean takes Bell as the hero of the novel and argues that "Bell does fail in his outer journey, but he succeeds in his inner one" (25). Vanderheide takes Moss and Chigurh as two "demons" of Bell. The former makes compensation for Bell's guilt about his conduct in battle and the latter for his proclivity to play it safe (30-5).

Besides the psychoanalysis group in the novel's criticism, the other group mainly focuses on the fiction's major thematic motifs, such as violence, morality, faith and consumerism and so on. Kenneth Lincoln assumes that the novel "scripts an old morality tale in a new context of precision weapons" (144). Similar to Lincoln, Linda Woodson holds that the novel centers on question of moral responsibility and determinism, as personified in the characters of Bell and Chigurh ("...you" 4-13). Robert Jarrett makes analysis of how the novel frustrates the genre reader's expectations and points out that the novel ends with an evocation of a very old fashioned idea: faith ("Genre" 36-46). Lydia R. Cooper also makes exploration of the relationship between story-telling and morality. She argues that the novel's plot "resembles the 'Pandora box'-type cautionary tale," and characters in the novel are typed ones in the tale, among which Moss "stumbles on a treasure, a bag of drug money, and, in stealing, awakens the wrath of the 'supernatural' evil power, Chigurh" (134). Raymond Malewitz takes Bill Brown's economic theory of "misuse value" to explore the relationship between man and man-made objects in the novel, and suggests that McCathy's work problematizes the inevitable penetration of exchange value into use value in American culture (721-41).

All in all, with the exception of Steven Frye, the mainstream literary critics of *No Country for Old Men* miss the fiction's narrative power in its aspect of chaos theory. Frye holds that chaos theory is the novel's defining metaphor, which can be evidenced from Chigurh's deterministic beliefs about the role of chance and fate in human affairs. Frye's vision of the novel as the metaphor of chaos theory and his interpretation of Chigurh as the epitome of power from both God and evil have touched upon the core of the novel. However, as an introductory book, Frye's work just gives a light brush over the chaos theory played in the novel and does not give a detailed analysis. Furthermore, it should be noted that Lydia R. Cooper's argument over the novel's "Pandora box-typed" plotting is analogous to that of butterfly effect in the fictional development, yet it is pity that she is not aware of the principle of chaos theory, which has been woven into the fabric of the novel itself.

For the current study, it might be argued that the novel develops with the premise of butterfly effect with its major conflicts centering on three characters, Moss, Chigurh, and Bell, who are combined to create a chaotic system. As the center of nonlinear dynamic system, Moss's capricious finding of large amounts of drug money causes his life journey in the desert as a deterministic chaos; similar to the judge in *Blood Meridian*, Chigurh is the symbol of chaos, both Satan and God, both yin and yang, whose appearance involves all of things in the novel into death or chaos, mysterious and unpredictable; as the witness and participator of the chaos system, Bell finishes the cycle of chaotic journey of these three characters, in which Moss chases after money, Chigurh after Moss, and Bell after Chigurh, constructing an actual escape-chase pattern in the narrative. The novel may be considered as a good example of narrative, in which the essence of chaos theory has been woven into its characterization and narrative pattern: the butterfly flapping its wings in New York causes a typhoon in Brazil.

ii. Periodic Three and Narrative Pattern as Chaos

The mathematician James Yorke discovers that in daily life, "the Lorenzian quality of sensitive dependence on initial conditions lurks everywhere," and "small perturbations in one's daily trajectory can have large consequences" (Gleick 67). In his famous essay, "Periodic Three Implies Chaos," Yorke proves that "in any one-dimensional system, if a regular cycle of period three ever appears, then the same system will also display regular cycles of every other length, as well as completely chaotic cycles" (Gleick 73). Yorke's observation demonstrates the association of the number "three" with the deterministic chaos, recalling the interpretation of the number "three" in *Tao Te Ching*: "Tao gives birth to the One; the One gives birth successively to two things, three things, up to every thing in the world" (Chap. 42). The number "three" is the combination of yin and yang, order and disorder, hence the symbol of chaos naturally. Number is one of the ways to present the world. Both chaos theory and *The Book of Changes* know about human world and chaotic cosmos by means of the number. The number "three" appears frequently in McCarthy's Southwestern novels. Sometimes it is associated with the three-body problem in science, presenting the chaotic life of characters, which will be demonstrated in the analysis of *All the Pretty Horses* in the following chapter. Sometimes it is associated with the self-similarity across scales, which is to be shown in the present study's examination of *The Crossing*. While, in *No Country for Old Men*, the number "three" is mainly associated with chaotic behavior in the cosmos. Events occurring by "three" times recur in the narrative, foregrounding the novel's narrative pattern as chaos.

In the opening section of the novel, Bell describes his sending a boy to the gas chamber. After that, he claims that he "visited with him two or three times. Three times" (COM 1; my emphasis). The novel follows the motion of three characters: Moss's survival journey from the pursuit of Mexican drug-runners, Chigurh, and Bell with his wits; Chigurh's unstoppable journey of producing death in his chasing of Moss to retrieve the money; and Bell's futile journey to track down Moss and Chigurh. Moreover, the escape-chase of these three characters constructs the major plot of the novel, which occurs in triplet. For example, Moss encounters Chigurh by three times. And he escapes from Chigurh twice, but is killed during the third and final encounter. First, Moss runs to Del Rio and cleverly outwits Chigurh, barely escaping him (COM

99-103); next, Moss goes to Eagle Pass, involves in a shoot-out with Chigurh, but manages to escape (COM 161); and last, Moss sends his wife Carla Jean to El Paso. After he puts her on the bus, he flees northward to Van Horn. But, he is caught and killed by Chigurh when he stops at a motel with a young hitchhiker (COM 201, 224, 236-9). Likewise, Chigurh narrowly escapes death by three times. First, He is caught with a murder instrument, which could be linked to his past crimes and earns him the death penalty, but he escapes by killing the deputy (COM 6-7); next, he gets shot by Moss in Eagle Pass, but lives with his wits and strength to survive (COM 161); and finally he goes to El Paso to kill Carla Jean and gets hit by a car in the street and hurts heavily, but lives still (COM 261). Bell almost encounters Chigurh, but just misses him by three times as well, complementing the triple-episodic narrative pattern for these three characters: first, Bell arrives at Moss's Desert Aire trailer after the moment Chigurh leaves, missing him (COM 93); second, he surveys the wreckage after the shoot-out in Ealge Pass at "nine-fifteen in the morning" having missed Chigurh who leaves the town when "the new day [is] paling" (COM 134, 122); and last, he arrives at the Van Horn motel while Chigurh is presumably still in the parking lot, but Chigurh manages to escape it (COM 242-5).

Violence still haunts McCarthy's ninth novel. In the hyper-violent society, McCarthy's characters, major or minor, are involved with violence. As "a kind of random totalitarian force with roots in the very origins of the nation" (Giles 7), in McCarthy's novels, violence is understood to be of "a fact of life, a certainty, a never-ending, unstoppable, unknowable force" (George 89). In *No Country for Old Men*, such an unstoppable and unknowable evil force centers around Chigurh, who takes the lives of those innocent victims by chance. Absurdly, each time he kills, he will speak to his victims philosophically with eloquence similar to Judge Holden. Recalling the principle of chaos theory, the novel arranges his odd talks about chance and determinism with the killed by three times: first, he almost kills the proprietor of a filling station, who escapes luckily through the coin toss (COM 55-8); second, he shoots Carson Wells, the bounty hunter from the drug-dealers (COM 173-9); third, he takes the life of Carla Jean after his killing of Moss and a hitchhiker in the motel (COM 254-60), which makes resonance with the narrative pattern as chaos.

iii. Chance, Chaos and Figures in the Narrative

No Country for Old Men centers around three figures, Moss, Chigurh and Bell, who are combined into a chaotic cosmos. In their chaotic life journey, chance plays with them, making their life involved into the trajectories of the chaos.

"As a representative American, Moss is on the run through the entire narrative" (Lincoln 143). A veteran Vietnam welder with a good heart, poor, hard-working, abiding by the law, living in the trailer-park, marrying a child-bride of sixteen, Moss is "every-man caught in the crosshairs of hell" (Lincoln 143), involving lots of innocents into his trajectories and death. Chance makes him meet with the briefcase with money from the failed drug dealing scene, and the consequence of such a lottery find is deterministic: danger and death. The temptation is so great that Moss decides to make adventures with his background, knowledge, crafts of killing and counter-detective survival capability. Thus, from the very beginning, the outcome of Moss's choice is doomed to be cataclysmic, yet its process is entirely unpredictable. Butterfly effect plays a great role in his life system, in which "a minor incident precipitates uncontrollable turbulence and results in large-scale catastrophe" (Slethaug 19).

Moss's dilemma is universal, and through his dilemma, the novel implies such a question for his reader: what would you do? Would you take the money? Moss is aware of the danger of his choice after his decision to go back to send water to a dying drug dealer, and he knows more about his situation. His farewell dialogue with his wife before his leaving home is a proof: "I'm fixin [sic] to go do somethin [sic] dumbern hell but I'm goin [sic] anyways. If I dont come back tell mother I love her." "Your mother's dead, Llewelyn" (COM 24). Moss's dilemma gives an example of order being suddenly thrown into turbulence due to chancy events in one's life. It is assumed that turbulence is a natural phenomenon for physical or biological systems, yet it is also an inherent part for human life. Moss's rapid transition from order to disorder, from steadiness to uncertainty, from a law-abiding citizen to an outlaw wandering along the border of Texas-Mexico, typifies a chaotic system, in which all depend on initial conditions sensitively, producing the disproportion of cause and effect.

Violence is the consequence of Moss's choice. In the novel, bloodshed becomes the constant, and at the end of the novel, almost all are dead, except Chigurh's receding into the background and memory of Sheriff Bell. McCarthy seems to suggest that violence is a kind of human experience, which results from a very trivial cause. Nevertheless, to make trivial cause develop into the catastrophe, chance works. At first, Moss's promise to fetch water for the dying drug-dealer makes him encounter other drug runners, causing him to get hurt and give up his truck and have to escape from home. Second, his deserting truck gives a clue for the pursuing killers and the policemen, leading to the interactions of parameters in the chaotic system: cause and effect. Third, his failure to discover the transponder in the money case allows the killer Chigurh to follow him step by step and almost kill him at some crucial moments. Fourth, it is chancy that his hunter is Chigurh, a trickster figure, who outwits him in every aspect; otherwise, his twisted American dream would be achieved with his crafts learned from experiences in the Vietnam war. We just give several examples. In effect, in the escape-chase process of characters, there are lots of evidences to show that chance works in the chaotic system.

When Moss gives a call to his wife, Carla Jean expresses her wish to return to their previous steady state. In their short telephone discussion of the misfortune in their life, Moss attributes his life's turbulence to "real money," while Carla Jean assumes that "a false god" plays in it (COM 182). What works in Moss's turbulence? The money or false god? or chances? The ambiguity of the causes enhances the chaos in Moss's life, which is as Frye notes, "the course of history and human lives proceed independent of free will, and prediction is impossible in the closed and highly complex physical system that is the world" (162).

As complicated as Judge Holden in *Blood Meridian*, Chigurh is an enigma figure in the novel, and in Moss's chaotic system of life, he plays the crucial role, making Moss's life much more complex and unpredictable. Chigurh's origin is as ambiguous as that of Judge, and we know little about his background or motive. As a good story-teller, McCarthy knows how to draw characters from a single detail. Although the text does not give the full description of Chigurh, we still notice his special exotic quality. In one meeting between Moss and Chigurh at the Hotel Eagle in Eagle Pass, Texas, the vision of Moss gives a glance at Chigurh: he wears "an expensive pair of ostrich-skin boots" and "pressed jeans"; "some foreign cologne" with "a medicinal edge to it." He looks "serene" with "blue eyes" and "dark hair," yet about him "there is something exotic," which is beyond Moss's experience. His "thoughts seemed elsewhere," even with a shotgun aiming at him, he appears to be "oddly troubled. As if this were all part of his day" (COM 111-2).

Similar to Judge, Chigurh is the epitome of evil or death. Just as what Sheriff Bell speaks of him as a "living prophet of destruction" (COM 2), Chigurh brings about catastrophic violence for others. As animalistic as the diabolic judge, Chigurh is pure evil in nature, who "watches the capillaries in his victim's eyes congeal as he shoots them through the forehead," either with a stun gun or a gas canister or the birdshot, and kills those meeting him with the motion "like swatting a fly, by surprise and in the instant, uneventful before and after the fact, perhaps no more than a small bullet hole in the forehead or a two-and-a-half inch indent from the cattle gun cylinder or a shotgun blast in the face" (Lincoln 146, 148). For him, "anything can be an instrument" (COM 57). In the text, he is shown with the devil's mastery of all kinds of weapons of destruction, from slaughter yard tools to rifles and handguns and sawed-off shotguns, from trucks to a transponder, the size of a Zippo lighter. He even knows exactly how to strangle a deputy with handcuffs cutting into his own wrists. As mysterious as sly Judge, in the end of the text, Chigurh disappears into the background after many of others meeting with him die swiftly.

As authoritative as the judge, Chigurh likes to be imagined as God or a lawgiver, who challenges against the authority from God and social institutions. Rather than a deity of benevolence and care, the God he imagines is "an abstract and indifferent lawgiver concerned with balancing the cosmic scales in the interests of principles beyond human understanding" (Frye 160-1). Before killing, he always gives a chance to his victims to save his or her life, playing with chances in one's life. Coin toss is Chigurh's means to help with his seemingly mysterious understanding of world and life, and via coin toss, he not only explains his ideas of determinism and chance but also determines the destiny of his victims to be saved or not. More than the evil in the inner mind of humans to bring about violence and blood without ration, or the demon in the life's turbulence to cause the chaos in one's life, Chigurh is the symbol of chaos, to be exact. To merge the imagery of chaos theory and the chaos theory itself into Chigurh's complicated and eloquent philosophical talkings about fate, chance and determinism not only foregrounds Chigurh's nature as the turbulence of chaos, but also makes the fiction a dynamic one.[①]

As an important imagery of chaos theory, coin toss is associated with stochastic probability. For Chigurh, he knows clearly that chance governs the fall of coin, so tails or heads for the bidding of the victim depend on chance when flipping the coin. In the beginning of the novel, he asks the attendant of a gas-filling station to flip the coin to determine his luck, then with Moss's wife Carla Jean at the end of the novel. Though chance plays the role in the coin's falling system, yet for Chigurh, he knows clearly that chance still depends on "all the intricate consequential moments that precede it" (Frye 161), that's why both encounters are opposite in the consequence. At the first time, the proprietor calls heads, the coin does fall with heads, then the man survives; while at the second time, Carla Jean also calls heads, but the falling coin turns out to be tails, then she is shot to death according to the negotiation.

Chigurh has his own understanding of fate and chance, which has been prefigured in the dialogue between John Grady Cole and Dueña Alfonsa in *All the Pretty Horses*, when they talk about the role of fate, chance and choice through the metaphor of the coin toss. The imagery of coin toss associated with fate and chance has appeared earlier in *Blood Meridian*, in which Judge Holden is a good magician with coin toss. The golden coin will return precisely and mysteriously to his hands in a mysterious arc after his flipping into the air: "The arc of circling bodies is determined by the length of their tether, said the judge. Moons, coins, men. His hands moved as if he were pulling

---

① The term dynamic fiction is suggested by Gordon E. Slethaug in his book *Beautiful Chaos*. Based on Heisenberg's distinction, dynamic fiction is taken to "describe the fiction in which chaos theory, complexity theory, or dynamic theory enter structurally as well as through figuration, model, and content" (Slethaug 8).

something from one fist in a series of elongations" (BM 245-6). Similarly, such an understanding of fate and chance echoes in *All the Pretty Horses*, in which Alfonsa talks with John Grady about the puppet show with a tether in one's hands when John Grady makes a proposal for Alejandra: "For me the world has always been more of a puppet show. But when one looks behind the curtain and traces the strings upward he finds they terminate in the hands of yet other puppets, themselves with their own strings which trace upward in turn, and so on" (Horses 231). The recursion of the imagery of coin toss in McCarthy's fiction suggests that the chain of causality for one's life and death has been broken in the postmodern society, and chance works in the chaotic system of life. All are uncertain, for "the portentous fortune in the toss is circumscribed by time and previous event" (Frye 161). In other words, any small change made in the temporal-spatial spot may cause certain consequences, great or small, for determinism and free will coexist in one's life, so one's destiny depends on chance, which decides on the probability of winning or not. Obviously, such an understanding of one's fate and chance is more or less in correspondence with that of the wisdom presented in Chinese Chaos, i.e. *The Book of Changes*.

Consistent with chaos theory, Chigurh believes that chance and happenstance constitute one's life process, yet one's destiny is the consequence of the coincidences of cause and effect. For him, the coin has traveled twenty years to "get here. It's here. And I'm here. And I've got my hand over it. And it's either heads or tails" (COM 56). From his point of view, "an irreducibly complex matrix of cause and effect has brought them [Chigurh and his victims] both to the present moments that precede it," for in one's life, after all, "there's an accounting" someday, though things are small and not noticed by people (Frye 161; COM 57). Thus in his dealing with the life of Carla Jean, he suggests that she has to "endure the dictates of determinism while enjoying the pleasure of free will" (Mackey 51). In the novel, he tells Moss that if Moss returns the money, he would like to offer Moss a chance to save Carla Jean. However, Moss does not trust him, thus losing a chance to save his wife with his free will. According to him, such a decision is one of the many events that leads to the here and now, so he asks Carla Jean to call a coin to determine her life. According to his logic thinking, "every moment in your life is a turning and everyone a choosing. Somewhere you made a choice. ...A person's path through the world seldom changes and even more seldom will it change abruptly. And the shape of your path was visible from the very beginning" (COM 259). By this, Chigurh "acknowledges the reality of volition, but the choice was Carla Jean's as well" (Frye 162).

Different from the gas station attendant, the turbulence in Carla Jean's life begins earlier than Moss's stealing of drug money in the desert, which perhaps can be traced back to her dream of romance in Wal-Mart. Carla Jean's choice of marriage with Moss seems inconsequential, yet the outcome of such a volition is totally unpredictable. Her romance with Moss is also a good example of the butterfly effect in one's life system. Just as Hayles puts it,

When time goes forward there is a role for chance, because small or random fluctuations near a bifurcation point can cause a system to take a different path than it otherwise would. ... But when time runs backward along the same track it took before, every juncture point is already predetermined and hence chance can play no further part in the system's evolution. (*Chaos Bound* 98-9)

Hayles' observation gives a hint how chance may allow for free will in a deterministic world and yet chance simply works in the irreversible temporal system, which just suits for the situation of Carla Jean.

In McCarthy's rhetoric, the butterfly effect has been implied earlier, though the novelist does not mention it apparently. When the ironsmith makes comments on the process of iron-making in his talking with Lester Ballard in *Child of God*, "it's like a lot of things, ... do the least part of it wrong and ye'd just as well to do it all wrong" (COG 74), obviously it may be associated with the butterfly effect in one's life system, especially for the turbulence in Ballard's life. Besides, in *All the Pretty Horses*, when the boys are talking, Rawlins says, "Way the world is. Somebody can wake up and sneeze somewhere in Arkansas or some damn place and before you're done there's wars and ruination and all hell. You don't know what's going to happen" (Horses 92), which is clearly consistent with the butterfly effect in chaos theory. Moreover, after John Grady is set free from the prison, Alfonsa remarks that "human decisions [are linked to, but] is more and more remote from their consequences" (Horses 230). The list may go on.

Of course, Chigurh might choose not to kill Carla Jean, he could have a choice to become a good person. However, from his sadistic logic, "I have only one way to live. It doesn't allow for special cases. A coin toss perhaps" (COM 259), we may sense that his evil, indifference and violence are bound within his character. Though capable with the power of God or Satan, Chigurh's own destiny runs along the trajectory of chaos system, too. After his killing of Carla Jean and departing from her home, he is struck by a car speeding through the intersection. Through the presentation of Chigurh as a symbol of chaos, McCarthy seems to suggest that violence is pervasive in the human world and "the cause and effect that constitute the universe are entirely determined and rife with suffering and bloodshed" (Frye 162). Consistent with the world as wilderness and chaos for the theme of his works, McCarthy shows his criticism of human nature as evil and violence in this hybrid of crime thriller and postmodern Western novel. For McCarthy, "There's no such thing as life without bloodshed, I think the notion that the species can be improved in some way, that everyone could live in harmony, is really dangerous idea" (Woodward, "Venomous Fiction" 31). McCarthy's vision of human nature as violence echoes in the talk of Bell with his uncle Ellis after he decides to leave his job (COM 293-5). Different from Bell's vision of the present country as corruption and violence changed from the past's being good and moral, for Ellis, evil is ever-present in the reality, and "[this country] was already in bad shape" (COM 294).

The title of the novel is from William Butler Yeats's "Sailing to Byzantium," which begins with the line "There is no country for old men," referring to transcendent world of art in contrast with the material world from the viewpoint of an aged man. Steven Frye holds that "the reference is clearly to Ed Tom Bell, his uncle Ellis ... as well as the harsh world of violence and struggle they work to control and understand" (156). Like the other side of a coin, Sheriff Bell stands opposite to the psychopathic killer Chigurh: good and evil; law-protector and destroyer; past and present; yang and yin, respectively, completing the chaos system with Moss and Chigurh as a witness and participator. Being a sheriff, he chases after the outlaw Chigurh and attempts to save the life of Moss and his wife, yet he is always out of luck. Bell is always late for the crime or just misses the killer when he arrives at the spot. Despite chance playing dramatically in the chaotic system, after all, Moss does not believe in law and just leaves his life in the chaotic system to play with determinism and free will. Bell's failure to stop the violence suggests that violence as an unknown and unstoppable force is inherent in human life, once born or chosen, it will spread with the effect of butterfly's flapping of wings and its consequence is unpredictable and uncontrollable.

The structure of the novel is peculiar, and each chapter begins with an italicized part, in which the old man Bell "grumbles along in monologues" (Ellis, *No Place* 225). Two narrative strands go throughout the novel in juxtaposition: one is about the journey of Moss being hunted by bounty hunters, policemen and Chigurh; and the other is about the journey of Bell's inner mind taking longer until the book collapses into one of his dreams. This narrative structure has been adopted before especially in McCarthy's *Outer Dark*, in which two narrative strands are juxtaposed together, one concerning the escape-chase journey of Culla, Rinthy and the Tinker, the other about the mysterious movements of the Triune in the wilderness. Similar to the narrative function of Culla, whom could go beyond the boundaries of the evil Triune from the human society and move freely back and forth between his world and the dark wilderness occupied by the evil Triune, Bell acts in the novel as an intersection between two narrative strands. Exactly, Bell could be counted as the bridge to join two different journeys together.

In his journey of the inner mind, Bell is so haunted by the past that he can only see the present as a dark and confusing mourning over the dead. Obviously, in Bell's observation, the post-sixties USA is decayed with violence. The young boy whom he has sent to death chamber kills his girl friend without any motivation, which foreshadows the evil force presented in the figure of Chigurh. Drug dealings go beyond national borders, igniting bloodshed and violence, and such an evil business even invades the world of the young and innocent, selling the drug to young school kids, or involving the ordinary persons into something illegal, in which Moss and Wells are examples: the former changes to be an outlaw from a law-abiding citizen and the latter, an ex-lieutenant colonel, transforms to be a bounty hunter for the drug corporation. For Bell, "this country was hard on people, but they never seemed to hold it to account" (COM 271). Nothing could do for a failed old man in the violent society, and at the end of the novel, Bell retires from his position. As an old man, what he can do is to evade into the dream to desire for a country with peace, love, soul, good manners rather than with "rape, arson, murder, drugs, suicide" (COM 196).

Different from his previous Faulknerian density of structure and expression with difficulty and complexity in language style, McCarthy's novels in New Mexico period are in the style of Hemingway's minimalist aesthetics. In line with the cosmos as chaos in the fiction, in which both the landscape and human society are in desert with blood, disorder and death, McCarthy's language tends to be desert-like, with its quick-pacing, clean, objective and local dialects and fragmented prose, echoing McCarthy's border country as "no country for old men."

As a fellow of the interdisciplinary Santa Fe Institute, McCarthy frequently works together with physicists there, and such a collaboration McCarthy has tersely attributed to his enduring interest "in the way things work" (qtd. in Bortz 13). For McCarthy, human life is a complex and dynamic system, in which there are so many variables involved in the complex networks of parameters, influencing one's life each moment. In the interactions of these variables, chance always plays, and any small alteration may produce large effects in a chaotic system.

In *No Country for Old Men*, chance makes Moss's life go astray and develop tragically. Chance also makes his tragedy cross beyond his personal realm and involve the whole society into violence and decay, making the catastrophic result go up exponentially. Moss's life is not a single example of the butterfly effect, but the consequence of the interactions of variables in the universe, which is a deterministic chaos. Chance plays dramatically in one's life, and nobody could escape from it. Besides, the absurdity of taking coin toss to determine one's fate disrupts the linear association of cause and effect, making human life meaningless and uncertain in the postmodern society. As the avatar of chaos, the psychopathic killer Chigurh appears together with the imagery of coin toss as stochastic probability in the novel, foregrounding the chaos in human life and society. Moreover, in the narrative, the recursion of major episodes in the plot development with the pattern of periodic three makes the narrative pattern correspond with chaos theory. All in all, McCarthy allows the narrative pattern of his novel and the destiny of his characters to follow the principle of chaos theory, particularly, the butterfly effect, making the fiction a dynamic one.

Chapter Four
Strange Attractor, Fractals and Self–Similarities: Spatial Configuration as Chaos

I have not spoken of the aesthetic appeal of strange attractors. These systems of curves, these clouds of points suggest sometimes fireworks or galaxies, sometimes strange and vegetal proliferations. A realm lies there of forms to explore, and harmonies to discover.

David Ruelle, Chance and Chaos

Clouds are not spheres, mountains are not cones, coastlines are not circles, and bark is no smooth, nor does lightening travel in a straight line. All of these natural structures have irregular shapes that are self-similar. In other words, we discovered that successively magnifying a part of the whole reveals a further structure that is nearly a copy of the original we started with.

Bernoit Mandelbrot, The Fractal Geometry of Nature

"Chaos is beautiful and develops itself in fantastic patterns and shapes" (Hawkins 10). Strange attractors and fractals are these "fantastic patterns and shapes," mapping the phase space of the deterministic chaos. In the wake of scientific work of chaos theorists, the concepts and patterns of chaos theory have been recognized by literary writers and artists, and meanwhile, with the "spatial turn" of narrative forms in the fiction, the basic patterns of chaos theory get well-known and become incorporated into literary writings gradually and consciously.

As regards McCarthy's literary texts, the concepts and principles of chaos theory have been demonstrated in the previous chapters with focuses on thematic presentation and narrative strategies. With basic patterns of chaos theory in mind, *All the Pretty*

Horses (1992) and *The Crossing* (1994), the first two books of the border trilogy will be taken as case studies to explore in this chapter, attempting to prove that McCarthy's fiction have got the spatial configuration as chaos in narrative forms: strange attractor and fractals respectively.[①] In terms of these two models or images of chaos theory, both are featured with common self-similarities. The final book of the border trilogy, *Cities of the Plain* (1998), does not offer as remarkable narrative forms for McCarthy's corpus as do *All the Pretty Horses* and *The Crossing*, yet in this serialized fiction, self-similarities could be found out to make it interrelated with theprevious ones, constructing a whole for the trilogy. For convenience of the study, such a work may be mentioned if necessary, and the extended examination of its narrative form will be left for another study in the future.

I. Strange Attractors, Fractals and Dynamic Spatiality

As the patterns or models to map the phase space of nonlinear dynamic systems, strange attractors and fractal have their specific aesthetic appeal. In contemporary fiction, they are taken as the spatial form for the narrative and thus making the fiction characteristic of dynamic spatiality. In the first chapter for the present study, they have been introduced in terms of the major content and concepts of chaos theory as well as spatial form fiction in contemporary period. In respect to their associations with spatial configuration in McCarthy's fiction, a brief review is necessary before our exploration of the dynamic spatiality of McCarthy's works.

First, consider the attractor and strange attractor. Generally, for physicists, there are two simpler kinds of "attractors": fixed points and limit cycles, representing "behavior that reached a steady state or repeated itself continuously" (Gleick 134). The motion of pendulum is a typical example. If the friction is considered, then the pattern of attractor may be a fixed point, as shown in Fig.1.3. If the mapping is done in the ideational state, that is to say, without consideration of friction, then we may get a

---

① The fourth chapter of the current study aims to foreground the spatial form of McCarthy's fiction as chaos, hopefully demonstrating that McCarthy's fiction has the aesthetic characteristic of dynamic spatiality. Therefore, both of the third chapter and the fourth one are different in terms of studying perspectives.

limit cycle, as shown in Fig.1.2. So it is easy for us to understand that the figure of an attractor is the "simulation of a system's behavior over time" (Jo Alyson Parker 22), and a particular attractor is created in a particular dynamic system within the parameters. As Hayles remarks, "an attractor is simply any point within an orbit that seems to attract the systems to it" (*Chaos Bound* 147), including a certain spot, a cycle, and predictable rhythms, in short, the shape that linear, predictable phenomena take.

Different from limit cycles and fixed points, strange attractors are shapes that nonlinearity and chaos take, which make combinations of infinite evolving points in a multiple-dimensional space, created in nonlinear dynamic systems. Each strange attractor has its own attraction point or attraction "basin," towards which the surrounding points are attracted in the evolving process, and yet their trajectories never intersect with each other. If the attracting point is not erased, then all the trajectories in the phase space may tend toward it forever. Additionally, in the formation of a strange attractor, bifurcations are also crucial. After bifurcations, the alternation between order and disorder may be quickened, then the state of nonlinear dynamic system may tend to be much more chaotic than ever before. The dimensions of strange attractors are usually fractal, for in the process of stretching, folding and squeezing, self-similarity may be created. By "strangeness," strange attractors refer to "pattern[s] with unpredictability, confinement with orbits that never repeat themselves" (Hayles, *Chaos and Order* 4). They usually feature instability, iteration and sensitive dependence on initial conditions, indicating the condition of deterministic chaos: regular irregularity, or orderly disorder. Butterfly attractor (Lorenz attractor) and Rössler attractor as shown in Fig 1.1 and Fig 1.4 are typical patterns of strange attractors.

Second, consider the fractals. With the feature of self-similarities across scales, local or global, whatever, fractals also map the trajectories of the motion of matters in a deterministic chaos other than strange attractor. Mandelbrot set, Julia set and "the fish of yin and yang," as shown in Fig. 1.5, Fig. 1.11, and Fig. 1.13, are typical images of the fractals. As simulations of nonlinear dynamic system, fractals are common for figures or shapes of things in nature. Coastlines, clouds, ferns, mountains, weather fluctuations, to name a few, lots of things in the natural world are structured with fractals rather than regularities in the geometrical figures like triangles, squares, cubes, as we learned from mathematical class in high school. In other words, "regular linear orders are the exception, not the rule" (Hawkins 161).

As Mandelbrot remarks, "Fractals are geometrical shapes that, contrary to those of Euclid, are not regular at all. First, they are irregular all over. Secondly, they have the same degree of irregularity on all scales. ... The rules governing growth ensure that small-scale feature become translated into large-scale ones" (qtd. in Hawkins 79). So we may note that fractals feature regular irregularities in the form, and they are the intriguing figure or immanent design for the deterministic chaos. Just as Slethaug points out, fractals "show an infinite nesting of pattern within pattern, repetition across scales (i.e. from large to smaller forms), and an area devoid of fixed coordinates" (110). In brief, fractals indicate traces and dynamic activity, not only referring to "fractal portions, fracture and fragmentation, and irregularity" (Slethaug 110), but also revealing the image of chaos theory: self-similarity across scales, or, a "recursive symmetry when the same general form is repeated across many different length scales" (Hayles, *Chaos and Order* 10).

II.Journey, Dream and Chaos: Strange Attractor in *All the Pretty Horses*

"McCarthy's characters are generally road people" (Ellis, "Horses" 105), and almost all of his male protagonists are wanderers on the road. Similar to his mobile characters, McCarthy himself also wanders extensively: from Rhode Island to Tennessee, then to England and El Paso, Taxas, and then, he moves to Santa Fe, New Mexico. Journey motif is favorite for McCarthy. Most of his fiction, despite their apparent episodic organization, rely on "the central structuring principle of the journey, through which his voyagers are brought into a series of conflicts and confrontations with themselves as well as with the various communities intersected by their wanderings" (Morrison 174).

Set in the Southwestern United States and parts of Mexico from 1949 to 1951, almost one hundred years after the end of *Blood Meridian* with the background of

Mexican-American war in 1848, *All the Pretty Horses* rewrites the myth of the frontier through the problematic presentation of its effects on the young man in the genre of the postmodern Western Bildungsroman. Although an outstanding cowboy with horsemanship, excellent skills of breaking and breeding horses, chivalry codes and courage, John Grady Cole, the stubborn and romantic protagonist of *All the Pretty Horses*, wanders on the road and experiences the chaos in his life journey. Due to its apparent anachronism, John Grady's dream of being a cowboy is just a pastiche in the postmodern time. All of his pursuits, including horses, land, ranch life and romance, are merely "all the pretty horses" in the picture book. His journey to and from United States and Mexico with the pursuit of his dream of a cowboy is the key structure of the fiction, around which order alternates with chaos; meanwhile, all the problems in the fiction, such as the gap between reality and dream, conflicts of determinism and free will, and the problematic myth of the west or frontier, develop with it.

As we know, strange attractors are charted by physicists and mathematicians to illustrate the nature and presence of basins of attraction via the work of computers, and writers are seldom tempted to do so, because "human motivation, social patterns, and cultural constructs cannot be turned into the physicist's models or the mathematician's computer-generated shapes" (Slethaug 148). However, for a literary text, once it is produced, the reader, writer, the text and the world will be involved together, because it has been changed to a post-text with the reader's interpretation. Jo Alyson Parker asserts that, since the change of the parameters in a particular system may effectually constitute the different interpretation of the data, "readers also vary 'parameters' in order to find what they consider the most accurate interpretation" (24). That is to say, different readers may interpret the same text differently as regards the ambiguity of language and contextual backgrounds of both the text and reader. Parker's observation goes up to the point for the interpretation of a literary text, especially its narrative configuration. In light of chaos theory's caring much more about the involvement of the observer, the reader (observer) may imagine the fiction's narrative form in the mind, or reconstruct the patterns of the texts into figures, shapes, or graphs, as the device of "reflexive reference" proposed by Joseph Frank does in the analysis of the narrative form.

Although McCarthy never mentions that chaos theory has been taken in his fiction, it does not mean that such an issue is closed in his works, and on the contrary, the models of chaos theory have been developed in his fiction. Since the strange attractor is the mapping of the trajectories of the matter's motion in the deterministic chaotic system, John Grady's journey back and forth between United States and Mexico may be taken as the examination subject within chaos theory. Through the exploration of changes from order to chaos within the frame of the journey of John Grady, the present study attempts to map out the fiction's narrative form as strange attractor, with the concern of certain key points like attracting points, bifurcation points and self-similarities along his motion's trajectories, hoping to understand better the spatial configuration as chaos in McCarthy's fiction.

Winner of both the National Book Award and National Book Critics Circle Award for fiction in 1992, *All the Pretty Horses* makes McCarthy achieve acclaim both in the public and academic circle. For McCarthy scholarship, such a remarkable work has been read through a variety of lenses. Slethaug has made its exploration from the perspective of chaos theory and points out that John Grady's journey "could be projected as a distorted torus attractor" (151). Charting John Grady's journey as a distorted torus attractor seems oversimplified so that Slethaug still falls into the trap of Newtonic thinking, for he simply maps out John Grady's trajectories of spatial motion between Mexico and United States without consideration of its temporal elements. According to Jo Alyson Parker, "The strange attractor is simultaneously a spatial configuration and a temporal continuum-a spatialization of temporal process and a temporalization of spatial form" (26). Furthermore, although Slethaug asserts that in this fiction, "there is a pattern of turbulence from order to chaos and back into a newly constituted and qualified order" (149), he does not make close analysis of such a pattern, but mentions it generally and then quickly shifts to his discussion of McCarthy's contemporary works. As regards to the strange attractor as the spatial configuration of the fiction, Slethaug's interpretation misses the point. Also, it is not persuasive for his assumption that the unpredictable death of grandfather Cole and the stochastic phenomenon of the lightning storm during John Grady's journey in the wilderness before descent into Mexico are the fiction's strange attracting points. Apparently, he mistakes the causes and phenomenon of turbulence in John Grady's life for attracting points in the chaotic system. Meanwhile, he ignores the significance of the attracting point for the narrative, which makes his study a bit general and rough. The problems exposed in the study of Slethaug are left for the present study to explore further.

i. Attracting Points

In *All the Pretty Horses*, it seems that all the stories develop around the dream of 16-year-old John Grady. His experience on the border journey and his attempts of the accomplishment of his dream construct the trajectories of the strange attractor. Dream means Utopian ideal, featuring emptiness and fictionality, and usually lying in the layer of imagination or fantasy. Centering around his dream, there is a deterministic chaos. Just in this chaotic system, there constitute different never-intersecting trajectories, and horses in the wilderness are the dream center of John Grady and naturally construct the attracting points or the basic attraction basin, towards which all the trajectories are attracted and merged in the chaotic system of his journey.

Life is a deterministic chaos. A trivial incident or a small accident may make one into the turbulence suddenly. With the death of John Grady's maternal grandfather in the old ranch house built in 1872, the end of Grady name is announced, too. For John Grady, such an accident in his family brings great changes for him, making his life have a turn from order to chaos. In the fiction, John Grady Cole is not titled by the single "John," but "John Grady," which signifies his identification with the posterity of an old frontiersman. Loss of his grandfather facilitates a series of other losses in John Grady's life: first, the ranch. After the death of his grandfather, John Grady's mother sells the ranch, and goes to town to pursue her dream of being an actress and social life in the city; while his depressed, gambling and alcoholic father is passive towards the ownership of the ranch, when facing the sudden change of life; second, the domesticity. Loss of the ranch has made John Grady lose the stability of cowboy life, while the divorce of mother and father enhances the disorder of John Grady's life, making him a wanderer in the wilderness; third, the romance. John Grady's girlfriend Mary Catherine falls in love with an older boy with a car, whose economic position is superior to John Grady. The dense imagery of death, loss and alienation from both the inside and outside of the house in the opening section of the fiction speaks out the loss of the young boy apparently. John Grady's turbulence is caused from the death of his grandfather, yet his loss of ranch life is in consistence with the penetration of machine in the Western prairie, recalling the general atmosphere of the chaos in the society. The process of industrialization and urbanization in the twentieth century denatures the wilderness. A great many of oil fields in the prairie and the howling and bellowing of the train passing from the wilderness are good examples, signifying the demise of the West and ranchers in the West.

As Kenneth Lincoln puts it, "in many ways a man and his horse redefined Western history" (103). As the direct tie to the ranch and the west, horses are necessary for John Grady's identity of being a cowboy and of course the means for his accomplishment of his dream to regain his lost identity, romance and landscape. In the fiction, the imagery of horses frequently appears together with each period of John Grady's journey, playing the great role in the progress of the plot and presentation of the fictional theme. After the funeral of his grandfather, John Grady walks out of the house. Standing on the road west from his grandfather's house, "where the Western fork of the old Comanche road coming down out of the Kiowa country to the north passed through the Westernmost section of the ranch," John Grady seems to see the Comanche warriors riding on that ancient road, which is "like a dream of the past where the painted ponies and the riders of that lost nation came down out of the north with their faces chalked and their long hair plaited and each armed for war which was their life and the women and children and women with children at their breasts all of them pledged in blood and redeemable in blood only" (Horses 5). As we know, the Comanches, as the natives in the west, almost disappear from that land after the Western expansion in the 19th century, and in *Blood Meridian*, they are enemies and victims of the Anglo-Saxon whites. Here, to make John Grady's situation analogous to the lost nation and ethnic group with martial codes and spirit of blood and violence not merely reminds John Grady of his loss of the rance life, which is similar to the loss of land of the Comanches, but also implies his inherent frontier spirit. Meanwhile, to juxtapose the past and the present, the history and the reality, the dream and factuality, foregrounds the gap between the dream and reality, foreshadowing the futility of John Grady's journey in Mexico with his frontier dream. Without awareness of the changes of time and space and the persistence in his dream of being a cowboy, John Grady's life is made much more disorderly, even though his later frontier journey in Mexico cannot help him regain his lost order.

In the fiction, John Grady does identify himself with horses. He could commune with horses through tender embrace and talking. More than that, for John Grady, "what he [loves] in horses [is] what he [loves] in men, the blood and the heat of the blood that [run] them" (Horses 6). In his imagination, walking together with him in his ride homeward are these ancient warriors, riding on "in that darkness they'd become, rattling past with their stone-age tools of war in default of all substance and singing softly in blood and longing South across the plains to Mexico" (Horses 6). The association of the love of the horse with a lost nation with martial codes in the west seems to suggest that John Grady's journey is caused by his dream to be a cowboy with colonial codes, which traces its origin back to the collective unconscious of American nation: the traditional myth of the frontier or the west.

The frontier in United States was closed in 1890, and the West as the "safety valve" proposed in Turner's frontier thesis has lost its value with the disappearance of the frontier. Despite that, in the minds of young John Grady, "Mexico" has been metamorphosed into his new "West" or "frontier" waiting for him to make frontier adventures and regain his lost ranch life and landscape, although he knows nothing about Mexican history, culture and society before his actions. With him and his friend Rawlins, is only "an oil company map that Rawlins had picked up at the cafe," on which, "there [are] roads and rivers and towns on the American side of the map as far South as the Rio Grande and beyond that all [are] white" (Horses 34). "White" means "blankness," which suggests that there will be something to fill in, to be occupied, to be penetrated, and "beyond that all was white," which implies that Mexico is a place with blankness, waiting for John Grady to "fill in," to "occupy," to "penetrate," to make his frontier adventures for the purpose to regain his lost "paradise." Indeed, in John Grady's mind, it is that "spread" of the ranch with beautiful scenery and large rich land that attracts him, which could be presented from his talking with Rawlins: "you got eyes for the spread? John Grady studies the fire. I dont know, he said. I aint though about it" (Horses 138). The adventures with colonial codes make the failure of John Grady's journey doomed, causing him into another turn of chaos in his life.

Before his descent into Mexico, John Grady gets a saddle as a gift from his father, though his father is aware that the ranch life has been passed, and "the country would never be the same" (Horses 25). He talks to John Grady, "People don't feel safe no more. We are like Comanches was two hundred years ago. ... We don't know what's going to show up here come daylight" (Horses 25-6). It is ironic that John Grady's father also draws an analogy between his lost identity as a ranch man and that of the Comanches, which facilitates the decision of John Grady's journey into Mexico to pursue his dream of being a cowboy, even though this dream may be a fantasy. Besides the saddle, one of the signifiers to be associated with horses, we are given the other image of horses associating with John Grady's dream. On his way home after the departure from his father, John Grady encounters a paper white horse skull in the wilderness. The juxtaposition of the broken horse skull with the saddle as a gift as well as the incorporeality of ancient Indian nations links discrete images in different temporal-spatial spots together, not only foreshadowing the futility of John Grady's later journey, but also foregrounding the temporal-spatial dislocation of John Grady's dream together with horses and cowboy life. More important, such a device of the juxtaposition of images recurring in the text makes the fiction synchronic rather than diachronic in its narration, hence the spatiality in its narrative form.

Furthermore, what impresses the reader most is the oil-painting of horses hanging in the sitting room of the Grady's house, in which "half of dozen of them breaking through a pole corral and their manes [are] long and blowing and their eyes wild" (Horses 15). The "wildness" of horses in the picture suggests John Grady's wildness in his dream, though he has been reminded that "those are picturebook horses" by his grandfather (Horses 16). The framing of wild horses in the picture implies the fictitiousness of John Grady's dream, which echoes in the title of the book, "all the pretty horses." The novel's title is from a child's lullaby: "Hushaby, / Don't you cry, / Go to sleep, little baby, / when you wake, / you shall have, / all the pretty little horses-/ Blacks and bays, / Dapples and grays, / coach and six-a little horses" (Luce, "When You Wake" 58). The lullaby introduces the motifs of dreaming and wishing. Just as Dianne C. Luce assumes, "Horses are literally what John Grady wishes for in his world, but through their association with the idealized picture-book horses in the painting, ... the pretty horses of the title come to represent any fantasy, dream, wish, or object of desire to which one might aspire or feel entitled" ("When You Wake" 58), John Grady's dream around horses is doomed to fail. All his dreams are simply "all the pretty horses" in the picture book finally. From the death of his grandfather, John Grady has suffered a series of losses in his life. The recurrent imagery of horses in the text, such as the warriors with horses for the lost Comanches, the horses in the picture, the saddle as a gift, and the horse skull in the wilderness, is to foreground the iteration of the chaos in John Grady's life, not merely reminding the reader of the falsity of the dream driven by frontier myth in its subtext, but also strengthening the dynamic changes of John Grady's life as a deterministic chaos.

As Jo Alyson Parker holds, "a strange attractor occurs when the attracting point in a chaotic dynamical system has become unstable, thus concurrently attracting and repelling the system trajectory. There is an actual attracting point (or points) in the system" (28). In effect, the attracting points of John Grady's turbulent journey are not stable. His loss and gain of horses correspond with his life's fluctuation between order and chaos, which causes his trajectories along the border of America and Mexico to shift back and forth, and even to go astray sometimes, foregrounding the chaotic nature of his frontier journey. In the second section of the novel, John Grady almost finishes his dream of being a cowboy through his excellent horsemanship to earn the recognition of the whole Rocha family at La Purisima in Mexico. He is once again together with horses and has the identity of a cowboy in this Mexican hacienda.

In the hacienda in Mexico, John Grady's identification with the strong and powerful stallion grows to be apparent in his riding out along the cienage road or the verge of the marshes or somewhere in the ranch. He could feel and sense as the horse does, "while inside the vaulting of the ribs between his knees the darkly meated heart pumped of who's will and the blood pulsed and the bowls shifted in their massive blue evolutions of who's will and the stout thighbones and knee and cannon and tendons like flaxen hawsers ... where the world burned" (Horses 128). However, such a life of peace and order with horses is only transient. Sooner, his life is shifted to a turbulence again. Due to his involvement with Blevins's stealing of horses and murdering, John Grady ends his transient orderly life and is sent to prison at La Encantada, where he suffers wounds and hurts physically and psychologically, experiencing another turn of chaos in his life journey.

Horses accompany every period of John Grady's life journey, making his chaotic life inseparable from the horses. Even in his dream of the sleep after his arrest, the lost paradise with horses as the center revisits him:

That night he dreamed of horses in a field on a high plain where the spring rains had brought up the grass and the wildflowers out of the ground and the flowers ran all blue and yellow far as the eye could see and in the dream he was among the horses running and in the dream he himself could run with the horses and they coursed the young mares and fillies over the plain where their rich bay and their rich chestnut colors shone in the sun and the young colts ran with their dreams and trampled down the flowers in a haze of pollen that hung in the sun like powdered gold ...". (Horses 161)

After his release from the jail, one of the important things for John Grady to deal with in Mexico is to go back to regain the lost horses, which causes him to have another journey into Mexico, making his life's chaotic system into another trajectory.

In the third section of the fiction, John Grady not only regains the horses of Rawlins and Blevins from the evil Captain in Mexico, but also tries his best to find the owner of the horse stolen by Blevins across the whole Texas. However, such a hard journey achieves nothing in that Blevins's name is "borrowed" from others, and in America, there are lots of Jimmy Blevins. Just as Father Jimmy Blevins comments, "There's any number of Jimmy Blevins out there in the world but its Jimmy Blevins Smith and Jimmy Blevins Jones. ...We get em [sic] from overseas you know. Jimmy Blevins Chang" (Horses 295), the ambiguity of the identity for his friend, Blevins, strengthens the sense of chaos in John Grady's journey.

Finally, John Grady gains one more horse after his adventures into Mexico, for he is sanctified to own the horse stolen by Blevins from the judge in Texas, who feels for John Grady's situation and even is moved by such a young boy's persistence in his dream of being a cowboy. Though John makes Blevins's horses with ambiguous origins legal and entitled, yet the ambiguity of horse's origin and the instability of its owner's identity further emphasize that John Grady's dream of being a cowboy with horses and his adventures with horses into Mexico are only fantasy. All that he gets through his frontier "conquest" are nothing but the bleached horse skull without flesh and soul in the wilderness sealed in the history and past, battered and broken, or the horses in his sleeping dream, coming upon "an antique site where some ordering of the world had failed" (Horses 280).

Horses visit John Grady again and again from the very beginning of the novel, in which horses of the ancient warriors are imagined to be together with him, to the final section of the novel, in which horses walking on the ancient road occur in his sleeping dream in his lonely journey in the wilderness. The reiteration of the imagery of horses from the very beginning to the ending of the fiction strengthens the importance of horses in John Grady's chaotic journey, and meanwhile foregrounds the "synchronicity" of the occurrence of events. Carl G. Jung has got the inspiration from the divination of *The Book of Changes* with the sixty-four hexagrams and suggests his idea of synchronicity. By synchronicity, Jung means the recurrent occurrence of an incident or an image in one's life, which is different from Newtonian causality (209). Rather than the delineation of the diachronic or linear progress of events in the temporal axis, synchronicity pays more emphasis on the disproportion of causality and spatial association of things in the world. According to *The Book of Changes*, the recurrence of an image or an incident in one's life presents the temporal-spatial accordance of certain events in life, which is chaotic itself and inexplainable from the diachronic or linear perspective. Apart from the synchronicity of horses occurring in John Grady's life, the juxtaposition of different images of horses in the text as mentioned in the previous passages also enhances horses to be the center of John Grady's frontier dream from the synchronic narration. Therefor, horses in the wilderness as the attracting points of John Grady's chaotic life system get foregrounded, towards which all the trajectories of John Grady's journey are attracted while they are never intersected with one another, making his journey more chaotic.

Seemingly the twin of *Blood Meridian* with the genre of postmodern Western, *All the Pretty Horses* is also self-reflective, critiquing the very genre of which it is a part. Both are "complicit" in their criticizing of the violence and emptiness of the myth of the frontier, although the former presents it through naked description of the blood and brutality hidden behind the history, while the latter exposes it through romantic presentation of the falsity and fictionality hidden in the reality. Like the "black hole" in the outer space, or Derridean "traces," which are "always already" present, the myth of frontier with horses in the wilderness as its images attracts John Grady to make his frontier journey into Mexico, and yet results in the chaos, indeterminate and inaccessible.

In sum, horses in the wilderness are the center of John Grady's dream, and even his incarnation. More importantly, horses are closely linked with him in his turbulent journey in the wilderness, and almost occur all the way from his decision of frontier journey into Mexico to his meeting of Blevins in the wilderness, to his romance with Alejandra in the Mexican haciendado, to his imprisonment, to his regaining of the lost horses through the fighting with the evil Captain. In a word, horses in the wilderness construct the attracting points of John Grady's chaotic life system. Just due to the instable nature of the attracting points, his life is made to be a deterministic chaos. The formation of the attracting points in John Grady's life system is one of the steps for the configuration of strange attractor in the fiction, and they are inseparable from some other important points, such as bifurcations and across-scaling self-similarities. However, for convenience of the study, we have to discuss them one by one. In the following part, the bifurcations of John Grady's chaotic journey will be further explored.

ii. Bifurcation Points

Chaos dominates the life of John Grady since the loss of his familiar style of ranch life. After his failure to persuade his mother to keep the ranch through his Southeast journey to the city of San Antonio, he decides to go Southward to Mexico to start his adventurous journey with the dream to rebuild the order in his life. However, the world is as complicated as chaos theory implies, decision may change one's life, yet uncertainties are on the road. As a 16-year-old young boy, his future life is unpredictable itself. His decision to make adventures in an unknown place brings him into the turbulence much more terrible than his expectation. In the presentation of John Grady's journey, McCarthy first puts him in the situation of turbulence with loss and death, then in the process of the journey, John Grady experiences the alternation between order and chaos due to the dynamic system's instability caused from its sensitive dependence on initial conditions, which exhibits the nature of chaotic behaviour in the dynamic system. In his chaotic life system, three persons, Blevins, Alejandra and Alfonsa construct bifurcation points, making his life system fluctuate between order and chaos.

The plotting structure in triplet seems to be popular for McCarthy's texts, *No Country for Old Men* is a good example. *All the Pretty Horses* consists of three sections: the ride into the Mexican highlands, the scenes on the hacienda (ranch) and in the prison, and the journey home to Texas, presenting the tripartite structure. Besides the tripartite structure in the fiction, the number "three" occurs in the fiction's plotting frequently. For instance, three characters are arranged in one group, adding the sense of chaos in each period of John Grady's journey; three days are spent for the manacled ride of John Grady and Rawlins to La Encantada, where Blevins steals back his horse; three days are taken for the interrogation of John Grady and Rawlins, who are counted as the horse-theft suspect at the jail; three times for the knifing of Rawlins in the stomach from a cuchillero (killer) in the prison; three guards for three prisoners on the way to the execution of Blevins; and three horses for John Grady to regain in the final section after his release from prison, and so on. All in all, the number "three" taken frequently in the plotting structure strengthens the chaotic feature for the narrative form.

The number "three" is sensitive, and it is chaotic by itself in chaos theory. Besides its association with the principle of periodic "three," as demonstrated above and in *No Country for Old Men*, it is also tangled with the three-body problem in science. Harriet Hawkins argues that, "the number three, ... is associated with predictable unpredictability in chaos science and discussions of three-body systems may explain why a triangular structure lends a measure of unpredictability to the drama in general" (156). In *Strange Attractors* (1995), Hawkins associates the three-body problems in science with the triangular structure of characters in Shakespearean drama. Hawkins assumes that "the three-body problem in science seems cognate to the ubiquitous triangles that pose comparable problems in literature (157). For Hawkins, "Othello and Desdemona might have had trouble, but might well have worked out their differences and settled down" without the tanglement of Iago in their affairs (156). Hawkins' interpretation of the triangular structure of characters in *Othello* is in accordance with James Gleick's understanding about the three-body problem in chaos science. As Gleick puts it:

The two-body problem is easy. Newton solved it completely. Each body-the earth and the moon, for example-travels in a perfect ellipse around the system's joint center of gravity. Add just one more gravitational object, however, and everything changes. The three-body problem is hard, and worse than hard. As Poincaré discovered, it is almost impossible. The orbits can be calculated numerically for a while, and with powerful computers they can be tracked for a long while before uncertainties begin to take over. But the equations cannot be solved analytically, which means that long-term questions about a three-body system cannot be answered. ... Binary star systems tend to form inside them, stars paring off in tight little orbits, and when a third star encounters a binary, one of these tend to get a sharp kick. (145)

Concerning *All the Pretty Horses*, the three-body problems for the figures in the text are crucial for McCarthy to add the predictable unpredictability in John Grady's journey. Without the participation of the third body, the relations of characters, no matter they are friends, or lovers, or family members, are harmonious with each other. Once one more partner is added in the system, there will appear the bifurcation point in the dynamic system, making the system much more turbulent than ever before. The mysterious person Jimmy Blevins is such a person, and his joining the party constructs one of the bifurcation points in the chaotic system, from which the journey of John Grady falls into predictable uncertainties.

Both John Grady and Rawlins are in good terms, for they are complementary in their character. John Grady is idealistic, while Rawlins is pragmatic, so John Grady can be warned not to be radical in some of his decisions. Their descent into Mexico is smooth and sound before the joining of Blevins, even harmonious with each other from the enjoyment of freedom and adventures in the wilderness. However, since Blevins joins their group, it seems that all are in chaos, hence changing the trajectories of John Grady along the border of Mexico and United States. First, the friendship. Both John Grady and Rawlins have quarrels over the problem of bringing Blevins together when crossing the border. Rawlins thinks that the riddle-like Blevins, horse and gun as well as his young age may bring disasters for their journey, getting them "throwed in the jailhouse" (Horses 41). Second, the destiny. Both John Grady and Rawlins are charged and then sent to prison at La Ecantada as two probable accomplices to Blevins, a suspect of the horse thief and murderer of a Mexican officer when attempting to regain his stolen horse from a stable after the lightening storm. In the prison, both John Grady and Rawlins experience the trials of life and death, and suffer hurts and wounds physically and spiritually, which directly leads to the decision of Rawlins to go back to Texas, and John Grady's change of his trajectories to make another adventure into Mexico on his own with the aim to revenge Blevins's unjust execution and regain the stolen horse of Blevins, even win back his love from Alejandra, having another turn of disorder in his life. More importantly, such a charge of the accomplice to Blevins makes John Grady lose the trust from the Hacendado and the Dueña Alfonsa, which leads to his loss of chance to regain his lost past forever and thus suffering the loss again from his almost accomplishment of dream: stable family, ranch life, and romance. Finally, the journey. For the purpose of making a revenge on the evil Captain, and finding out the owner of the stolen horse, John Grady even kidnaps the evil Captain and thus suffering another severe wound in the thigh in his return journey to Mexico on his own. Of course, such a trial in Mexico alters his life view and life journey. In the end of the fiction, when meeting Rawlins to send back his horse Junior in San Angelo, John Grady's opinion about his home town or home country is different from that of his friend. For Rawlins, San Angelo is still a good country, where he could find a position in the oil field, while for John Grady, "it aint my country. ... I dont know where it is. I dont know what happens to country" (Horses 299). This country with the frontier myth tells him that he could accomplish his American dream through his frontier adventures, and going South (i.e. West) into the wilderness can help him acquire what he wishes, just like his fore-fathers, yet he still fails and has to go on with wandering on the road. All in all, a series of losses in the later journey of John Grady begin with the join of the third body, Jimmy Blevins, in the system, causing the trajectories of his journey into the total turbulence and instability.

To a certain extent, it might be argued that Blevins is the sensitive bifurcation point, from which sensitive dependence on the interior changes produces unpredictable disasters for John Grady's journey. Dianne C. Luce speaks right, "Many of the trials John Grady endures derive from Jimmy Blevins, the human lightening rod who appears on the scene almost the moment John Grady and Rawlins set off for Mexico and almost mysteriously as Judge Holden appeared to Glanton's gang, out of nowhere" ("When You Wake" 62). Besides his mysterious origin and nature of being a human "lightening rod," Blevins has a legendary family history, in which lots of his family numbers are struck to death by lightening. In the fiction, lots of minor details associated with stochastic force of nature are built up to create the concept of turbulence for John Grady's journey. For instance, the lightening storm after the boys cross the border into Mexico, frightens Blevins, leading to his loss of horse, gun, boots and clothing; small gray nameless birds are driven by the storm and impaled against the roadside cholla, some "[espalier] in attitudes of stillborn flight or hanging loosely in their feathers. Some of them [are] still alive and they [twist] on their spines as the horses [pass] on and [raise] their heads and [cry] out" (Horses 73). Just as Slethaug points out, "These are unpredictable and sometimes tragic phenomena, which dramatically alter the lives of those affected" (153). Finally, even though John Grady and Rawlins do return to San Angelo and presumably resume a more stable existence, yet they never return back to their original sate, for they have been changed. They are no longer that pair of young boys, riding "at once jaunty and circumspect, like thieves newly loosed in that dark electric, like young thieves in a glowing orchard, loosely jacketed against the cold and ten thousand worlds for the choosing" (Horses 30).

Bifurcation points make the chaos accessible in the dynamic system. After bifurcations, the system tends to become more chaotic, causing the fluctuations of the order and chaos never to settle down, even going fast exponentially. In the strange attractor, bifurcation points may cause the trajectories of matter's motion to move towards different directions unpredictably, yet never intersecting with each other. Besides Blevins, Dueña Alfonsa might be the other "the third body" character in the party, nevertheless, this time the partner changes to be a lover rather than a "buddy" for John Grady, creating the other bifurcation point in his motion's trajectories, and hence leading to his life's falling into turbulence once again from the transient peace and order.

The second section of the fiction gives a description of John Grady's brief and happy, free and peaceful cowboy life on the hacienda at La Purisima after the chaos in the barren wilderness, and then falls quickly into the turbulence of violence and brutality in the prison at La Encantada. The hacienda at La Purisima seems to be thenew Eden for John Grady after hardship in his journey:

The Hacienda de Nuestra Señora de la Purisima Concepción was a ranch of eleven thousand hectares situated along the edge of the Bolsón de Cuatro Ciénegas in the state of Coahuila. The Western sections ran into the Sierra de Anteojo to elevations of nine thousand feet but South and east the ranch occupied part of the broad barrial or basin floor of the bolsón and was well watered with natural springs and clear streams and dotted with marshes and shallow lakes or lagunas. In the lakes and in the streams were species of fish not known elsewhere on earth and birds and lizards and other forms of life as well all along relict here for the desert stretched away on every side. (Horses 97)

In this ideal place, John Grady seems to regain his lost landscape and find his expected position due to his excellent skills for a cowboy, who could break a herd of horses in four days and work all day on no sleep. He achieves appreciation and trust from the Hacendado and the Dueña at La Purisima. More important, he obtains the favors of the daughter of this paradise-like ranch at first sight. He even decides on staying there for "about a hundred years," and McCarthy's iteration device in language foregrounds his happiness with love: when he rides the wild stallion bareback, he "loved to ride the horse. In truth he loved to be seen riding it. In truth he loved for her to see him riding it" (Horses 96, 127).

However, happy life never lasts long, and "the hacienda is not the location of a recovered cowboy paradise, but rather an alien world" (Cant, *Cormac McCarthy* 127). John Grady quickly falls into turbulence again due to his romance with Alejandra, which happens just as Alfonsa remarks that "between the wish and the thing the world lies waiting" (Horses 238). Although his involvement with the case of Blevins is one of the causes for him to lose the trust of Alejandra's father and her grand-aunt, yet the differences between lovers in class, position and identity directly lead to the disagreement with their romance from both Alfonsa and Rocha. Jay Ellis assumes, "John Grady is remarkably unsuccessful as a potential husband. In Alejandra, he chose a woman so highborn and virtuous that his relationship degraded her" (*No Place* 212). Ellis' viewpoint is reasonable, at least John Grady's rashness does influence the reputation of Alejandra, whose living country is sill constrained with patriarchy. There, "a woman's reputation is all she has" (Horses 136). As for the young lovers, they are so innocent that they do not consider the consequence of their continuous dating at night. Alfonsa reminds John Gray of the reality that "society is very important in Mexico. Where women do not even have the rote" (Horses 230). In her long talk with him, some imageries associating with randomness and uncertainties, such as chess-playing and coin-producing, are taken to remind him of the gap between reality and dream, anticipating the unsanctioned romance and turbulence for John Grady in Mexico.

Morrison holds that John Grady's banishment from the hacienda is due to the intervention of Alejandra's grand-aunt and father, and he even considers John Grady's situation similar to that of "the fallen Adam," who is driven out of Eden "by the vengeful father and defeated by the wily serpent (in the guise of Alejandra's godmother)" (180). Morrison's understanding is partly reasonable and partly wrong. It is proper to take Rocha as the angry God, for both young man and old man do commune with each other in the way that Adam does with God. In the talk during their billiard-playing, Rocha warns John Grady to give up his romantic idea to stay together with Alejandra in Mexico through the case of failed romance between Alfonsa and Gustavo. In Rocha's mind, Mexico is a special place, even Spanish culture cannot change it, so he believes that John Grady's attempt to achieve his purpose with European culture is "the idea of Quixote. But even Cervantes could not envision such a country at Mexico" (Horses 146). More importantly, in Rocha's vision, "One country is not another country. Mexico is not Europe" (Horses 145). Rocha means that John Grady is wrong for he tries to achieve his frontier dream through his "culture penetration" via the romance with a noble Mexican lady. With regard to his attempts of imposing the codes and regulations of the frontier myth onto Mexican culture and society, that's simply illusionary. Different from Rocha, a strong-minded keeper of the benefits of his family and nation, Alfonsa is a lady with liberal ideas, and feels for John Grady. It is unfair to take her as the serpent in the garden, after all, she buys John Grady out of the prison and provides him and Rawlins with a large sum of money to return home. We may consider her reasonably. As the surrogate and God mother of Alejandra, what she cares most is only her grand-niece's reputation and happiness, so she has to stand on Rocha's side from the perspective of a failed lady in romance and ideals.

As regards the failure of romance of John Grady and of course his chaotic life journey, Alejandra is also one of the elements to be considered. Similar to Blevins and Alfonsa, her joining of John Grady's life brings about catastrophic effect on him. As the third party of the group (both John Grady and Rawlins), her romance with John Grady ends his peaceful cowboy life in his paradise, thus constructing another bifurcation point of the trajectory for John Grady's motion. Just as the chaos implies, everything in the world are made up of *yin* and *yang*, or order and disorder, both alternate sensitively depending on the interior changes of initial conditions. The romance with Alejandra almost makes John Grady achieve what he wishes to acquire in his frontier journey, such as horses, land, ranch, romance and domesticity, while, the romance with this Mexican noble lady also plunges him into chaos once again from the transient order in his life. Just as Rawlins' parodic cowboy discourse tells, "A goodlookin horse is like a goodlookin woman ... They're always more trouble than what they're worth" (Horses 89). The spoiled Alejandra indeed responds to John Grady's worries that "you're fixin to get me in trouble" with the challenge that "you are in trouble" (Horses 131). Similar to Blevins, John Grady's "Eve" brings him into the jail, making him suffer imprisonment, hurt, trauma and loss. Such an incident ends his peaceful cowboy life in his paradise. More importantly, it directly causes his another crossing into Mexico, hence another turn of disorder in his life.

The great differences between the lovers are crucial factors to consider in the turbulence of John Grady. In spite of their differences in nationality and culture, the vast gulf of class and status between them is hardly passable for them. John Grady is only a cowboy, i.e. a common worker at the ranch. Although he has had Abuela as his wet nurse in his house, he is still lower-classed, and his family at most traces back to the early frontiersmen in West Texas. For Americans, cowboys are romanticized. Actually, they are not self-reliant, independent figures as that depicted in literature, rather, historically, they were dependent "wage-slave[s], tied to an arduous existence controlled by the often-absent owners of ever-large ranches" (McGilchrist 154), and they were "badly fed and badly paid," their status "was little higher ... than a tramp, wandering from ranch to ranch in search of a job or driving another man's beef to another man's railroad for salt pork, beans, and forty dollars a month" (Kollin 575). Whereas, Alejandra is a noble lady from an old aristocratic family, which can trace its lineage back to lots of generations, and even associated with the royal family in

Mexican history. The social class differences between the lovers are made obviously from each of their respective horses at the first sight. The horse Alejandra rides is a spirited Arabian, famous for beauty, class, endurance, speed and purity, while John Grady rides a newly broken-in mesteño, or quarter horse, namely, a cross-bred horse used for working the ranch and cattle. Superficially the failure of romance is caused from the transaction between Alfonsa and Alejandra on the condition that both of lovers never meet each other after John Grady's release with the purpose to keep the family reputation, yet in effect, various variables interacting with each other in the system lead to the failure of the romance. In the end, Alejandra also decides to be responsible for her family and her own self. Therefore, once again, John Grady suffers loss due to the denial of the mother figure in the incarnation of Alfonsa, and also the refusal of the lover, Alejandra; however, this time it is the romance that he he fails to regain, and of course the failure of the romance causes his loss of the chance to regain the ranch. Before his descent into Mexico, the denial of his mother makes him fail to be a cowboy with his beloved horses in the ranch, and also the refusal of the lover, Mary Catherine, makes him suffer the failure of romance. The recurrent losses in his life add more chaotic color for John Grady's life system.

Nevertheless, John Grady's life is doomed to be chaotic from the beginning. His turbulence and dilemma result from the motion of deterministic chaos. Strange attractor features with sensitive dependence on initial conditions, so all the variables in the system are necessary to consider. Apart from three bifurcations consisted of Blevins, Alejandra and Alfonsa, in John Grady's life system, a great many variables may be combined or singly work to make his life journey chaotic, such as his grandfather's death, his mother's selling of the ranch, his enchantment of horses and cowboy's life, his involvement with Blevins's stealing horses and murdering, his disagreement with the vision of life from Alfonsa, his ignorance of Mexican culture and society, his disregard of the changing of time and space, the impassable gap of position and class between lovers, and some other minor causes he does not pay attention to in his life. The list may go on. Though he crosses the border physically, yet spiritually he fails and has to be "banished" from his Eden. Jarrett speaks right, John Grady "has not recovered or reopened the frontier but merely ... crossed into another 'closed' landscape, possessed by an aristocratic culture impervious to the cowboy myth" (*Cormac McCarthy* 101).

For McCarthy, "John Grady Cole's dilemma is an example of steady-state activity and order suddenly thrown into disorder and turbulence" (Slethaug 19), which is produced from the disproportion between cause and effect. Everything in the world is interconnected, and nothing can be considered singly or separate from the others. Such an idea has been reiterated first through Rawlins, who says, "Way the world is. ... you don't know what's going to happen," then by the Mexicans at La Purisima, who believe that "it was no accident of circumstance that a man be born in a certain country and not some other," and last, from Alfonsa, after John Grady's release from prison, who remarks that things are in mutual connection, and "human decision could never be abandoned to a blind agency but could only be relegated to human decisions more and more remote from their consequences" (Horses 92, 226, 231). In brief, bifurcations facilitate the changes of variables in the system, making John Grady's life fluctuate between order and chaos.

iii. Self–Similarities

Strange attractors in nonlinear dynamic systems can present very complicated geometrical properties, and usually they contain self-similarities across scales through stretching and folding. In the design of turbulence of John Grady's journey to and from United States and Mexico, McCarthy makes it in accordance with some features of strange attractors like the self-similarity from the iteration of the motion's trajectories. Due to uncertainties caused by sensitive dependence on initial conditions in the voyage, John Grady's journey presents the nonlinearity or the disproportionate cause and effect, making his dream a pastiche in the postmodern time. For the process's turbulence, the text also constructs some imageries or characters with self-similarities, creating lots of mutual mapping for human beings and animals, or human beings and natural surroundings, or characters in the fiction and reality, or the narrative structure, hence making the text the dynamic and spatial form of symmetrical asymmetry or orderly disorder locally and globally.

In the final pages of the novel, we confront a similar vision with that of the opening pages of the novel, in which the lonely wandering hero riding on the horse is juxtaposed with living Indians camped just outside of Iraan, Texas. These Indians "stood watching him," with "no curiosity about him at all. As if they knew all that they needed to know. They stood and watched him pass and watched him vanish upon that landscape solely because he was passing. Solely because he would vanish" (Horses 301). Unlike the earlier descriptions of those Indian warriors, who ride on "in that darkness ... singing softly in blood and longing South across the plains to Mexico" (Horses 6), these scattered Indians in the prairie are made to be apparently indifferent and dull. Similarly, unlike the earlier image of John Grady with youth, courage and vigor, in the end of the novel he is presented to be a single man, riding and passing "like the shadow ... . Passed and paled into the darkening land, the world to come" (Horses 302). The tone of melancholy in the passage suggests the loss and futility of John Grady's pursuit of his ideals: the ranch; horses; domesticity (due to the death of his father and surrogate mother); and romance (with Alejandra). Additionally, the juxtaposition of the young rider after adventures in Mexico with the lost ethnic group and nation implies "an equality between John Grady and the Comanches, who have passed out of the existence" (McGilchrist 154), making his life journey tragic with his pastiche of cowboy's frontier life in an unsuitable time and place with historical anachronism.

Despite the obvious self-similarity of the opening and ending sections of the novel to describe the situation of John Grady before and after his turbulent journey, some other similarities are frequent in the details of the novel, creating the mutual mapping in the narrative text. In the beginning of the novel, when standing outside the house, John Grady listens to the bawling of a little calf, which is confronted with the train's passing from the prairie, causing the shake of the earth, making John "feel it under his feet" (Horses 3); while in the end of the book, John Grady meets "a solitary bull rolling in the dust against the bloodred sunset like an animal in sacrificial torment," and just in the barren country without the cattle, "the pumpjacks in the Yates Field ranged against the skyline rose and dipped like mechanical birds" (Horses 302, 301). Perhaps, McCarthy suggests the similarities of the destiny of animals with his young stubborn "hero" through the mapping of the lonely wanderer with the animals in the wilderness, for both are doomed to pass into the "darkening land" with the fictional ideas of penetration into the modern time with the coming of industry and technology (Horses 302). It might be argued that the novel does not merely tell the destiny of a young boy, but serves as an allegory to warn all of the young Americans with the cowboy dream soaked in the myth of the frontier or the west. More exactly, it is also "a model for all of humankind" in its subtext (Slethaug 153). We human beings go from one ideal to another without meditation, which is just like the way of our reading of a book. Without reading the previous page, the following one will not be known, for each page in the book predicts something new. Such is the implication of the tragic destiny of John Grady: any pursuit in life will not have a satisfactory ending, for the desired object is so abstract in the distance that our failure of pursuit has been doomed from its beginning.

The similar destinies between humans and animals appear in other minor details from the book, for example, the hurt and dead birds in the lightening storm when crossing the border into Mexico also map out the tragic destiny of young "hero" in the later turbulent storm of life. The sad eyes of a dying deer sacrificing to keep John Grady alive on his way back to Texas map out the sorrow of Alejandra, who promises to depart from his lover and turns out to be a sacrifice for her passion, her lover and her family. The Dueña is right, the world's heart beats at a terrible cost and its pain and beauty are intertwined with each other. Also, horses are taken to map out the destinies of each of the respective owners. For instance, Redbo (i.e. "redbone"), the horse of John Grady's father, with the color of red, on which John Grady rides to revenge Blevins, seems to imply the wildness in his character, and simultaneously foreshadows the bloody quality of John Grady's another Mexican adventure on his own. In his journey to and from USA-Mexico, John Grady's riding horse is Grullo, a kind of pale horse. "Pale horse, pale rider," as the *Book of Revelation* prophesies. Besides its association with death, the horse with the color "pale" is also an omen for John Grady's chaos in his journey. Interestingly, Blevins' horse is dark, which anticipates the instability of his whereabouts, identity, destiny, and even mysterious disasters he brings to both John

Grady and Rawlins, and of course himself involved, too. As for Alejandra, a noble lady from an aristocratic family, her spirited Arabian horse matches her nobleness in the status and character.

Moreover, the fiction arranges some self-similarities in its choices of imagery. For instance, the book begins with the funeral of John Grady's grandfather, and ends with the burial of Abuela in the cemetery, "the last remaining tie to the ranch" for John Grady (Morrison 177), which indicates the total ending of the frontiersman family with the name of Grady in the west. Before conducting the journey into Mexico, John Grady rides on that ancient Comanche road, when the sun "sat bloodred and elliptic under the reefs of bloodred cloud before him"; while, after his adventures in Mexico, the "solitary bull in the dust" in the wilderness rolls against "the bloodred sunset like a sacrificial torment" (Horses 5, 302). In *All the Pretty Horses*, McCarthy frequently employs "blood" in his description of the landscape, which is like what he does in Blood Meridian. The reiteration of the imagery of bloodred sunset in both the opening and ending section seems to suggest the quality of John Grady's journey, mapping the situation of human beings with natural surroundings.

After the decision to go to Mexico, John Grady meets his ex-girlfriend in the street. Mary Catherine's fragmented reflection "in the windows of the Federal Building across the street standing there" (Horses 29) maps the later futile romance with Alejandra at La Purisima, implying something void for the expected romance of John Grady through his journey, which is just like the flower in the mirror or the moon in the water, beautiful and yet inaccessible. Indeed, in the second section, the novel's presentation of the romance of John Grady with Alejandra is set in the lake at a moonlight-lit night. McCarthy fully makes uses of the cinematographic device to produce the beautiful spectacle, with the gaze from both John Grady and the reader:

The water was black and warm and he turned in the lake and spread his arms in the water and the water was so dark and so silky and he watched across the still black surface to where she stood on the shore with the horse and he watched where she stepped from her pooled clothing so pale, so pale, like a chrysalis entering, and walking into the water. (Horses 141)

Furthermore, the novel also builds up the similarities between various characters, creating the textual symmetries in the characterization. For example, John Grady's actress mother dislikes the dull life on the ranch and lives in the hotel of the city with her lover. Similarly, Alejandra's mother also lives together with Alejandra in Mexico city, and Alejandra goes back to the ranch occasionally. Interestingly, John Grady's mother is also similar to Alejandra's surrogate mother in their refusal of the objects John Grady dreams in his life: the ranch from the former, and the girl from the latter. Despite Rawlins' disagreement with bringing Blevins into Mexico, John Grady still persists on. This deals with the other point of self-similarity constructed by McCarthy when mapping out the trajectories of John Grady's journey. Both John Grady and Blevins are similar to each other: both are homeless orphans from the loss of domesticity due to the divorce of father and mother; both have a dream of the west to be a cowboy; both are excellent in their horsemanship and marksmanship; and both are rash in the character without consideration of the consequences for their actions. Seemingly, John Grady admires Blevins in his sub-consciousness, so that's why he refuses to sell Blevins to the wax man from Mexico and insists on bringing him together to Mexico. More importantly, both are ethnocentric psychologically, when Blevins asks John Grady to bring him together to go to Mexico, his only reason is that "[he] is an American" (Horses 46), obviously displaying his sense of superiority as an American. Though the novel is the pastiche of popular Western to raise questions about the genre and values upon which it is based, the struggle between good and evil still exists in it. Obviously, Blevins is the symbol of evil concerning his being a thief and a murderer, yet through the presentation of similarities between Blevins and John Grady, McCarthy makes the enchanting effects of the frontier myth on the young boy universal, and thus exposing its problematic essence.

As regards major characters in the novel, both Alfonsa and John Grady are similar to each other in several points. First, both are wounded. Alfonsa loses her ring finger in her girlhood when practicing shooting, implying her loss of passion in her womanhood;

while John Grady gets a severe scar in his visage during the fighting with the assassin sent by Pérez, the head of hooligans in the prison at Saltillo, foreshadowing his loss of the lover, Alejandra in *All the Pretty Horses* or another Mary, Magdalena in Cities of the Plain. Second, both are left-handed and good at playing chess with their left hands. Third, both are failed idealists. When she is young, Alfonsa studies in Europe, where she is cultivated to be a free thinker with democratic ideals, yet the cruelty of Mexican society, such as violence, hierarchy, revolution and patriarchal politics, changes her to be a conservative old woman from a girl with ideals and passion in the mind. She has to place all her ideals in Alejandra and separate the lovers from each other with the hope that her grand-niece will lead on a happy life instead of following her tragedy, although she admires John Grady, who may be considered as her foil, or the foil of her previous lover, Gustavo Madero. For John Grady, his adventures in an alien country with ideals lead to a series of loss in his life and his final wandering as a single shadow in the wilderness with wounds and traumas physically and psychologically.

However, we should note that both are merely self-similar to each other; actually, they are different in their attitudes towards life and destiny. For Alfonsa, life is a puppet show, "when one looks behind the curtain and traces the strings upward he finds they terminate in the hands of yet other puppets, themselves with their own strings which trace upward in turn, and so on" (Horses 231). So in her mind, determinism decides on one's destiny, for humans live in an interconnected web. Whereas, for John Grady, dream clouds his reason. Like a Quixote-like hero with free will, his sticking to the ideals makes his life into chaos. The novel's open ending anticipates that he will ride on with his futile dream into "the world to come" (Horses 302). By means of the open ending to describe the destiny of John Grady with the mentality of the frontier dream, McCarthy suggests its poisonous effects on young men with its nature of fictionality. Nothing can be helpful but death to stop its enchantment with young men like John Grady. Alfonsa has reminded John Grady of the gap between dream and reality and even teaches him a lesson: "In the end we all come to be cured of our sentiments. Those whom life does not cure death will. The world is quite ruthless in selecting between the dream and the reality, even where we will not" (Horses 238). Indeed, in *Cities of the Plain*, John Grady is finally killed by Eduardo due to his attempt to save a girl from the whorehouse and dies at a roadside shed built up for the puppies tragically. For John Grady, his life with Utopian ideals goes on just like what Eduardo remarks, "Men have in their minds a picture of how the world will be. How they will be in that world. The world may be many different ways for them but there is one world that they dream of" (Plain 134), though futile and hopeless. Despite their differences, neither of them can escape the constraints of chaos in their life. By means of the device of self-similarities, we may sense the artistic beauty of the strange attractor in the narrative.

Besides the local self-similarity in the characterization or choices of imagery, in effect, the fiction also presents the global self-similarity in the structure. As we mention above, the opening section and the ending one construct the mutual mapping. More than that, the narrative has its own interpolated narrative or embedded tale: the story about Alfonsa's chaotic life journey is framed in the story of John Grady's turbulence; and meanwhile the story about tragic historical figure Gustavo Madero is framed in the story of Alfonsa by means of her long monologue with John Grady as the silent listener, constructing the tales-within-the-tale form. Gustavo is a radical figure in Mexican political history and has been the lover of Alfonsa when young in the fiction. Similar to his brother, Francisco Madero, both the leader of the revolution against the regime of DÍAZ and the first (and only) elected president of Mexico, Gustavo sacrifies his life and passion for the pursuit of the progressive career, hoping to build up a democratic government in Mexico with his help of the poverty-stricken population of Mexico. Similar to Alfonsa, he gets his education in Europe and United States and develops to be a person with Enlightenment ideals; likewise, similar to both Alfonsa and John Grady, Gustavo also suffers from physical wound and has an artificial eye due to an accident in his life. Interestingly, similar to both Alfonsa and John Grady, he is an idealist, too. Finally he is violently killed by the mob in Mexico city in the coup d'état launched by Francisco's political adversaries. Like the mapping of John Grady's life journey, Gustavo's life journey also witnesses the brutality, bloodshed and violence in the reality, falling into the turbulence due to life system's deterministic unpredictability.

The framing of the story of Gustavo in the story of Alfonsa of the story of John

Grady creates three-fold self-similarities among fictional characters, fictional characters and historical personage in the reality. Such a tale-within-the-tale device not only makes the futile pursuits of characters map each other and hence foregrounding the novel's thematic motif, but also creates the symmetrical asymmetry in the fictional text and hence constructing the self-similarity in the narrative structure globally. In brief, the local and global self-similarities in the text finish the spatial form of the strange attractor in the chaos. The framing device has been taken in the first section of the fiction, in which John Grady's father talks about the divorce of Shirley Temple with John Grady shortly after they discuss the selling of the ranch, not only mapping the divorce of John Grady's parents and thus the dispossession of his inheritance of the ranch from his grandfather, but also reflecting the demise of the West for John Grady and thus the loss of the possibilities for the accomplishment of his dream to be a cowboy. As "a national symbol and an icon for American values" (Kollin 570), Shirley Temple, the child actress, "ceases to function as a reliable and stable entity but instead loses her innocence" (ibid), through her growing-up and divorce, which is much like the changing of the West, the nation's young region, growing distant and lost from young John Grady gradually with the loss of his grandfather's ranch. Furthermore, in the third section of the novel, John Grady also talks about his tale to a group of Mexican children before his final dating with Alejandra after his release from the jail, which is in the same way as Alfonsa talks with him, for both he and these kids are almost silent listeners. Such a textual device builds up the self-similarity across the scale. More than that, it makes the text a bit self-reflexive in its effect, which will be explored further in the following section when talking about the fractals as the other spatial configuration of the chaos in *The Crossing*.

In brief, the device of self-similarities makes the text into symmetrical asymmetry in the spatial form and meanwhile orderly disorder in the dynamic form. By means of its combination with attracting points and bifurcation points in the turbulent process of John Grady's journey, the spatial configuration of strange attractor is created in the narrative form, making the fiction remarkable with its unique dynamic spatiality.

Jo Alyson Parker notes that the advantage of examining the text's structure through a chaos-theory lens requires that we be aware of the content that prompts the chaotic structure. Parker means that the combination of form and content is necessary in the interpretation of a chaotic narrative (29). In our exploration of narrative form in All the Pretty Horses, both the content and form of the narrative are combined to draw upon a gestalt of the narrative's spatial form. In view of the journey presented in the fiction as the deterministic chaos, it is possible for the pattern of chaos theory to be taken to map the state space of the chaotic system for John Grady's life.

As the simulation of the motion of the deterministic chaos, strange attractor is taken in *All the Pretty Horses* concerning the turbulence of John Grady's journey to and from America and Mexico. Centering around the utopia ideal of John Grady, there is a deterministic chaos, featuring sensitive dependence on interior changes in initial conditions in a dynamic system. Horses in the wilderness are attracting points in the system, making John Grady's journey chaotic due to its temporal-spatial unstableness. Since the pattern of strange attractor is not fixed but evolving, all the trajectories of matter's motion may tend towards the attracting points or basin. If the attractor points cannot be erased, the matter's motion never stops. Therefore, through the presentation of the failure of John Grady's frontier dream, McCarthy not only points out the poisonous effect of frontier myth on young Americans, but also problematizes the Western literature with the frontier myth as its structure, making his fiction self-reflective. Along with the futile journey of John Grady, Blevins, Alejandra and Alfonsa construct bifurcation points in the chaotic system, facilitating John Grady's journey to alternate between order and disorder, and much more turbulent than ever before. In addition, a large quantity of self-similarities are made from the choice of imageries, characterization, and narrative structure in the fiction, creating multiple-dimensional reflexivity in the text. With its foregrounding attracting points, bifurcation points and self-similarities presented within the chaotic system of John Grady's journey in the narrative, the fiction finishes its spatial configuration as strange attractor, making the text symmetrical asymmetry or orderly disorder in the form and characteristic of dynamic spatiality.

III. "All Tales are One": Fractals in *The Crossing*

Like the companion of *All the Pretty Horses* rather than the serialized novel, *The Crossing* is parallel with its previous one in lots of points, such as the rewriting of the myth of the frontier, the presentation of the conflict of the reality with dream, the deterministic chaos in a young boy's life. However, much more complicated than *All the Pretty Horses*, *The Crossing* presents its philosophical meditations[1] about life, myth, and narrative[2] through the tales embedded in the tale. Much more remarkable than *All the Pretty Horses*, the fiction's chaotic narrative structure echoes its overt philosophical thinkings in the narrative content. Although the interpolated tales are taken earlier in the McCarthy corpus, such as *Child of God*, *Blood Meridian*, and *All the Pretty Horses*, they are much foregrounded in *The Crossing*, in which the interpolated tales accompany the major part of the narrative (i.e. not the interpolated tales), mapping mutually in their presentation of major thematic motifs.

Fractals refer to self-similarity, and self-similarity indicates the across-scaling symmetry. Usually in one figure, the other similar one is embedded, as shown in the snowflake-like Koch curve, or the ginger man-like Mandelbrot set, or carpet-like Julia set (see Fig 1.9, 1.5, 1.11). These odd fractal shapes "are formed by the iterated process in the complex plane" (Gleick 221), and thus getting the infinite reiteration of the interpolated figures in a finite space. John Barth once suggests that there is an "uncanny prefiguration of a meeting ground" for the arabesque, chaos theory, and postmodernism in Friedrich von Schlegel's application of the term Arabeske to the use of framing narratives in his theorizing about the genre of the novel (284). Barth is also free to mention that his working ethic taken in his newly written novel *The Last Voyage of*

---

[1] *The Crossing* is remarkable in its depth of philosophical thinking, and in this point, it can be considered as the companion of *Blood Meridian*. John Cant even argues that *The Crossing* is "the most overtly philosophical and profoundly human of all McCarthy's works" (*Cormac McCarthy* 195).

[2] *The Crossing* is rich in its thematic presentation, and critics have different understandings. For example, Kino McMurtry argues that the novel "is filled with discussions of existence, God, and destiny" (150); Stacey Peebles holds that the novel talks about God, reality, history, and the nature of the storytelling itself (135); John Cant asserts that the novel addresses more directly the question of the role of culture, language and narrative (*Cormac McCarthy* 195).

Somebody the Sailor (1991) is "chaotic-arabesque postmodernism" (289). According to Joseph Conte, Barth's arabesque design in his text is parallel with Mandelbrot's fractal geometry and both reveal the nature of regular irregularity, or orderly disorder that is prevalent in the natural world (105-6). Besides, the arabesque "reinforces the reflexivity that one associates with postmodern fiction" (Conte 106). Basing on understandings of Barth and Conte, we may assume that fractals featuring recursive symmetry and reflexivity could be taken as a model for the design of the postmodern fiction.

In *The Crossing*, a border fiction (in the natural world, borders are also in the shape of fractals), McCarthy resorts to fractals as his narrative configuration. Fractals are presented in both the content and structure of the narrative. Framing device is the major means to construct fractals in the structure, which creates multiple-dimensional reflexivity in the text. The recursive presentation of its thematic motifs in the major part of the narrative and three major interpolated tales as well as some minor tales creates fractals in the content, making resonance in the fiction's thematic content. The complicated combination of the major part of the narrative and main interpolated tales as well as some other minor tales embedded in the narrative create across-scaling self-similarities in the text, and hence the spatial configuration as fractals in the narrative form. Just as the ex-priest in the fiction declares, "For this world also which seems to us a thing of stone and flower and blood is not a thing at all but is a tale. And all in it is a tale and each tale the sum of all lesser tales and yet these also are the selfsame tale and contain as well all else within them ... Rightly heard all tales are one" (C 143), the priest's words are helpful to make sense of the fiction's narrative form as fractals. By means of the fractal, the self-reflexivity of the narrative gets foregrounded, too, strengthening McCarthy's persistent notion for his narrative: "Everything is talk," or "All is telling" (Horses 28; C 155).

i. Wolf, Wilderness and Myth: Billy's Journey as Chaos

Chaos dominates our living cosmos. Recalling "the call of the wild," Billy starts his wilderness journey. However, his kindness to send a wounded she-wolf back home changes them, making both of their lives into the chaos. As important as the horses for John Grady's dream, the wolf in the wilderness is also the center of Billy's ideal, constructed and driven by the myth of frontier. By means of the tale of Billy's journey with the wolf, the problems hidden in the frontier myth are exposed.

Similar to *All the Pretty Horses, The Crossing* is made up with three sections. Each section contains one part of the narrative. The number "three" is still favorite for McCarthy. In the text, the number "three" is taken to foreground the fractals in the narrative structure.[1] The major part of the narrative contains three border-crossing stories about Billy: sending back a wounded she-wolf to the Pilares in Mexico on his own, retrieving the stolen horses with his younger brother Boyd after the death of his parents, and bringing back the bones of Boyd after the failure of the joining of the army from the heart murmur. Together with the tripartite structure of the narrative text, three tales told by three wise persons are embedded in the major tale of Billy's border journeys, suggesting the self-similarity across scales in the narrative structure. Different from John Grady's "buddy" Rawlins, Billy's initial adventurous partner is a she-wolf, who is wounded in one leg and has to walk on three. Oddly, a ruined church in Caborca he meets in the journey and a crippled dog he encounters in the end of the book also stands on three "legs." His attempts to join the army with the knowledge of the country at war are rejected three times. Billy weeps by three times in the book. Billy has three dreams embedded in the narrative. These minor details associated with the number "three" make resonance within the narrative, constructing the recursive symmetry in the text locally.

Similar to John Grady, death, loss and alienation accompany Billy's life journey, too: the loss of family and horses due to his hospitality paid to an wandering Indian in the woods to seek for food, which incurs the murdering of his parents and the stealing of horses from that Indian; the death of the she-wolf due to his utopia ideal to send her back home without following his father's request to report the success of trapping the wolf to his father; the death of his younger brother Boyd after being brought to Mexico to regain the lost horses; loss of all his kin in the final ending of the

[1] Edwin T. Arnold also mentions the frequency of the number "three" in his exploration of the spiritual issues with the lens of Jacob Boehme's mystic and philosophical thinking, yet obviously he associates the number "three" with the Trinity in Christianity ("McCarthy" 231).

fiction, becoming a lonely wanderer alienated from American and Mexican society, although he experiences a lot from his journey. To sum up, Billy's life system is also a deterministic chaos, dominated with randomness. Although the fiction does not point out directly the sensitive dependence on its initial condition in the chaotic system, the disproportion of cause and consequence still could be sensed in his life. The choice of fetching food for the wandering Indian in the plain without telling his parents perhaps brings about disasters for Billy and his family, and incurs a series of tragic events in his journey, which changes his destiny and even influences the life of those around him. Likewise, the choice of making the cross-border journeys to send back the she-wolf to her living natural world or to retrieve the stolen horses or to bring back his deceased brother's bones causes the death or loss each time. Billy still suffers the failure of his dream in spite of experiencing lots of hardships in his voyage. Decisions change one's life. Billy's turbulence in his life, such as loss, alienation, and the death of his family numbers and the she-wolf, are almost associated with a trivial incident in life, just as the ganadero (rancher) comments in his talking with Billy, "you do not know what things you set in motion. ... No man can know. No prophet foresee. The consequences of an act are often quite different from what one would guess" (C 202).

Frontier myth still makes effect in Billy's life. According to Barcley Owens, there are two frontier myths, "one that champions progress and Anglo-American might and one that champions the preservation of wilderness and its idealized natives" (68). The frontier myth Billy attaches to is the second one. As the emblems of the wilderness, both the wolf and the native Indian function at the same as horses and the Comanches do in John Grady's adventurous journey into Mexico. Both appear in Billy's life mysteriously, and attract him to go back to wilderness from civilization. However, different from Ballard's passive regression from civilization to wilderness due to the evil forces in his living surroundings, Billy's response with "the call of the wild" is his active choice, even becoming his pursuit of ideals. However, one may assume that their going back to wilderness is the effect of the chaos, for all are interrelated in our living cosmos. Small perturbation may cause large consequences in the system. So in this point, both are a bit similar in the destiny. Like the horses frequently appearing in John

Grady's sleeping dream and even becoming the center of his ideals, wolves also attract Billy. Horses are necessary for John Grady to achieve his frontier dream, while wolves are also the means for Billy to go to the wilderness. Although originally, Billy's purpose is to trap the wolf for the bounty, yet with his knowledge of the wolf better and better, he transforms to be the caretaker of the wolf and even gradually identifies himself with the wolf.

The wolf's attraction to Billy starts earlier at his young age. Similar to the opening section of *All the Pretty Horses*, in which the imagery of horses and the Comanche warriors is made to symbolize the frontier dream of John Grady, the imagery of a pack of running wolves in the opening section of *The Crossing* is taken to construct the center of Billy's dream. On a winter's night, Billy does encounter the wolf pack:

They were running on the plain harrying the antelope and the antelope moved like phantoms in the snow and circled and wheeled and the dry powder blew about them in the cold moonlight and their breath smoked palely in the cold as if they burned with some inner fire and the wolves twisted and turned and leapt in a silence such that they seemed of another world entire. (C 4)

Despite the coldness, Billy waits patiently and later seven of them approach him in a close distance, and he "could hear their breath. He could feel the presence of their knowing that was electric in the air." These mysterious animals even stop and look at him, then "they turned and quietly trotted on" (C 4). Such a surreal vision recalls the encounter of Ike McCaslin with the bear in Faulkner's *The Bear*, and the text's intertextuality with *The Bear* strengthens the tie of Billy with the wilderness. Barcley Owens argues that such an encounter with the wolf is "a transfiguring moment of epiphany for Billy" (74), and more than that, it has planted the seed of the wilderness in the mind of a 16-year-old young boy.

As the symbol of the wilderness, wolves are animals favorite for the Western literature and frequently appear in some legends in the west. With the love of the wilderness, McCarthy has been attracted to wolves. In one of his rare interviews, it is reported that he has discussed with Edward Abbey about a "covert operation to reintroduce the wolf to Southern Arizona" (Woodward, "Venomous Fiction" 30). Wolves frequent McCarthy's works. In *Blood Meridian*, they are used to describe the brutality and blood of the wilderness, constructing the "optical democracy" with these evil wandering mercenaries. While in *The Crossing*, the she-wolf is the combination of terror and beauty, and hence the incarnation of the wilderness, or more exactly, the chaos. The old wolf-trapper Don Alnulfo knows the wolf better. For him, the wolf is like the snowflake. "You catch the snowflake but when you look in your hand you dont have it no more. Maybe you see this dechado. But before you can see it is gone. If you want to see it you have to see it on its own ground. If you catch it you will lose it. And where it goes there is no coming back from" (C 46). In effect, the wolf in the mind of this Mexican old man is no more the single wolf, or a physical object in the physical world, but the soul of the wilderness with a kind of mysterious or supernatural power. Much more important, in Don Alnulfo's vision, "by its very nature the wilderness cannot be owned because-like the snowflake which melts in your hand-as soon as it is held, it ceases to be the wilderness any longer" (McBride 77). Don Alnulfo's vision of the wolf is close to that of chaos theory, which pays emphasis on the holistic relation of the cosmos, in which all are interconnected, and man is symbiotic with wilderness (nature). Chaos theory suggests that man should have "a new dialogue with nature,"[1] instead of simply taking it as a determinate or submissive system to subdue at man's will and control. Edwin T. Arnold notes that "in moving west McCarthy developed a worldview more in keeping with Native American cosmology than with traditional Eurocentric Christian perspective" ("McCarthy" 215), Arnold's argument is reasonable, yet we may further his view to be much exact to sum up McCarthy's worldview in his Southwestern works: his world vision has kept with the perspectives of chaos theory.

Don Alnulfo's words anticipate the failure of Billy's journey with the wolf, in which he initially wishes to trap the wolf for the bounty, then hopes to "save" her by making himself the wolf's master, custodian and care-taker, and finally transforms

---

[1] The scientist Ilya Prigogine has got a famous book about chaos theory, *Order Out of Chaos: Man's New Dialogue with Nature* (1984).

to be an unwilling executioner by shooting her to death. Similar to native Americans in the west, wolves are also victims of American frontier development and progress movement. They are dispossessed of living land and resources and even wiped out from the wilderness. McBride notes that "by Billy Parham's time, the U. S. Government has been successful in all but erasing the wolf from the Southwestern landscape" (74). *The Crossing* presents some of the stories of bygone wolf trappers and their multiple kinds of traps or medicine taken to catch the wolf, echoing such a historical context. In his personified description of the she-wolf, McCarthy endows her human nature like loyalty to her mate ("He'd bitten her because she would not leave him" [C 24]); vulnerability ("She was carrying her first litter and she had no way to know the trouble she was in" [C 25]); loneliness (she would "howl and howl again into the terrible silence" [C 26]); and intelligence ("She circled the set for the better part of an hour sorting and indexing the varied scents and ordering their sequence in an effort to reconstruct the events that had taken place here" [26]). Instead of ignorance with the "old protocols" made between human beings and animals, the she-wolf's border-crossing adventure is made for the purpose of regaining her lost companion (C 25). However, her journey into the human world makes her life into the chaos, much more turbulent than ever before. Time has been changed, and the wilderness has been destructed with the encroachment of the ranches in the west. The text gives some details in the explanation of the perplexity for the survival of wolves, anticipating the danger of her journey: "her ancestors had hunted camels and primitive toy horses on these grounds. She found little to eat. Most of game was slaughtered out of the country. Most of the forest cut to feed the boilers of the stamp mills at the mines" (C 25). Sensitive dependence on initial conditions is universal for every dynamic system. At the moment when the lonely she-wolf crosses the border to find her lost companion, her tragedy has been doomed.

The Crossing arranges a large amount of self-similarities in the narrative, linking different images or characters together to make them free from the temporal-spatial constraints, and thus making the novel characteristic of dynamic spatiality. The failure of the journey of the she-wolf is parallel with that of Billy's first wilderness journey. The she-wolf's loss of her companion foreshadows Billy's later loss of his young brother in his second journey, in which he brings his brother to Mexico to regain the stolen horses. Billy's trailing of the dead body of the she-wolf to her home maps out his bringing back his brother's bones to home in his third journey, and of course his carrying the body of John Grady in Cities of the Plain, in which both the protagonists meet together. These textual self-similarities construct fractals in the narrative form locally.

Similar to John Grady, who is able to break 16 horses in 4 days, Billy also shows his capacity as a cowboy. In his efforts to trap the wolf, he employs "all the ingenuity of bygone trappers and some of his own in trying to think like a wolf, to understand the very nature of it" (Owens 79). While, with the success of his catching the wolf, Billy's dilemma occurs. Though the fiction does not give the direct description of his perplexity in his mind, yet from the narrator's telling, "he sat on the horse for a long time," we can sense his dilemma (C 53). To send her back or to return to report to his father, that's a question. Perhaps due to "the world waiting" (C 53), Billy finally decides to rebel against his father's request and follows "the call of the wilderness" to become a "catcher" in the wilderness. Just as Edwin T. Arnold puts it, "in the course of his journey with the wolf, Billy grows more aware of this other world. He has always had a sense of kinship with this aspect of nature, as indicated by his early dreams and visionary experiences" ("McCarthy" 220). During the first night in the mountains, Billy looks into the wolf's eyes reflected in the campfire:

When the flames came up her eyes burned out there like gatelamps to another world. A world burning on the shore of an unknowable void. A world constructed out of blood and blood's alcahest and blood in its core and in its integument because it was that nothing save blood had power to resonate against that void which threatened hourly to devour it. ... When those eyes and the nation to which they stood witness were gone at last with their dignity back into their origins there would perhaps be other fires and other witnesses and other worlds otherwise beheld. But they would not be this one. (C 73-4)

Rather than taking the she-wolf as his lover as Owens assumes to be parallel with the love between John Grady and Alejandra,[①] Billy actually identifies with the wolf, and appears to understand the other world inhabited by wolves, although the fiction does present tender feelings of Billy towards the she-wolf. Both are alienated in the world, and lonely wanderers in the wilderness.

On his way to send the she-wolf to her living mountains, Billy suffers misunderstandings from a great many persons in both Unites States and Mexico. Some of them assume that Billy is to collect her for the hide or sell her for the bounty (invoking the bounty-hunting prevalent in McCarthy's works, especially that of the Apaches in *Blood Meridian*). Some of them think that his taking care of the she-wolf and attempts to send her back home are crazy or peculiar. A group of Mexican government officials even rob Billy of the she-wolf with the power and make her confiscated as contraband and then sell her to a traveling circus. Finally she is sold again to a hacendado who pits her against a pack of hunting dogs just for amusement. Like one of the fractals for Billy, the she-wolf also suffers the misunderstandings of discursive power from humanity. Since her appearance in the narrative, she has been mystified. Concerning her experience, there are lots of different tales. "An old woman said that the wolf had been brought from the sierras where it had eaten many schoolchildren. Another woman said that it had been captured in the company of a young boy who had run away naked into the woods" (C 102). A third one tells how were wolves follow the hunting party and howling at night from the darkness. The hacendado, who arranges the she-wolf to fight with the hunting dogs, tells the tale of the wolf differently: an American was caught stealing the wolf from the Pilares Teras and had been "intent on taking the wolf to his own country where he would sell the animal at some price" (C 118). "The story-teller's task is not so simple," the ex-priest speaks right, for "he appears to be required to choose his tale from among the many that are possible" (C 157, 155). Obviously, the subtext of the myth's chameleonlike ability in factual construction makes

---

[①] Barcley Owens argues that "Billy's romantic dream of returning the she-wolf to its mountain home parallels John Grady's love for Alejandra. The wolf becomes his wilderness lover as they share food and sit side by side" (82).

correspondence with Billy's wilderness journey in the text.

The wilderness myth is culturally and historically constructed. Euro-Americans assume that they are "out of the natural order and protocol of things, that [they] can impose [their] own order upon and thus conquer the wilderness" (McBride 78). The fences, the railroads, and the highways built up in the wilderness, are textual evidences of human exploitation of the wilderness. In American history, esp. in the process of American Western movement, large quantities of wolves and other animals like American mountains cats and buffaloes have been wiped out because they are thought to compete with humans for resources. The stupidity and lust of human beings finally dispossess the wolf's freedom, humiliate her nobility and even almost torture her to death. When a horse-rider proposes to buy the she-wolf on his way to the Pilares, Billy replies that "the wolf was the property of a great hacendado and that it had been put in his care that no harm came to it" (C 90). "A great hacendado" mentioned by Billy might refer to God or wilderness. His assumption of being the custodian or protector of the property owned by God or wilderness makes what he does for the wolf reasonable and justified. However, it is such an idea of taking the wolf as his subordinator that makes Billy complicit with those people, who misunderstand him and she-wolf. For those persons, the wolf and the wilderness she symbolizes could be taken as the commodity to buy and sell or exploited without constraints. The she-wolf is only a physical object without spirit and might be taken as a play toy to amuse them. It is ironic that Billy's shooting her to death with his own gun is his final care of the she-wolf. The disproportionate cause and effect once again plays with figures in McCarthy's fiction. McCarthy seems to imply that the wilderness myth Billy believes in is ill-founded, which is parallel with the frontier myth John Grady entrusts on. By means of the tale of Billy's journey with wolf to the high Pilares, McCarthy not only critiques the cruelty and violence of humanity, but also exposes dangers of the anthropocentrism and problems hidden in the national consciousness. At the same time, in the process of his textual construction, McCarthy deconstructs the myths driving his protagonists to pursue their hopeless ideals.

All work as Don Alnulfo understands, "there is no order in the world save that which death has put there" (C 45), the she-wolf finally returns to her home in the Pilares as Billy promises, yet only a carcass brought back, and once again blood deals with the chaos. Like a prophet, Don Alnulfo suggests before the tragedy, "if men drink the blood of God yet they do not understand the seriousness of what they do" (C 46), and the poignant passage written in the ending of his first journey after Billy buries the body resonates with the warnings of Don Alnulfo, leaving many unresolved problems for humans to meditate besides sorrow and pain:

... he could see her running in the mountains, running in the starlight where the grass was wet and the sun's coming as yet had not undone the rich matrix of creatures passed in the night before her. Deer and hare and dove and groundvole all richly empaneled on the air for her delight, all nations of the possible world ordained by God of which she was one among and not separate from. ... he reached to hold what cannot be held, what already ran among the mountains at once terrible and of a great beauty, like flowers that feed on flesh. (C 127)

The wolf's extinction foreshadows the calamities to come for human world in the end of the book, when Billy witnesses the first successful detonation of an atomic bomb. The "white light" wakes him up in the early morning and he mistakes the explosion for the sunrise, but its light fades and he is left in "the inexplicable darkness" until the "right and godmade sun did rise, once again" (C 425, 426). The false light caused by the atomic test blast implies the massive destruction waiting for the human race. Just before his witness of the explosion of the atomic bomb, Billy drives away a crippled dog, "repository of ten thousand indignities and the harbinger of God knew what" (C 424). As "a sort of avatar for the nuclear age" (McBride 81), the lamed dog with grotesque shape might be a fractal of the she-wolf. By means of the self-similarities between the wolf and the mutated dog and the juxtaposition of the false light in the morning and the sunrise, McCarthy suggests the failure of Billy's wilderness journey. A lonely wanderer in the wilderness, Billy "[sits] in the road," and "bow [s] his head and [holds] his face in his hands and [weeps]" (C 426). His final weeping in the book might be thought to cry for the she-wolf, for the crippled dog, for the wilderness, for himself, of course, for all the humans on the earth.

As the symbol of the wilderness or chaos, the wolf's destiny images that of human beings. Small perturbations in the system may cause a great effect. The wolf's journey into human world brings about her tragic ending in the wilderness, and Billy's journey into the wilderness also makes his life into the deterministic chaos. Both map out mutually, constructing recursive symmetry in the text. By means of the presentation of the chaos in Billy's journey with the wolf in the wilderness, McCarthy not only exposes the fictionality of frontier myth but also suggests the interconnection of the cosmos, in which both man and nature are symbiotic.

ii. "All is Telling": The Interpolated Tales as Fractals

Just as John Cant puts it, "Few critics write of *The Crossing* without mentioning the many interpolated tales told to Billy Parham on his wanderings" (*Cormac McCarthy* 197), the interpolated tales are so foregrounded in the fiction that they cannot be ignored concerning the narrative form of the fiction. One may note that almost all of these interpolated tales that Billy hears on his three wilderness journeys are constructed to be self-similar to the major part of the narrative concerning their foundational thematic motifs about myth, life and narrative, which builds up the fractals in the narrative content and form. Also, almost all of these story-tellers are as discursive and metaphysical as the judge in Blood Meridian, and in their long philosophical "monologues," most of them concern the truth of the narrative through reflections of or comments on happenings in the major part of the narrative, making the text self-reflexive.

After his burial of the she-wolf and wandering in the mountains, Billy comes across a keeper of the ruined church in Huisicheptic abandoned after the earthquake. The man claims himself to be a one-time Mormon coming here to seek "evidence for the hand of God in the world," yet the world he found is "not a thing at all but is a tale" (C 142, 143). Twenty-one pages in length, the ex-priest's tale of a "heretic," or a "certain man," more exactly, all men, is taken in the form of history to make explorations of the nature of life and story-telling, which not only involves the witness or spectator or reader into, but also puts forth the problems of narrative when telling the story to Billy.

The tale of the man in the ex-priest's tale is self-similar to that of Billy not only in their thematic presentation of life as chaos but also in some minor details in the tale itself, constructing mutual mapping between the major tale and its embedded tale. Similar to Billy's orphanhood, the man's parents are killed in the Caborca church when he is a boy. The man has once traveled with his father to the town, where he remembers his father "lifting him to see puppets performing in the alameda" (C 144), which recalls the puppet show as metaphor of the net in Alfonsa's long tale about Mexican political history in *All the Pretty Horses*. Life is a puppet net, in which all are uncertain, yet interconnected, as is shown in the life of both the man and Billy. Years later the man gets married and has had his son, with whom he starts his journey, in which his boy "rides in the bow of the saddle before him" (C 144). Rick Wallach notes that the man's way of riding with his son is similar to that of "Billy transporting Boyd on his saddle at the opening of the novel" ("Theatre" 168). Similar to Billy's second tragic journey with Boyd, in which Boyd is wounded in their shooting at the bandits stealing his family's horses, and later dies before Billy's returning to fetch him, the man in the tale leaves his boy with his relatives and goes on with his business journey, in which his son dies in the earthquake before he returns to Bavispe. The ex-Mormon comments that "life is a memory, then it is nothing" (C 145). True to his words, the man in the tale beholds amid the carnage "a dead clown," which recalls the clown in the traveling circus seen in the fair from him and his son. In his own childhood, the man is also brought by his father to see the puppet show in the traveling circus (C 145). Just as Billy transports the bones of his brother from Mexico to Unites States, the man (the father) in the tale "returns to Huisiachepic bearing across the mule's haunches the corpse of the child with which God has blessed his house" (C 146). In terms of the destiny of human beings, especially those dreamers like John Grady, Alfonsa, Billy and Boyd in the border trilogy, the ex-priest's words are true: "such a man is like a dreamer who wakes from a dream of grief to a greater sorrow yet. All that he loves is now become a torment to him. The pin has been pulled from the axis of the universe" (C 146). The ex-priest means that life is nothing with linear causality, but a deterministic chaos with orderly disorder. For him, a story-teller, the world is like a tapestry weaved by God. God is the weaver, "seated solely in the light of his own presence. Weaving the world" (C 149). Taking God as a weaver implies that human beings are controlled by fate or determinism, recalling that of Alfonsa and his father, who take God (fate) as a myopic coiner, who "peers with his poor eyes through dingy glasses at the blind tablets of metal before him" (Horses 231). Paradoxically, for such a weaver to control one's destiny, his texture is simply self-same, which works as the priest says, "ultimately every man's path is every other's. There are no separate journeys for there are no separate men to make them. All men are one and there is no other tale to tell," and then the weaver fails in his weaving (C 157). If the weaver is considered as the story-teller, then his tapestry might be the writing. Therefore, to tell such a tale of the man similar to that of Billy is to construct the recursive symmetry in his text, through which McCarthy implies self-referentiality of his own tale about Billy's journey.

The ex-priest's tale is obviously about the notion and function of narrative, which might be the most significant passage from McCarthy to make comments on the narrative:

The task of the narrator is not an easy one, he said. He appears to be required to choose his tale from among the many that are possible. But of course that is not the case. The case is rather to make many of the one. Always the teller must be at pains to devise against his listener's claim-perhaps spoken, perhaps not-that he has heard the tale before. He set forth the categories into which the listener will wish to fit the narrative as he hears it. But he understands that the narrative is itself in fact no category but is rather the category of all categories for there is nothing which falls outside its purview. All is telling. (C 155)

The ex-priest means that all the stories are constructed for the convenience or benefits of story-tellers. In terms of Billy's tale, McCarthy seems to suggest that it is constructed, too, because "those seams that are hid from us are of course in the tale itself and the tale has no abode or place of being except in the telling only and there it lives and makes its home and therefore we can never be done with the telling" (C 143). The man, who loses the son in the earthquake, becomes a heretic and a wanderer finally, which foreshadows and maps the later destiny of Billy. After the death of the she-wolf, Billy wanders in the mountains, and later, after his trailing of the bones of Boyd northward, he wanders in the country all the time. Until the final ending of the fiction, he is still a wanderer. The mutual mapping of the stories of the man and Billy constructs the self-similarity between the embedded text and the main text.

The second interpolated tale from a blind revolutionist constructs the other fractal of Billy's failed journey. When he meets the blind, Billy has started his second journey, in which he and his younger brother Boyd attempt to retrieve the stolen horses of his family. Just as Barcley Owens asserts that McCarthy's frontier heroes "go to Mexico on the flimsiest of pretexts: to retrieve stolen horses, to relocate the wolf, to find a lost brother" (67), Billy's second journey with rashness brings about the disorder for his life again. In his first journey, the good intention to send the she-wolf back home causes the tragic death of the wolf, and simultaneously, it brings disasters within his family, because he is carrying off the only rifle in his family makes his parents incapable of making responses when encountering attacks. In his second journey with his brother, with the ignorance that "the world works according to its own device and not those of the individual" (Arnold, "McCarthy" 226), Billy repeats the same mistake by demanding a personal justice, or an accounting, and once more he encounters disaster with his brother shot and the horses lost again. In effect, Billy fails to understand the hints of both Don Alnulfo and the ex-priest suggested in his first journey. The former reminds him of the emptiness of imposing order on the wilderness (to relocate the wolf in the world) and the latter implies that the significance of one's acts is only from his own imagination, rather than out of the necessity of the reality, because "every word we speak is a vanity. Every breath taken that does not bless is affront. ... In the end we shall all of us be only what we have made of God" (C 158). Apparently, McCarthy takes their words or tales to make comments on the tale of Billy's journey and his own narrative as well.

The tale of the blind is told alternatively between the blind's wife and himself, and Billy (listener or reader) acts as an interlocutor. When young, the blind takes part in the campaign in 1913 to be against the rebels under Contreras and Pereyra, in which he keeps on his duty as a cannon-shooter in the war with the rebels at Durango. He and his comrades-in-arms are sent to prison after the failure of the campaign and later are shot for their refusal to swear oaths of loyalty to the government. One of the most violent scenes in McCarthy's works occurs to him, when a German Huertista named Wirtz seizes him by the face and "suck [s] each in turn the man's eyes from his head and spit [s] them out again and leave[s] them dangling by their cords wet and strange and wobbling on his cheeks" (C 276). The violence that the blind man encounters recalls that of Gustavo, whose artificial eye is pried out with a pick by the mob and then being passed "among the crowd as a curiosity" (Horses 237) and of the she-wolf, who is tied in the pit to fight with hunting dogs to satisfy man's lust of violence. Chaos plays with him, too. He gets survival from the cárcel due to his blindness and after wandering long he comes across his present woman, who is the story-teller of his present tale.

Crossing the boundaries of light and darkness, even life and death (after the loss of sight, he gives in to his grief to attempt to commit suicide), makes the blind understand life, humanity, and world deeply. For him, the world is in chaos, nothing different between good and evil, light and darkness, life and death, dream and reality, beauty and ugliness, everything is not real but illusionary from one's mind. The physical world is not real but fragile and "perilous": "that which was given him to help him make his way in the world has power also to blind him to the way where his true path lies. The key to heaven has power to open the gates of hell" (C 293). Mexico is a country, in which colored birds, wildflowers and young girls "whose own eyes [are] pools of promise deep and dark as the world itself," are in company with "the figure of death in his paper skull and suit of painted bones strode up and back before the footlights in high declamation" (C 277). Obviously, the blind man echoes the perspective of chaos theory towards life and world and humanity and even tale-telling.[①] For him, the world contains little in the way of justice, and evil is so powerful that the good man "will not know that while the order which the righteous seek is never righteous itself but is only order," thus "all is plain, light and dark alike" (C 293). The blind man makes a summary of the "truth" of his life story, for he says to Billy that "every tale was a tale of dark and light and would perhaps not have it otherwise. Yet there was still a further order to the narrative and it was a thing of which men do not speak" (C 292). Superficially, the story of the blind is different from that of Billy, yet both are self-similar with each other in terms of their life as a chaos, and in effect, it is also a fractal of the major part of the narrative. Furthermore, the blind's tragedy is the anticipation of that of Billy in his life journey, even the warning of all the dreamers (Boyd included) on the earth that nothing is real but telling at all.

Billy's final journey is undertaken to return Boyd's bones to his native country after the failure of joining the army in the second world war. On his third border-crossing journey, he has heard the last tale told by the gypsy, who stops to treat Billy's wounded horse. The gypsy's tale reiterates those intellectual thinkings about life, myth, and narrative from the blind and the ex-priest, constructing another fractal of the major part of the narrative. The gypsy is employed by one American old man to regain his dead pilot son's airplane lost in the high desert mountains of Sonora. The gypsy's trailing of the wreckage of the airplane maps out Billy's trailing of the bones of Boyd, while the gypsy knows better the emptiness of his journey than that of Billy. For the gypsy, he is aware that some facts in the history cannot be known, and even though some known facts in the history cannot be true. The airplane that their client hopes to regain is a case, for "men assume the truth of a thing to reside in that thing without regard to the opinions of those beholding it while that which is fraudulent is held to be so no matter how closely it might duplicate the required appearance" (C 405). The gypsy implies the ambiguity of the identity of things made from its beholder and interpreter, which not

---

① *The Crossing* is a fiction with the depth of metaphysical and philosophical thinkings, yet these philosophical passages are in fragmentation, seemingly not easy to find coherence in the context. Concerning the long passage from the blind's tale, Edwin T. Arnold associates the blind's talkings with Boehme's theology, which appears to overlap with chaos theory ("McCarthy" 227).

only indicates the emptiness of Billy's journey from his efforts of regaining the body of Boyd, but also comments on the ambiguous identity of Boyd, hence the ambiguity of myth and narrative.

Before Billy finds out the bones of Boyd, Boyd has been mystified into a national hero for Mexicans in the corrido (ballad or folk song) due to his accidental killing of the gerente, a one-armed overseer at La Babicora ranch, where the horses of Billy's parents are appropriated. The death of the gerente is an accident made from his falling off horse to break his back when trying to reappropriate the horses of Billy's parents, and yet Boyd has no way of knowing that the gerente is detested by the local people due to his being a traitor in the revolution. In effect, the situation of Boyd is self-similar to that of the she-wolf as we mentioned in the previous section, both are mystified and constructed in the people's imagination. Just as Quijada tells Billy: "The corrido is the poor man's history. It does not owe its allegiance to the truths of history but to the truths of men" (C 386). For Billy, he just knows that Boyd "kills two men in Galeana. No one knows why" (C 384); while for Quijada, he knows obviously the truth of the myth: "the corrido tells all and it tells nothing" (C 386). Like the myth or story-telling, the corrido plays the role of the narrative, too, "not only in structuring accounts of the past, ... but also in creating our sense of personal identity" (Cant, *Cormac McCarthy* 206).

Furthermore, by means of the tale told by the gypsy, McCarthy reiterates the idea of life as a deterministic chaos. The gypsy tells to Billy, "if a dream can tell the future it can also thwart the future, for God will not permit that we shall know what is to come" (C 407). For the gypsy, both the journeys of the dead pilot's father and Billy to regain something in the past are meaningless, but "vanity" for the dreamers (Billy, Boyd, and the father of the dead pilot included), because "the world was made new each day and it was only men's clinging to its vanished husks that could make of that world one husk more" (C 411). The gypsy tries to show that the failure of the journey for Billy or Boyd or his client is made from the chaos in the world, for "He [God] is bound to no one that the world unfold just so upon its course and those who by some sorcery or by some dream might come to pierce the veil that lies so darkly over all that is before them may serve by just that vision to cause that God should wrench the world from its heading and set it upon another course altogether "(C 407). Taking the dreamer as the sorcerer with sorcery suggests the unreliability of dream, for man cannot cope with God, of course, the world or the universe. This point has been demonstrated through Billy's romantic desire to relocate the wolf, or to regain the horse, or to transport the body to home. The same is true for Boyd, whose romantic desire to impose the order on Mexico and save a young girl from the raping of some horsemen makes him "a man of the people" in his violence and death.

Just as John Cant argues, "McCarthy is much more concerned with his own activity as a writer of narrative and he uses the interpolated tales to foreground the nature of the teller's art. At the same time he suggests both the significance and limitations of that art" (*Cormac McCarthy* 206). These interpolated tales told to Billy are in the form of the history and these tale-tellers are witnesses or participators of the history, which makes the text complicated. The question is that, what are the true facts of the history? Can we believe in the tales of these story-tellers? As we know, the blind man's perceiving the world is via touch rather than sight, and some of the experiences the blind in the story knows are from his wife, particularly his interpretation of the words of the sepulturero (caretaker) in the church, spoken to the girl, his present wife, which he invests with meanings drawn from his own life experience into his narrative (C 287-8). As for the version of the heroic events of Boyd in the corrido and that of Billy's knowledge with him, the gap is large or small? For the gypsy, he is aware that "the tale must be read for what it tells us about the teller" (Cant, *Cormac McCarthy* 209), which is the purpose of the tale. As for the history of the airplane, it is of no consequence to them. The construction of the tale or the history is for the teller's benefits. Concerning the gypsy's situation, the history of the plane is to show the resourcefulness, courage and strength of the gypsies themselves; and as regards to the father of the dead pilot, the history of the plane is to make solace of a father in grief. McCarthy seems to make his reader fall into the trap of the narrative, and in his fiction, some facts can not be known, some known facts are not true. With regard to the hospitality of both Billy and Boyd towards the Indian in the woods, why does it incur the murdering of their parents and the stealing of their horses? Even though the reader can get bits of textual hints from the novel. Just at the scene with the Indian, Billy uses the name of Boyd, and later Boyd tells Billy about the killers, "They knew my name. ... They called for me. Called Boyd, Boyd" (C 173). However, it is still uncertain for the Indian as the thief and murderer, because the narrative does not provide reasonable cause-consequence explanation of his acts after the acceptance of hospitality from the kids. Through textual uncertainties, McCarthy seems to suggest the uncertainty of life and fictionality of the narrative, for "all is telling" (C 155).

The problem of the narrative has appeared in McCarthy's works previously. In *All the Pretty Horses*, although John Grady maintains that "there aint but one truth," the vicious captain at La Encantada still insists that the reality is malleable for "we can make the truth here" (Horses 168). In *Child of God*, Ballard is sent to prison due to the sheriff's taking his committing crime for granted without investigation. Different from some of his contemporary postmodernist writers, who may expose their fiction's fictionality through self-referentiality or self-reflexivity made by their own comments or devising some of different clues of plotting or ending for their fiction, McCarthy excels at his staying behind his stories as a "weaver" or "coiner" or "stonemason"[1] and making some of his characters into speakers (narrators) to make comments on their own stories and meanwhile cunningly reminding the other character of their own stories.

In *The Crossing*, these interpolated tales from the priest, the blind, even the gypsy are in parallel with each other in order to explore the significance and truth of life, myth, narrative and even chaos itself, constructing the fractals of the major part of the narrative. Furthermore, almost all of them are presented in the discourse of chaos theory, which renders the novel to be remarkable. To describe life into a deterministic chaos, and then make comments on what he tells with chaos theory, McCarthy explores how to make use of chaos theory to write down a story about chaos, which makes The Crossing remarkable in his corpus and even contemporary American fiction.

---

[1] McCarthy also takes God as the image of the stonemason in his play *The Stonemason* (1994), which echoes the images of God as weaver mentioned by the ex-priest: "According to the gospel of the true mason God has laid the stones in the earth for men to use and he has laid them in their bedding planes to show the mason how his own work must go. A wall is made the same way the world is made" (TS 10).

iii. Some Other Fractals in the Narrative

Apart from the fractals created by major interpolated tales, self-similarities presented in the minor details of the narrative construct some other fractals in the text, completely achieving the gestalt of the narrative text as fractals. The subtext of Boyd's romantic adventures in Mexico underlying the major narrative builds up one of the fractals in the text. Pared characters frequent McCarthy's works and appear to become protagonists in the fiction usually. Concerning the party of Boyd and Billy, the former is more remarkable and romantic than the latter in terms of horsemanship and marksmanship as well as life vision, which is similar to the relationship between John Grady and Rawlins in *All the Pretty Horses*. Similar to John Grady, Boyd also has had a romance in his Mexican journey. John Grady suffers loss of the ranch due to his romance with an Mexican noble lady, and even at the cost of his young life in his attempts to save a Mexican whore in *Cities of the Plain*. Boyd suffers his life from his romance with Mexican girl, too. Though girls might not be the direct cause for the disasters of young boys, they function as bifurcations in the chaotic system. As the third party, Mexican girl's appearance causes the fluctuations of order and disorder within the journey of young boys. Boyd's failure maps that of Billy, which can be evidenced from Billy's futile journey with the she-wolf in the wilderness.

Besides those characters with wisdom in these interpolated tales, the lessons Billy gets in the journey are reiterated from some other people, constructing other fractals in the narrative. The primadonna in one traveling opera company tells Billy: "The road has its own reasons and no two travelers will have the same understanding of those reasons. ... The shape of the road is the road. There is not some other road that wears that shape but only the one. And every voyage begun upon it will be completed. Whether horses are found or not" (C 230). In American culture, Robert Frost's understanding of the road is popular, different roads may cause different lives once the road is chosen. However, for the primadonna, all the road are the same, yet their differences depend on understandings of different voyagers, in one word, it is dreamers (readers) that endow significance for their dreams (texts). Her words echo that of the ex-priest, "All tales are one," which depends on the reader in his involvement with the tale (C 143). Besides, the problem of the art of the narrative is reiterated in the minor detail about the acting of the primadonna in a melodrama. She tells Billy that the world is like stage, on which the massages are something true, for all are in pretense. It is life that imitates art rather than art imitates life, and thus "the actor has no power to act but only as the world tells him. Mask or not mask is all one to him" (C 230).

Violence in *The Crossing* can be found everywhere, which evokes the comments on the evil of humanity from a man on the road: "he said that if they were old enough to bleed they were old enough to butcher" (C 209). The tale about her grandmother from Boyd's young Mexican lover is the fractal of the tale of the blind revolutionist, for both are about blood in the revolution, recalling that of the story from Alfonsa about the tragedy of Gustavo. The girl's grandmother "has been widowed the revolution" and by the third time she weds no more, though she has chance to marry again for she is "a great beauty and not yet twenty years of age" (C 321). While, the death of Boyd makes the girl's destiny self-similar to that of her grandmother, constructing another minor fractal in the narrative.

In *The Crossing*, dreams occur frequently. As a a kind of narrative device, dreams can be taken as another kind of the embedded story to construct self-similarities between dream and reality in the plotting events. After the departure with the blind and his wife, Billy has had his first dream, in which he meets wolves in the moonlight, "they touched his face with their wild muzzles and drew away again ... . When the last of them had come forward they stood in a crescent before him and their eyes were like footlights to the ordinate world and then they turned and wheeled away and loped off through the snow and vanished smoking into the winter night" (C 295), recalling his meeting the wolf packs in the snow night in his childhood. In his dream, his parents are sill alive and Boyd tells him that "he'd had a dream and in the dream Billy had run away from home," making the sharp contrast of the reality with dream (C 295-6). The arrangement of the self-similarity between the dream and the events in the plotting constructs the recursive symmetry in the text, meanwhile the dream-within-the-dream structure maps out the structure of tales-within-the-tale in the narrative text, building up the fractal in the narrative structure.

In Billy's second dream, "he held his dying brother in his arms but he could not see his face and he could not say his name. Somewhere among the black and dripping streets a dog howled" (C 325). Billy's dream turns out to be the reality presented in his third journey, in which he crosses the border to send back the bones of his brother Boyd. In the final book of the border trilogy, the dying John Grady is held in thearms of his buddy Billy, forming the picture of the pieta. As a narrative device, dream has been taken to create the self-similarity between the dream and reality in the border trilogy, which links them together into the wholeness. After the release from the jail, John Grady returns back to La Purisima and meets Alejandra for the purpose of regaining his lost love. Both meet at a hotel in Zacatecas. After waking up, Alejandra tells her sleeping dream to John Grady, in which John Grady is dead, and carried "through the streets of a city ... It was dawn. The children were praying. *Lloraba tu madre. Con Más razón tu puta* [your mother is crying, with most reason your whore][1] (Horses 252). Alejandra's dream echoes the final death of John Grady in the duel with the pimp Eduardo for the whore Magdalena in *The Cities of the Plain*. The accordance of the dream with the reality even constructs the across-scaling self-similarity between books of the border trilogy, making them a whole finally.

Chaos theory encourages the reader's non-linear thinking in his participation in the writing, and his "reflexive reference" is necessary to make when exploring the spatial configuration of the narrative text. As the other pattern or model to map the phase space of the deterministic chaos, fractals are presented in both the content and structure in the second book of the border trilogy. In *The Crossing*, the tripartite structure for the major part of narrative text and its three interpolated tales as well as some other textual details associating with the number "three," make the text in accordance with the pattern of chaos theory, constructing the recursive symmetry in the text. If the number "three" in *No Country for Old Men* is taken to refer to chaotic nature of things in the world, and in *All the Pretty Horses*, the number "three" is mainly associated with the three-body problem in science to present the chaotic state of John Grady's journey, then in *The*

---

[1] A translation of the Spanish in *All the Pretty Horses* is from Brent Stevens at <www.cormacmccarthy.com>

Crossing, the number "three" is taken to show across-scaling self-similarities in the narrative form, creating the textual resonance.

Billy Parham's three border-crossing stories are made to be parallel with three interpolated tales in terms of their major thematic motifs about life, myth and narrative, constructing fractals in the narrative content and form. Furthermore, some other minor tales underlying the major narrative part, such as the tale of the she-wolf, of Boyd, of Boyd's Mexican girlfriend, of the primadonna in the troupe, and so on, construct some other fractals in the narrative. All in all, the complicated and organic combination of the major part of the narrative and the interpolated tales as well as some other minor tales underlying the major tale makes the text remarkable with its spatial configuration as fractals, not only creating the self-referentiality in the text, but also making the text recursive symmetry in the form. McCarthy takes the fractals, one of the spatial patterns to map the phase space of nonlinear dynamic system, to construct his fiction's spatial form, making his fiction exceptional in contemporary American literature.

Conclusion

Each man is the bard of his own existence. This is how he is joined to the world.

Cormac McCarthy, Cities of the Plain

In the second half of the 20th century, postmodern science brings about the epistemic shift for our knowledge of living cosmos. Chaos theory completely turns away from Newtonian mechanical sense of the world as a machine with order to a turbulence with orderly disorder. Order refers to stability, regularity, certainty and determinacy of the world as well as the interconnection of events to make up the world; while disorder refers to instability, irregularity, randomness and indeterminacy of the world as well as the isolation of events in the world. Classical science thinks that the essence of world is order, and the purpose of scientific studies is to find out order and rules of events in the world hidden in the disorder and noise of the surface; while chaos theory suggests that both order and disorder constitute the essential existence of events in the world, and both even shift alternatively with dependence on initial conditions sensitively. For chaos theory, in a deterministic system, the innate randomness may occur necessarily, which means the deterministic unpredictability of things' development. In its emphasis on description rather than prediction, chaos theory destroys Laplace's dream of solving the mysteries of the universal machine. As a deterministic chaos, the world in which we live is uncertain and unpredictable rather than of absolute laws and mechanic process, interconnected and open rather than of isolated, closed system, holistic rather than something global or local. Chaos has become an important metaphor entering into the vision of philosophers and writers since the 1980s. The overlapping of chaos theory and postmodernism in their recognition of world makes both the arts and science tread on the same ground in the contemporary period, bringing in the radical changes of American literature within the twentieth century.

Chaos constitutes the core of McCarthy's works, and becomes the tension to understand McCarthy's aesthetic force. The central argument of my study has been that McCarthy's works are both complex and dynamic due to their association with the chaos in their thematic content, narrative strategies, and narrative forms. The metaphorical meanings of chaos have been applied to present McCarthy's understandings of humanity, society and nature as orderly disorder and nonlinearity in regard to the themes in his profoundly informed novels. Besides the fictional world, McCarthy's textual world is also "chaotic" in terms of its application of both core principles of chaos theory into narrative strategies and important patterns of chaos theory into spatial configuration, making his fictional writings a whole featuring chaos.

McCarthy is a mobile person. He never stays in one place permanently, but shifts from Rhode Island to Tennessee, then to England and El Paso, Taxas, and finally to Santa Fe, New Mexico. The mobility of his life parallels with his mobile writings, too: from his early period's Appalachian writings to his middle period's Southwestern works, and finally to his latest New Mexico period, with the apparent characteristic of geographical setting in his span of writings for almost 40 years. Compatible with the mobility of writer and writings, most of his characters are on the road, moving from "civilization" to "wilderness," due to all kind of reasons, passive or active, or both, just like that of Lester Ballard in *Child of God*, or John Grady Cole and Billy Parham in *The Border Trilogy*, or the Kid in *Blood Meridian*, or Llewellyn Moss in *No Country for Old Men*, or Father in *The Road*, which are involved into the deterministic chaos. In correspondence with these wanderer characters, seemingly all of his fiction fall into road novels, associating with journey or voyage. It is such characteristic of mobility that makes McCarthy's works tend to be associated with chaos and chaos theory, because chaos theory is to study the trajectories of matter's motion in a nonlinear dynamic system; simultaneously, it provides the basis for my study's choice of chaos theory to make examination of his dynamic works.

McCarthy loves the wilderness, and his childhood's hunting and roaming in the wilderness of his Appalachian hometown make his knowledge of wilderness rich. Most of his characters are good frontiersmen in American wilderness, and deserts, mountains, caves, and plains, are their habitats. However, just as I have suggested in the study, most of them are wanderers in the wilderness, and Lester Ballard, the Kid, John Grady, Billy Parham, Llewellyn Moss, Father, are good cases. The denaturing of the wilderness with the process of industrialization, urbanization, and even the detonation of atomic bombs in the late twentieth century dispossesses their living places and causes their wandering "on the road." It seems that there is no corner of life, no matter how remote it is, which could be unaffected by changes to life brought in by late twentieth century consumerist modernity. McCarthy understands evil, violence, and darkness of humanity and even human society, and he has acknowledged that "There's no such thing as life without bloodshed, I think the notion that the species can be improved in some way, that everyone could live in harmony, is really dangerous idea" (Woodward, 1992: 31). Alongside the wilderness which McCarthy is able to observe so minutely is the wider world, enmeshed in the blood and violence caused from various wars, the World War II, the cold war, Korean War, Vietnam War, Golf War, Anti-terrorist wars, even the threat of nuclear wars, McCarthy points out the "wilderness" in the human mind and human society, which is similar to or even much darker and bleaker than Joseph Conradian "heart of darkness," or T. S. Eliot's "wasteland" for modern Western society.

As a "meta-narrative" of McCarthy's works, wilderness is presented in McCarthy's works metaphorically, geographically, politically and even mythically. As the great metaphor of chaos, wilderness is synonymous with chaos in the presentation of themes of McCarthy's works. Just as I have suggested in this study, chaos theory focuses on nature, and nature's re-enchantment for postmodern science makes people know more about himself in nature. Nature is nonlinear and in it both symmetry and asymmetry, both order and disorder, both beauty and ugliness, both regularity and irregularity, are parallel with each other. McCarthy's fictional world is full of paradoxes, just as the "chaotic" wilderness presents us humans, and in his works, nature, society and humans are in the chaos or wilderness, which is no longer preoccupied with dualistic assumption about good and evil, order and disorder, center and margin, subject and object, rather, the eclecticism of ambiguity and nonlinearity. By means of his "boundary-crossing" in the presentation of humans, human society and nature as chaos or wilderness, McCarthy makes himself important in the field of contemporary literature. As a serious writer, McCarthy could focalize on the crucial problems in contemporary culture and in his questioning of the capitalized order, he not only points out its malaise of his living postmodern age, but also critiques and dismantles it with his vision of world as chaos.

McCarthy believes that "words are things," and life is narrative, just as he expresses through the words of the evil captain in *All the Pretty Horses*, "we can make truth here" (Horses 168) or the ex-priest in *The Crossing*, "all is telling" (C 155). Being narrative means construction and fictionality, featuring uncertainty and unpredictability, which makes McCarthy's recognition of world contrary to Newtonian sense of world as stability and certainty. For McCarthy, life is a deterministic chaos, in which everybody is involved into its trajectories, full of chances and randomness. Most of characters in McCarthy's works are on the edge of chaos, where the alternation between order and chaos sensitively depends on the interior changes of initial conditions, and any small perturbations may cause great changes in their life systems. Lester Ballard, John Grady, Billy Parham, Moss, and Father are good examples to demonstrate the butterfly effect on human life in a chaotic system, and the turbulence in their lives proves the paradoxes of the deterministic chaos: all things in the world are both cause and consequence, both the subject and object, both the node and core, and they are interconnected in a web.

Besides his presentation of the destiny of his characters as interconnection in the chaotic web, McCarthy's holistic world view causes his works connected with each other on the one hand and even with other canon works in American literature on the other hand, not only making his works a whole with different fractals, but also making him in line with American literature tradition. Though self-similarities could be found out through both *All the Pretty Horses* and *The Crossing*, as I have suggested in my studies of both of works concerning spatial configuration, such a means is taken throughout McCarthy's corpus. Self-similarities are made through the rich intertextuality and intratextuality in McCarthy's works. Intertextuality refers to the relation of different works by different writers, and intratexutuality indicates the connection of different works by the same writer, implying the progression of the works for a given writer. Just as I have suggested in my study of the iteration *in Blood Meridian*, the intertextuality has been made in McCarthy's presentation of both of the figures in the work: the Kid and Judge Holden. Besides, in my studies of *The Crossing*, the intertextuality could be traced in the presentation of Billy Parham's wilderness dream. Intratextuality is dominant in McCarthy's works, which has been suggested in the studies of the border trilogy. Besides the parallel characterization of major figures in McCarthy's works, such as both John Grady and Billy Parham, both Alejandra and the she-wolf, both John Grady and Boyd Parham, both John Grady and Dueña Alfonsa, both John Grady and the Kid, both Alejandra and Magdalena, both Don Héctor Rocha and Eduardo, which has been suggested in my studies of both *All the Pretty Horses* and *The Crossing*, the reiteration of some minor characters in McCarthy's works also makes them interconnected, such as the idiot in *Outer Dark*, *Child of God*, and *Blood Meridian*, the blind in *The Crossing*, *Cities of the Plain*, and *The Road*, and the wise hermits to give warnings for the protagonists in *Blood Meridian*, *The Crossing*, and *The Road*. Furthermore, most of McCarthy's minor characters are philosophers in their understandings of life and world as chaos, which could be evidenced from the blacksmith in *Child of God*, the hermit wanderer in *Blood Meridian*, Dueña Alfonsa in All the Pretty Horses, and these three stroy-tellers including the ex-priest, the blind, and the gypsy, the wolf trapper, the ganadaro, and the primadonna in *The Crossing*, Chigurh in *No Country for Old Men*, and Ely in *The Road*. Echoing the interconnection of characterization, some important imageries associated with chances and chaos are prevalent in McCarthy's writings, such as tapestry, maze, puppet net, coinage, maps, coin-tossing, chess-playing, and snowflake, which makes McCarthy's writings interconnected with each other locally.

The intratextuality might be foregrounded in McCarthy's four important Southwestern works, namely, the tetralogy of Southwestern works, *Blood Meridian*, *All the Pretty Horses*, *The Crossing*, and *Cities of the Plain*, as regards their characterization, genre of postmodern Western, critiques of the myth of frontier or wilderness, landscape descriptions, and expression of McCarthy's world view of chaos. For McCarthy, history and myth are socially and culturally constructed, and in his presentation of the poisonous effects on Americans for the myth of the frontier through the futile journey of these protagonists in the wilderness, McCarthy presents the "reality" of simulacra in the postmodern age. In his choice of the genre of postmodern Western for his Southwestern works, McCarthy makes his complicit critique of the history and myth constructing the convention of American Western, and meanwhile his works are made to be self-reflective, critiquing the genre of which they are inside. McCarthy's rewriting of the myth of frontier or wilderness makes him in correspondence with the current of revision of history after the 1960s in America, and thus gaining the important position with these contemporary writers, such as E. L. Doctorow, John Barth, Thomas Pynchon, Ishmael Reed, and James Welch. More importantly, via the rich intratextuality in his works, McCarthy makes his novels reflexive in multiple dimensions. The glance of intertextuality and intratexuality in McCarthy's works can prove the dialogic characteristic of McCarthy's textual world. More significantly, so many self-similarities created by intertextuality and intratextuality make his works interconnected, constructing a whole for McCarthy's corpus. Meanwhile, the close intertextual links with works of Fenimore Cooper, Herman Melville, Mark Twain, William Faulkner, F. Scot Fitzgerald make McCarthy's writings in connection with the tradition of American literature with its eclecticism, making himself outstanding in the world of American literature.

As an interdisciplinary translator working actively at Santa Fe Institute, which describes itself as an "independent research and education center ... for multidisciplinary collaborations in the physical, biological, computational, and social sciences ... in attempts to uncover the mechanisms that underlie the deep simplicity present in our complex world" (Brosi 11), McCarthy is not new to chaos theory or complexity science. His friendship with the physicist Murray Gell-Mann, one of the founders of the Santa Fe Institute, makes his writings in accordance with the principles of chaos theory self-consciously, which has been suggested in my studies of narrative strategies of his representative novels, *Blood Meridian*, *The Road* and *No Country for Old Men*. Iteration, indeterminacy and butterfly effect are taken in McCarthy's narrative, making his novels as complex as beautiful chaos. To sum up, the complexity of McCarthy's works stems from his knowledge of chaos theory and his scientifically complex vision of world as well as the innovative ways he takes to convey that view through his fiction. The adoption of the principles of chaos theory as narrative strategies of his important works makes McCarthy innovative and his bringing the scientific features into fictional writings makes him much closer to these master writers such as Kurt Vonnegut, Thomas Pynchon, John Barth, and Don DeLillo in contemporary American literature.

Deeply concerned about how to construct a novel form suitable for the reality of chaos, McCarthy has made artistic innovations in making chaos both the content and form of his novels. Besides taking the principles of chaos theory as his narrative strategies, both patterns of chaos theory are taken in McCarthy's narrative to make his texts into symmetrical asymmetry or orderly disorder in their spatial configurations as both strange attractor and fractals, which has been demonstrated in my study of both *All the Pretty Horses* and *The Crossing*. The principles and patterns of chaos theory have been taken in his narrative structures and forms, which makes McCarthy's fiction into dynamic ones, "in which chaos theory, complexity theory, ... enter structurally as well as through figuration, model and content" (Slethaug 8).

Chaos theory pays emphasis on the participation and intervention of observers, just as the length of English coastline depends on the scales, which has been suggested by Benoit Mandelbrot. McCarthy's works are hard to make categories, even though some critics have paid pains to demonstrate them to be realism, or naturalism, or modernism, or postmodernism, or late-modernism, concerning their writing modes, or to be Southern or Western or South-Western, as regards their regional features. To be honest, it is parochializing and limiting to label one writer with any-isms in the literary criticism, for such a general categorization tends to constrain and misunderstand him and his writings usually. In effect, in view of his narrative content and form as chaos, McCarthy's works have gone far beyond any boundary constraints of theoretical discourses, "offering the reader not a multiplicity of meanings, but rather a meaning which encompasses multiple interpretations" (McGilchrist 153). By this I suggest that McCarthy's reader is asked to participate in the process of fictional writings and he is made aware that meanings of a given text may be different seen from different readers, and that there are ways in which all these interpretations are somehow true. If we have to point out what McCarthy's works are, they might fall into the types of the writerly texts termed by Roland Barthes, and his metafiction *The Crossing* is a typical example. For Barthes, the distinguishment of the readerly texts with the writerly ones is not absolute, but distinct for their differences. The readerly texts generally refer to those realistic works with attempts to imitate the reality, or to create something real, towards which the reader's attitudes are simply acceptable or refusable, for their rights of creation have been dispossessed. Contrary to the readerly texts, the writerly texts are generally "intransitive" works, which are made to focus on the writing itself rather than the worlds they create, and the reader is asked to join in the creation of writings. Seen from the perspective of semiotics, the readerly texts are orderly and explicit, while the writerly ones are ambiguous and implicit, of signifiers rather than signifieds. McCarthy has expressed his ideas about his texts through the ex-priest in *The Crossing*, "Always the teller ... sets forth the categories into which the listener will wish to fit the narrative as he hears it. But he understands that the narrative is itself in fact no category but is rather the category of all categories for there is nothing which falls outside its purview. All is telling. Do not doubt it" (C 155).

I pass, like night, from land to land;

I have strange power of speech;

The moment that his face I see

I know the man that must hear me;

To him my tale I teach. (Coleridge, II, 619-623)

Such a poetic stanza from Coleridge's "The Rhyme of the Ancient Mariner" may be good to be taken as my ending of the study of Cormac McCarthy and his works. As a remarkable writer in contemporary American literature, McCarthy shifts from the South to the west, from Appalachian mountains to Southwest deserts and prairies, and his "strange power of speech" in his story-telling makes us sense both the force and glamour of chaos. McCarthy is a poet, and his deep observation of evil, violence, deformation and morbidity of humanity and even our living cosmos in his works gives us warnings of those deep in ourselves and makes us aware that we are evil and violent. Likewise, his presentation of terrible beauty in our living cosmos dismantles the Western metaphysics of dualism of subject and object, man and nature, nature and culture, order and disorder, center and margin, providing us insights when observing the world as a deterministic chaos. McCarthy is a philosopher, and his radical criticism is made to make a diagnosis of the malaise of his living postmodern age without dread, which produces the alienation of human beings, encodes the violence fetishism, and denatures the wilderness, challenging against the Western epistemology since Enlightenment. Meanwhile, his observation of human life as narrative in one chaotic system teaches us to be dialectic towards life, society, and nature, in which chance and randomness are dominant. McCarthy is a writer with political consciousness, his disclosure of history and myth as construction not only satirizes the corruption of history and myth and their penchant violence in American national consciousness, but also subverts the conventions of their construction of national identity. In his critique of the poisonous effects on young Americans for the myth of wilderness or frontier, McCarthy aims to "derail the mythic machine which still runs wildly down the tracks of American identity, dominating national discourse" (McGilchrist 198). McCarthy is a good story-teller, even though most of his contemporary writers believe in the exhaustion of narrative, and his innovative ways of conveying his vision of world as a deterministic chaos by means of chaos principles and patterns as narrative strategies and forms make him a remarkable artist, ranking together with Vladimir Nabokov, John Barth, and Thomas Pynchon. More important, his fictional writings with the span of almost forty years are under both the currents of postmodernism and chaos theory, reflecting the merging of science with arts for the tendency of contemporary literary writings. McCarthy has gone beyond any constraints of regional literature and writing modes, becoming a unique writer in contemporary American literature. His contribution to American literature will make him get more and more "listeners," appreciating his great tales about chaotic and systematic humans, society and nature.

To be a good "listener" of McCarthy's tales is not easy due to their complexity and ambiguity, even though we seem to "see his face." If what I do at present is just a glance casting at his power as a good storyteller, that is enough, because I am also a lone traveler at night passing "from land to land," hoping to explore the treasure house of his works with the perspective of chaos theory, which appears to be "strange," yet powerful, to tell my "tale" of McCarthy's works from aspects of narrative content, narrative strategy, and narrative forms, which have been constructed together into that beautiful chaos. To be a good "listener" of McCarthy's tales is still a long way to go, because McCarthy is still on "the road" with his writings at present, and for us, we are only beginners.

Works Cited

[1] Arnold, Edwin T. "McCarthy and the Sacred: A Reading of *The Crossing*." [A] *Cormac McCarthy*: *New Directions* [C]. Ed. James D. Lilley. Albuquerque: Univ. of New Mexico Press, 2002.

[2] Arnold, Edwin T. "The Mosaic of McCarthy's Fiction." [A] *Sacred Violence: A Reader's Companion to Cormac McCarthy* [C]. Eds. Edwin T. Arnold and Dianne C. Luce. Jackson: Univ. of Mississippi, 1995.

[3] Arnold, Edwin T, Dianne Luce. "Introduction."[A] *Perspectives on Cormac McCarthy* [C]. Eds. Edwin T. Arnold and Dianne Luce. Jackson: Univ. Press of Mississippi, 1993.

[4] Barrera, Cordelia Eliza. *Border Places, Frontier Spaces: Deconstructing Ideologies of the Southwest* [D]. The Univ. of Texas at San Antonio, 2009. Ann Arbor: UMI, 2009. ATT 3368769

[5] Barth, John. "PM/ CT/ RA: An Underview." [A] *Further Fridays: Essays, Lectures, and Other Nonfiction 1984—1999* [C]. Boston: Little, Brown and Co., 1995.

[6] Bartlett, Andrew. "From Voyeurism to Archaeology: Cormac McCarthy's *Child of God*." [J] *Southern Literary Journal*, 1991 (24).

[7] Baudrillard, Jean. "*Selected Writings*." [C] Ed. Mark Poster. Standford: Standford Univ. Press, 2001.

[8] Bell, Robert. *Dictionary of Classical Mythology* [M]. Santa Barbara: ABC-clio, 1982.

[9] Bell, Vereen M. *The Achievement of Cormac McCarthy* [M]. Baton Rouge: Louisiana State Univ. Press, 1988.

[10] Berry, K. Wesley. "The Lay of the Land in Cormac McCarthy's Appalachia." [A]

Cormac McCarthy: New Directions [C]. Ed. James D. Lilley. Albuquerque: Univ. of New Mexico Press, 2002.

[11] Bloom, Harold. *Novelists and Novels* [M]. New York: Checkmark Books: 2007.

[12] Boon, Kevin A. *Chaos Theory and The Interpretation of Literary Texts: The Case of Kurt Vonnegut* [M]. The Edwen Mellen Press, 1997.

[13] Bortz, Maggie. *Paradoxical Journey Towards the Mature Masculine: Telos in the Cultural Dream of No Country for Old Men* [D]. Pacifica Graduate Institute, 2010. Ann Arbor: UMI, 2010. ATT 1481840

[14] Bowers, James. "Reading Cormac McCarthy's *Blood Meridian*." [A] *Western Writers Series* [C]. Ed. John P. O'Grady. Boise: Boise State Univ. Press, 1999.

[15] Brewton, Vince. "The Changing Landscape of Violence in Cormac McCarthy's Early Novels and the *Border Trilogy*." [J] *Southern Literary Journal*, 2004 (37).

[16] Brickner, Richard P. "A Hero Cast Out, Even by Tragedy." [J] *New York Times Review*, 1974 (13).

[17] Brosi, George. "Cormac McCarthy: A Rare Literary Life." [J] *Appalachian Heritage,* 2011 (39).

[18] Cambel, A. B. *Applied Chaos Theory: a Paradigm for Complexity* [M]. New York and London: Academic Press, 1993.

[19] Campbell, Neil. "Beyond Reckoning: Cormac McCarthy's Version of the West in *Blood Meridian or the Evening Redness in the West*." [J] *Critique*, 1997 (34).

[20] Campbell, Neil. *The Culture of the American New West* [M]. Edinburgh: Edinburgh Univ. Press, 2000.

[21] Cant, John. *Cormac McCarthy and the Myth of American Exceptionalism* [M]. New York and London: Routledge, 2008.

[22] Cant, John. "Oedipus Rests: Mimesis and Allegory in *No Country for Old Men*." [J] *The Cormac McCarthy Journal*, 2005 (15).

[23] Christman, Phil. "A Tabernacle in the Dark: On the Road with Cormac McCarthy." [J] *Books and Culture: A Christian Review,* 2007 (13).

[24] Coleridge, Samuel T. "The Rhyme of the Ancient Mariner [1798]." [A] *Poems: Samuel Taylor Coleridge* [C]. Ed. J. Beer. London: Dent, 1995.

[25] Collett-White, Mike. "Movie Remark for McCarthy's Bleak Novel *The Road*." [J] *Thomas Reuters*, 2009 (3).

[26] Conte, Joseph. *Design and Debris: A Chaotics of Postmodern American Fiction* [M]. Tuscaloosa: Univ. of Alabama Press, 2002.

[27] Cooper, Lydia R. *Cormac McCarthy's Heroes: Narrative Perspective and Morality in McCarthy's Novels* [D]. Baylor University, 2008. Ann Arbor: UMI, 2008. ATT 3316047

[28] Cremean, David. "For Whom the Bell Tolls: Conservatism and Change in Cormac McCarthy's Sheriff from *No Country for Old Men*." [J] *The Cormac McCarthy Journal*, 2005 (5).

[29] Culler, Jonathan. *On Destruction: Theory and Criticism after Structuralism* [M]. Ithaca, NY: Cornell Univ. Press, 1982.

[30] Curtis, James M. "Spatial Form in the Context of Modernist Aesthetics." [A] *Spatial Form in Narrative* [C]. Eds. Jeffery R. Smitten and Ann Daghistany. Ithaca and London: Cornell Univ. Press, 1981.

[31] Dacus, Chris. "The West as Symbol of the Eschaton in Cormac McCarthy." [J] *The Cormac McCarthy Journal* 1, 2009 (1).

[32] Deresiewicz, William. "It's a man's, man's world." [J] *The Nation*, 2005. Online. <http://www.thenation.com/doc/20050912/deresiewicz>

[33] Donahue, James J. *Rewriting the American Myth: Post-1960s American Historical Frontier Romances* [D]. Univ. of Connecticut, 2007. Ann Arbor: UMI, 2007. ATT 3265766

[34] Donnelly, Brian. " 'Coke Is It!': Placing Coca-Cola in McCarthy's *The Road*." [J] *The Explicator* 68.1 (2010): 70-73.

[35] Donoghue, Denis. "Reading *Blood Meridian*." [J] *The Sewanee Review*, 1997.

[36] Eaton, Mark A. "Dis(re)membered Bodies: Cormac McCarthy's Border Fiction." [J] *Modern Fiction Studies*, 2003 (49). Rpt. in *Contemporary Literary Criticism*. Ed. Jeffrey Hunter. Vol. 295. Detroit: Gale, 2011. *Literary Resource Center*. Web. 13 Nov. 2010. <http: //go.galegroup.com>

[37] Ellis, Jay. *No Place for Home: Spatial Constraint and Character Flight in the*

Novels of Cormac McCarthy [M]. New York and London: Routledge, 2006.

[38] Ellis, Jay & Natalka Palczysbki. "Horses, Houses, and the Gravy to Win: Chivalric and Domestic Roles in the *Border Trilogy*." [A] *Sacred Violence: Volume 2: Cormac McCarthy's Western Novels* [C]. 2nd ed. Eds. Wade Hall and Rick Wallach. El Paso: The Univ. of Texas at El Paso, 2002.

[39] Foucault, Michel. "Of Other Spaces." [J] Trans. Jay Miskowiec. *Dicritics*, 1986 (16).

[40] Foucault, Michel. "Panopticism." [A] *Discipline and Punish: The Birth of the Prison* [C]. Trans. Alan Sheridan. New York: Pantheon, 1977.

[41] Foucault, Michel. *Power/Knowledge: Selected Interviews and Other Writings 1972-1977* [M]. Ed and Trans. Collin Gordon. New York: Pantheon, 1980.

[42] Foucault, Michel. *The Order of Things* [M]. New York: Vintage Books, 1973.

[43] Frye, Steven. *Understanding Cormac McCarthy* [M]. Columbia: The Univ. of South Carolina Press, 2009.

[44] Gallivan, Euan. "Compassionate McCarthy?: *The Road* and Schopenhauerian Ethics." [J] *The Cormac McCarthy Journal*, 2008 (6).

[45] George, Sean M. *The Phoenix Inverted: The Re-birth and Death of Masculinity and the Emergence of Trauma in Contemporary American Literature* [D]. Texas A & M Univ. -Commerce, 2010. Ann Arbor: UMI, 2010. ATT 3405822

[46] Geyh, Paul et al. *Postmodern American Fiction* [M]. New York and London: W. W. Norton & Company, 1998.

[47] Giles, James R. *Violence in the Contemporary American Novel: An End to Violence* [M]. Columbia: Univ. of South Carolina Press, 2000.

[48] Gillespie, Michael Patrick. *The Aesthetics of Chaos: Nonlinear Thinking and Contemporary Literary Criticism* [M]. Cainesville: Univ. Press of Florida, 1996.

[49] Girard, René. *Violence and Sacred* [M]. Baltimore: The John Hopkins UP, 1977.

[50] Gleick, James. *Chaos: Making a New Science* [M]. New York: Penguin Books, 1987.

[51] Grant, Iain Hamilton. "Postmodernism and Science and Technology." [A] *The Routledge Companion to Postmodernism* [C]. Ed. Stuart Sim. New York &

London: Routledge, 2002. 65-77.

[52] Graulund, Rune. "Fulcrums and Borderlands: A Desert Reading of Cormac McCarthy's *The Road.*" [J] *Orbis Litterarum*, 2010 (65).

[53] Grimal, Pierre. *The Dictionary of Classical Mythology* [M]. Trans. A. R. Maxwell-Hylop. New York: Blackwell, 1951.

[54] Grove, Loy. "Gaddis and the Cosmic Babble."[N] *Interview with William Gaddis. Washington Post* (23 Aug. 1985): B10.

[55] Grubic, Royce P. *Cosmos, Chaos, and Process in Western Thought: Towards a New Science and Existentialist Social Ethic* [M]. VDM Verlag Dr. Muller, 2008.

[56] Guillemin, Georg. *The Pastoral Vision of Cormac McCarthy* [M]. College Station: Taxas A & M Univ. Press, 2004.

[57] Guinn, Matthew. "Rude Forms Survive: Cormac McCarthy's Atavistic Vision." [A] *Myth, Legend, Dust: Critical Response to Cormac McCarthy* [C]. Ed. Rick Wallach. Manchester and New York: Manchester Univ. Press, 2000.

[58] Handley, William R. "Western Fiction: Gery, Stegner, McMurtry, McCarthy." [J] *The Oxford Encyclopedia of American Literature*. Vol. 4. Ed. Jay Parini. New York: Oxford University. Press, 2004.

[59] Harvey, David. *The Condition of Postmodernity* [M]. Massachusetts: Blackwell Publishers Ltd, 1990.

[60] Hassan, Ihab. *The Postmodern Turn: Essays in Postmodern Theory and Culture* [M]. Ohio State Univ. Press, 1987.

[61] Hawkins, Harriett. *Strange Attractors: Literature, Culture & Chaos Theory* [M]. Hertfordshire: Prentice Hall/ Harvester Wheatsheaf, 1995.

[62] Hayles, N. Katherine (ed.). *Chaos and Order: Complex Dynamics in Literature and Science* [C]. Chicago and London: The Univ. of Chicago Press, 1991.

[63] Hayles, N. Katherine. "Chaos as Orderly Disorder: Shifting Ground in Contemporary Literature and Science." [J] *New Literary History,* 1989 (20).

[64] Hayles, N. Katherine. *Chaos Bound: Orderly Disorder in Contemporary Literature and Science* [M]. Ithaca and London: Cornell Univ. Press, 1990.

[65] Hayles, N. Katherine. *The Cosmic Web: Scientific Field Models and Literary*

Strategies in the Twentieth Century [M]. Ithaca and London: Cornell Univ. Press, 1984.

[66] Hebdige, Dick. "Subjects in Space." [J] *New Formations*, 1990 (11).

[67] Herzog, Tobey C. *Vietnam War Stories: Innocence Lost* [M]. London: Routledge, 1992.

[68] Holloway, David. "A False Book is No Book At All: The Ideology of Representation in *Blood Meridian* and the *Border Trilogy*." [A] *Myth, Legend, Dust: Critical Responses to Cormac McCarthy* [C]. Ed. Rick Wallach. Manchester and New York: Manchester Univ. Press, 2000. 185-200.

[69] Holloway, David. *The Late Modernism of Cormac McCarthy* [M]. Connecticut and London: Greenwood Press, 2002.

[70] Huang, Kerson. *I Ching: The Oracle* [M]. Singapore: World Scientific Publishing Co., 1984.

[71] Hutcheon, Linda. *A Poetics of Postmodernism: History, Theory, Fiction* [M]. New York and London: Routledge, 1988.

[72] Hutcheon, Linda. *The Politics of Postmodernism* [M]. New York and London: Routledge, 1989.

[73] Jameson, Frederic. *Postmodernism, or, The Cultural Logic of Late Capitalism* [M]. Durham: Duke Univ. Press, 1999.

[74] Jarrett, Robert. *Cormac McCarthy* [M]. New York: Twayne, 1997.

[75] Jarrett, Robert. "Genre, Voice and Ethos: McCarthy's Perverse Thriller." [J] *The Cormac McCarthy Journal*, 2005 (5).

[76] Joseph, Peter. "Blood Music: Reading *Blood Meridian*." [A] *Sacred Violence: Volume 2: Cormac McCarthy's Western Novels* [C]. 2nd ed. Eds. Wade Hall and Rick Wallach. El Paso: Texas Western Press, 2002.

[77] Kestner, Joseph. "Secondary Illusion: *The Novel and the Spatial Arts*." [A] *Spatial Form in Narrative* [C]. Eds. Jeffery R. Smitten and Ann Daghistany. Ithaca and London: Cornell Univ. Press, 1981.

[78] Klinkowitz, Jerome. "Spatial Form in Contemporary Fiction." [A] *Spatial Form in Narrative* [C]. Eds. Jeffery R. Smitten and Ann Daghistany. Ithaca and London:

Cornell Univ. Press, 1981.

[79] Kollin, Susan. "Genre and the Geographies of Violence: Cormac McCarthy and the Contemporary Western." [J] *Contemporary Literature*, 2001 (42).

[80] Kristeva, Julia. *Powers of Horror: An Essay on Abjection* [M]. New York: Columbia Univ. Press, 1982.

[81] Kuberski, Philip. *Chaosmos: Literature, Science and Theory* [M]. Albany: State Univ. of New York Press, 1994.

[82] Kuhn, Thomas S. *The Structure of Scientific Revolution* [M]. 2nd ed. Chicago: Chicago Univ. Press, 1970.

[83] Kundert-Gibbs, John Leeland. *No-Thing is Left to Tell: Zen/Chaos Theory in the Dramatic Art of Samuel Beckett* [M]. Madison/ Teaneck: Fairleigh Dickinson Univ. Press, 1999.

[84] Kunsa, Ashley. "'Maps of the World in Its Becoming': Post-Apocalyptic Naming in Cormac McCarthy's *The Road*." [J] *Journal of Modern Literature*, 2009 (33).

[85] Kushner, David. "Cormac McCarthy's Apocalypse." [J] *Rolling Stone*, 2007 (27). Online. <http://members. authorsguild. net/dkushner/work3.htm>

[86] Laing, Ronald D. *The Divided Self: An Existential Study in Sanity and Madness* [M]. London: Penguin Books, 1967.

[87] Lang, John. "Lester Ballard: McCarthy's Challenge to the Reader's Compassion." [A] *Sacred Violence: A Reader's Companion to Cormac McCarthy* [C]. Eds. Edwin T. Arnold and Dianne C. Luce. Jackson: Univ. of Mississippi, 1995.

[88] Lao Tzu. *Tao Te Ching* [M]. Trans. Stephen Mitchell. New York: Harper Perennial, 1988.

[89] Lincoln, Kenneth. *Cormac McCarthy: American Canticles* [M]. New York: Palgrave Macmillan, 2009.

[90] Lorenz, Edward. N. *The Essence of Chaos* [M]. Washington: Univ. of Washington Press, 1993.

[91] Luce, Dianne C. "Beyond the Border: Cormac McCarthy in the New Millennium." [J] *The Cormac McCarthy Journal*, 2008 (16).

[92] Luce, Dianne C. *Reading the World: Cormac McCarthy's Tennessee Period* [M].

The Univ. of South Carolina Press, 2009.

[93] Luce, Dianne C. "The Cave of Oblivion: Platonic Mythology in *Child of God.*" [A] *Cormac McCarthy: New Directions* [C]. Ed. James D. Lilley. Albuquerque: Univ. of New Mexico Press, 2002.

[94] Luce, Dianne C. "'When You Wake': John Grady Cole's Heroism in *All the Pretty Horses.*" [A] *Sacred Violence: Volume 2: Cormac McCarthy's Western Novels* [C]. 2nd ed. Eds. Wade Hall and Rick Wallach. El Paso: Texas Western Press, 2002.

[95] Lyotard, Jean-Francois. *The Postmodern Condition: A Report on Knowledge* [M]. Minnneapolis: Univ. of Minnesota Press, 1993.

[96] Mackey, Peter Francis. *Chaos Theory and James Joyce's Everyman* [M]. Cainesville: Univ. Press of Florida, 1999.

[97] Maguire, James H. "Fiction of the West." [A] *The Columbia History of the American* [C]. Ed. Emory Elliott. Beijing: Foreign Language Teaching and Research Press, 2005.

[98] Malewitz, Raymond. "'Anything Can Be an Instrument': Misuse Value and Rugged Consumerism in Cormac Mccarthy's *No Country for Old Men.*" [J] *Contemporary Literature*, 2009 (50).

[99] Mandelbrot, Benoit B. *The Fractal Geometry of Nature* [M]. San Francisco: W. H. Freeman and Co., 1983.

[100] McBride, Molly. "*The Crossing*'s Noble Savagery: The Wolf, the Indian, and the Empire." [A] *Sacred Violence: Volume 2: Cormac McCarthy's Western Novels* [C]. 2nd ed. Eds. Wade Hall and Rick Wallach. El Paso: Texas Western Press, 2002. 71-82.

[101] McCarthy, Cormac. *All the Pretty Horses* [M]. New York: Vintage International, 1992.

[102] McCarthy, Cormac. *Blood Meridian, or The Evening Redness in the West* [M]. New York: Vintage International, 1992.

[103] McCarthy, Cormac. *Child of God* [M]. New York: Vintage International, 1973.

[104] McCarthy, Cormac. *Cities of the Plain* [M]. New York: Alfred A. Knopf, 1998.

[105] McCarthy, Cormac. *No Country for Old Men* [M]. New York: Alfred A. Knopf,

2005.

[106] McCarthy, Cormac. *Outer Dark* [M]. New York: Vintage International, 1993.

[107] McCarthy, Cormac. *Suttree* [M]. New York: Random House, 1979.

[108] McCarthy, Cormac. *The Crossing* [M]. New York: Alfred A. Knopf, 1994.

[109] McCarthy, Cormac. *The Orchard Keeper* [M]. New York: Vintage International, 1993.

[110] McCarthy, Cormac. *The Road* [M]. New York: Vintage International, 2006.

[111] McCarthy, Cormac. *The Stonemason: A Play in Five Acts* [M]. Hopewell, N. J.: Ecco Press, 1994.

[112] McGilchrist, Megan Riley. *The Western Landscape in Cormac McCarthy and Wallace Stegner: Myths of the Frontier* [M]. New York & London: Routledge, 2010.

[113] McHale, Brain. *Postmodernist Fiction* [M]. London and New York: Routledge, 1987.

[114] McMurtry, Kim. "Some Improvident God: Metaphysical Explorations in McCarthy's *Border Trilogy*." [A] *Sacred Violence: Volume 2: Cormac McCarthy's Western Novels* [C]. 2nd ed. Eds. Wade Hall and Rick Wallach. El Paso: Texas Western Press, 2002. 143-157.

[115] Metress, Christopher. "Via Negative the Way of Unknowing in Cormac McCarthy's *Outer Dark*." [J] *Southern Review*, 2001 (37).

[116] Mickesen, David. "Types of Spatial Structure." [A] *Spatial Form in Narrative* [C]. Eds. Jeffery R. Smitten and Ann Daghistany. Ithaca and London: Cornell Univ. Press, 1981.

[117] Milton, John. *Paradise Lost* [1674] [A]. *John Milton: Complete Poems and Major Prose* [C]. Ed. Merritt Y. Hughes. *New York: Odyssey Press*, 1957.

[118] Monk, Nick. "An Impulse to Action, an Undefined Want: Modernity, Flight, and Crisis in the *Border Trilogy* and *Blood Meridian*." [A] *Sacred Violence: Volume 2: Cormac McCarthy's Western Novels* [C]. 2nd ed. Eds. Wade Hall and Rick Wallach. *El Paso: Texas Western Press*, 2002.

[119] Moran, Terence. "The Wired West." [J] *The New Republic*, 1985 (5).

[120] Morrison, Gail Moore. "*All the Pretty Horses*: John Grady Cole's Expulsion from Paradise." [A] *Perspectives on Cormac McCarthy* [C]. Eds. Edwin T. Arnold and Dianne C. Luce. Jackson: Univ. Press of Mississippi, 1993.

[121] Nabokov, Vladimir. *Strong Opinions* [M]. New York: Random House, 1990.

[122] Nash, Gerald D. "The West as Utopia and Myth." [J] *Montana: The Magazine of Western History*, 1991 (41).

[123] Newman, Charles. *The Postmodern Aura, The Act of Fiction in An Age of Inflation* [M]. Evanston: Northwestern Univ. Press, 1985.

[124] Oates, Joyce Carol. "The Treasure of Comanche County." [J] *The New Yorker Times Review of Books*, 2005. Online. <www.nybooks.com/articles/18359>

[125] Occupy Wall Street Movement. Protest against the Collateral Auctions [OD]. Oct. 15, 2011. <http://grwww.net/portal.php?mod=view&aid=14544>

[126] Owens, Barcley. *Cormac McCarthy's Western Novels* [M]. Tucson: The Univ. of Arizona Press, 2000.

[127] Owens-Murphy, Kate. "The Frontier Ethic behind Cormac McCarthy's Southern Fiction." [J] *Arizona Quarterly,* 2011 (67).

[128] Parker, Jo Alyson. *Narrative Form and Chaos Theory in Sterne, Proust, Woolf, and Faulkner* [M]. New York: Palgrave Macmillan, 2007.

[129] Parkers, Adam. "History, Bloodshed, and the Spectacle of American Identity in *Blood Meridian*." [A] *Cormac McCarthy: New Directions* [C]. Ed. James D. Lilley. Albuquerque: New Mexico Univ. Press, 2002.

[130] Peebles, Stacey. "What Happens to Country: The World to Come in Cormac McCarthy's *Border Trilogy*." [A] *Sacred Violence: Volume 2: Cormac McCarthy's Western Novels* [C]. 2nd ed. Eds. Wade Hall and Rick Wallach. El Paso: Texas Western Press, 2002.

[131] Petrides, Sarah I. *The Postregional Turn in Contemporary American Literature* [D]. Brown Univ., 2008. Ann Arbor: UMI, 2008. ATT 3318350

[132] Phillips, Dana. "History and the Ugly Facts of Cormac McCarthy's *Blood Meridian*." [J] *American Literature*, 1996 (68).

[133] Pitts, Jonathan. "Writing On: *Blood Meridian* as Devisionary Western." [J]

Western American Literature 33.1 (Spring 1998): 7-25. Rpt. In *Contemporary Literary Criticism*. Ed. Jefferey W. Hunter. Vol. 204. Detroit: Gale, 2005. *Literary Resource Center*. Web. 13 Nov. 2010.<http://go.galegroup.com>

[134] Porush, David. "Fictions as Dissipative Structures: Prigogine's Theory and Postmodernism's Roadshow." [A] *Chaos and Order: Complex Dynamics in Literature and Science* [C]. Ed. N. Katherine Hayles. Chicago and London: The Univ. of Chicago Press, 1991.

[135] Powers, Richard. *Galatea 2.2* [M]. New York: Farrar, Straus &Giroux, 1995.

[136] Prigogine, Ilya & Isabelle Stengers. *Order Out of Chaos: Man's New Dialogue with Nature* [M]. New York: Bantam, 1984.

[137] Rabkin, Eric S. "Spatial Form and Plot." [A] *Spatial Form in Narrative* [C]. Eds. Jeffery R. Smitten and Ann Daghistany. Ithaca and London: Cornell Univ. Press, 1981.

[138] Ragan, David Paul. "Values and Structure in *The Orchard Keeper*." [A] *Perspectives on Cormac McCarthy* [C]. Eds. Edwin T. Arnold and Dianne C. Luce. Jackson: Univ. Press of Mississippi, 1993.

[139] Rebein, Rick. *Hicks, Tribes, and Dirty Realists: American Fiction after Postmodernism* [M]. Lexington: Univ. Press of Kentucky, 2001.

[140] Rice, Thomas Jackson. *Joyce, Chaos and Complexity* [M]. Urbana and Chicago: Univ. of Illinois Press, 1997.

[141] Rikard, Gabriel D. *An Archaeology of Appalachia: Authority and the Mountaineer in the Appalachian Works of Cormac McCarthy* [D]. The Univ. of Mississippi, 2008. Ann Arbor: UMI, 2009. ATT 3358514

[142] Ruelle, David. *Chance and Chaos* [M]. Princeton: Princeton University Press, 1991.

[143] Sanborn, Wallis. *Animal Presentation in the Fiction of Cormac McCarthy* [D]. Texas Tech Univ., 2003. Ann Arbor: UMI, 2003. ATT 3083343

[144] Schaub, Thomas H. "Secular Scripture and Cormac McCarthy's *The Road*." [J] *Renascence*, 2009 (61).

[145] Schopen, Bernard A. "They Rode On: *Blood Meridian* and the Art of Narrative."

[J] *Western American Literature* 30.2 (Summer 1995): 179-94. Rpt. In *Contemporary Literary Criticism.* Ed. Jeffrey W. Hunter. Vol. 204. Detroit: Gale, 2005. *Literature Resource Center.* Web. 13 Nov. 2010. <http://go.galegroup.com>

[146] Shakespeare, William. *Othello* [A]. *Four Tragedies* [C]. Ed. David Bevington. New York: Bantam Books, 1988.

[147] Shaviro, Steve. "'The Very Life of Darkness: A Reading of *Blood Meridian.*" [A] *Perspectives on Cormac McCarthy* [C]. Eds. Edwin T. Arnold and Dianne L. Luce. Jackson: *Univ. Press of Mississippi*, 1993.

[148] Shaw, Robert. *The Dripping Faucet as a Model Chaotic System* [M]. Santa Cruz: Aerial Press, 1984.

[149] Simpson, Lewis P. "The Closure of History in a Postsouthern America." [A] *The Braze Face of History* [M]. Baton Rouge: Louisiana State Univ. Press, 1980.

[150] Slethaug, Gordon E. *Beautiful Chaos: Chaos Theory and Metachaotics in Recent American Fiction* [M]. Albany: State Univ. of New York Press, 2000.

[151] Smith, Henry Nash. *Virgin Land: The American West as Symbol and Myth* [M]. Cambridge: Harvard Univ. Press, 1973.

[152] Smitten, Jeffrey R. "Introduction: Spatial Form and Narrative Theory." [A] *Spatial Form in Narrative* [C]. Eds. Jeffery R. Smitten and Ann Daghistany. Ithaca and London: Cornell Univ. Press, 1981.

[153] Snyder, Phillip A. "Hospitality in Cormac McCarthy's *The Road."* [J] *The Cormac McCarthy Journal*, 2008 (6).

[154] Soja, Edward W. *Postmodern Geographies: The Reassertion of Space in Critical Social Theory* [M]. London & New York: Verso, 1989.

[155] Spurgeon, Sara. "The Sacred Hunter and Eucharist of the Wilderness: Mythic Reconstructions in *Blood Meridian."* [A] *Cormac McCarthy: New Directions* [C]. Ed. James D. Lilley. Albuquerque: Univ. of New Mexico Press, 2002.

[156] Stadt, Kevin. *Blood and Truth: Violence and Postmodern Epistemology in Morrison, McCarthy, and Palaniuk* [D]. Northern Illinois Univ., 2009. Ann Arbor: UMI, 2009. ATT 3358996

[157] Stevens, Brent. "A Translation of the Spanish in *All the Pretty Horses.*" [OD] *The*

Cormac McCarthy Society. June 23, 2010. <www.cormacmccarthy.com>

[158] Stewart, Ian. *Does God Play Dice? The New Mathematics of Chaos* [M]. London: Penguin Books, 1990.

[159] Sullivan, Nell. "The Evolution of the Dead Girlfriend Motif in *Outer Dark* and *Child of God*." [A] *Myth, Legend, Dust: Critical Responses to Cormac McCarthy* [C]. Ed. Rick Wallach. Manchester and New York: Manchester Univ. Press, 2000.

[160] Sullivan, Walter. *A Requiem for the Renascence: The State of Fiction in the Modern South* [M]. Athens: Univ. of Georgia Press, 1976.

[161] Sullivan, Walter. "About Any Kind of Measures You Can Name." [J] *Sewanee Review*, 1985 (93).

[162] Sun, Wanjun. *Chaos and Order in Thomas Pynchon's Fiction* [M]. Baoding: Hebei Univ *Press*. 2008.

[163] Tabbi, Joseph & Wutz Michael. *Reading Matters* [M]. Ithaca & London: Cornell Univ. Press, 1997.

[164] Vanderheide, John. "Varieties of Renunciation in the Works of Cormac McCarthy." [J] *The Cormac McCarthy Journal*, 2005 (5).

[165] Wallach, Rick. "Judge Holden, *Blood Meridian*'s Evil Archon." [A] *Sacred Violence: Volume 2: Cormac McCarthy's Western Novels* [C]. 2nd ed. Eds. Wade Hall and Rick Wallach. El Paso: Texas Western Press, 2002.

[166] Wallach, Rick. "Foreword." [A] *The Late Modernism of Cormac McCarthy* [M]. By David Holloway. Connecticut and London: Greenwood Press, 2002.

[167] Wallach, Rick. "Theatre, Ritual, and Dream in the *Border Trilogy*." [A] *Sacred Violence: Volume 2: Cormac McCarthy's Western Novels* [C]. 2nd ed. Eds. Wade Hall and Rick Wallach. El Paso: Texas Western Press, 2002.

[168] Walsh, Chris. "The Post-Southern Sense of Place in *The Road.*" [J] *The Cormac McCarthy Journal* 6, 2008 (6).

[169] Weiss, Daniel. *Cormac McCarthy, Violence, and the American Tradition* [D]. Wayne State Univ., 2009. Ann Arbor: UMI, 2009. ATT 3359585

[170] Weissert, Thomas P. "Representation and Bifurcation: Borges's Garden of Chaos Dynamics." [A] *Chaos and Order: Complex Dynamics in Literature and Science*

[C]. Ed. N. Katherine Hayles. Chicago and London: The Univ. of Chicago Press, 1991.

[171] West-Pavlov, Russel. *Space in Theory: Kristeva, Foucault, and Deleuze* [M]. Amsterdam and New York: Rodopi, 2009.

[172] Wilhelm, Randall S. "'Golden chalice, good to house a god': Still Life in *The Road*." [J] *The Cormac McCarthy Journal*, 2008 (6).

[173] Winchell, Mark Royden. "Inner Dark: or, The Place of Cormac McCarthy." [J] *The Southern Review*, 1990 (26). Rpt. In *Contemporary Literary Criticism Select*. Detroit: Gale, 2008. *Literature Resource Center*. Web. Nov. 13, 2010. <http://go.galegroup.com>

[174] Woodson, Linda. "Mapping *The Road* in Post-Postmodernism." [J] T*he Cormac McCarthy Journal*, 2008 (6).

[175] Woodson, Linda. "...You are the Battleground: Materiality, Moral Responsibility, and Determinism *in No Country for Old Men.*" [J] *The Cormac McCarthy Journal*, 2005 (5).

[176] Woodward, Richard B. "Cormac Country." [J] *Vanity Fair* (August 2005). July 18, 2011. <http://proquest.umi.com/pqdweb>

[177] Woodward, Richard B. "Cormac McCarthy's Venomous Fiction." [J] *The New York Times Magazine*,1992 (19).

[178] Zamoria, Lois Parkinson. *The Apocalyptic Vision in Contemporary American Fiction: Gabriel Garcia Marquez, Thomas Pynchon, Julio Cortazar and John Barth* [D]. University of California, Berkeley, 1977. Ann Arbor: UMI, 1977.

[179] Zhan, Shukui. *Vladimir Nabokov: From Modernism to Postmodernism* [M]. Xiamen: Xiamen Univ. Press, 2005.

[180] 汉娜·阿伦特，杰罗姆·科恩.责任与判断 [M].陈联营，译.上海：上海人民出版社，2011.

[181] 彼得·贝格尔.神圣的帷幕——宗教社会学理论之要素 [M].高师宁，译.上海：上海人民出版社，1991.

[182] 约翰·布里格斯·F，戴维·皮特.混沌七鉴：来自易学的永恒智慧 [M].陈忠，金纬，译.上海：上海世纪出版集团，2008.

[183] 恩斯特·卡西尔. 人论 [M]. 上海：上海译文出版社，1985.

[184] 迈克·克朗. 文化地理学 [M]. 杨淑华，宋慧敏，译. 南京：南京大学出版社，2003.

[185] 约瑟夫·弗兰克等. 现代小说中的空间形式 [M]. 秦林芳，等译. 北京：北京大学出版社，1991.

[186]（清）郭庆藩. 庄子集释（辑第 1 册，第 3 卷下）[C]. 北京：中华书局，1961.

[187] 葛瑞姆·汉卡克. 上帝的指纹（下册）[M]. 胡心吾，译. 北京：新世界出版社，2008.

[188] 胡铁生. 美国文学论稿 [C]. 长春：吉林大学出版社，2011.

[189] 江宁康. 美国当代文学与美利坚民族认同 [M]. 南京：南京大学出版社，2008.

[190] 荣格. 东洋冥想的心理学——从易经到禅 [M]. 杨儒宾，译. 北京：社会科学文献出版社，2000.

[191] 赖俊雄. 晚期解构主义 [M]. 台北：杨智文化事业股份有限公司，2005.

[192] 莱辛. 拉奥孔 [M]. 朱光潜，译. 北京：人民文学出版社，1979.

[193] 李杨. 美国南方文学后现代时期的嬗变 [M]. 济南：山东大学出版社，2006.

[194] 陆扬，朱立元，主编. 空间理论 [A]. 当代西方文艺理论 [C]. 上海：华东师范大学出版社，2005.

[195] 罗小云. 美国西部文学 [M]. 合肥：安徽教育出版社，2009.

[196] 杰弗里·帕克. 地缘政治学：过去、现在和未来 [M]. 刘从德，译. 北京：新华出版社，2003.

[197] 伊利亚·普利高津. 确定性的终结：时间、混沌与新自然法则 [M]. 湛敏，译. 上海：上海世纪出版集团，2009.

[198] 斯拉沃热·齐泽克. 意识形态的幽灵 [A]. 齐泽克，阿多诺. 图绘意识形态 [C]. 方杰，译. 南京：南京大学出版社，2002.

[199] 沈小峰. 混沌初开：自组织理论的哲学探索 [M]. 北京：北京师范大学出版社，2008.

[200] 奥斯瓦尔德·斯宾格勒. 西方的没落（下册）[M]. 齐世荣，等译. 上海：商务印书馆，1995.

[201] 山海经 [M]. 冯国超，译注 . 北京：商务印书馆，2009.

[202] 徐道一 .《周易》与当代自然科学 [M]. 广州：广东教育出版社，1995.

[203] 杨仁敬 . 论美国后现代派小说的嬗变" [J]. 山东外语教学，2001.

[204] 张天勇 . 社会符号化——马克思主义视域中的鲍德里亚后期思想研究 [M]. 北京：人民出版社，2008.

[205] 张小平 . "所有的故事都是一个故事" ——论麦卡锡《穿越》中分形的空间构型 [J]. 国外文学，2014.

[206] 赵一凡 . 从卢卡奇到萨义德：西方文论讲稿续编 [M]. 北京：生活 读书 新知 三联书店，2009.

[207]（宋）朱熹 . 周易本义 [M]. 北京：中华书局，2009.

Acknowledgments

Life is a deterministic chaos. Chance makes me accomplish my dream of going on with Ph.D studies in my late thirties, and chance makes me a student of my respected supervisor, Professor Zhan Shukui and lucky to study and live in Xiamen University for three years after working as a teacher for a great many years.

This dissertation would not have been completed without the advice and support of a number of people, and I am deeply appreciative of their help. I would like to extend my deepest and foremost thanks to Professor Zhan's acceptance of my being his student, and in my study life in Xiamen University, he gives me a lot of help and instruction in my academic studies as well as care and love in my life. Without his consistent help and illuminating instruction, my present project would not be possible. All the way from the initial proposal to the outline, and then to the present draft of my dissertation, every step in my Ph.D program's progression would not have forwarded without Professor Zhan's efforts and encouragement. Professor Zhan is more like a family member, whose care and help are always there when I encounter difficulties both in life and studies.

My heartfelt thanks are also paid to my respected Professor Yang Renjing in Xiamen University. For me, he is a kind and wise father, instructing me to grow mature in all aspects of life. In my choice of the current project, Professor Yang's wisdom and original ideas about American literature inspired and helped me a lot. His devoted spirit of academic studies encourages me to go on with exploring in the literature world, though it is hardly romantic, even torturing sometimes when facing this noisy world and society.

I am also deeply indebted to Professor Zhao Yifan in China Academy of Social Sciences, and Professor Chen Shidan in China People's University, and each of their excellent lectures in Xiamen University instructed me in the studies of difficult theoretical discourses. My special thanks should go to those professors and teachers in Xiamen University, who have contributed to this study and my Ph.D program in one way or another: Professor Zhang Longhai, Professor Li Meihua, Professor Zhou Yibei, Professor Liu Wensong and Ms. Chen Wenna; and the librarians in the library of Xiamen University, particularly Mr. Lai Shoukang, whose instant help in my collection of research materials provides the foundation for the accomplishment of my project.

I would like to express my thanks to my friends: Professor Xu Feng in Zhengzhou Institute of Aeronautics, who paid time and efforts to collect my studying materials in America; Professor Chen Baorong in Henan University of Traditional Chinese Medicine and Professor Wang Lili in Zhengzhou Engineering Institute, whose care and love offer warmth in my life in Xiamen; Ms. Ban Guihong, whose poetic ideas about life make my academic studies romantic and colorful; Mr. Luo Zhangyi, who inspires me always with his deep understanding of traditional Chinese thinkings; Dr. Feng Anbo and Dr. Wang Chenghui, who always give me hands in my studying in Xiamen; and Ph.D candidates in Xiamen University: Ms. Zhao Qingli, Professor Jiang Chunlan, Ms. Wang Yanhua, Mr. Du Kaihuai, Ms. Ma Qunying, Mr. He Zhaohui, Ms. Liao Bailing, Ms. Wang Yanping and Ms. Xu Jing, whose friendship supports me in my long-day journey in American literature.

Last, but not least, I owe a word of thanks to my family members. My parents, parents-in-law, brothers-in-law, sisters and sisters-in-law, and my beloved daughters, though they might not have very clear ideas of what I have been engaged in, have been side with me and supported me all these years. My final thanks will be paid to my beloved husband, Professor Li Hailong, whose love is my staunchest support forever. Without his help, advice, and support, I could not have completed this project.

致小说家科麦克·麦卡锡

（代后记）

一

麦卡锡，每次看到你
看到的是你双眸里的远山
蓝色的湖泊
燃烧的天堂和地狱
黎明刺破的长空里
巨大而喀迈拉似的战马
荒凉盆地里嗜血的骑手
他们飘荡如游魂
踽踽前行
世界俨然一个病人
一个狂徒
一个瘦骨嶙峋的老人

麦卡锡，每次看到你
看到的是你患了白内障似的
冷寂的蓝月
啜饮着红色的蓝色的
灰色的白色的准确地说五颜六色

的阴影与血浆的大地

习习的阴风

吹过那湖那水那山那高不可及的

子午线

仿佛远古的传说

巨龙与武士的搏斗

红色的天空飞起

野鸭似的箭羽

麦卡锡，每次看到你

战马的嘶鸣子弹的呼啸

兵戈相击

地心里隆隆的轰鸣

火山口沸腾的岩浆

风吹打着地面上的干草

稀稀疏疏

暑天里的寒冰

白骨森森

一双枯瘦的双眼睥睨着

走过的人

天边的云

静默的树

边陲渐行渐远

血色残阳

一弯惊恐的蓝月

默默对峙

2017. 12. 01

二

从黑暗到黑暗。麦卡锡，你的眼中
人性的沼泽，遮蔽不了贪婪与爱欲的毒草
亚当夏娃的故事，显然不是耶和华的寓意
你将它写入灵魂，写入人类，写进
三十万年人类演化的记忆。崖壁上
赫然有血的印迹，灵的冲击
风化的白骨，苍白、无力

春风已然吹过南北东西。麦卡锡
你的眼里，我读不出春意
料峭寒风，古道瘦马，长滩戈壁
万物都是耶和华神漂白的骨头
一夜狂风，晚来雨急，那飘落一地的
樱花，是否诉说着挣扎、沉沦的爱欲

从黑暗到黑暗。从阿帕拉契亚山区
到新墨西哥。开满白色花朵的树木
张扬着魅惑的春意。麦卡锡，今天
你，是否走出了德克萨斯的书斋
看辽阔大地，看世事沧桑变迁
看人间从冬到春
是否一样的真理

恶，是你不变的故事
善，却随春姗姗来迟

2018.03.16

三

众神已然退场。此时
你是宇宙的王

长满青苔的小径，从此
可有深夜叩门人？

月光，可浅酌
也可独饮

2018. 10. 14

四

万物都是他漂白的骨头
除了他。谁的爱
堪以如此浓墨重彩

2019. 05. 24